Judgment of Blood

Timothy Black

Dreamsphere Books
Winnipeg, Canada

Editor: Sanford Larson
Proofreader: Francisco Feliciano

Published October 2023 by Dreamsphere Books, an imprint of Story Perfect Inc.

Dreamsphere Books
PO Box 51053 Tyndall Park
Winnipeg, Manitoba R2X 3B0
Canada

Visit http://www.dreamspherebooks.com to find out more.

Judgment of Blood

Chapter 1

BEING ELECTROCUTED AIN'T HALF as fun as you might think.

Then again, waking up next to a beautiful woman had a way of making everything seem better.

"Sarah!" Maggie called out as she rolled over from cuddling me on the forest floor.

She was fuming as she spat half-chewed bones out of her mouth, taking no notice of the claw marks dug into the ground. She'd almost got me last night.

"Sarah, get out here!" Maggie shouted more insistently. "Did you let me eat a raccoon again? You know I despise those vermin!"

I stifled a snicker at her plight; in response, Maggie stared deadpan at me as she brushed the dirt and leaves away from her front. I turned redder than her hair and looked away, trying to maintain some of the manners I'd been raised with. Damn it, she knew that I was doing my level best not to take advantage of the unnatural bond between us. But she sure wasn't making it easy.

Of course, it didn't help none that we were both naked as the day we were born.

The summer morning was already making us sweat. Cicadas chattered in the underbrush even as heat lightning flashed silently in a cloudless sky. The weather had been weird lately, and the shifting telluric currents that controlled it felt off somehow. My stomach kept doing flip-flops that had nothing to do with Maggie pressing up against me.

Giggles preceded Maggie's little sister before the girl emerged out of the bushes, gap-toothed grin flashing. She wore the ramshackle surge pack I'd managed to cobble together, powering the lightning rod she twirled in a playful fashion. Sarah took a perverse pleasure in letting Maggie and me almost tear into her before she put us down with the rod. Sometimes we'd awake to find she had let us run wild the whole night through.

Sarah was young enough that the change hadn't taken her yet, but it was close. It wasn't just for her sister's company that the girl had left their werewolf pack behind when we'd left Sacramento; shifters were a danger to everyone until they settled into their final fur, and Sarah was on the cusp of starting her transformations.

"Gimme my britches, brat," I called out. It was hard as hell keeping leaves and mud covering my privates, but she was a kid, and I was a halfway-decent man.

She waggled her eyebrows and laughed when I turned a deeper shade of red.

"Enough, Sarah," Maggie scolded. Sarah stuck out her tongue and tossed me the bundle of clothes I'd stripped out of the night before. "Elijah is correct; your behavior is inappropriate for your age."

I stole a look over to where the naked Maggie stood sternly, trying to keep a straight face as she lectured her sister on manners. She felt my hungry stare through the link we shared and snorted at me while rolling her green eyes in exasperation as I turned away.

"You are the strangest sort of hypocrite, Elijah," she sighed. "When we are lost to the fur we alternate between rutting and attempting to murder each other. We do not need Sarah's taunting to tell us that. Why then must you insist on acting as if we are blushing virgins when we wake?"

I shrugged into my patched pants, avoiding her gaze. "It ain't the same when we got our senses, and you blasted well know it."

Maggie's presence was suddenly behind me, and with it the heady scent of her. It was a mixture of soft and wild, strawberries amid thorn bushes, the sinuous movement of beautiful monsters in the dark. It made my heart race; when her fingertips brushed across my neck, I nearly jumped out of my skin.

"I am well aware of the difference. When we run as wolves, the bond draws us together, to both love and devour each other. When we wear skin, I choose to be with you. I know you feel the same. Your insistence in playing at chastity when we walk as humans is ... irritating."

"Don't matter," I said, gruff as I put on the ruined hot-suit jacket with its multiple claw tears. "Like you said: the bond is still there. Should we go and get hitched just because I was the first one you turned? That might be enough for some folks, but it ain't enough for me. You got to know me and I got to know you, down to the soul, before I'll let this happen when we got hold of our minds."

I turned around and met her gaze, for once able to ignore her nakedness as I hardened my resolve. "We were forced together because I was the first victim you bit. That ain't romance. That ain't love. Now, get dressed."

The joy and playfulness in the air drained away, and Maggie turned away with a smoldering look. I cussed myself. Is there a pretty naked lady with a temper claiming love standing in front of you and teasing? How about you question her feelings for you and remind her how she infected you with a disease that turns you into a bloodthirsty werewolf every full moon?

Yep. I was a genius.

I sighed and stared south, toward what kept me from just letting go of my inhibitions and enjoying life on the ground.

Although the flying metropolis of Wardenclyffe was just a dot on the horizon, there were better than ten thousand men and women on the salvation city relying on me. They didn't even know it, either. The last remnants of humanity sailed along atop the invisible telluric currents, shepherded by a secret society of wolf-infected scientists that kept their inner beasts in check through constant electric shocks. I had to admit, it was probably for the best they hid their affliction from the rest of the city. If folks knew what was beneath their obscuring goggles and respirators, they'd riot and crash the city within hours of the discovery.

I was just as much a secret as the Tellurians, though. When Sarah wasn't fast enough and had to put me down with the surge pack during the full moon, my flesh reacted differently than most. Instead of being just stunned by the electricity, I'd revert to being human again, and my body would need shocks throughout the night to keep me down. Otherwise, I'd wake up, sprout fur, and start the chase again. Most werewolves could be downed by the lightning for the entire night; it was just one more strange mystery to how my body had reacted to the infection. Only a few people even knew I'd survived it, or that I was ranging ahead of my abandoned home and trying to find any threats before they got to Wardenclyffe. The folk up there might have written me off, but I still loved the old sanctuary city.

"What's wrong with you, Eli?" Sarah asked, breaking the silence imposed by Maggie's huff. She dutifully passed over the surge pack so I could make sure the thing had survived another night of use. Rigorous maintenance was the only thing keeping the ramshackle thing working.

Although she'd been raised by her sister and their wolf family without any contact with uninfected people, Sarah had adapted quickly to my presence, finding to her delight that she didn't have to be stuffy around me. Maggie was too set in her ways to follow her sister's example, but it was nice to talk to someone that wasn't a walking textbook.

"Just thinking a bit too much," I hemmed, poking at a couple of raw wires. They sparked with a cracking sound. Good enough. The surge pack would need to passively charge from the local telluric currents, but it would be fully juiced back up by the next full moon. An unexpected arc zapped my finger, making me jerk my hand back.

"Hey, don't electrocute yourself; that's my job!" Sarah giggled, but her laughter petered out in the empty air. It was getting harder and harder to pretend that there wasn't doom on the horizon.

For three months we'd been trailblazing north of the city, barely outpacing its ponderous flight. Wardenclyffe was caught in a strange riptide in the electromagnetic currents, being drawn toward the mysterious Menlo Station where Edison and his vicious Cabal of flunkies waited. But we'd been pulling ahead from the city steadily the last week. Wardenclyffe had slowed down to a more stately pace. But why? Had the Tellurians somehow wrested control back of its path, or was this just more of Edison's tricks? We hadn't caught sight of his bastard followers yet, nor did we know why they'd attacked Wardenclyffe with one of their Thunder Trains three months ago.

What was abundantly clear to anyone with the wolf in their blood was that the telluric currents we were following were becoming unstable. I'd never heard of the streams ebbing and surging before in all my years aboard Wardenclyffe. Sure, a salvation city passing through would leave a disrupted wake of energy they couldn't double-back on without shaking the city apart, but nothing could permanently change the eternal flows.

At least, that was what I'd thought.

"Something approaches from the city," Maggie said, standing next to me as she shrugged into her patched prairie dress. "Do you see?"

My heart hammered with hope as I followed her pointing finger, straining my eyes. Maggie had been born as a werewolf, so she tended to keep some of her supernatural senses in human form, but I lacked her inborn abilities. Briefly I considered using the blinder goggles Sarah had taken to wearing around her neck like a talisman, but I shuddered at the thought. Sure, the black obsidian lenses wouldn't burn my eyes out thanks to the wolf inside me; that said, it would still leave me with a headache for hours from viewing the world as a ghostly shadow of electromagnetic currents.

Instead, I closed my eyes and reached out my senses. I'd been trying to train myself to identify the telluric currents over the last few months. Lately, I'd begun to doubt my progress, as the electromagnetic streams north of us surged and flashed away in my mind. They had to still be there, but for some reason I couldn't sense them.

At least my troubles with the currents didn't extend to the south. I was able to tell that an object had launched from Wardenclyffe. But it was far too small to be a Thunder Train.

Maude had only been able to visit me one time since I'd been exiled from Wardenclyffe by Beta Steinmetz, the Tellurian who had de facto control of the city. Although my grandmother was the undisputed mistress of the *Heaven's Grace*, the big Double T was the workhorse of the city and would be missed if it went haring off on a side trip without explanation, so she'd been careful to not draw too much attention to us. While I felt disappointment that the craft riding the currents toward us wasn't the *Heaven's Grace*, my curiosity was piqued by the size of it. Even the *Tammany's Troubles*, the smallest Double T on Wardenclyffe, made more of a disruption in the telluric streams than whatever was heading our way.

The strange anomaly darted back and forth along its path, jagged and erratic. Between that and the distance it had to cross, the object was a good half hour away, even at the surprising speed it was traveling at. But it was definitely coming toward us.

"Should we flee?" Maggie asked.

"Not much reason to," I sighed. "Likely they're tracking the residual from the surge pack. I'm sure as shit not leaving that thing behind. Besides, only folk that know we're down here are friendlies. Mostly. But there ain't nobody wants me dead that thinks I'm still alive."

"Why do you even bother protecting those people?" Sarah asked, holding up the blinders and peering through them. Even though she hadn't experienced her first change into a beast, being naturally born to it like her sister let her endure the goggles' destructive nature without much discomfort or danger.

"My friends and kin are there. Don't matter much that there's people I don't like in the city. I ain't deserting Wardenclyffe just because of a few assholes."

"But you're here," Sarah protested. "Not there. They don't want you. We do. You don't belong to their pack anymore. You're one of us now."

I fought back an irritated sigh. To her it seemed very obvious; either you were part of something, or you weren't.

"Leave Elijah alone, Sarah," interjected Maggie. "He will learn soon enough the folly of clinging to such incongruent notions."

I struggled to hold my temper, stalking off to rummage through the gear Sarah had kept safe. There were some dried squirrel strips in there. I tore into them with a little more vigor than was needed.

We spent the rest of the wait in uncomfortable silence, while I fumed over what the girls thought of me and my obsession with keeping Wardenclyffe safe. But nothing Maggie could say or do would ever get me to give up on my family and home. Nothing.

As our flying visitor rocketed closer, I forgot my temper, fascination instead taking over. My initial impression had been correct: the oncoming craft was far too small and fast to be a Thunder Train.

The object looked like a shooting star had knocked boots with a lightning bolt; their offspring was a glowing sphere of electricity that streaked across the sky with a tail of sparks instead of fire. Within a few moments the mass at the center resolved itself into a man riding a device three times his size, his legs locked hard against its sides, his body hunched down against the wind. My senses screamed at the brutal effect his steed had on the telluric currents, cleaving through them like a knife rather than sailing atop them like a Thunder Train.

"Elijah!" Maggie hollered in warning.

The lightning comet was coming right for us.

We went to ground, scrabbling away from the path of the oncoming disaster. The sisters melted into the trees and underbrush, but I lacked their grace and knowledge. I just took off running at a right angle to the rider's path, holding on to the surge pack for dear life. The lightning generator was the only thing that let me keep a shred of my humanity, and I wasn't going to let some idiot suicide into it.

The comet rider altered his course to cut me off.

"Son of a bitch!" I panted, skidding to a stop.

My arm hairs stood up as the comet shot straight at me, static electricity heralding its arrival. Squall tubes, steel-hard glass containers filled with an alchemical sludge that allowed flight when electrified, were bolted onto the machine from front to back. I didn't need to see the pilot's bald head, goggles, and respirator to know there was only one kind of madman that could be responsible for such a thing.

Tellurian.

The air shrieked at being violated by the contraption, but above its roar I heard the muffled shout of the storm prophet riding it as he desperately waved me away.

"Eli, move!"

I managed to twist away just as the thing blasted past faster than a cannonball, its lightning shroud caressing me like the fingers of a demented lover. The force of the near-miss tossed me against a tree with bone-cracking impact. My teeth chattered from the voltage passing through me, but the battered hot-suit managed to shunt some of the energy away.

Still hurt like a bastard though.

The comet crashed into a line of trees, smashing through them like a fist through paper. Wood blew apart as the machine and rider plowed a narrow swath through the forest.

At least the impacts managed to slow the iron horse a bit. The man nosed it down into the dirt, cutting a trench fifty feet long as the contraption finally came to rest.

The Tellurian riding the thing fell off, his arms and legs shaking with exhaustion from clinging to such a rough ride. Maggie popped out of the underbrush, eyes narrowed in suspicion. There was no sign of Sarah, but the kid was skittish around strangers. She was probably watching from the shadows, ready to toss out all the fury her skinny teenage fists could bring to any that threatened her sister.

"Successful test," the storm prophet croaked with a half-laugh. "Well . . . I'm still breathing, at least."

He was burnt all over with his head smoking, but the man wasn't in any danger of dying. Despite what most folks on the salvation cities thought, the full-length lab coat, boots, and gloves that the Tellurians wore didn't protect them from the electricity they worked with. In fact, the garments were laced with copper, conducting shocks and jolts directly to their skin to help keep their wolf-born infection under control.

I pulled out a heavy wrench from my pack and smacked it in my palm, all menacing-like. Well, as menacing as my tall, beanpole frame could muster.

"Who are you?" Maggie asked, unlimbering her delicately-filigreed Winchester rifle and taking aim at the intruder's head. Damn. One of these days I'd learn to just let her take the lead with her gun, rather than trying to posture like an idiot.

"You're going to hurt my feelings," the storm prophet rasped. "After saving your life, I figured you might at least remember me."

"Henry!" I shouted in realization.

"Of course it's me, you idiot," my oldest and truest friend laughed, pulling himself into a sitting position on the crashed craft. "Who else would ride a dangerous prototype down to see you?"

Maggie lowered the rifle, but she wasn't grinning like me. While it was true that Henry had saved her life, she had a superstitious distrust of Tellurian technology and those who used it.

A hundred questions bubbled up, but Henry waved them off. He pushed up his blinder goggles, staring at me with the too-blue eyes that the Tellurians hid from the world. Wolf eyes, hungry and savage, kept in check only by constant low-level electrocution. Despite carrying the virus, Henry had no trace of hair on him, a side effect of the constant electric shocks he endured to keep him human.

"Eli, we need your help. Something's wrong with the currents in Wardenclyffe's path."

"I knew it!" I hollered, slapping my thigh in triumph, before the expression on his face sobered me up. "Everything's been feeling off for a few weeks. Like the streams are migrating. But that's impossible, isn't it?"

Henry shook his head. "It's worse than you know. The telluric currents aren't just shifting around. They're disappearing. There's a dead spot coming up where there's no currents whatsoever, and the city is heading right for it. We have two weeks, maybe three, tops.

"After that, Wardenclyffe is going to crash."

Chapter 2

T HAT'S ... A BAD THING."

It was the best I could do.

"Brilliant deduction, Eli," Henry snorted. "I knew you were the man to talk to, the great thinker who would clear it all up."

"Fine. It sounds really, *really* bad. Is that better? I didn't think there was anywhere on Earth without telluric currents. Hell, I've never even heard of one ending, just thinning out too much to follow."

Henry shrugged, squinting at the bright sunlight in his unprotected eyes. "It's supposed to be impossible. But nobody told the dead spot ahead of that. From what we can tell, there's a place coming up where the currents simply converge and disappear, like a giant sinkhole."

"And the riptide dragging the city toward Menlo Station?" Maggie asked.

"Gone. Too late for us to hop streams though. There's nothing substantial enough to hold up the city anywhere close. And if we try to reverse direction, the disruption wake of our own passing will swamp us and tear the city apart."

I cussed like a sailor. This was all Menlo Station's fault. We'd thought the city dead long ago; right up until a Thunder Train from her, the *Shrieking Sally*, crashed into Wardenclyffe, carrying Maggie in her werewolf form. Although we didn't have any hard evidence yet, there was plenty of suspicion and troubled history with the Howling City to build on. We figured the Cabal that ruled them had sent the wolves our way as infectious cargo, trying to set loose the plague that had wiped the ground clean of humanity long ago. I wanted to find out why they'd attacked us.

Right before I kicked their ass for it.

"So, what do the Tellurians think? Is this more of Menlo's shenanigans?" I asked.

Henry shook his head. "Nobody knows for sure. They don't think so though, as it would ground the Cabal too. But since we can't launch Double Ts to investigate, there's no way to tell for sure. That's why I had to pull the *Bantam* out."

He gestured over to the contraption he'd ridden in on. Despite knocking down a few trees, the vehicle was relatively unscathed. There was a saddle bolted on for a rider toward the rear, behind a confusing array of controls and dials barely shielded from the wind by an angled iron plate. Flat pedals were operated by the pilot's feet, and squall tubes sparked down the length of its entire hull. The iron and steel gadget was built like a bullet-shaped battering ram, with no elegance or grace to its form.

Size-wise, it was a midget when compared to a real Thunder Train. Although it had to weigh a few hundred pounds, the thing wasn't more than fifteen feet long and about five feet high at the tip of the windshield. Its main frame had obviously been cut down from a wrecked Double T's boiler, overlaying a confusing set of pistons and hydraulics. Lining the secondary hull were several lead-acid batteries for holding a charge if there were no storms nearby. I'd have lain odds that Henry had cobbled the machine together from one of the train graveyards on Wardenclyffe. In fact, I could see the lettering from its former life spelled out on part of the ramshackle hull.

"Hang on a damn minute. *R-o-o-s* . . . Henry, tell me you didn't cut up the old cock!"

My friend winced at the accusation, and his tone was defensive. "I didn't have much choice. Besides, neither of us were ever going back there, and his boiler was already riddled with our old experiments. He was perfect!"

"I can't believe you mutilated him," I grumbled, patting the frame of the contraption. The *Iron Rooster* had been a junked Thunder Train that Henry and I had damn near grown up in. It'd been our fort, our sanctuary, a wreck in the forgotten depths of Wardenclyffe that we'd cut our engineering teeth on like a surgeon slicing and stitching a corpse.

"At least he's found new life in this form," Henry said, trying to console me. "Before, he was just a rusting hulk in the yard, waiting for the day he had to be parted out to keep the others running. But now he's reborn as the *Bantam!*"

"I suppose so," I admitted. "How'd you get this little feller to fly, anyway? He don't seem big enough to be out of the nest."

"Layered steel between the gear work to increase surface charging area by three hundred percent, triple the normal amount of squall tubes, a column of the best batteries I could steal, and an unprotected saddle that shocks my ass when I twitch wrong."

I smiled, but real laughter was a horizon a little too far away right now. There were other things on my mind.

"Will it still fly? That landing was two trees short of an explosion."

Henry blushed. "Yes. I'm just not very good at piloting it. This . . . well, this is the first time it's been out of the launch tube. Although Beta Steinmetz approved the project, he wanted it kept secret. Nobody else knew about it, outside of Maude. So, no test flights before this."

"Why now?" Maggie asked.

He waved north. "Whatever is going on out there, we need eyes on it. But the telluric currents can't support a Double T anymore, and they're too chaotic for a telepulse to work, even if you had a receiver. A few more miles north, and even the *Bantam* won't be able to fly in the weakening current. Somebody had to come down and let you know what was happening. Eli, Maggie: we need your help."

We looked at him in confusion.

"Exactly what do you expect us to do about the disappearance of your magic?" Maggie asked.

"It's not magic, it's science," Henry snapped.

"My mistake," she responded, sarcasm lacing the words. "That is why your precious telluric currents only surged into existence after the appearance of werewolves. Historical documents are replete with accounts of people tapping into and using these mythical energy lines, correct? How silly of Newton to forget about your 'science' when he was describing the Laws of the universe. I am amazed he overlooked such an obvious violation of his precious rules!"

"Typical of the ignorant. Just because we can't explain an event doesn't mean that you can automatically throw it into the lap of a preacher or mystic."

"Careful, Henry," I said. He was getting under my skin a bit with his tone. "She did grow up bedding down with more books than the Tellurians got hidden in the Tower. I don't give a good goddamn what we call it, but the telluric currents are real, and there's thousands of people whose lives depend on them staying real. Can we at least agree on that?"

Maggie and Henry exchanged smoldering glares, but both nodded. Henry didn't have any way of knowing, but Maggie had plenty of reason to distrust the Tellurians. The Cabal that had stolen her away to Menlo Station were an awful lot like a demented mirror to the storm prophets, and even had a few traitors from the Telluric Society in their ranks. Maggie had been loath to talk about her short time in the Howling City, but it was obvious that she thought of all those who dabbled in the storm technology as monsters, madmen gone wild with magic they didn't understand.

I couldn't argue much with that point of view. It was rumored that even Tesla himself could barely comprehend the technology he was working with. But needs must when the Devil drives, and, crazy or not, the half-understood telluric technology had saved tens of thousands of folks when the furbacks took over the ground.

But if the telluric currents were disappearing . . . well, the world was about to get a whole hell of a lot more interesting for the last human city.

"Eli, I know you must have your hands full with dodging the fully-turned lycanthropes down here all the time, but if you could get ahead of the city's path . . . why are you two looking at each other like that?"

I scratched my head and grimaced.

"We haven't encountered any furbacks in the last couple of weeks."

At Henry's amazed stare, I could only shrug. We were raised on Wardenclyffe to believe that the ground was teeming with savage beasts, werewolves that had finally succumbed to the disease and were animals for the rest of their lives. And, for the most part, that was true. It might take a few months, maybe even a year, but eventually the change from beast back to human wouldn't happen, and the poor bastards would remain a hulking abomination for the rest of their lives.

We'd had troubles after leaving the ruins of Sacramento, dodging through the territories of several packs as we crossed the mountains toward Oregon. Fortunately, the three of us carried the curse in our blood, and the inhuman stamina that came with it allowed us to travel faster than a horse-mounted man over the rough country.

The full furbacks generally avoided the presence of shifters like us. They seemed to know instinctively about the insane fury of the shifters, how the wolf in the blood went crazy during its transformation and attacked anyone and anything. Despite what I'd been taught all my life, fully turned werewolves were less bloodthirsty than those caught between human and beast, managing to even form packs that functioned as primal families.

But still, we were pissing on someone else's tree the whole trip, and we'd had our fair share of wolf attacks. Although they'd steer clear during the full moons when we could bite back, we'd had to use the surge pack and Maggie's firearms a half dozen times when the moon was waning. She was running low on ammunition when we crossed into Oregon a few weeks ago, and I didn't know how much longer the surge pack would last. We'd pretty much been down to praying and running.

And then the other werewolves just up and disappeared.

"What Elijah claims is true," Maggie said, glancing around the forest uneasily. "We saw one or two stragglers, outcasts without packs, fifteen days ago. Since then, there have been no signs of any inhabitants. It does not bode well. By our nature, we of the wolf's blood spread out and avoid infringing on each other's domain. This area is teeming with prey; it would make an excellent territory for any pack. Yet there are no signs, no scent markers or claw slashes on trees, claiming this land. It is . . . unsettling."

"Could this be related to the telluric currents disappearing?" I asked Henry.

"It's entirely possible" he replied. "We know there's some sort of resonance between the disease and the telluric currents; after all, we

Tellurians process our own blood into ascension fluid for the squall tubes. Call it magic, call it science, but the connection is one that can't be denied. Our infection is what allows us to feel the streams, to chart courses through them. A disruption might be enough to drive off those wolves who are most attuned to it."

"No," Maggie stated flatly. "For years, lycanthropes tore each other apart, until there were few enough that the land could sustain us. Fertile hunting territories like this would not be abandoned simply because the area feels odd. Although the savagery of those that have grown fully into their fur is lessened, the hunger that drives them would overcome any hesitation they would have about laying claim to this area."

Henry shrugged. "A beast is a beast to me. Put whatever face you want on it, but the infected are all just poor, doomed bastards. And yes, that includes us storm prophets. Speaking of which, I need to get back to Wardenclyffe before the currents peter off around here. There's no telling how long they'll stay strong enough to support the *Bantam*."

"Figured so," I said. "But if you could spare a minute, I could use a hand. I scrounged a surge pack out of parts from the supply depots we've run across. It's been acting a bit squirrelly lately. I think we been running it too hard, between the shocks to keep us down during the moon and the fighting use it's been drafted into."

"I can risk a few more minutes. Where is it?"

"Sarah, come on out from hiding and show Henry your toy!"

Silence greeted me from the woods around us.

"Sarah?" Maggie called out, worry creeping into her voice. "This is not the time for games."

We were used to the girl wandering off on her own a ways. Whether letting me and Maggie have some alone time, or just plain boredom, the kid tended to range out while we were hiking. It was the reason I let her hold onto the surge pack; more than once she'd had to defend herself against an irate furback. The crash landing of the *Bantam* had sent her scurrying into the underbrush, and we'd figured she was still out there lurking, shy around Henry. When Maude had brought the *Heaven's Grace* down before, the girl had done the same thing, hiding until they were gone again. So, we hadn't paid any mind to her disappearance.

This was different.

Each of us took to calling Sarah's name out, hoping for a response. But the forest remained silent, with nary a sound. That in itself was getting worrisome. I understood animals clearing out when the *Bantam* crashed, but the woods should have had critters and insects chirping away again by now. There was only one thing that I knew of that could cause the forest to go still like that. And then we heard it.

A werewolf howling.

I'd been around the girls long enough to decipher the howl. The beast was hungry and desperate, never a good combination. Worse yet, a second howl carried with it the certainty that it had found something.

Prey.

We took off running toward the commotion. I took some comfort in knowing that Sarah was still carrying the surge pack.

As if in answer to my thoughts, there was a sizzling crack and a flash of light through the trees ahead. The boom of artificial thunder shook the forest, and an animal's yelp of pain rose up. Suddenly there came a sound that none of us expected to hear.

Gunfire.

And then Sarah screamed.

Chapter 3

BRANCHES WHIPPED OUR FACES as we barreled through the woods toward the noise. Maggie led the way, her feet finding a path surer than any I could imagine, her hands readying the Winchester to shoot the bastard making her sister scream.

I followed close by, smashing through the underbrush like a drunken bull. While I lacked Maggie's grace, I had more than enough muscle to make the heavy wrench I was carrying lethal. Sarah wasn't my kin by blood, but the kid had grown on me over the last few months. I was kindly fond of her. That made my wrench want to meet her attacker.

Henry stumbled along behind us, unaccustomed to the wild terrain. I wasn't exactly sure what he was planning to do, as he was missing the arc bracers Tellurians used to electrocute their foes. But it still felt good that my friend was backing me up, and that he didn't waste no words on excusing himself to escape on the *Bantam*. You could say a lot of things about Henry. But he wasn't a coward.

Another gunshot. Sarah's screams came to an abrupt stop.

The underbrush parted ahead of us, and out stepped a beast from my nightmares.

It had started life as a werewolf, but that time was long behind it. All four of its limbs had been replaced with steel replicas, armored to cover the hydraulics and gear work within. Thick blades extended from its hands and feet, lengthy knives curved to resemble the claws they had replaced. A long red stripe had been dyed down the back of its white fur, and it had small loops of metal pierced through both its ears and nose.

A pair of small furnaces and boilers had been implanted into its lower rib cage on each side, with exhaust pipes leading off its hips.

The critter was a Broken, one of the mechanically-augmented beasts we'd tangled with back in the ruins of Sacramento. I'd thought all of them killed when the *Dead Man's Hand* exploded, but apparently they had kin out this way.

The mutilated wrong-wolf rose up on its hind legs to its full nine foot height, opened its jaws, and roared. Maggie skidded to a stop, shouldered her rifle, and fired in one smooth motion.

It would have been a clean head shot if the striped Broken hadn't suddenly brought its arm up with inhuman speed; the bullet ricocheted off the tempered steel with a spark and a whine. Maggie worked the Winchester's lever and fired again. This shot found exposed flesh on the body, but the ironhide didn't show any reaction to it.

Henry and I hung back to clear her field of fire, feeling useless as Maggie continued to fire round after round into the Broken. The ironhide only reacted by covering its head; otherwise, it allowed the bullets to impact its flesh and steel without complaint.

"Let us try another tactic then," Maggie snarled when she'd emptied the rifle.

Her hands darted down to the leather apron she wore with its innumerable bullets. Although her usual load for the Winchester was lead, she did keep a few special surprises on hand for any furback we couldn't drive off with normal bullets.

Silver.

"Neshomne! Back!"

The shout came from behind the Broken. The big beast dropped its guard, turned, and bounded back the way it had come, ignoring the cussing Maggie while she struggled to get the silver loaded fast enough to take a shot. As quick and practiced as she was, it didn't compare to the wrong-wolf's speed; by the time she'd brought her rifle up, the critter had disappeared.

"Stop shooting, you damned fool!" the voice in the woods called out. It was deep, mannish, and annoyed.

"Come on out; I'm guessing this one is with you, and I got better things to do than ride herd over your young'un!"

We moved cautiously through the leaves; I took the lead, with Maggie covering me, and Henry watching our rear.

Deep growling with a metallic tinge greeted us as we emerged into a clearing. The wrong-wolf was sitting on its haunches like a dog, ears folded back, rumbling a warning snarl. Sarah was on her backside, glaring up at the Broken, her arms crossed in defiance..

Next to the ironhide was a man in a midnight-black duster and cowboy hat, with matching vest, britches, and holsters. Under the vest he wore a tucked-in button-down shirt, as bloody red as his leather gloves and boots. His skin was pale with a bluish hue, as if he'd drowned in an icy pond and forgotten to stay dead. White hair peeked out from under his hat, matching the muttonchops and handlebar mustache. Despite his unhealthy-looking hair and skin, the man was built solid, and his stance was unwavering. He stroked the Broken's massive head like a favorite pet, and the ease with which he wore the twin pistols on his hips spoke of a practiced gunfighter. But the weirdest thing of all were his eyes.

Even from here we could see that his irises were a deep red, almost glowing in luminescence.

"Howdy," he said, tipping his hat all neighborly-like.

Maggie raised the Winchester. But before she was halfway up with it, the stranger had drawn both pistols and aimed them at her head. If I'd blinked I would have missed it. Sarah yelped and flattened herself out on the ground, trying to clear the field of fire.

"I wouldn't try it, darlin'," the stranger said. "Be a shame to end you just as we met, but don't you doubt for a second I will. Why don't ya'll just go ahead and toss down your weapons?"

There was something off about the man's mouth, something shiny flashing around in it. More than that though, there was a scent around him, a feeling that made my wolf-born senses want to retch.

The surge pack Sarah had been carrying was on the ground, and I cussed at seeing the bullet hole in the power converter. I could fix it, but the chore would be impossible without the proper parts.

Maggie carefully laid her rifle against the pack, never taking her eyes off the stranger. At his nod I followed suit with the wrench. Even after we were disarmed, the wrong-wolf kept growling.

"Tell your partner back there in the trees to come on out. Can't fool Neshomne's nose."

When Henry emerged from the underbrush, the stranger gave a strangled grunt and half-lowered his weapons.

"What in the happy hell is a Talon doing out this way?" the man in black asked.

Henry stared at us in confusion, and we could only shrug back.

"Hang on a minute," the stranger muttered, raising the pistols back up. "You ain't no Talon. You got their eyes, but you ain't deformed like them, and you're keeping the company of a halfbreed. Who the blue blazes are you people?"

"We could ask the same of you," Maggie shot back.

"Fair enough. Malakhai is what my mama named me. And ya'll are . . . ?"

"Just travelers passing through," I put in, trying to figure a way out of the gun sights. Well, as Maude would say: when in doubt, try the truth. Just be sure to keep a couple of your cards back. "Me and the ladies are ground folk, just making our way through. The man with the pretty eyes is Omega Thomas, a Tellurian. You know about them, right?"

Malakhai's eyes widened, and he gave a low whistle. "Nice of you high and mighty to come down here with the rest of us peons. Although you might consider heading back up in the clouds, if you know what's good for you."

"Ah, that old friendly greeting of 'you ain't from around here, are you, boy?'" Henry spat. He was a bit more sensitive than I was to folk looking down on me for my skin shade. "Now could you lower the damn guns and tell your mutt there to calm down?"

"Oh, he ain't growling at you," Malakhai said, bringing the pistols back up.

Henry and I went flat on our bellies like Sarah, trying to avoid getting hit as Maggie rolled forward and snatched her rifle back up. As she took a firing position, though, two shots rang out from Malakhai's guns.

Pained snarls startled us as something big and heavy smashed through the woods behind us.

The werewolf that we hadn't noticed stalking us was black-furred with white streaks on her paws. Malakhai's first two bullets destroyed her elbows, rendering her arms temporarily useless.

"Stay down, you damn fools!" Malakhai shouted as he fired off three more shots. The first two hit the attacking werewolf's kneecaps, blowing blood and bone out the other side; the third one was a head shot that jerked the furback to a stop.

"I have silver loaded; I will dispatch the lycanthrope," Maggie said, swiveling her rifle around to the more immediate threat.

"No!" Malakhai yelled, darting forward in a blur of speed.

He knocked her Winchester off target just as she fired. Instead of center mass, Maggie's bullet caught the werewolf in the shoulder. Muscle and blood exploded from the howler as the silver reacted violently with her tainted flesh. The critter snarled as she was flipped around by the force of the shot.

"Stop trying to kill the poor bitch!" Malakhai snapped. "Neshomne! Lockjaw!"

The Broken wrong-wolf dug its steel claws into the dirt and sprang forward, quickly crossing the distance to the injured werewolf. Those same claws sank deep into the furback's flesh as Neshomne drove her to the ground. The black-furred wolf tried snapping at her mechanically-augmented attacker, but her joints hadn't healed back yet, and the head shot had knocked her senseless. Neshomne maneuvered to get behind his victim and latched down hard on the nape of her neck with his jaws, pinning her to the ground.

Maggie worked the lever on the Winchester and pointed it at Malakhai.

"Really? We're back to this again?" he said, arching an eyebrow. "Ma'am, if you want a good old-fashioned draw-down after I'm done, I'll oblige you. But right now, I got other business to attend to."

There was a blur of motion, and he was gone before she could pull the trigger.

In a streak of black and red he was on the pinned werewolf's back, pushing aside the growling Neshomne to get access. With his red-gloved hands, Malakhai pulled the werewolf's fur back, digging deep to look at her roots.

"Damn. I was afraid of that."

I could barely hear him, but I could see him well enough. He gritted his teeth with a grimace, and that's when I realized what was wrong with his mouth.

Malakhai had a pair of silver fangs.

A gurgled cry of pain came from the pinned furback as Malakhai bit into her. Rather than create the explosion of gore that silver usually did, his fangs simply penetrated through the howler's tough hide and into the flesh underneath like a hot knife through butter. There was a ghastly sucking sound, and my stomach roiled.

Malakhai was drinking the werewolf's blood.

We just stood there in shock. After about a minute of the terrible tableau, Malakhai raised his head up.

His eyes were wide and white, with no sign of pupil or iris to them. Blood matted his mutton chops, but not as much as I'd expected from the sounds.

Malakhai let out an inhuman scream and blurred.

His body was vibrating so fast and violent it threw out dirt from under him in small clouds. Then, just as suddenly as he'd started, he stopped shaking.

Malakhai was obviously exhausted. He staggered back from his victim for a moment, waving Neshomne off. The big white Broken released its jaw-hold on the other werewolf's neck. The wounded beast didn't move, save to whine. With a sigh of resignation, Malakhai went back to draining the poor furback.

"I really want to shoot him. Now, please," Maggie said, her voice breaking a bit. Sarah nodded with her sister's suggestion, her face white with fear.

Maybe it reminded them a bit too much of how they lost their mama to the Broken. Maybe they were just plain creeped out by the weird antics of the stranger. Either way, I couldn't blame either of them for wanting to put a stop to what was going on. But I also couldn't let Maggie kill the only other person we'd run into on the ground, not when we desperately needed information on what lay north of us.

Still, I'd grown tired of watching the sideshow as well. I stepped forward to put a stop to Malakhai's bloody feast and get some answers.

Neshomne leapt in front of Malakhai, protecting him from my

interference, a deep and metallic growl vibrating from his throat. Maggie raised her rifle and Henry stepped forward with balled-up fists, but the wrong-wolf wasn't advancing on me. He was just making sure I didn't move any farther.

"Enough," Malakhai said from behind his big friend. "It's done."

Neshomne gave us one last warning rumble before backing up a bit. I expected to see the other werewolf dead, drained dry of her blood.

Instead, Malakhai was crouching over the naked form of a brown-skinned woman in her forties. Fur and quickly rotting flesh surrounded her like a macabre halo, the tell-tale signs of a werewolf that had returned to human skin and shed its bestial form. Malakhai shrugged off his heavy black duster, using it to wrap the unconscious woman as he staggered upright.

His red eyes had returned to normal, although there were blood-shot veins lacing them. Looking like he'd been on the bad end of a week-long bender, he called Neshomne over.

The big wrong-wolf went to all fours and knelt down obediently. Malakhai grabbed a handful of the white back fur and swung himself up onto the Broken's back, still holding onto the woman. With a nudge of his heels and a click of his tongue, he brought Neshomne parallel to us.

"Get on out of here. Take your young'un there and head back the way you came."

"I'm afraid we can't do that," I said, setting my jaw stubbornly.

Malakhai frowned and shook his head. "I'm serious, kid. Don't follow me. Ain't nothing but pain and death where I'm going."

"Eli's not the kind to take anyone's advice," Henry said, the ghost of a grin tugging the edges of his mouth.

The man in black sighed, turning Neshomne away. Malakhai shouted over his shoulder as he rode the ironhide north.

"Then I'll see you all in Hell!"

Chapter 4

THE SQUALL TUBES ON the *Bantam* sparked bright blue as it flew away, laboring to stay atop the weakening currents and carrying Henry back to Wardenclyffe. He'd only been able to spare a few hours, but it had been enough to cobble together repairs on the surge pack.

"Now, then," I said, turning back to Sarah. "What have we learned from today's shenanigans??"

"Not to wander off," Sarah replied with a roll of her eyes.

"Nope. The lesson here is 'shoot strangers on sight before they put a hole in your lightning generator.'"

Sarah giggled, stifling it at Maggie's scowl.

"You are too lenient with her."

I shrugged. "I ain't her daddy. Besides, there's no way she could have knocked down that gunslinger before he pulled on her. She's just lucky he didn't have murder on his mind."

Maggie was incredulous. "Are you blind? He was using her to lure out the lycanthrope. She was naught but a stalking goat to him, put out to draw the hungry beast in."

"Maybe. Or maybe he just ran across her while hunting the furback. No way to really know, and I'd rather assume better than worse. Besides, if all he was interested in was drawing out the critter, he'd have shot Sarah instead of the surge pack. Fresh blood from a wound would have brought the wolf running faster than anything else."

"Perhaps," Maggie admitted. "Does this mean you intend to follow his advice then and turn back from our journey north? Surely if you are willing to give him the benefit of the doubt in endangering Sarah, then you must also heed his words on the folly of proceeding."

In response, I just pointed at the dot of Wardenclyffe on the horizon.

"Madness," she grumbled, but let it go at that.

"I figure him and his kin are why this area is so clear of wolves."

A troubled expression passed over Maggie's face.

"Possibly," she allowed, fetching a map out of the pack she'd ransacked from her old den in Sacramento. "According to this, that abandoned city we passed, Salem, used to be the state capitol. Why did his people not reclaim it, if they are so adept at holding the lycanthropes at bay?"

I poked at the map. "There. They likely holed up in Portland, farther north. It's got a river and easy access to the sea. Fishing and hunting would be better. Seems like a decent place to refound a civilization."

"Then why would Malakhai warn us off from following him?"

"Does it really matter? We're not even going that way. From the triangulation that Henry and me managed to do, the telluric sinkhole lays somewhere in the Cascade Mountains to the northwest, not in the valley itself. Whatever is affecting the currents, it's up there."

Sarah popped her head up with a big grin.

"Does that mean we get to climb another mountain?"

I snorted at her excitement, but Maggie shook her head in worry.

"This is not going to be as easy as you think, Sarah. We used passes to avoid scaling peaks when we were attempting to stay ahead of Wardenclyffe, but this is an actual feat of strength and endurance that we are ill-equipped to undertake. We have none of the gear explorers possessed in the old stories, nor do we have a knowledgeable guide. It will be dangerous."

"Then stay behind," I snapped. Anger flashed hot and bright as a gunshot. "I've had a bellyful of your complaining."

I instantly regretted my outburst. Ever since the wolf had infected my blood, I'd found myself jumping salty more easily, taking offense and biting back in normal everyday conversations. But Maggie's constant attempts to get us to turn back to Sacramento, to accept my fate to become one with her pack and let Wardenclyffe go its own way, were starting to wear on my nerves.

It didn't help that she was right.

Our beast-born stamina and strength had helped us win the footrace against Wardenclyffe, but we'd been tackling deer trails during summer. The Cascades were lined up like solemn monoliths to the east, all the way up the valley. I had no idea what to expect on the climb up, nor was I looking forward to the hardships involved. But that didn't matter much when lives were on the line.

"You know I will not abandon you," Maggie said, her face going rigid at my tone. "If my counsel is no longer useful to you, however, feel free to get yourself killed. Surely your precious flying city will not suffer the same fate as its idiotic champion if he chooses to sacrifice his life so meaninglessly."

She had me there. I couldn't very well toss my nuts in the fire without it coming back to burn Wardenclyffe. Rushing in headlong to climb a mountain range without proper gear or training wasn't the brightest idea I'd ever had.

"We could always ask Malakhai's people for help," Sarah said. She hated it when we fought.

"Didn't sound like the folks in Portland are too keen on visitors." I shrugged. "Still, without any alternatives, a bad plan is still better than none at all. Maggie?"

"I do not like it," she grumbled, folding the map back up. "Still, there may be a way to split the difference. We can do a reconnoiter around the lowlands of the Cascades as we approach before splitting off east toward Portland. After all, we do not know precisely where the source of the telluric interference is located. Perhaps it will be at the foot of the mountains, and we may avoid the fool's errand altogether."

"You really think we'll get that lucky?"

"We will not know until we try, Elijah. Besides, it will also give us the opportunity to locate the precise area Malakhai's people reside in. After all, we are merely assuming that is where he went. He did not name his origin, he only said it was to the north. If Portland has not been resettled as you suspect, then we should be able to acquire equipment there to facilitate the scaling of the mountain."

"A perfectly reasoned plan," I agreed. "Not a chance in the world that it'll go off without a hitch though."

Sarah laughed at my wry grin. After a moment Maggie joined in, and the tension between us eased.

We were still about twenty miles away from the Cascades, so we pushed ourselves hard the rest of the day. It didn't matter how much wolf you had running through your blood when you go jogging with fifty pounds of gear on your back; the trip still takes a bit out of you. But we pressed on, and by the time darkness fell we were a lot closer to the mountains than we'd started.

The strange heat lightning that had been playing across the sky for the last few weeks had intensified, and the dusk was lit by erratic snaps and pops going off high above us in the clouds. I felt sick to my stomach, and it had nothing to do with the running, or the fact we'd still not seen another living soul in our journey. I'd thought that the telluric currents would just disappear into the sinkhole as we got closer.

I'd been wrong.

Instead, it was like someone had wrenched the streams out of the earth and shoved them up in the air. Everything was topsy-turvy, with us feeling the echo on the ground while they faded into nothingness above.

Maggie and Sarah appeared queasy too; their supernatural senses had been turned inside-out. It didn't take much for us all to agree to bed down for the night and to tackle the rest of the trip in the morning.

The night was deader than we'd come to expect. Without werewolves on the prowl, the last few weeks we'd heard the animal kingdom just going at it every night, hooting and hollering to each other. None of us had ever heard such a chorus before. It gave me hope that maybe the world wasn't quite as doomed as I'd been brought up to believe.

But there was nothing tonight. The clouds above blocked out the starlight, and the night seemed malevolent in the way it pressed in on us. For the first time in a couple of weeks, we set up a watch routine, with each of us taking a three-hour shift to keep a weather eye out for trouble. Even knowing there was someone on guard, none of us slept well that night.

The morning dawned humid and heavy, and we ate in gloomy silence. Flashes of lightning continued to crackle above us in the clouds, and our feet felt like they were filled with lead as we started the hike up the mountain again.

After only an hour walking, I had to call a break.

"What's wrong?" Sarah asked. There was no trace of her normal jubilation, no sign of bubbly excitement barely contained. She had dark circles under her eyes, and there was a slur to her words that was only matched by my own. It took a moment for me to remember why I'd stopped us.

"We're going the wrong way."

"That is ridiculous," Maggie scoffed. "See? The sun is . . . wait, it is not in the correct position."

She was pointing west, but the sun was climbing the sky in the east. I toed the still-warm ashes from the remains of a familiar campfire.

"We just backtracked to where we started."

Sarah and Maggie both stared at me like I was going mad. But as they took stock of our surroundings, they slowly realized I was right.

"My stomach hurts," Sarah whimpered.

"Mine as well," Maggie said, placing a concerned hand over her sister's gurgling guts. "Could our disorientation be an artifact of whatever is happening with the telluric streams?"

"How the hell should I know?"

I stopped myself. This was wrong. I'd gotten irritated with Maggie before, same as she had with me. But we were snapping at each other more than normal, and there wasn't any good reason for it. The same realization flitted across her eyes. We moved a little distance off from Sarah, and bent our heads in.

"Her mind is untroubled by whatever is inciting our tempers," Maggie whispered to me.

"Maybe because she hasn't gone through her first change yet?"

"It is the only possibility I can think of. Does that mean she might be less affected by the strange loss of directional sense as well?"

I snorted. "It's worth a shot. She'll never let us live it down, though."

Sarah was all too happy to be nominated as the trailblazer. After the first couple of times that we began wandering off her steps, we tied ourselves to her. For two hours she tugged at us, making sure we kept going in the right general direction.

After a while though, we noticed we'd again started backtracking on our own footprints. We kept trying to head toward the mountains, keeping the sun in the same position relative to us in the sky. But we all felt sicker and sicker, as if someone had force-fed us a whole bottle of castor oil mixed with rancid grease.

"I'm sorry," Sarah mumbled, as the sun started to dip toward the horizon. "Whatever got hold of you, has me now, too."

"Don't blame yourself," I said, struggling to keep the bitter pit in my heart from lashing out at her. It wasn't the girl's fault, and damned if I'd take my mood out on her. "It's stronger on us, too. I'm not sure how much more of this I can take. My stomach is about to climb up and start slapping me if we don't get some distance between us and the source. There's got to be another way around this shit."

As soon as we began moving away from the mountains, the queasiness and discomfort started fading. The farther we traveled away from the Cascades, the better we felt, and the faster our feet moved. Maggie and I shared a worried glance over what that could mean. But Sarah's bubbliness has started to come back, and it was enough to buoy our spirits as well.

Wardenclyffe was still a ways off. We'd find Malakhai and his people, get what help we could, then return and bust through the sinkhole's effects. The farther away we got from the mountains, the more I was certain of that plan.

It took another day and change to hike the foothills back toward Portland. The woods were silent and still throughout the trip, and game was scarce. Rations sustained us, but there was a pall over the group that even Sarah's antics couldn't dispel.

Full night had taken us again by the time we saw the first lights in the distance below. The stamina lent by our infection was flagging after the long slog, but it was nearly done. We'd figured the ruins of Portland were where Malakhai's folk had set up camp, and it looked like we were right. The three of us marveled at how many lanterns we saw being lit in the valley below.

"Could they really have done it?" Sarah asked her sister, her cheeks flushed with excitement. "Restarted everything, I mean. Is this what all the old books were talking about, the wonders of civilization?"

"Perhaps. But remember Malakhai's exhortations. He seemed fairly certain we would not find a warm welcome."

"Fat lot of choice there is," I grumbled. "We got a powerful need. We'll just have to come to some kind of understanding."

Despite the confidence I shoved into my words, it wasn't the telluric sinkhole behind us that made my belly shudder as we descended toward Portland.

It was fear.

Chapter 5

W E ARRIVED ON THE outskirts of the town a few hours later. I'd become more and more impressed on the approach at how many lights were firing up across the valley, and about halfway there we saw cables crisscrossing across the fields ahead. That's when I realized the inhabitants weren't lighting torches or oil lanterns.

"Holy hell," I said. "They've got power."

Maggie shrugged, avoiding a tree root and making sure I didn't sprain my fool ankle with the same. "Why is that such an amazing fact to you? Your city has power, your flying locomotives have power. Sarah bears your own creation, a portable lightning generator cobbled together from spare parts. It releases quite a bit of power into us every full moon cycle."

"It's not the same. Wrangling storms, energizing the squall tubes, hell, even the surge pack; these are all seat-of-our-pants things. We don't have a consistent ability to generate electricity. In some ways, we're like parasites living off what nature provides, draining the energy out of the world to keep our own asses safe. But to provide stable power to a large community, without the need to drain storms and race for the next charge? It's something you can only do on the ground, with access to a wide range of resources."

Sarah did a little jump, stomping and sending up a puff of dust. "Wow . . . ground. Hey, Maggie, did you know that was what we were walking on? I could've sworn it was unicorn hide!"

"Very funny, wise-ass. I meant it was amazing to see it happen now, post-apocalypse. Whoever's running Portland has done something amazing: they've taken the first step to reestablishing a foothold for civilization. Imagine not having to hide in the clouds anymore!"

Maggie and Sarah had the same insulted expression.

"Elijah, we, and others like us, are not hiding. We live here."

"But not as people, as real folk! Eventually you all go down to the fur, become wolves permanently!"

Sarah scrunched up her face somewhere between a pout and a scowl. "We're not real people to you?"

"That ain't what I'm saying, I just meant—"

"We are fully aware of what you meant, Elijah Aloysius Kelly," Maggie said. "That we take issue with your words is not an indication that we did not comprehend their meaning."

Suddenly I remembered Maude, calling me by my full name, right before she lit into me for breaking a rule. Was it just common womanly courtesy to give men such a warning before they brought the hammer down? Should I keep trying to dig myself out of the hole as the walls fell in, or accept that I'd been stupid and try to distract her?

For once, I chose wisely.

"That's some mighty big corn over there."

I pointed out across a field at the edge of the forest, desperate to get her focused on something, anything, other than me. Maggie stared hard at me for a minute, before turning to see the wondrous corn that would save me from my own stupidity.

The rows of neatly tended vegetables did their job. I wasn't sure how high corn grew naturally, having lived most of my life in the sky, but I was pretty sure the green ears weren't meant to be as thick as my thigh. The stalks were at least twice our height, bowed down by the weight of their bounty. If it wasn't for the incline leading down from the woods, we wouldn't have been able to see the field in its entirety.

Cables crisscrossed the field in a grid pattern, and I could feel the electricity surging through them, generating a current that made my teeth buzz. The top of the stalks were damn near touching the lines, and a couple of scorch marks on them showed where they'd actually brushed against the high cables.

A lone scarecrow hunched down in the middle of the field, just as over-sized and distorted as the corn he guarded. On the other side of the field a farmhouse and barn sat, both with electric lights burning, where folks were working. Lanterns were also spaced along the cables overhead, sputtering and low, giving off as much illumination as starlight.

Sarah stepped down into the field, brushing one of the corn stalks, and I hissed at her to stop. Something was very, very wrong.

The scarecrow had moved.

Maggie had seen it as well, and she'd shouldered her Winchester before Sarah had taken another step. The ornate rifle stood silent and steady; Maggie knew as well as I did that gunfire would announce us long before we'd be able to figure the situation out.

A few tense moments passed as we waited, barely breathing for fear we'd make too much noise. The malformed scarecrow shuddered once, and then, with a clanking of chains, raised its head to the sky.

And howled.

Sarah handed up the blinder goggles, and I slipped them over my eyes. The searing headache hit right away, but I could see the ghostly outlines of the electromagnetic world. Blue-white phantoms flitted across the world from the bright cables, their energy coursing through the air and into the plants below.

At the center of the shimmering web was the lupine form of a Broken, its mechanical limbs bright with the patterns of internal wiring. Brutal enhancements ran through the wrong-wolf's fleshy body, the pulsing of energy showing where it had been surgically upgraded. Unlike Malakhai's companion, this Broken had a larger, cruder furnace and boiler square on its back. The poor ironhide's spine was fused into the metal itself. It was in perpetual agony just by being alive.

"That's a hell of a thing," I breathed, handing the goggles over to Maggie. She took a quick look-see then passed them back to Sarah.

"Barbarous."

"Ain't it just?" I spat. Whoever Malakhai's people were, they seemed to have an unnatural need to use the mutilated ironhides. After seeing the man use one as a mount, I fully expected a guard or soldier of some type, but this? Using one to keep your corn safe was just downright demeaning.

The Broken lifted its muzzle to sniff the air. A deep growl thrummed out from its chest and it swung its head over to stare at us.

Maggie brought her rifle down and motioned with her head back to the forest. I nodded and reached down to help Sarah find her footing as she backed up.

"Pa! Something's got John worked up!"

We all froze at how close the boy's voice was. He was somewhere nearby in the tall corn. The lantern above the wrong-wolf flared to life, casting the world around him into stark relief.

"We don't have time to coddle his nightmares tonight. Muzzle him and get back here," came the answering shout from the boy's father.

My heart skipped a beat when the stalks nearest to the Broken parted and a young teenage boy stepped out within claw-range of the big wrong-wolf. It took me a moment to realize the kid wasn't showing any fear of the ironhide. The big critter actually whined as the boy approached, and went down to his belly.

"It's all right, John," the kid said, reaching out to scratch behind the abomination's ears. "Sorry I have to do this, but Pa's got a point. We have to get this place ready before the Judge gets here tomorrow."

The wrong-wolf lifted one of its steel arms up, pointed straight at us, and growled.

The boy turned, squinting his eyes. The light above wasn't helping him any, and we stood motionless, willing him not to see us among the shadowed woods.

"Someone out there? Hello? Don't make me let John loose on you!"

"Jimmy! What's taking you so long?" the man called out from the farmhouse.

The boy, Jimmy, narrowed his eyes one more time at the vexing shadows that cloaked us, before giving up with a sigh.

"Sorry, John. We don't have time to play."

The timbre of the boy's voice changed, and he made an effort to enunciate his words clearly.

"Engage muzzle."

There was a click, then a whirring noise. The wrong-wolf snarled in resistance, opening his maw wide for a moment. Tiny metal hooks shot out from the critter's upper and lower jaws and latched onto each other. The ironhide whined as the hooks retracted, slamming his mouth closed with a teeth-crushing snap.

The abomination whimpered, and Jimmy gave him one last pat on the back of his head with gentle murmurings before taking off back through the corn to the farmhouse. The light above the ironhide dimmed down again, leaving him in the shadows with his pain.

"Monsters," Maggie whispered, shaking her head.

Somehow, I didn't think she was talking about the wrong-wolf. Maggie had reasons to hate the mechanical monstrosities more than most, but she was still a human being under the cold exterior she wore for the world. No decent soul could see what had been done to the Broken and keep from feeling sorry for them. They were still human, somewhere down through the fur and metal.

We made our way back along the edge of the forest, careful to keep to the shadows. You could tell where the people were working in the field by where the lanterns glowed. I was just happy they were still at it this late at night; the last thing I wanted was to use the blinders to keep watch for more folks.

Although I could tune the engineering goggles to the electrical frequency of people's bodies, it would necessitate wearing the blasted things for a bit longer than I was comfortable with. They might not blind me like they had my grandma, but that didn't mean the goggles were a welcome companion. Lately, they'd come to symbolize the difference between Maude and me, and why I couldn't live with my kin up on Wardenclyffe anymore.

The forest tapered off as we circled the farm, leaving us darting around in the wild grass. As I'd hoped though, soon we came across a dirt road, free from weeds and well-traveled. Portland's resurrection had brought with it usable roads, and it was a relief to travel along something other than deer paths.

"Why not just contact those farmers and request supplies?" Maggie asked as we followed the track into Portland.

"Backwoods folks ain't always the friendliest." I shrugged. "These people are at the edge of town, and if living on Wardenclyffe taught me anything, it was that those on the outskirts are there either because they don't fit in with other folk, or because they're mean enough to hate company. If there's any shifters come traipsing through, it'll be a farm like this that's hit first. They'll be well-armed and antsy about visitors. Do you really think that Broken was only chained out there for the crows?"

"You know way too much about how mean people can be to each other," Sarah said, tightening her grip on the surge pack's lightning rod.

"Ain't that the God's honest truth," I agreed.

Shadows surged out of the field next to the road, and three figures rose up, all carrying double-barreled shotguns. I swallowed hard at the scattergun pointed at my gut.

"Um . . . howdy?"

Chapter 6

THE BARN WAS CLEAN, crowded with tools, and smelled of deep summer. Overhead bright lights burned, illuminating the trio that had captured us. The two girls and boy, Jimmy, were obviously siblings, all of them in their early teens.

Our captors pushed us down into a corner, handling the shotguns with skill, never letting us have the chance to disarm them.

"Go get Pa," the older girl said. Jimmy nodded and ran off. I smiled friendly-like at the girls left behind, but they kept their faces blank, and the shotguns trained on us. So much for any delusions of charm.

A few minutes later a man in his late thirties stepped into the barn. His scowl marred otherwise benign features, but the expression wasn't for the trespassers on his land.

"Why in God's name did you do this?" he asked, turning to the children.

The kids glanced at each other with surprise, and the oldest girl spoke up.

"Pa, they didn't use the right way in, or the call, and they—"

"Enough!"

There was panic on their daddy's face that I didn't understand. He shushed his children and turned on us; I didn't particularly care for what I saw lurking in his eyes. It got my hackles up, and I couldn't help but to start imagining the farmer doing all manner of unspeakable things to the girls. The wolf in my blood perked its ears up and bared its teeth.

"Who sent you?" the farmer asked, voice kept carefully neutral. "Are you with the Advocates?"

We stared at him, baffled.

"Who are they?" Sarah piped up.

"Well. That's a fair start," the man grunted. "At least you're not claiming to be something I know you're not."

"What in the blue blazes are you talking about?" I asked.

"Let's start from the beginning. My name is Frank Grant," the man said. "These are my children: Jimmy, Ethel, and Louise. And you are?"

"Confused as hell."

Frank smiled ruefully, and pulled a pistol out of his waistband. "That may be true, but I'll have names in addition to attitude. Please."

"Maggie and Sarah Butler," Maggie put in, sighing at my stubbornness. "The obstinate fool is Elijah Kelly. And we apologize for trespassing on your territory."

"That part I don't mind so much," Frank said. "In fact, I'd rather have not known about you at all. But since my children apparently don't have enough chores around here to keep them out of trouble, I'm afraid I must insist you all take your clothes off."

The kids giggled nervously, and their daddy sighed like a long-suffering man. "After, of course, those same children vacate the barn."

"You might as well get to shooting," I said, my teeth bared. "Ain't no way that I'm letting you have your nasty way with no one. I'll kill you first, no matter how many bullets you put in me."

Frank curled his lip in disgust.

"What kind of man do you take me for?"

"The kind that wants a twelve-year-old girl to strip in front of him," I spat back, gesturing at Sarah.

Frank shook his head. "Either you're one hell of an actor, young man, or you really have no idea what you've wandered into."

He reached up and pulled the collar of his blue work shirt away from his neck. There were scars there, pairs of them, as if he'd been attacked multiple times by some critter. Calling his oldest girl over, he showed us a set of healing cuts on her neck too.

"Do you know what these are?"

"Should I?"

"Well, that's what I'm trying to determine. I don't want to see your friends naked; but I need to, if I'm to keep my family safe."

"Fine," Maggie put in, pulling her dress away from her neck. "See? No marks."

"Sorry, little miss," Frank said. "The scars can be just about anywhere on a body. I'm afraid I must insist on checking every inch of skin."

"Ain't happening," I snarled, taking a step toward him, paying no attention to the guns.

"Enough posturing, Elijah," Maggie said. "We have your word that the only thing that will touch our bodies are your eyes?"

"Of course," Frank said, insulted at having to answer the question. "Ethel, take your brother and sister and get back to work. We still need the farm ready for tomorrow's inspection."

The oldest girl nodded, handing over her shotgun to Frank before ushering her siblings out of the barn. She wasn't none too happy to be leaving her daddy with three belligerent strangers, but it was obvious he was used to being obeyed.

"Not Sarah," I said, catching Frank's gaze and holding it. "I'll strip down, but not her. And I swear, if you lay one hand on either of them ..."

Frank nodded. "Fine. The girl might be too young to bear the purification marks, anyway."

Maggie and I exchanged puzzled looks. But Frank had agreed to our terms, so we did what we had to do. Despite the summer heat, I felt a chill as we shed the last bit of our underclothes. It was still weird to me to be naked around the girls, even with the full moons we'd experienced, and to have a stranger staring at us in our birthday suits was downright unsettling.

I could tell that Frank was trying to be quick about his inspection, but he was thorough too. He even went so far as to ask, politely, to see our inner thighs. All through it he was red in the face; it was obvious he wasn't enjoying the ordeal either.

When it was all said and done he nodded for us to put our clothes back on, and pulled out a handkerchief to mop his brow.

"Thank God that's over," he muttered.

"I weep for your discomfort," Maggie said, raising an eyebrow.

"Sorry. I just had to be sure, is all."

"Sure of what?" I asked, exasperated.

"That you weren't spies."

"What? Spies? Who needs spies anymore, the world is dead!" I said. "Are you telling me that here, the only place we've found any civilization on the ground, you people have already managed to split into different factions and start shit with each other?"

Frank fidgeted. "Actually . . . well, yes, I suppose. But it isn't as simplistic as you make it sound."

I threw my hands up in the air and turned back to the girls. "Unbelievable! Maybe you two were right: wearing the fur permanently ain't such a bad thing after all, if this is all we can accomplish as people."

"Enough, Elijah!" Maggie said. "We have proven ourselves to this man. Surely he will now be able to explain why we had to endure such an embarrassing exhibition."

Although Frank didn't know Maggie, a deaf man could've heard the threat in her voice. He nodded apologetically, putting his pistol away and leaned the shotgun up against the wall of the barn. Frank sat on a hay bale, inviting us to do the same across from him. I didn't miss the fact that he kept the weapons close at hand, nor did he return ours. We might not bear the scars he was worried about, but the farmer was no fool.

"First things first: have you ever heard of the Cabal of Purity?"

A shudder ran through me at the mention of those bastards, and terrible memories of Dr. Trent's horrific journal rose up. "I've read about them. Bunch of racist pricks that worked on diseases and ways to kill us colored folk for decades. They were responsible for creating the werewolf virus."

Horror broke over Frank's face. "Oh, dear Lord in Heaven. I didn't know about that. How? Why?"

"Well, it wasn't exactly their original intent," I said. "The Cabal just wanted a mixture of rabies and smallpox that would wipe out the Indians. But the red man fought back, tried to cure themselves with the Ghost Dance. Best I can tell, the werewolves are what happened when science and magic collided head-on. Both sides had a hand in the final mess, but if the Cabal hadn't tried to exterminate the Indians none of this would have ever happened."

"They told us it was all the savages' fault . . ."

"Wait; what do you mean by that? You've actually met the bastards?"

Frank was embarrassed, and cleared his throat a few times before answering.

"Not face to face. They prefer to act through their agents, the Blood Judges, and the puppet government they've installed here in Portland. The Cabal are the ones behind our re-founded civilization.

"They're also the ones that keep us from turning back into werewolves."

Chapter 7

THEY WHAT? THAT'S IMPOSSIBLE!"

"And yet, Elijah, there he sits, without the fur," Maggie said. "Unless he was recently bit, at his age he should have become a lycanthrope permanently by now. That he is not supports his claim."

"The little lady's right," Frank said. "I don't quite know how long I've been infected, but I've been human full-time for the last thirteen years."

"But how?" I asked, amazed. "Even the Tellurians don't know how to cure it."

Confusion was writ large on Frank's face. "Who are they?"

"How could you not know about the storm prophets? The men and women that built the salvation cities, that oversee our very lives, the order of scientists that saved the last of humanity?"

The farmer shifted uncomfortably. "I don't remember much before I was pulled out of the fur. Some people don't even recall their names, and what memories most of us have are fragmented and scattered. The beast takes us deep; returning to humanity costs us dearly."

"Quite traumatic, I am sure," Maggie said dryly. "It is not quite as terrible a fate to be a wolf as you make it out to be. Still, a method to control shifters until their time of rage has passed would be useful to those of us that look forward to the day our evolution is complete. How have you accomplished it?"

"Have you ever heard of how you're supposed to suck out rattlesnake venom to save someone's life?"

"An ill-advised and fraudulent medical myth, but yes, I am aware of the folk tale."

"They suck out the disease," I realized, thinking back to Malakhai's attack on the werewolf.

Frank nodded. "Essentially, yes. The Blood Judges can't get enough of it out to cure us, but something about how they were altered by the Cabal lets them feed on the infection in our blood, cleansing it."

"I will never understand the penchant of 'civilized' people for dancing around the truth," Maggie sighed. "I have read of such blood-feasting creatures before. They went by another name in the ancient legends: vampires. As I recall, they were not the heroes of those stories."

"Call them whatever you want, this is a hell of a discovery!" I grinned. "A way to control the virus, a way to get humanity back on its feet!"

Frank avoided my jubilant gaze, clearing his throat and getting up off the hay bale. He slid open the barn door and breathed in the night air, his forehead creased in worry. "Not quite, friend. 'Humanity' doesn't figure into what's happening here."

It took a moment for that to sink in past the rush of finding out there was hope after all. Then I realized what he meant: the Cabal had created the Blood Judges. Their goals and reasons were anything but pure. Even the Devil shuddered at their attitude toward other folk.

Frank led us outside, motioning for us to follow him to the big wrong-wolf chained in the middle of the cornfield. I didn't like the fact he hadn't returned our weapons; we were a might too close to the big abomination for my peace of mind.

"Have you met John?" he asked, patting the ironhide's flank like a pet. "Don't worry, you can get closer. Jimmy engaged the muzzle, so he's relatively harmless."

"Yes, we saw your captive earlier," Maggie said, venom lacing her voice.

"She ain't wrong," I said "You chained him up, but he's not a dog. He might be an abomination of a werewolf now, but that John of yours used to be a man. Is still one, somewhere down deep."

"I know," Frank said, regret lacing his words. "Of all people, I know. But this is the world we live in. What's better: for the Judges to gun them down in the wild, or for them to capture the poor bastards and alter them to serve civilization? I have to believe that life is better than death."

"I'm pretty sure cutting into them and enslaving them answers that little philosophical question all by itself," I spat. "Just how many Broken have your people put into chains?"

Frank seemed confused for a second, before realization hit him. "There's a rumor or two floating around about a group of altered werewolves that rebelled and escaped into the wild. Is that who you're talking about? That's rather frightening. Even with the surgeries, the Augmented can be quite a handful. Regardless, John's not one of what you call Broken. I suppose you could call him 'Fixed,' in relation to those others."

"You mean . . ." I made snipping motions with my fingers.

"Thank God, no. Despicable as it is, they leave their parts intact to breed another generation of slaves." Frank said. He tapped John's metal arms and legs. "Most of the Augmented have their limbs encased in steel, with an in-built muzzle. Safety features, you understand. The hive collar John wears controls it all. The Talons can control him remotely, but it also responds to our voice commands, allowing us to work with him. It'll lock him down if he tries to attack his owners."

I found myself growling, echoed by Maggie and Sarah.

"Sorry," Frank said, holding his hands up. "But not talking about it doesn't change anything. Technically, I'm John's master. I don't treat him like property, but I do have to keep up appearances on occasion."

"Why?" Sarah asked.

"Because not all of us are resigned to a life of running on all fours chasing prey," Frank said. "I get that you people are born to this. I'm not. And I don't want to live that way. Despite what you might think, nobody should be destined to lose themselves to being a wild animal. Werewolves are not natural. This is a disease, more deadly than any plague people have ever faced in history. To preserve the human race, aren't some compromises worth it?"

I toed the chains latched onto John's arms.

"Are they?" I said bitterly. "If the compromise hollows out what it means to be human, if it degrades us by turning us into slaver filth, could it ever be worth it? What are you saving, if this is the cost?"

"So says the man without children," Frank said, shaking his head. "You saw Ethel; without the Blood Judges, she would have already turned by now. Jimmy and Louise are on the cusp. Should I abandon them to the wild, let them go feral and hunt and kill each other? Or me? Or you?"

"There's got to be a better way."

"You're starting to sound like an Advocate now," Frank sighed, staring off at the mountains. "I don't disagree with them; for God's sake, I turn a blind eye to them using the barn as a hideaway when they're sneaking through. That's why I was irritated with my children at capturing you; I don't want to know what the Advocates are doing. It keeps my family safer that way. But the longer this whole mess keeps going, the more I think they're just fooling themselves."

"All right, enough's enough!" Sarah threw her hands into the air in frustration. "First we're not them, then we are. Make up your mind. It sounds like you can't even decide if they're the good guys or the bad guys."

"Some call the Advocates rebels; most regard them as criminals," Frank said with a shrug. "The Cabal has tried to stamp them out before, but they're well-versed in covering their tracks. They call the mountains home, but make periodic raids and sorties into Portland and the outlying farms."

"For what? Corn?" Sarah asked.

"Not quite. They come for the Augmented."

"But why?"

Frank motioned John down. The wrong-wolf went to his belly without resistance.

"Come here." Frank parted John's fur, and Sarah peeked in. "What do you see?"

"Lots and lots of fur."

"And under that, little miss?"

"Skin, I guess."

"Brown skin," he corrected.

"So?" Sarah said. "He must've been a brown man before turning.

Doesn't affect fur color though, and other lycanthropes don't care about that stuff anyway. So what?"

"None of the Augmented that have white skin."

Son of a bitch.

Sarah didn't understand what Frank was driving at. But I did. The Cabal hadn't been experimenting on just anyone. They'd chosen the infected they'd considered subhuman before the Wendigo virus had run rampant across the world. Under the fur of the Augmented the skin would be a variety of colors and shades. But there would be one common theme: they were all colored folk.

The Cabal had brought back slavery.

"This is the trade you're willing to make?" I demanded, hauling Frank up by his work shirt "Seriously? This is what you're going to defend?"

He didn't fight me, and there was a haunted shadow in his eyes. "I know the price."

"You may know it, but you are not the one paying it," Maggie said, disgust on her face. "To cling to your precious 'humanity,' you will deprive another of theirs. I will say this: you are correct. You do not belong among the lycanthropes. For no beast is as low as you."

John growled, deep in his throat. But the ironhide stayed down on his belly, despite his body shuddering. The complicated metal collar ringing his throat emitted a series of pops and sparks with smoke; I could only assume it was keeping him from ripping our throats out for threatening his master.

"Why don't you release your dog?" I asked, teeth bared, shaking Frank with every word. His feet were off the ground, and I could feel the wolf surging in my blood with my anger. "Ain't that what he's for? Barking at intruders, protecting the family farm? It's not like he was, he is, a man, with hopes, and dreams, and family somewhere. No, his life is something that's fair game to be traded for yours, right?"

"Don't you understand?" the farmer said, still not releasing his wrong-wolf from its muzzled state. "I don't have a choice in this. I hate the system, hate their ideals. But I have to watch out for my children, do what's right by them."

"Bullshit," Sarah said, surprising us all. I'd never heard her cuss before, as Maggie disapproved of it.

"You talk like kids are fragile, like we're some sort of treasure to be squirreled away and protected at all costs. I'm sitting here listening to you justify this, this *mutilation*, for your kids' sake? What kind of future do you think you're buying for them by paying this cost? They're not stupid; you're their daddy, and you're telling them that this is their fault!"

Frank was horrified. "No, not at all!"

"Yes," Maggie put in. "You say you accept this travesty for them. Do you think they do not hear your words? How many others in Portland say the same thing to their children? 'This evil is for you.' That is not proving love. That is telling them that they are a curse upon your existence. 'If it were not for you, I would be a better man.' You use your offspring as an excuse to hide your own cowardice, to obscure the fact that you are willing to engage in slavery and to stand with evil rather than face your own fears."

"No!"

The denial hadn't come from Frank this time; it was voiced by Ethel, as she and her two siblings stepped out of the corn. The racket from our argument had brought them running, and they hadn't forgotten their shotguns. The kids didn't seem too happy that I had hands on their daddy, and the boy saw that their wrong-wolf was still muzzled.

"John!" Jimmy cried out. "Disengage muz—"

"Stop!" Maggie shouted, walking straight into their scatterguns. She got so close they had to back up a step. "Say that second word, and I will murder you, child."

We all stopped arguing and turned a horrified stare at the fiery woman.

"I make no apologies," Maggie said, a hand coming to rest on the shotgun barrel poking in her belly. "If you attempt to harm Elijah, I will kill you where you stand. Any of you. You will not be able to stop me before I murder you all. On this, you have my word."

"Maggie, don't do this," her sister pleaded. "You're too close to your final change; if they . . . please, I don't want to lose you yet!"

The ghost of a small smile tugged at Maggie's thin lips. "I smell no silver shot loaded into these weapons. Tear me in half with them if you wish, but I will rise again, and I wager the lycanthrope version of me will be quite peeved. Frank Grant may hide his choices in the illusion of protecting his children from the world, but I am honest in mine. Elijah is my mate. Those who seek his life will die by my hand. There are no exceptions to this rule."

"Damn it, stop trying to kill yourself to save me!" I said, exasperated. I let go of Frank and turned to her. "I made my choices, and I'll not have you spilling your blood to pay for them."

"You may not honor my feelings for you, or reciprocate them," Maggie answered, her voice tight and controlled. "But that does not diminish my own. I love you, Elijah Kelly. You are kind, intelligent, and you do what is right. Beyond that, though . . . I . . . I just love you. Damn it. Were you a cowardly dullard with the morals of a Tellurian, I would still love you. I cannot help it, cannot stop it. Nor do I desire to. You may do as you wish with your own heart.

"But you have mine. Now and forever."

I was stunned. While it was true that Maggie had made no secret about her feelings for me, I'd written them off as a side-effect of the curse we shared, the infection that she'd transferred to me when she'd bitten me that first time. I had no idea that her emotions ran that deep for me. Maggie didn't seem like the type of woman that had that kind of capacity. I'd sold her short, though. Under the controlled exterior, she was just as passionate as anyone else.

She loved me.

"Maggie, I—"

"Please; save whatever excuse you are going to use to deny my feelings until later. I am trying to preserve your life, wretched man."

"Fair enough. You can start by not getting yourself dead."

"Elijah . . ."

"I don't particularly like the situation either," I said. Her sudden and intense display of emotion had thrown a tub of cold water on my own anger. "Hell, I'm the one that started you and Sarah after his hide over his excuses. I should have held my temper better though. We can't afford to climb up on this soapbox just yet. Otherwise, ten thousand people in Wardenclyffe are going to pay the price for our ideals."

The ladies looked like they were going to argue for a moment; but both reluctantly nodded their heads. Maggie backed away from the kids slowly. At least they didn't sic their wrong-wolf on us right away.

"You just keep your distance from my children," Frank said, pushing his kids behind him a bit. They were the ones with the shotguns, while we were still unarmed. But I didn't think now was the time to point that inconsequential fact out to the man. He was a bit too worked up for my liking, what with Maggie threatening his children and all.

"We have to get back to work," Frank said. "Judge Tillman isn't exactly the most forgiving lawman wearing the fangs, and we need him to drain the infection out of Ethel and myself. There's a small room hidden under the barn that the Advocates use. It has bedding, and whatever other supplies the last group left."

He waved us off as we went to thank him.

"Don't. Listen, I know you don't agree with what I'm willing to trade for keeping my children safe. I don't care. Being a father doesn't mean asking for other people's permission to protect your son and daughters. Keep your heads down, and wait until the Judge is gone before you leave the room under the barn."

Frank shooed his kids back to the farmhouse, then turned to us. Gone was the gentle father watching out for his children, the good man struggling to keep his morals in a bad time. His face held only hostility. Maggie had crossed a line with him. He pointed his finger at his chained wrong-wolf.

"If you're not gone before tomorrow night, I swear to God above that I'll let John loose on you and bury what's left in the field. Don't ever darken my doorstep again."

I swallowed hard and nodded at the farmer.

"We understand. Thank you."

Somewhere down in Portland, a lone werewolf howled in misery and confusion, the note ringing clear across the valley.

I kindly agreed with him.

Chapter 8

CLOUDS GATHERED ABOVE. LIGHTNING flashed, and thunder rattled my teeth. The well-worn planks of Wardenclyffe's streets shuddered with the storm's rage. The buildings grew indistinct as a heavy fog descended around me.

Something growled in the dark.

A pair of glowing eyes, blue-white like the lightning above, burst into existence behind me. Teeth wreathed in sparks lined an impossibly large muzzle as it opened, roaring with hunger. The werewolf's form coalesced from the storm, its body nothing more than an outline of sizzling electricity.

Deep rumbles from it echoed the storm above. The elemental monstrosity reached out toward me with a clawed hand as large as a horse. One word came through the roar, a word that shattered my very bones with its power.

"MINE."

My eyes shot open.

Sunlight filtered through the wooden slats above me as a rooster crowed in the chilly air.

"Shh," Sarah whispered from across the small space separating us.

My breathing was ragged, and my throat was sore like I'd been crying out in my sleep. A weight was pressed up against my side, and in the gloom my sleep-addled mind panicked for a second, thinking the stormwolf had followed me out of my dreams.

Then the lump snored.

I tried to cover my laughter, so as to not wake Maggie up, but Sarah was giggling right along with me. We both shook with barely-suppressed snorts, although mine was more out of relief than anything else. Maggie mumbled something, and then scooted closer, her arm circling my waist as she snuggled her face into my chest.

My giggles faded as something else took hold. Even in the half-light under the barn, Maggie's hair caught the rays of the rising sun, setting the strawberry-blonde strands ablaze. The stern expression she cultured during waking hours was relaxed with sleep, and I couldn't resist brushing one of the errant hairs away. Her cheek was soft, softer than I'd expected. Maggie smiled at my touch, lost in her dreams of a better world.

"She really does love you," Sarah whispered.

"I know," I sighed. "But how can she be sure it's not just the bite forcing her feelings on her?"

"You're giving that stuff way too much credit. Haven't you realized by now? The emotional effect fades within a full moon or two."

"Sarah, that doesn't make sense. I mean, I still feel the same pull toward her; if anything, it's only intensified."

"Yeah, of course," she grinned. "That's because you love her back, you dummy."

Stealing a glance at Maggie, I felt my heartbeat faster. "I . . . I just thought . . ."

"Did you?" Sarah teased. "Did you really?"

"No." I grinned. "I suppose I didn't."

I'd spent so much time and energy denying that there was anything between me and Maggie that I'd missed that very thing growing stronger. We'd been there for each other time and again, whether it was fighting the Broken back in Sacramento, or staying ahead of Wardenclyffe and all the werewolf packs we'd encountered since then. More than that, though, there was just a weird combination of desire and certainty between us. Maggie had made up her mind and her heart a while ago it seemed.

She'd just been waiting for me to catch up.

"Hell of a time to fall in love," I whispered, stroking Maggie's cheek again.

Sarah just grinned back, passing over a piece of dried fruit. I munched on my breakfast in silence, trying my damnedest not to shift and wake the sleeping lady snuggling me. I wanted this to last as long as it could.

Sarah had found a stash of supplies down here. Given Frank's insistence on not knowing what was going on below his barn, it didn't surprise me that what he thought of as a small alcove had been enlarged and fairly well-stocked. The Advocates hadn't been shy about taking advantage of his willing ignorance, and it was pretty obvious this was a major jumping-off point for them.

In addition to the food, there were a variety of clothes packed away in a couple of crates. There was also one that had, of all things, theatrical supplies; makeup, wigs, and spirit gum. But the strangest find of all was at the bottom of the crate: an all-too-familiar skull and neck brace.

"Look what else I found while you were snoozing." Sarah pulled a strange leather helmet out of the corner. A dozen cables and connectors led from it back into the wall. It had a chin strap, and the eyes had been covered by a pair of metal discs that sprouted more of the cables. We'd missed it during the night, hidden as it was in its own tiny indentation in the alcove.

"That appears . . . unfriendly," Maggie yawned, stretching out next to me. I covered my sigh of regret with a cough, and offered her part of my breakfast. She sat up, absentmindedly chomping on the desiccated apple slice.

"Here, let me see that," I said. Sarah let me take hold of the odd helmet. I flipped it over; it had copper and gold wires running throughout the interior, and a familiar set of obsidian lenses mounted within the eye-plates.

"Figures," I snorted in amusement. "Some wise-ass modified a pair of blinder goggles and put them in this contraption. I wonder what they were after?"

Sarah rolled her eyes at me. "Well? Put it on and find out!"

I stared down at the helmet dubiously. Blinders weren't something I wanted over my eyes in the best of circumstances. It was a pretty good bet that whoever had integrated them into the helmet didn't possess the technical know-how of the Tellurians that invented the blasted things.

Still, there was only one way to be sure.

"Be sure to wear black when you bury me," I said, trying to make it sound like a joke. But there was a tension I couldn't hide in my words.

I slipped the helmet over my head. With the eyes covered like they were, it felt as if the world had disappeared, like some giant leech had latched onto my head and was consuming me. Fighting down the panic, I pulled the chinstrap tight and braced myself.

Nothing happened.

"Hey, there's a switch in here," Sarah said. I could barely hear her through the helmet.

"Don't—"

Whatever I'd been about to say was suddenly blanked out by a spike of intense pain. It was like someone had driven steel bolts into my brain and heated them up, roasting my head from the inside-out.

And then, just as quickly, it was gone.

I found myself floating above a ghostly version of the Grant farm. Unlike proper blinder goggles, though, the world did not resolve itself into the beautiful pulse and flow of electromagnetic currents. This seemed muddier, less distinct. The only thing that shined in this washed-out world was the grid pattern of the cables that were stationed above the cornfields. Waves of energy emanated from the cables, directed into the vegetation below. I could see the resonance of the corn itself, reacting to the electric field generated by the network.

"Are you all right, Elijah?" Maggie asked. Her voice barely penetrated, like she was speaking over a great distance.

"I think so." My own voice sounded foreign to me, strange and disconnected. "I can see the whole farm. There's movement toward the edge, if only I could . . . whoa, Bessie!"

As I fixated on the movement I saw at the edge of the cornfield, my view smeared, like watercolor in the rain, and suddenly my perception was exactly where I'd been staring at. Everything past the farm itself existed in a hazy ghost-world, with shapes silhouetted in the mist. But the movement that had drawn me in was close enough to make out.

A man in hat and duster rode astride a Fixed wrong-wolf, just as Malakhai had. Like the other Judge's mount, the new ironhide had the more advanced double furnace system and pipes, allowing it to be ridden. There weren't any colors in this washed-out world, but it didn't take a genius to know the man would be sporting the same scarlet boots and gloves with a midnight-black coat and hat. He had to be the Blood Judge that Frank's family had been worried about.

Instead of the easygoing, friendly smile that Malakhai had worn, the man's clean-shaven face was set in a perpetual scowl. He was old, sixty at least, with short hair and a hook nose. But it was his eyes, or rather, one eye, that pulled the attention. His left eye was a different frequency than the rest of him; I'd seen the effect before, when viewing Tellurians through the blinders. The eyeball was artificial, which meant that the Cabal had technology equivalent to the Tellurians. Not for the first time, I wondered at all the similarities between the two groups. There was a secret connecting the two factions, no matter how much Henry and Theta Clemens denied it.

"What do you see?"

I couldn't tell whether it was Maggie or Sarah asking. The voice was indistinct, far away.

"Judge Tillman has come a'calling."

I hadn't shouted, or raised my voice. But somehow, the ironhide the Judge was riding heard me. She stopped, turned her head to where my ghostly perception floated, and growled, ears back and teeth bared. It took me a second to realize something important.

I'd heard her growl.

Blinders and their like didn't grant the ability to perceive sounds; but whatever had been done to tie the odd helmet into the grid system over the farm had a wondrous side effect.

"What's wrong, Adeline? Someone out there?"

Tillman's voice was querulous, the kind where you could hear the man spoiling for a fight with every word. He stared hard out at the field. His artificial eye pulsed, changing frequencies several times.

"Easy, sugar," he murmured, pulling a pistol and pointing it right at me. "Anyone out there? Show yourself, or be gunned down!"

I didn't dare move, for fear of him seeing me. The girls were asking more questions in the distance, but I couldn't answer them. Despite how silly it seemed, somehow I knew that if I did anything, said anything, that would be the end of me.

Tillman stared hard a few minutes, his gun tracking across the field and ready to kill. The wrong-wolf kept growling at where I was, but the Judge was less observant than his mount. He grumbled and brought his wolf to heel. The Fixed reluctantly obeyed, still growling and tossing the occasional glance back at where my perception lingered as she trotted on.

Finally, I felt safe in pulling off the helmet. Reality hit with a blazing headache, and I gasped like a drowning man.

"Painful?" Sarah asked, her voice too loud in my ears.

"Like a bear trap on my brain," I whispered, trying to keep my voice from splitting my skull open.

Maggie brought a rag soaked in cool water from the canteen to my head, mopping the sweat away that I hadn't known was there. Her eyes were creased with worry, her lips pressed into a thin line of concerned disapproval. She wasn't exactly the picture of beauty, dirty and grumpy like that. But her gentle touch, the way she tended to me, it just crystallized what had been bubbling under my conscious for months now. Sarah had been right. It wasn't the disease making Maggie love me. She just did. It was about damn time I fessed up as well.

I loved Maggie too.

"This isn't so bad," Sarah said. To my horror, I saw that she'd put the helmet on.

"Get that thing off your fool head," I managed to wheeze out through my splitting headache.

"Do not worry, Elijah," Maggie said. "Remember, the blinder technology has a different effect on those born with the wolf blood."

"Then at least get her to stay quiet. They can hear what you say through the helmet."

Maggie scooted over to her sister, whispering just loud enough for Sarah to hear. The girl nodded in understanding; I got the impression she was concentrating on what she was seeing and hearing.

After about a half hour the headache began to subside, but it simmered right below the surface like bubbling tar. Sarah had been in the helmet the whole time, and didn't show any signs of discomfort. To keep my mind off the pain waiting in the bushes like a rattlesnake, I reached over and unfurled the oilcloth bundle that contained the metal brace I'd discovered the night before.

"What is that?" Maggie asked, keeping her voice low as she shuffled back over. Even through her prairie dress and my britches I could feel her warmth as she cuddled up against me, and it made me blush.

"I figure it's how the Advocates move around," I said. "It's a Vocalator's brace."

Maggie shuddered, and I couldn't blame her. We'd met only one Vocalator so far: Barbara, a little girl that had been enslaved to the Broken we faced in Sacramento. She'd served as the mouthpiece for the wrong-wolves, who used an iron spike from their palms shoved into the base of the girl's head to talk through her. It stood to reason that she wasn't unique, and the butchers that had created the ironhides would have altered other victims to allow their mutilated wrong-wolves to speak. Discovering the brace in the supplies confirmed it.

"Why would they need such a thing?"

I smiled. "You and Sarah might be all right trying to pass in the white-skinned Portland; something tells me though that the Advocates are a might more colorful, like me. I sure as shit can't pass for a Fixed, so I suppose that leaves only one option."

The spirit-gum in the supply bundle served well-enough to attach the Vocalator's brace to the back of my neck.

"How do I look?" I asked. "Slave enough?"

"I suppose," she said, picking up the makeup. "I will have to blend the edges; it does not sit quite right. Have you considered what happens, though, when one of these 'Fixed' attempts to interface with you?"

She had a point. Nothing like getting a six inch metal spike shoved through your skull to put a crimp on your day.

"Guess you'll just have to say 'bad dog' to any that try," I said with a fake grin, hoping to jolly her out of worry. But Maggie wasn't buying what I was selling.

We were both startled when Sarah tore off the helmet and tossed it to the side. She'd been quiet the whole time, and we figured she'd just been too entranced with following Judge Tillman and his Fixed around with her ghost-form. Even with her natural resistance to the effects of the blinders, though, Sarah had a hollow-eyed stare. I recognized the same pain I'd experienced.

She tried to say something, but her voice broke, and she tried again. "... coming ... go ..."

"Here, Sarah, drink this." Maggie handed over the canteen. Her little sister took a long swig, and handed it back over.

"We've got to get out of here," she gasped.

"Why?" Maggie asked.

"Because the Blood Judge knows this room exists. And he's headed this way."

Chapter 9

W E GATHERED ALL THE supplies we could and popped open the trap door above that led up into the barn. Sarah was still bug-eyed from the effects of the helmet, so I helped Maggie haul her out and sat her on a hay bale.

"Let us depart," Maggie said, hoisting herself over the lip of the hole.

"It don't make any sense," I said, shaking my head. "If Tillman knew about the Advocates' secret alcove, why not come straight here instead of fooling about with Frank?"

Sarah snorted. "He said he was giving Mister Grant the chance to act like a proper white man. Said nobody would hold it against him if he didn't know the dirty animals had dug a hole under his barn."

"The farmer did not speak of our presence?" Maggie asked, eyebrow cocked.

"Nope. In fact, it seemed to me he was playing for time when I snatched the helmet off. My guess is that the Judge doesn't think there's anyone here right now."

"Funny that he'd know about this place, and how he was so sure there'd be no one here. Almost like he had the inside track. The Advocates got a rat or two running around in their midst." I checked around the barn. No animals, only a few tools, just a few hay bales to make the place seem like it actually had a purpose beyond hiding the Advocates. Frank might profess to grudging support of Portland, but his actions spoke louder than his words. Time for me to do the same.

"We have to burn this place down."

"Eli! After all that farmer's done for us?" Sarah asked, aghast.

"That's why we have to destroy this building," I said. "You really think Frank will last more than a minute once the Judge sees this place? It's pretty damn obvious he ain't using the barn for farming. After Tillman sees how the Advocates have tied into his power system, it'll all be over for Frank except the screaming. Him, and his kids."

The girls got my meaning.

"So how do we do it?" Sarah asked. "Flint and tinder will take too long. Even with all this dry hay. And the thunderclap from letting loose with the surge pack would be like yelling out Mister Grant's guilt."

"We use what we got," I said, opening the trap door back up again. I hopped down, and pulled out the cables hooking the helmet into the grid. "Accidents happen, especially on a farm wired for power. There's plenty of current running through the alcove. A bit of stripping the wires, then short-circuiting . . ."

There was a snap and a spark, followed by the smell of my skin burning.

"Ouch. Um, there might be a bit more voltage here than I figured . . . better start running now."

The ladies grabbed our stuff and headed for the door, sneaking as best that they could. I yanked the cables from the mooring in the alcove and touched the sparking ends to the nearest hay bale. It went up in an instant, sending a flash of fire and smoke right into my face. I passed the arcing cable from bale to bale, tossing it against the barn wall before heading for the exit myself.

Choking black smoke followed me out, and the three of us ran into the cornfield. Cries rose up behind us, along with the sounds of chains being unlimbered. We got a fair distance into the field, and risked a glance backwards.

Leaping flames clawed at the sky. The barn was engulfed in an inferno that could be seen even above the gigantic cornstalks. I gave Sarah a boost to see what was going on, careful to keep her head from popping up like a gopher.

"They set John loose to haul water," she reported. "But the Fixed is acting clumsy, spilling most of it. I think Mister Grant's figured out what you were trying to do; he's keeping the Judge's attention on the fire."

I lowered Sarah back down, and cracked my back.

"Well, that's rent for the night paid."

"Of course, Elijah," Maggie said. "I am sure he regards a burnt-out building ample recompense for his kindness."

"Given the alternative?" I said, grinning. "If we hadn't happened by, he would have gotten a much worse outcome. We're square as can be."

Maggie grudgingly agreed, starting down the road that led into Portland. The power cables from the farm connected into a set of lines that ran alongside the dirt road, and we followed them like a trail of buzzing breadcrumbs. My wolf-born senses went a bit screwy this near to the lines. It was pretty clear that whatever was causing the telluric doldrums in the area hadn't knocked out generated power. We passed side roads with an inordinate amount of cables going down them, spaced out every mile or so.

"Do we wish to explore where these paths lead?" Maggie asked, after we'd passed the third one. "They appear to have some importance."

"I'm not sure. Normally I'd say they were more farms, but there's way too many lines running to and from them. It just doesn't make any sense." I peered down the dirt track and its multitude of cables. There was a bend around a rock outcropping that hid what lay at the end of the path.

"Before tackling Portland head-on, perhaps it would behoove us to discover the purpose of these strange roads."

"Well?" Sarah put in. "Let's get to behooving and see what's down there!"

The path had once been well-traveled, but there was plenty of fresh green growing across it now. Whatever business had spurred the creation of the route had fallen by the wayside since then.

As we approached the bend in the road, the sound of heavy chains clanking made us cautious. Rather than continue blindly, we instead decided to climb a rock at the edge of the path, doing our best to scrabble up the broken granite as quietly as possible. I'd thought I was ready for anything when we crested the top.

I was wrong.

Below us, a set of logs like spokes on a wagon-wheel sprouted out from a thick steel column. The cables we'd followed for a mile fed into the top of the post, and I could see the various gears and rings around the midsection that marked its mechanical nature. It was a bit like a crank generator, the kind that lawbreakers back on Wardenclyffe served time on when they stole or fought too much. It produced electricity from nothing but kinetic energy, as the crankers shoved the central turbine around in its housing. Essentially, it was a glorified dynamo, highly inefficient, but good for putting backs to work when there was nothing else. It was thankless labor, and it paled to the energy brought in by storms. It was nothing a man with any other choice would willingly do for any length of time, for any reason.

The Portlanders weren't using normal men though.

There was a Fixed wrong-wolf chained to each log, their mighty backs bent to the work. Restraints jangled in time to the cracking of a whip wielded by man who leaned out from a platform above the abominations. The slave driver was tall but fat, and so dirty it was hard to tell he was white; if it weren't for the methodical whip snaps I would have laid odds that he'd never seen any kind of strenuous activity before. He was muddier than a pig's ass, with a stink that wafted over the fifty yards or so to us. Baths weren't exactly something we'd been able to take regular either, but there wasn't one of us that didn't wrinkle their nose at him.

"It's a power generator," I whispered to the ladies. "A damned wasteful one, but still good enough down on the ground I suppose, when you got slaves to work it."

I pointed over to a group of six by six foot cages, situated next to a rundown shack. They were made of layered iron, crude but strong. "See there? My bet is that the overseer lives in that little house, and locks down the wrong-wolves during the night."

"They keep the Fixed in those cages? Those things are tiny!" Sarah said, horror lacing her voice.

"You expected more from these so-called people?" Maggie spat.

"C'mon, you mangy curs!" the slave-driver hollered at the ironhides. "My arm ain't getting tired, and neither are you!"

"Is every road that splits off from the main thoroughfare populated the same?"

"I don't know, Maggie. I'm trying not to think about it."

Her comforting hand on my arm would usually turn my thoughts to more pleasant areas; but this time even her touch wasn't enough to wipe away what I was seeing. My imagination conjured encampment after encampment, all at the end of the small side-roads. How many whips cracked over how many backs?

"No wonder we didn't run into anyone the last few weeks," I muttered. "They went and enslaved the whole damn countryside."

"We should go before they see us," Maggie whispered. "The solution to your city's imminent doom will not be found here."

"All right, you goddamn auggers!" the overseer shouted. "Feeding time! Sit on your worthless asses while I fill your trough, you useless animals!"

Maggie was right; there was nothing here that would help Wardenclyffe, or solve the mystery of the dead zone in the telluric currents. But to turn my back on what was right in front of me? I just wasn't that kind of bastard.

"Give me the spyglass," I said. My tone wasn't pleasant. But Maggie understood. She handed it over without comment.

The ironhides below were a sight to see. I'd expected a similar level of sophistication in their augmentations as I'd seen in the Fixed on Frank's farm and ridden by the Judges; but these were closer to the Broken in Sacramento, a hodgepodge of half-completed experiments that barely functioned. But there was something they all shared: the same brutal surgery had been performed on each one of them.

They had their jaws welded shut.

Unlike the muzzle contraption that the 'luckier' ironhides had been implanted with, the poor abominations below had suffered the indignity of simply having metal plates bolted across their snouts and then welded together. Breathing holes had been punched through the iron at regular intervals, but damned if I knew how they got food into their bellies.

My answer came with the reappearance of the overseer, who unchained each ironhide in turn and led it to a long metal trough in front of the cages before locking it into place. Once he'd moved them all, the dirty man went to the head of the trough and pulled a lever.

A rancid slurry of corn meal and ground meat poured down the trough from a spigot. The ironhides shoved their metal muzzles down into the mixture. Their bodies shuddered as they tried to get the foul food into their bellies, sucking the slurry in through the holes in their iron muzzles.

"Disgusting."

"The culinary mixture was likely not formulated for its pleasing taste, Elijah."

"I wasn't talking about the feed."

I'd seen enough. There was nothing I owed the critters below; they were no kin to me or mine. But there was only so much I could stomach of the cruelty in the world.

After a hasty discussion, Sarah and I scrabbled back down the rock, leaving Maggie up top with her rifle. The last thing I wanted was gunfire announcing our presence to everyone in the area; but it was a damn sight preferable to dying if the plan fell through.

The slurping sounds of the Fixed at their trough covered our approach until we were almost up to the overseer. His stench at this range was the stuff of legends.

"Mister?" Sarah said, startling the dirty man.

He spun around, half-pulling a pistol out of his trousers. When he saw Sarah and me though, he relaxed right away. I cast my eyes down, trying not to meet his gaze. The overseer seemed satisfied that I was just another servant, and instead took to leering at my twelve years old 'owner.'

"Well, hey there, little girl," he said, smiling with a rotten grin.

"Hey there yourself," she responded, and I repressed a shudder. Sarah was doing her best to match his lecherous tone. She wasn't good at it, but that didn't make it any less creepy and strange.

"This ain't no place for a blooming flower like yourself, honey," the overseer said. "How'd you and your augger get this far out without an escort? It's a mighty dangerous country out here, what with Sister Blister and her Advocate curs running round."

"My what?"

I'd shuffled closer and closer while she was talking with the overseer, but I was brought up short when he poked me in the chest with his fat finger.

"Your augmented nigger, here," he said with a sneer. "You think an augger like this can protect you out here in the wild country? Why, any manner of unpleasantness could befall a fresh little young'un like you."

I let the big wrench I'd hidden up my coat sleeve slip down into my waiting hand.

"What the—"

Whatever the bastard had been about to say was lost in blood and teeth as I swung the heavy steel wrench up, catching the overseer right under the jaw. The hit dropped him like a sack of bricks.

Sarah turned away as I laid into the man with the heavy wrench. He gargled something, trying to get me to stop. But the wrong-wolves around me brought their muzzles out of the trough and stared at me. I could hear their silent roars of pain and degradation and rage in my mind, feel them in our shared blood. The weight of their gaze lent strength to my arm. The wolf took over.

There was nothing of humanity in me as I smashed the overseer's mouth and head in with the heavy steel tool. The slaver tried to defend himself at first, but the wrench broke his arms in the first flurry of blows. After a while he stopped moving. Only wet crunching sounds remained as I hammered the fragments of his skull and brains into oblivion.

Panting, I fell to my knees and let the wrench drop. I was sweating and covered in the dead man's blood. Sarah was nowhere to be seen.

The ironhides stared silently, nary a growl nor a snarl among them. After I was done, the closest bent down and picked the overseer up. He shook the body, as if wondering if my victim would wake up.

Satisfied that the slaver was dead, the Fixed rolled his master's body over into the trough. As one, the wrong-wolves began to smash into the dead body, their chains adding more weight to furious steel fists.

The trough buckled under their blows, spilling their feed onto the ground. I stared in horrified fascination as they continued to beat the overseer's dead body, reducing it to the consistency of the slurry before shoving their muzzles down into the bloody mud with gut-churning slurping sounds.

They were having a second lunch.

Neither Sarah nor Maggie were anywhere to be seen as I went through the overseer's shack, searching for a way to break the ironhides' chains. I happened upon a pickax, and went back outside to free the beasts. There was no way to tell if they'd turn on me or not, but I wasn't going to leave no one as a slave.

I managed to get out two blows before one of the wrong-wolves had snatched the pickax away from me. He turned to the chains with the tool, shattering the links in a single blow.

Backing away, I let the ironhides see to their own freedom.

What water there was in the overseer's shack sufficed to wash his blood out of my hair and off my hands. I cleaned up the hot-suit rags I was wearing best I could. Stains that were too obvious I rubbed dirt from the floorboards over.

I hadn't been able to shear my hair down to my skin for the last couple of months, so it didn't surprise me when a couple of longer strands came loose in my haste to get clean. But the color of the roots made my eyebrows raise.

My hair was turning white.

I plucked a couple more out to check. Sure enough, they were the same way. Their normal dark brown color shifted into pure white at the root.

"Well. Ain't that a thing."

Was it some weird side effect to being electrocuted? I already knew my body went squirrelly when current was applied to it, reacting in different ways than most folks due to the experimentation the Cabal had done on my daddy before I was conceived. It didn't really matter though; by the time my hair could grow out enough to show the peculiar albino shade, I'd either be done with Portland or dead.

The sobering thought accompanied me back to where the ladies waited. Although the sounds of the ironhides freeing themselves had ceased, they didn't seem to be much interested in us. Once they had gotten loose the wrong-wolves took off east toward the Cascade mountains. I wished them better luck in those screwy hills than we'd had.

As we made our way back to the main road, neither of the sisters seemed inclined to conversation. Nobody seemed too eager to mention that I'd just beat a man to death in cold blood. It didn't matter how much the bastard had done to deserve it; he'd never raised hand against me personally, and the savagery I'd unleashed on him must have been hard to watch. They'd never seen me like that before. There wasn't much I could say about it. So we all just let the silence fester.

The road angled down as we trudged on, until a turn along the ridge let us see over the treeline, revealing the city below in all its terrible splendor.

Portland was like nothing I'd ever seen before. I'd expected something akin to a grounded salvation city, but the denizens had taken full advantage of the land space available to spread out across the valley. Buildings crowded together toward the center of the city, but there were also clusters of structures with a lot of nothing in-between, like Portland couldn't decide if it was one city or a bunch of smaller towns set on being close neighbors. The power cables along the road turned into a haphazard sprawl of ugly black lines crisscrossing the city like weeds choking the life out of what was below. Cranker stations sat every mile or so, amping the power up and keeping it going along the lines.

"Stupid bastards." I shook my head. "Why the hell are they using direct current? That's about the dumbest way to set up a grid I've ever seen. No wonder they got so many generators set up along the lines. It's the only way to get electricity out to the farms in the sticks."

"Is that so different than how Wardenclyffe does it?" Maggie asked.

"Absolutely. Alternating current is really the only way to efficiently transmit . . . oh my God, was that petty bastard really one of them all along? I never thought . . . but the Dragon of Science mentioned in Trent's journal. It has to be him."

"Who?"

"Edison! He hated Tesla's A/C so much he electrocuted animals, people even, to prove how dangerous it was. That the Cabal is using his ideas . . . hell, I should have known, should have seen it all along. The Cabal pricks didn't just take over Menlo Station. They were in charge of it the whole time.

"Thomas Edison was a member of the Cabal of Purity."

Chapter 10

I T SHOULD HAVE BOTHERED me more that I was a murderer.
Oh, sure, I'd killed before; there were a whole hell of a lot of
dead wrong-wolves scattered around Sacramento whose burnt
bodies attested to that. But that had been in defense of my home,
stopping a plague-bomb before it had impacted Wardenclyffe. If I'd only
known their true destination, Menlo Station, I might have even let them
finish what they'd started, if only to deliver destruction back on the
heads of those that had created them. But I'd acted on my best instincts
and assumptions at the time, and I'd never felt guilty about it.

The overseer had been different. I'd gone hunting for trouble. I
could forgive myself if I'd been surprised, and we'd had to kill to escape.
That was defending Maggie and Sarah, after all. Even though they were
tougher than any man I'd ever met, there was always going to be
something primal deep down in me that wanted to hold a shield in front
of them. But I couldn't even make that excuse this time. Hell, I'd used
Sarah as a distraction, letting her walk into danger so I could shed the
overseer's blood.

It was a cold bastard that sought to end another life, no matter how
foul the person. I should have felt guilty. I didn't.

Killing the man hadn't bothered me one damn bit.

And that troubled me more than the murder itself.

"Eli, you okay?"

"Shush, Sarah," Maggie whispered. "Remember, if he speaks, we
could all die from the discovery."

She was right. Vocalators were seen, not heard; the operation rendered the Vocalator mute when they weren't under an ironhide's control. They were forever after unable to object to what had occurred to them.

We'd just started to enter the city proper, and the population had taken a sharp spike up. It was fast approaching late afternoon, and belatedly it occurred to me that we were going to have a hard time finding a bed in the town for the night.

The city wasn't like any other I'd read about. The books we had back on Wardenclyffe had described northern cities as dirty and crowded, but full of a peculiar kind of life. Even the few cities of size in the Deep South had their own active heartbeat, albeit fueled by the crimes of slavery and decadence. Then again, that was all before the world went the way of the apocalypse.

If Portland had a pulse, it was a sluggish one, pumping thick bile laced with pure pain through arteries long-ago replaced by iron and steel. Maude had told me of the times before the Civil War when she'd witnessed slaves bought and sold in Alabama. Poor white sharecroppers like the Deveroux family didn't see much of colored folk off the auction block, unless they ended up toiling in the fields alongside them or holding the whip. They had more in common with the black men and women than the rich plantation owners that manipulated it all, who used slavery as a way to keep their own kind down as well. The affluent used the threat of cheaper slave labor to keep their fellow whites broke and scraping by. My grandma had filled my head with the memories she had of the Deep South, making sure it wasn't forgotten, and that we'd never repeat those same mistakes again. Even the best of cities in the antebellum were rife with inhumanity and abomination, riddled through with corruption of the spirit and flesh.

Portland was much, much worse.

Its citizens weren't shy about using the wrong-wolves as slaves. More than that though, they embraced the mockery of life and liberty like an old friend too long missed. By the time the road had turned from dirt to cobblestone it was hard to turn your head without seeing some new disrespect inflicted on the poor wretches. Construction on the edge of the city was in full swing, with Fixed used to haul, hammer, and dig.

Quite a few of the unlucky wrong-wolves had gotten their limbs chopped off and replaced with tools: shovels, picks, sledgehammers, and a strange mechanism that drove nails through wood with gouts of steam.

Coal wagons, hauled by more of the Augmented, visited each building under construction to resupply the furnaces the Fixed had implanted into their spines and backs. Fur and skin burned and blistered from the foreign objects, and thick black smoke belched out from the crooked pipes on their backs as the ironhides worked.

In stark comparison, their masters were clean and colorful.

As we progressed further and further into Portland proper, the work crews of Augmented were less prevalent, eventually disappearing completely. The cobblestone streets here were well-tended, and there was even a raised walkway off to the side for us foot-sloggers to use. The only skin color other than white belonged to the Vocalators, who were dressed in the style of their masters and used as manservants, to carry and fetch and be generally ordered about.

The few Fixed we saw were relegated to pulling coaches and wagons, most of which contained families in gaily-colored linen suits and dresses, lemon and blue and scarlet. There was a carefree air about them that nauseated me, especially when I saw a smiling man crack a horsewhip across the flanks of the wrong-wolf that pulled his family around in their buggy. The men and women demonstrated a casual cruelty to the Augmented that beggared belief, wallowing in brutishness with their hollow smiles in a way that no beast would ever lower itself to mimic. I longed for the days when we were running from our lives from werewolves defending their territory. At least those monsters were honest about what they were.

"What a dirty little trio," someone twittered from behind us. "That's the filthiest augger I've ever seen!"

Maggie and Sarah turned slowly, the grimace on their faces matching the feeling in my gut. I waited half a step and then turned as well, keeping my eyes downcast. Our lives depended on each of us acting according to role.

In our shared disgust of what we'd been witnessing, the Butler sisters and I had turned a brisk walk into a stupefied amble. Unfortunately, there were more than a few folks out for their daily constitutionals. Behind us were a pair of older women with enough white powder on their faces to frost a field, attended by a Vocalator carrying packages. It took me a moment to realize that the women were actually closer to Maggie's age than my grandma's, what with their fancy getups. Their Vocalator was totted up like a Victorian gentleman, although by the look on his face he wasn't exactly happy about it. Looking at the trio behind us was like staring into a distorted fun-house mirror.

"Oh my, Joy, it's even worse than we thought. Look, that one has come armed into the city!" the taller of the two exclaimed, pointing at Maggie's holstered rifle. They lacked the sense to realize the bulky sack on Sarah's back concealed the deadly surge pack. The sisters had brought all our gear along, hiding what they could in the packs, but Maggie's exquisite rifle just took up too much space to be concealed easily.

I wasn't familiar with the particular lip-dance of the two harpies in front of us, but I'd seen such behaviors before: we had our own share of bullies on Wardenclyffe.

The shorter one snapped a fan open, using it to hide her mean-spirited grin coquettishly. "Why, you'd think these country bumpkins would learn to at least take a bath before mixing with civilized people."

Sarah snorted once and then stifled it, but Maggie couldn't help herself. She let out a belly-laugh that turned heads across the street to us.

The duo that had been looking to start a war of words with Maggie and Sarah blushed bright enough to be seen through the cake batter on their cheeks. The pair of useless peacocks had no way of knowing just how ridiculous they appeared to the hard-bitten sisters. We'd faced down deadly challenges over the last few months, and the vapid idiots thought they could provoke Maggie and Sarah by making fun of how rough and tumble we all looked. The ghost of a smile flitted across their Vocalator's lips.

It took all I had not to crack a grin too.

A sudden commotion down the road drew our attention. The savage roar of rebellion and pain sliced through the dusty air like a claw. I squinted at the glare of the afternoon sunlight, and could just make out an intricate set of pulleys and rope mounted on thick wooden beams built in the shape of an 'X' on a platform. It looked a bit too much like a gallows for my liking. But there was no hangman's noose waiting.

Strapped down to the beams was a wrong-wolf, naked and vulnerable. The poor critter's artificial arms and legs were immobilized by heavy ropes tied to its hands and feet, and its spinal furnace had been starved of fuel.

An old man in a white suit walked out on stage, carrying a black wood cane with a brass top. He quieted down the crowd by waving the cane back and forth imperiously. They obeyed faster than I'd have thought.

"On this day, August 21st of the 1910th year of our Lord," he said, steely eyes sweeping the crowd. "Witness here the judgment of God, leveled on the spawn of the Advocates and their sinful ways. For the crimes of murder, thievery, and the abomination of cannibalism, this acolyte of Sister Blister and Bloodrath is sentenced to death by quartering."

As if on cue, the crowd roared in approval and support, before quieting down again.

"Since this beast's crimes were against the community, so too will the community carry out the judgment against this animal."

Again, the crowd cheered. The man didn't make any effort to quiet them this time, and instead saluted with his cane before leaving the gallows stage. People began surging toward the platform as he stepped out of sight.

"Gracious, these backwoods bumpkins are going to make us late for the Quarter!" the taller idiot said, wrinkling her nose at us.

Give Maggie credit, she didn't shoot the twit in the face. Rather, she just grimaced and pulled Sarah out of the way. I bowed low, trying to hide the fire in my eyes from their withering gazes.

The duo and their servant joined the thickening throng of people pulsing towards the makeshift gallows.

The wind shifted, and a scent I knew all too well drifted in.

Blood.

A heart-wrenching howl sounded; the crowd roared its approval. Different spectators were taking turns at a spoke-handled wheel connected to a set of pulleys. The ropes attached to the Augmented wolf's artificial limbs fed into the pulleys, through them. With each turn of the spoked wheel, the howls of agony from the beast grew louder.

They were ripping him apart. Slowly.

Blood pooled and dripped from where the metal arms and legs had been surgically grafted onto the wrong-wolf. The rapid healing of the critter was working against it, keeping the poor beast from dying as its limbs were slowly wrenched out of their sockets. I'd read about folks being drawn and quartered back in the ancient days, but this used the werewolf's own regeneration to take the horror to a whole new low. How long could the poor thing survive? Would it be left like a mutilated turtle on its back, arms and legs missing as its supernatural healing refused to let it perish?

The crowd that had gathered around the quartering gallows laughed and shouted obscenities, calling out encouragement to those who took their turn at the wheel to spin it faster or slower. Those who cut short their time at the control wheel were mocked for being cowards and weaklings. The bastards that took their time were applauded and cheered.

"Can we kill them?" Sarah whispered, her eyes wet with unshed tears.

As much as I hated watching the critter get tortured to death, the experience was much worse on her and Maggie. They'd been raised by their werewolf pack, at least the ones that had passed through the shifter phase of their life. The same beasts that had haunted the nightmares of those on Wardenclyffe were instead cherished kin for the sisters. I'd been around them long enough to hear stories of family, adopted and otherwise, forming into packs to protect the young among the furbacks. And I'd borne witness to their own wolf-gone mother, a great gray beast with courage and grit to spare, attack a pack of Broken to try and rescue children that the ironhides had stolen away. It wasn't a beast the sisters saw getting tortured on the gallows with all the white folks in their colorful suits standing around, laughing.

It was a person.

And they were right. It was all too easy to forget that under the fur and fangs, under the surgical alterations made by the Cabal of Purity, that men and women lurked, poor souls twisted by a disease into something monstrous. That the wolves eventually evened out in their temper once they'd taken to the fur all the way made it all the worse.

"Eli, I think something's wrong with Maggie," Sarah said, drawing my attention away from the terrible spectacle.

Maggie's hands were shaking, and her cheeks were flushed red. Sweat beaded across her face, and her eyes were unfocused. The reaction was one I'd seen before, but it caught me off-guard. We had both just ended our lunar cycle; it seemed impossible at first blush, but there was nothing else that made sense.

Maggie was shifting into a werewolf again.

There was only one way that could happen.

Damn.

I cast a glance around and, seeing everyone focused on the quartering of the Augmented, risked a whisper back.

"Sarah, we have to get Maggie out of here."

"Why?" Sarah's sister asked, a bloodthirsty look coming into her eyes. "These fine citizens deserve to find out what happens when a wolf gets loose among them. Add some red to their fine clothes."

"Two things. One, while I'd like to lay into them with all manner of unspeakable violence, do you think they don't know how to put down a rabid wolf for good? They're playing with their victim on the gallows rack, but I'd bet dollars to doughnuts that these assholes have cut down more than their fair share of furbacks in their day. And two, this ain't like the other changes. The day I've been dreading has finally come.

"Maggie is going to become a werewolf permanently."

Chapter 11

W E'VE GOT TO GET her off the street."

Sarah nodded, her face scrunched up with worry for her older sister. As we looked around for an alley or shadowed spot to duck into, Maggie started spasming. I grabbed hold of her while Sarah took the Winchester. Maggie's skin rippled as the muscles underneath strained to tear and reform. But she wasn't one to give up so easy to the inevitable: she was fighting the transformation tooth and nail.

And there was nothing I could do to help.

There wasn't much I knew about the final transformation from shifter to full-time furback. Maggie had been loathe to talk about it, even though we both knew she was coming up fast to the point where she'd stop turning back into a human altogether and stay a wolf. Hell, I didn't even know if her temper would calm down right away, or if she'd be a murder-machine on the loose for weeks looking to kill me and Sarah. All Maggie had been willing to say was that it would be the end of our time together, at least until I went down to the fur permanent too. It made sense; even if we were willing, I wasn't the kind of man turned on by a nine-foot tall werewolf, and she'd be able to rip me apart as long as I was human. Even when I was transformed during the full moons, I'd basically try and kill her since I was still caught in the halfway-world of being a shifter. Those kinds of problems put a crimp in any relationship.

But none of that mattered now. Sarah didn't dare unlimber the surge pack and zap her sister, even assuming it could stop the transformation. Maggie was about to shed her human skin in the worst place possible. Portland was well-acquainted with wolves. Even if she wasn't put down out of hand by a mob, the last thing we wanted was to get a Blood Judge on our tails. We had to find somewhere safe, calm Maggie down, and hope for the best.

"What's wrong with the lady, little miss?"

An older man with a salt and pepper beard had come out of a nearby building at the sounds of Maggie fighting her transformation.

He seemed a benevolent sort; the man wore an ink-stained leather apron over crisply-pressed shirt and pants, and the scent of a printer's shop wafted out the door he'd left open behind him. But the gleeful roar of a crowd for the torture of their slave, a crowd filled to the brim with folks like him, was reason enough to not trust him. The man barely gave me a glance, but even in that brief moment I saw his lip curl in disgust, confirming my suspicions.

"Bring your lady inside to rest, little miss," he offered, making a short bow. Looking at me holding Maggie, his face hardened. "Your augger, of course, must wait outside. After getting his filthy hands off of that white woman."

Maggie shuddered in my arms. Her eyes rolled back in her head, and she started shaking uncontrollably. I could feel the printer's harsh gaze on me as I lifted Maggie up. I wasn't letting her go, no matter the consequences.

"Please, sir," Sarah pleaded. "I am far too frail and weakly to carry my sister inside, and this Vocalator has been tasked by our father to guard us both on pain of death."

I was impressed. I'd never heard Sarah lie before the encounter with the overseer, but the girl was getting better at it by the second. While I wasn't normally on the side of teaching a kid those lessons, her burgeoning ability to spin a believable tall-tale was coming in handy now. She managed to sell the lie of frailty even with a Winchester rifle across her back. That was talent.

The man took another long look at me, then sighed in resignation. "Fine. But you better keep your hands off that white skin, you hear me, boy?"

Inwardly I bristled, but held my tongue for the moment and

nodded, trying to keep my eyes downcast like the slave he expected. Apparently satisfied, the man ushered us into his shop. Sarah shucked our gear off at the door, careful to make sure the clothes and supply bags were hiding the surge pack's bulk.

Maggie's rifle was laid gently atop the pile; it was the only possession their mother had been able to bequeath them before the fur took her, a fine thing with intricate filigree won long ago by the sharpshooting skill that ran in their family. In the midst of my panicked worry over Maggie, the strangest thing drew my attention. The electric lights in the print shop caught the filigree at just the right angle. I'd never noticed their mother's maiden name inscribed near the trigger, hidden within the swirls: Annie Oakley. The implications of the Butler sisters' ancestry rolled over me, but there was no time to think about that.

Racks of drying newsprint cluttered the front room, but the man moved them a bit to allow me to put Maggie down. My throat went dry at the double-barreled shotgun hanging behind the counter, out of place in a print shop and ugly. I slid my eyes off it quickly before he could notice my fearful interest.

The printing press taking up the back of his shop didn't look much like the ones we had on Wardenclyffe. It was smaller, sure, but my mechanical knack told me right away that it was also more efficient. When you ain't hiding in the clouds trying to stay safe, I guess you got lots more time to fiddle with making things better, rather than just hoping you can survive the next week.

Newspapers weren't the only thing the print shop dabbled in. Copies of the Bible were stacked up on the edge of a table, alongside something called *The True History of the United States of America*. Maude always had a rule with folks that led in with the word 'true' when talking to you: they were probably liars, and anyone who took them at face value was a blasted idiot. It and the Bible were the only book titles in the shop, forming neat piles on different shelves. There were at least a hundred of each.

The printer took Maggie out of my arms with a disapproving huff, and I barely restrained a growl at his laying hands on her. I didn't trust a man who only printed two books when he had the capability to create more. There weren't any signs of literature beyond the Bible and that single history tome; not a Poe, not a Twain, nary a Jules Verne or Oscar Wilde in sight. It seemed . . . unnatural.

"Here, we'll lay her down. She's your sister, little miss?" the man asked, not unkindly.

Sarah shot a glance at me, and I tried not to meet her eyes. The man was watching us close, and he didn't need to be given the impression I had any say in the matter. Sarah was on her own for this.

"Yes," she answered after a beat. "I apologize, but the heat seems to have affected her."

The man shook his head. "I don't think so. Looks more like your sister is about to turn into a werewolf than suffering from sunstroke. We'd better call a Judge."

Sarah and I stiffened like we'd been struck by a lightning bolt.

He stood up and moved behind the counter, cranking a handle and picking up a device that he started shouting into.

"Send a Judge!" he hollered into the handset. "Wolf drain! Send a Judge! Wolf drain!"

"What are we going to do?" Sarah whispered, letting the man's shouted repetition cover our conversation. I could see in her eyes the same fear I had: a man in a black duster with red gloves gunning Maggie down as she transformed.

But we couldn't let fear rule us. Sure, there wasn't anything to say they'd let Maggie and us go after a Judge had seen to her, but the girls hadn't done anything to warrant suspicion, and as long as I kept my own trap shut, Sarah might be able to bluff our way out of the whole mess. And, as much as I hated dwelling on it, the people of Portland seemed the kind to not let a white woman go down to the fur forever. I didn't want to trust them with anything. But there was only one real choice.

"We give the Blood Judge his shot," I whispered back. "The printer ain't wrong. Maggie is fighting against the wolf, but she got pissed enough to trigger a change. And we both know this might be her final one. It's out of cycle, which ain't good. If a Judge can bring her back to herself, then we got to let him try."

Sarah nodded. The worried look stayed on her face though.

"There we go," the man said, having finally gotten the message across the device. He replaced the handset and moved back from around the counter. "Sorry about the racket. Although the Talons keep us flush with their new technology, some of the inventions work better than others."

He rummaged around the shelves and brought down a couple of empty burlap sacks. "Here, have your augger put these under her head. Then I'd back up, little miss. No telling if your sister is going to go rabid or not, and better to let the Vocalator be her first victim if she does."

Maggie thrashed around on the floor, and I had trouble getting her head to stay on the makeshift pillow. Every time I tried to hold her arms down, I saw the printer's eyebrows go up and felt his gaze crawling over me like spider legs.

"Excuse my manners," he said, turning back to Sarah and holding out his hand. "Never properly introduced myself. My name is William. William Greene."

"Sarah," she responded, letting William take her hand and plant a light kiss on it. "Sarah . . . Grant."

I groaned inwardly, but she wasn't wrong in trying to lie. We didn't know anyone else in Portland, so it was a calculated risk to use the Grant name.

"Oh, so they finally got Frank to adopt a Returned that wasn't his blood?" William asked, chuckling. "It's about time. Just because he's on the edge of town doesn't make him any less accountable to the community. Are you both back from the fur? You look a little young to be a shifter."

Sarah nodded, a little too eager to answer. "I started my change early. We were both thrown out from the pack keeping us captive, and found each other. Then the Judges found us."

Bless that girl, she was faster on the draw than I was. It dawned on me that many of the inhabitants of Portland were Returned from the fur; there was no telling how many folks were left uninfected by the time the Cabal got their forces up and running in this town. There was only one way to bring people back once they'd permanently changed: Blood Judges. Since most people wouldn't have any kin, at least none they remembered, it made sense that people would be adopted into different families, and raised up in the 'morals' of the Portland community. Sarah had realized all of that quickly, and was building on the lie.

"I'm surprised Frank let you come into town unsupervised, with only that dirty augger for protection. Well, I'm just glad you little ladies were found and brought back from savagery," William said, smiling like a genial grandfather. He jerked his head at me, and the smile disappeared. "It's a damn shame to think of all the good, decent folks still stuck out there with his kind."

"Yes," Sarah said, trying to keep her voice neutral. "It's terrible."

Maggie thrashed on the floor with the most violent spasm yet, crying out. It took everything I had not to reach out to her, to comfort and hold her. William pulled his leather belt free of his pants and knelt down by Maggie, shoving it in her mouth.

"Ain't the first Returned I've seen try to go back feral on us," he said over his shoulder. "Don't worry, little miss, I'll keep an eye on her and make sure that tongue doesn't get bit through. You just don't worry your pretty little head about it. Go on, now, you can't do anything about this. I think I've got a little hard candy behind the counter if you want a treat to take your mind off of your sister."

Sarah's eyes beseeched me to move away. I realized that I was tensing up, ready to attack William for daring to manhandle Maggie like that. I unclenched my fist and turned away. Sarah was right, of course. He was just trying to help Maggie. But there was something inherently repellent about the man, a casual unearned superiority that rubbed me the wrong way even more than the expected racism.

I shadowed Sarah as she moved behind the counter. Although she was smiling and nodding at the constant stream of inane chatter now coming from William, her gaze passed right over the proffered candy jar without interest. Sarah gave a small gasp of excited discovery and reached under the counter, pulling out a crumpled map.

"You be careful over there with that augger," William warned off-hand. He was leaning into Maggie's chest to keep her still with his knee. Despite needing to quiet her, he didn't look to be using any real gentleness with her. "Don't let him near the register. Can't trust them not to steal, even when they don't know what they're taking."

"Yes, yes," Sarah muttered for his benefit, unfolding the map and keeping it out of sight behind the counter.

Maggie strained against William's grip, trying to bite him. While he was distracted, I bent my head in to take a look at Sarah's discovery. It was an old map of the Willamette Valley, published before the Blood Panic of '93, but someone had been writing notes on it since then. The outlying areas of Portland were sectioned off, with the word 'purged' written in different handwriting over each area. A set of notes had been jotted down on the eastern edge of the map, and I had to lean in to make out a familiar name.

Carnegie City.

It was all I could do not to let loose and start cussing everyone and everything. Carnegie City had been the last salvation city flying that the Tellurians on Wardenclyffe had known of, the only island of humanity other than our own to have survived the decade and a half since the first of the cities lifted off of the ground. Carnegie City had been built by the millionaire of the same name, and it had shown. Although the government seized industrial assets after the Blood Panic, Carnegie and the other robber barons had still exerted an immense amount of influence. The city that bore his name attracted the richest and best, and in the end even the U.S. Congress had decided to move the seat of government there, along with the library that bore their name. Carnegie had been obstinate in following Tesla's example of egalitarianism, and had opened the doors of the city to uninfected of many classes and skin tones, despite the complaints of his peers.

In many ways, Carnegie City had been the prettier, richer sister of Wardenclyffe. It had hurt to lose telepulse contact with them two years ago. We'd feared the worst. And, according to the map, we were right to.

The wreckage of Carnegie City was scattered across Mount Hood.

Chapter 12

T HAT DOESN'T MAKE ANY kind of sense," I muttered. Sarah raised her eyebrows in question. "Salvation cities don't just crash into mountains. They're physically incapable of it, as long as their squall tubes are working. Carnegie City had even better equipment than Wardenclyffe. The other cities falling out of the sky over time due to aging equipment and mistakes by folks, sure, I'll buy that. But Carnegie? She should have been flying long after Wardenclyffe rusted away."

"Hey, what are you doing over there?" William asked suspiciously, half-raising up off of Maggie. Her thrashing had grown weaker, and I cussed myself as I realized he might have heard me whispering. I was terrible at acting like a mute Vocalator.

"Nothing, sir," Sarah said, shoving the map back under the counter. The sound of the aged paper's concealment was loud in the silence.

"Now, wait just a minute," William said, standing straight up. Maggie's fit had calmed down, and despite me loving her, I couldn't help but wish she was pitching a bit more of a fuss right now. Had William heard me? He wasn't acting very neighborly any more, and the way he looked at me could have skinned a catfish still on the hook.

"You're messing with my books back there!" he said. "Teaching that augger to read? Right in front of me, like I'm some kind of simpleton!"

I realized that with the two of us huddling our heads together over the hidden map, teaching me to read was probably the most benign interpretation the old racist could have come up with. William stalked toward us, and Sarah and I scuttled out of his way as he made his way behind the counter.

"Sir, it's not what you—" Sarah tried to explain.

"Enough!" William bellowed, turning to the wall behind and its shotgun. He pulled it down and aimed the double-barrel right at us.

"We're going to see what Judge Tillman has to say about all this."

I couldn't decide whether to cry, retch, or laugh at the situation. I'd heard from Maude about how in the antebellum days it'd been illegal to teach slaves to read, and it seemed that Portland had resurrected that bit of idiocy alongside the whole 'let's own a person' crap. God only knew what other insane things they'd tossed on the pile alongside it. Even the worst of the folks on Wardenclyffe would blanch at the unrepentant hatred on display.

It made me want to kiss Maggie right then and there, just to spite them with how we felt about each other.

"Please, mister, don't . . ." Sarah said. She was all out of stories and excuses. The girl might be pretty good at lying, but there was only so much shit someone could pass through their teeth before their stomach started giving them trouble. She spared a look for Maggie's rifle, twenty feet away. It might as well have been on the other side of the world for all the good it did us.

"Why don't you go ahead and put down the scattergun, Mister Greene," a familiar voice said from outside the door. I followed where Sarah was staring and felt my blood race in panic.

Malakhai, the Blood Judge who'd warned us off Portland, was standing in the door frame, with the white fur of his wrong-wolf companion blocking out the street beyond.

Thoughts and fears raced through my head. There was no talking our way out of this; we'd been pretty honest with the Judge in our dealings with him, and it had left us at a disadvantage. All the fibs and fabrications were about to come unraveled.

"I'm guessing she's the reason you called for a Judge?" Malakhai gestured to where Maggie groaned and twisted on the floor, the veins in her neck standing out as she ground her teeth together. Her tendons popped with the tension as she fought against the wolf inside, and Malakhai's brows knitted together in concern.

"This ain't your neighborhood, Malakhai. Where's Tillman?"

"Running down leads on the Advocates, or at least that's what they told me. Not that it's none of your business."

"The girl might be too far gone," William grunted, not lowering his shotgun. "These two on the other hand, well, they're a bit more of current events."

"You weren't too far gone when Ramirez pulled your sorry ass out of the fur," Malakhai drawled. There was a slow threat to his voice, like a cougar stalking its prey through the underbrush. "I do believe I said to put that weapon down, Greene."

William's face blanched at the Judge's tone, and the shotgun lowered. The print shop owner deflated and sullenly gestured for us to come out from behind his counter.

"No need to remind me of Ramirez," he groused.

"Shut up, William. I was the one who had to put him down after your little incident, so I'll mention it any blasted time I want to. Especially to you. Now, you raise that weapon again, and I'll drain you so dry you'll be laid up for a week, you got that?"

William nodded, never quite meeting the Judge's scarlet gaze.

"What about these two?" the print shop owner asked, gesturing at Sarah and me. "The little miss there was teaching that augger how to read—"

"I could swear I told you to stop flapping your lips, Greene. I don't give a good goddamn about anything but keeping the girl human. Hold her down."

The cowed man did as he was told without any more backtalk, kneeling next to Maggie and holding her shoulders down. She'd started up kicking again though, and even leaning his weight into her legs Malakhai was unable to keep her still.

"You," Malakhai said, nodding his head toward me. "Come over here."

A disgusted snort escaped William's lips. "You're not going to let a dirty augger touch a white girl, are you?"

The Blood Judge stared hard at William, seeming to weigh the words on an internal scale that we weren't privy to. There was a heavy silence, the only sounds being those of Maggie's struggles. Claws burst forth from her fingertips, spraying blood across her clothes. Sharp teeth slid over her human ones, hardening into a jagged line of death.

"So you don't mind if Neshomne there breaks the wall down to help instead, Greene? He ain't going to fit any other way," Malakhai finally said. "If you think we can hold down a werewolf in mid-transformation by our lonesome, you're a hell of a lot dumber than I thought. And that would take some doing."

William's face grew flushed with anger, but he bit his tongue against further objections as I moved to hold Maggie's legs down. Her patched prairie dress was straining as her bones cracked, muscles tearing and knitting themselves back into the body of an aberration. Malakhai took his hat off and bent down, baring his silver fangs as he gently bit into her neck.

Maggie bucked and struggled against our grip, but three grown men holding her down managed to keep her from ripping her own throat out. After a few seconds her struggles grew weaker, and the bestial growls and snarls escaping her turned into a soft weeping, like that of a child. The claws fell out as human fingertips replaced them, the rejected flesh smoking into nothing with her wolf-teeth following suit. Despite how far along she'd been, the only signs that Maggie had almost been lost to the beast were a few strained seams on her bloodstained dress and a thick sheen of sweat. Her color was paler than normal, but her breathing had fallen into the regular rhythm of an exhausted sleep.

"She'll be all right for now," the Judge said, pulling back from the bleeding puncture wounds he'd made with his fangs.

The human teeth marks where he'd bit her bruised and healed almost instantly, but the pair of holes from the silver fangs wept blood in a slow drip, as if crying for how close Maggie had come to being forever lost.

"Still, she'll need to be kept in the isolation cells for a while. For her own protection," Malakhai said, wiping the blood on his mouth with a handkerchief. "I'm assuming the young'un there is her sister, and this is their Vocalator?"

Malakhai's irises were glowing scarlet from draining Maggie's blood, and I felt the pressure of the warning look he shot me like a heavy blow. For some reason, the Judge was content to play at us not knowing each other. That was fine by me.

"Yeah, you guessed right," Sarah chimed in, as quick on the uptake as always.

"What are you going to do about her, then?" William asked, regaining some of his confidence and pointing at Sarah. "Even though I'm sure the augger tempted her somehow, the girl broke the law; you can't ignore that."

"I can't?" Malakhai asked softly, taking a step closer to the print shop owner. "Did I blink and miss the part where your opinion mattered?"

William shuddered, and seemed to draw in on himself a little. Malakhai put a single red-gloved finger under the other man's chin and forced William to look him in the eye.

"Don't ever think you can tell me what I can and can't do, you little shitstain. Got that?"

William swallowed hard, not daring to break the gaze, and grunted a 'yes.'

"Good," Malakhai said, letting the other man scuttle back. He turned to Sarah. "Darlin', what's your name?"

"Sarah Grant. And this is our servant, Elijah."

One of Malakhai's white eyebrows went up at her using Frank's family name. But he kept his questions silent, and instead instructed us to carry Maggie outside. She was making small sad noises as Sarah and I lifted her up, one under each shoulder. Once outside, the massive Neshomne knelt down and gathered her up in one arm, holding her like a sleeping child. We darted back in to grab the gear we'd piled up at the entryway. Sarah slung the Winchester against her shoulder, but by the look on her face she'd rather be using it on Greene. Working together, we made sure the surge pack was hidden again before scooting clear.

Malakhai exited behind us, putting his black hat back on and nodding at a passerby who'd become a bit too interested in the commotion. The stranger in question saw the red glow in the Judge's eyes and decided we weren't quite as captivating as he'd first thought. He hurried on past without a second glance.

"Judge Tillman will hear about this," William threatened. Now that we were back out in public, the print shop owner had found his balls again.

"I'm sure he will," Malakhai drawled, turning back to William. "Be sure he hears how you nearly let a girl go down to the fur over it, too. I'm sure he'll be interested in how a Vocalator being within five feet of a written word was more of a danger to the city than an uncontrolled werewolf sprouting up in the middle of town. Kisses to the missus, Greene, unless you want to keep them all for yourself."

William sputtered at the Judge as he turned back to us. There was a grim line to Malakhai's jaw that I didn't like, and he took both me and Sarah by the back of our shirts like two errant children, marching us down the wooden sidewalk until we got the hint and started walking that way on our own. Neshomne lumbered next to us on the road, moving like a gorilla on his hindquarters and one arm's knuckles as he kept Maggie nestled safely in the other.

"See now, here I thought I was speaking perfectly good English before when I told you three to not come here," Malakhai growled, pushing us ahead of him. "Did I not make the point that this was not the place for you kids?"

"Yes," Sarah said, casting an accusing stare at me, "you did. But some people got it into their heads that there was no choice."

The folks on the sidewalk parted at the sight of a Judge herding two people down the way, but there were still far too many people around for me to risk talking. Instead, I limited myself to an irritated clearing of my throat.

"He thought we had get here before the city crashed," Sarah sighed, recognizing the look on my face and rolling her eyes at it. "Everybody is depending on us, blah, blah, excuses, thousands of worthless sky-huggers dead . . . personally, I wouldn't mind Wardenclyffe dropping right down in the middle of your town. You and the Tellurians deserve each other."

"Hang on a second there, missy," Malakhai interjected. "I've heard tell of that particular salvation city. Didn't think she was still flying after all these years, especially what with Carnegie City's fate."

Sarah translated my look of alarmed interest well enough. "We saw on the printer's map that the wreckage is near here," she said. "Do you know what happened to them? Eli said it should have cleared the mountain easily."

"Yeah, I suppose it would have," Malakhai replied. "But it floated into the wrong territory."

All the pieces started falling into place suddenly, and my stomach felt like it was churning with molten lead. I realized it wasn't just time and age felling the mighty salvation cities. Maude had always said it was suspicious that we'd lost telepulse contact with so many so quickly after all the years of survival. Malakhai's voice was somber, and I could hear the impotent anger and grief underlying his words as he confirmed my newborn fear.

"The Cabal destroyed Carnegie City, and it sounds like they got your Wardenclyffe lined up for the next bullet."

Chapter 13

"WHY WOULD ANYONE EVER do such a thing?" I asked. Malakhai's black duster rustled as he squared his shoulders behind us. "Refined resources are a might scarce these days, but with the Hedrickson foundry starting up next month, there's only one thing I can think of that nothing but a salvation city can offer: test subjects."

I stumbled a bit at that, and Malakhai was 'nice' enough to shove me back into pace. Despite his size and the recent infusion of infected blood, I could tell he had to put his size into bulling me down the way. It didn't make a lot of sense, but for some reason he wasn't carrying the muscle his frame suggested.

"Looks like you're doing fine when it comes to victims for your cruelty," Sarah said, fidgeting under the weight of the hidden surge pack.

She gestured at all the Vocalators we still saw scurrying about. While the Augmented wrong-wolves might be purposely kept out of the center of the city, there were plenty of their smaller cousins serving as everything from doormen to valets. Portland seemed as much black as white. There couldn't possibly have been that many Augmented that the masters wanted to hear from; then again, I suppose robbing a man you'd enslaved of his ability to talk was its own reward when you were an asshole. I wondered how many Vocalators would trade the 'reward' of being human again for keeping the Cabal from cutting up their brains and putting them back in chains. Being a werewolf for the rest of your life didn't seem so bad in comparison.

"These poor bastards?" Malakhai snorted. "Cabal ain't got any use for them, really. They give the townsfolk control over these wretches to keep their minds off the fact they got more in common with their servants than they do the Talons in charge. Ain't nothing like telling a man he was born special just cause he's white to make him a worthless son of a bitch. But there's one particular thing that folks on salvation cities got to offer the world below."

"They're not infected," I whispered. I didn't need the warning shove from the Judge to button my lip back up. Although people weren't exactly lining up to cheer him, there were still enough about to raise a fuss if they overheard me.

"You must be getting sick, Miss Grant, to have your voice go all baritone like that on you."

Despite Malakhai's attempt at humor, Sarah wasn't smiling. "Why would it matter? I mean, your butchers just chop up whoever they want, so being picky doesn't get them much."

"It's downright adorable how you keep lumping us all together, including the man who just saved your sister from going down to the wolves," Malakhai said, an edge to his voice. Neshomne let out an irritated huff of air. "Because it can't be that some of us didn't choose the life we live, and are just trying to make the best of the hand that got dealt."

Sarah frowned, but tilted her head in acknowledgment.

"Not all of the Cabal's experiments can be done on folks with the Wendigo virus in their blood," Malakhai continued, mollified. "Take the Blood Judges, for instance."

"You were from a salvation city?"

Malakhai gave a short, guttural laugh. "Not even close. I wasn't the kind they wanted to save, even if I did wear tin before the world went down to the beasts. No, the Cabal snapped me up from a survivor's camp in the last days. They came in offering help with lies of safety, and the folks who bought their snake oil came out mostly dead."

I cast a glance back at him meaningfully.

"I said mostly," he barked. "It's not like I'm the picture of health, and I beat the odds to be where I am."

"What did they do to you?" Sarah asked.

Malakhai's boots came to a halt behind us, causing us to both pause and look around. His hat was pulled down to where we could barely see the gleam of his eyes, staring hard at nothing. Neshomne's ears were down, and an almost inaudible growl was rumbling in his chest. The massive Augmented and the Judge were both tense as steel cabling, ready to fight ghosts of a past we couldn't see.

"That's . . . complicated," Malakhai finally said. "It ain't something I want a young'un to hear, and it lasted longer than you'd think, but not the eternity it felt like. In the early days, before the well ran dry, they used us up fast, putting us through every experiment and test they could think of. The creation of the Judges took a lot of trial and error, and even then, only one in a thousand of us survived.

"They didn't have much choice on who made it through; Ramirez and me were proof of that. Tillman, Johnson, and Glover were their lucky breaks, though, and they been figuring out over time just how many of us is enough to keep Portland out of the fur. Losing Johnson to an Advocate attack hurt that number. The day another survives the process though . . . well, let's just say that I ain't got any illusions about my chances if it's a good old boy that makes it."

"I don't know," Sarah said, injecting a come-hither tone to her voice. "You look like you're a pretty good specimen."

It was all I could do not to shudder. She was trying the same trick on Malakhai as she'd used on the overseer, trying to curry favor. For all I knew, it'd work like a charm, and she'd convince him to let us loose. But damned if it wasn't disconcerting watching a twelve-year-old try to be seductive.

From the look on the Judge's face, he was of the same opinion.

"I surely hope you ain't implying something improper, kid. There's a whole slew of reasons it's a bad idea, but let's stick to the two big ones: you're way too young for those thoughts, and even if you weren't, you sure as shooting ain't my flavor of ice cream."

Neshomne rumbled low, but his ears were perked up and his mouth hung open. It took me a second to realize he was laughing.

"What's wrong with me?" Sarah asked, and there was a definite note of hurt in her voice.

"Don't take it the wrong way, kid. I'm sure when you're all growedup that men will melt like butter in the sun to you. But you're barking up the wrong tree with me, darlin'."

Malakhai was struggling to put something into words. He was distinctly uncomfortable, and Neshomne wouldn't stop laughing. The giant white wrong-wolf chortling sent the townsfolk around us to the other side of the road, leaving the sidewalk all to us. Not that there were that many left; despite going deeper into Portland, there seemed to be fewer and fewer people around.

"Shut up, hairball," Malakhai said to Neshomne, shaking his head in irritation. "Let me put it this way: you seen how each Blood Judge got themselves a furry companion? Well, they ain't chosen by a roll of the dice. It takes a special Augmented to carry a Judge. We smell wrong to werewolves, and we're one of the few things they won't eat. But they'll sure as shit kill us. You might even say they're driven to it."

Given the lack of folks in our immediate vicinity, I decided to risk a bit of talking.

"What makes you so special?"

"Keep your voice down. And nothing. Nothing makes me special, in particular. But since a werewolf uses his nose more than you use your eyes, they tend to take a dislike to anyone that has silver running in their blood. They'll run from us if they can, but murder is a close second on their to-do list when they meet my kind."

"I knew something was off about you," Sarah muttered, wrinkling her nose.

"Silver nitrate injections," Malakhai nodded. "It's part of the reason that the infected can't be subjected to the Blood Judge protocols; they blow up like a topped-off boiler with the first injection. Details got a might fuzzy when they knocked me out, and nothing when I was awake is anything I want to remember. But the chemistry they do to our blood is what keeps us from permanently contracting the Wendigo virus when we bite into werewolves. Thing is, without regular infusions of the red from the infected, Judges would croak faster than a bullfrog in the chorus. Turns out the human body's got a pretty bad reaction to silver poisoning on such a large scale. So it's a careful balance of 'not quite dead' and 'oh, look, the Judge went crazy from the disease in his brain.'"

"Neshomne looks pretty infected to me," I said.

"True enough. And in a pinch, he would provide me with blood; even then, I have to be careful. You don't want to see an Augmented that loses his fur. Their healing is gimped from all that's been done to them, and the metal through their body does nothing but put them in agony. But mostly he's here to be muscle. I might look like a prizefighter, but outside of my speed I'm actually a featherweight. All the Judges are. I probably couldn't beat little miss there arm-wrestling without a fresh infusion."

There was a gleam in Sarah's eye with that admission I didn't like. Apparently, Neshomne saw it too, and a low rumbling warning growl reminded her he was right there. It seemed to snap Malakhai back into action as well, and he prodded us forward.

"We can jaw while walking. Anyways, you need a special werewolf to serve as a Judge's companion. Blood relation is good, loved one is even better. Tillman got his daughter back, after a fashion. Johnson, before she got taken down last year, had her brother. Ramirez had his wife, as does Glover. And me . . . well, there ain't no blood shared between Neshomne and me, but we been together since this land weren't nothing but timber and the Chinook tribes."

"Together?" Sarah asked, confused. It took her a moment to catch on, and her eyes widened. "Oh, together-together!"

"Yeah, that," Malakhai laughed. "Like I said, the Cabal had no choice on what made it through their experiments intact, so they had to take us as we were. There just weren't enough Judges that survived to let them be picky. Neshomne's people had no problem with two men loving each other, but I got no illusions about anyone else. I've paid the price plenty of times for being who I am, but there ain't nothing no one can do to change it, so it was either roll over and die or fight back."

"So that's why the Cabal will murder you as soon as they get an 'acceptable' replacement," I murmured, keeping an eye out for anyone. The road and sidewalk were both empty, abandoned as if a plague had passed through. After the hustle and bustle of a half-mile back it was eerie.

"That and the fact I don't believe in what they're doing here. Bringing people back from the fur is all well and good, but slavery wasn't right the first time, and it sure ain't right this time either. They're just bound and determined to keep making the same mistakes as the old world though. And there's still idiots buying their pitch."

"So you have to do this because the situation makes you?" I didn't bother to keep the scorn out of my voice. "It was a bullshit argument from Grant, and he had children to think about. It sounds even weaker coming from you."

"Listen, kid, it might look easy from your end, but . . . ah, hellfire." Malakhai's voice turned hard as a huge building came into view. "Talking time is done. Keep your wits around you, as this is more of Tillman's stomping grounds than mine, and there ain't none you can trust within those walls."

The building in question was two stories of meanness given walls and a roof. I couldn't rightly identify its full size from here, but what the place lacked in height it more than made up for in sheer girth; there was no way to tell where the place ended, as the sides of the building were hidden by smaller houses crowding in. Dirty white concrete was marred with dark spots in a telltale stain pattern that said 'yes, there was killing here.' Rusted iron spikes laced the edges of the roof in pairs, the first set pointing down like God's accusing fingers, the other set straight up. A raven croaked from one of the angled iron shafts, pecking at a rotten piece of meat that was still hanging from the point. I tried not to notice that it looked an awful lot like a chunk of human forearm.

"If there was a heart of Portland, this would be its rotten core," Malakhai muttered. "Even the zealots who support the Cabal keep a fair distance from here. The Talons and their lackeys like to call it the Foundation, but I prefer the other name it's earned round these parts: the Tombstone."

There were no windows set in the walls, and the only way in was a pair of iron-shod doors that belonged back in medieval Europe. Atop the building a tower flickered with electrical arcs, and into it ran dozens of cables from the web crisscrossing the town. But the most surprising sight of all bore letters down its side that spelled out *Purity's Pride*.

The Tombstone had a Thunder Train sitting idle on its roof.

Chapter 14

THE *PURITY'S PRIDE* CURLED around the edge of the Tombstone's roof like a rattlesnake enjoying the last rays of sunlight. It was a Skybreaker, a sister of the *Heaven's Grace*, the only line of engines built specifically to serve as Thunder Trains, as opposed to being converted over from its rail-born cousins. Technically the Alleghenies were supposed to be nearly identical, but there was something that immediately put me off this Double T. The primal part of my blood that the wolf had soaked into wanted to latch teeth onto the snake-train and shake it until its head snapped off. Maude always believed that something of the engineer soaked into their engine, for better or for worse. I'd doubted my grandma's superstitions, but the way that the *Purity's Pride* was affecting me made me a believer.

"Nice roof ornament," I said. "I'm guessing the dead zone is keeping them grounded, right?"

"You like risk, don't you, kid?" Malakhai said with a sigh. "What if someone sees you talking?"

"We're going to jail, right? What difference does it make?"

Malakhai rubbed his face with the palm of his red-gloved hand in frustration. "It's not like that. Look, your lady friend there needs to be in one of the isolation cells for now, to be sure she doesn't shift again. It's dangerous to catch someone in mid-transformation; there's a distinct possibility it ain't over for her yet. I figured you young'uns would want to be near her to watch over. Was I wrong? Feel free to cut loose and run around Portland again, although I'm guessing you'll be in trouble again sooner rather than later, and I won't be there to pull your fat out of the fire this time."

"Eli, he's got a point," Sarah said, her voice soft as the Tombstone loomed before us. "Maybe we should play along a little while longer."

"Fine. For Maggie's sake," I grumbled. "But none of this is getting us any closer to killing the dead zone before Wardenclyffe hits Portland."

"You're looking in the wrong place for that one, kid," Malakhai said, glancing around to make sure we were still alone. "The Advocates are the ones generating the disruption that keeps the Double Ts grounded. We got trapped Talons that's gone batshit trying to figure out how to take it down. The Dragon isn't one to take failure lightly."

"What? Wait, the Cabal isn't creating the telluric interference field? But I thought . . ."

"That they'd want to ground themselves here? And, according to you, with a huge salvation city on its way to crash into their little social experiment?" Malakhai asked. "They're evil, and got themselves some serious delusions of grandeur, but they ain't stupid, kid."

"But that doesn't make any sense," I said, shaking my head. "These Advocates you people keep talking about sound like freedom fighters, like they're trying to help folks. Why would they want to crash a city of innocents into Portland? I mean, I understand their hatred of this place, but there's got to be a better way of wiping it off the map."

Malakhai shrugged. "My best guess is they don't know what they're doing; not like they got a bunch of Tellurians running around up there on Mt. Hood. They're using the interference field to keep the Cabal from tracking them into the mountains. By the time the Cabal realized the Advocates posed a real threat the deadzone had gone up. We've had some goddamn bloody skirmishes since then. Emanuel has more than earned the name 'Bloodrath;' brutality ain't just a Cabal trademark. And there's no way to root them out of there either. Can't send up an army of Augmented without having them chasing their own tails all over Creation."

"So that's why we couldn't follow the ridge line like we wanted to," Sarah muttered.

The Judge nodded. "The Cabal can't get to the Advocates to shut it off. And since they don't exactly chat, none of the rebels know about your city bearing down on us. Not that they'd care. There's already another salvation city on a collision course with Portland thanks to the riptide in the currents: Menlo Station. I suppose that's why the Advocates threw up the field in the first place, to get rid of two birds with one giant flying city."

"What about you?" I asked, watching his reaction. "It's obvious you're gentle toward the Advocate cause. Maybe you even work for them. Why don't you tell them about Wardenclyffe?"

I didn't see Malakhai draw his pistols, but suddenly their barrels were under mine and Sarah's chins. The Judge's eyes were blazing red, and Neshomne was growling low.

"You best keep those kind of thoughts to yourself, kid," he said, voice grating with threat. "Seeing as how me and Neshomne rely on Cabal treatments to stay alive, and there's good folk in this city that need us to keep them out of the fur, any hint that we ain't loyal would be bad for quite a few people. We toe the line betwixt bastards and traitors as much as we're able; you young'uns don't know shit about that square-dance, or the toll it takes. Keep your opinions buried deep down along with your snotty questions, or bad things will happen. We clear?"

I started to answer, but stopped when I saw the Tombstone's doors open. A nod from me and Sarah was enough though.

A teenage boy with fiery red hair stepped out, his freckled brow furrowed in a sad imitation of Malakhai's own scowl. "Brought us some troublemakers, Judge?"

After one last warning glance to us, Malakhai lowered his pistols, spinning them with a flourish before holstering them. "Not so much, Rawlson," he called out. "The girl here nearly went to the wolf at Greene's shop; we need to keep a weather-eye on her until we're sure she's out of the woods."

The gangly teen frowned in disappointment, and his gaze lingered on me. "You sure? That Vocalator looks a bit uppity to me."

I dropped my gaze and slumped my shoulders. I'd have to get better at pretending I wasn't on the edge of knocking everyone's teeth down their throats.

"Everyone looks uppity to you," Malakhai said with a humorless smile. "I'm willing to bet you sneer at Talon Thompson behind his back. He catch you at it, yet?"

Rawlson's face went white as a sheet, and he disappeared back in, leaving the door ajar.

"Remember what I told you," Malakhai grunted, taking us by the scruff of our shirts again, although not unkindly. "Watch your asses, and remember: you're here for your friend to get better. Get through this clean, and we can get you gone easy."

Going in the double doors of the Tombstone felt like stepping into the underworld. Even the light of the setting sun outside was brighter than the dull yellow electric bulbs that sputtered in the darkness of the building. They were placed too far apart to light the way, giving the shadows ample playground between. The hallway was long and wide, with sturdy doors leading off it every twenty feet or so. Stained tile work covered the floor, and something told me I was glad the light didn't quite reach all the corners of it. Although the double doors were obviously meant to accommodate most Augmented, Neshomne still had to duck his huge lupine head coming in.

Greeting us by the door was Rawlson's station, a ramshackle desk with a gun cabinet behind it holding a couple of shotguns and rifles. On the desk rested three circles of steel, thick as a fist and less welcoming than one. They were studded with tiny glass tubes in which filaments lay dead, with thick cabling leading into a battery pack on heavy leather straps with a lock on it. It didn't take a Tellurian to figure out what the circlets were.

Shock collars.

Malakhai directed us to unload our possessions onto a crude blanket. In went the bags and pouches of our life, including the surge pack from Sarah's shoulder. The Blood Judge widened his eyes at the contraption when some of its obscuring cloth slipped. But he didn't say anything, letting Sarah cover it in the pile. Once we'd finished Neshomne scooped the blanket into a hobo's bundle with one hand, easily shouldering the weight.

Rawlson snapped his fingers and pointed at the Winchester rifle that Sarah still had shouldered. "Give it over, girl. No weapons allowed, even for white women. You just have to trust in our protection."

The last was accompanied by a rotten-toothed grin. I could tell Sarah was fighting the urge to level the rifle and take his head off. But when Maggie shuddered in Neshomne's arms, it threw a bucket of cold water on her sister's ire. Sarah handed over the Winchester. The Deputy wrote a receipt for it before locking the rifle up in the gun cabinet behind him.

"All right, then, let's get your augger fitted out," Rawlson said, matter-of-factly. He picked up a collar and opened it. As soon as I heard the click, my fists balled up, but I held my temper and straightened my hands out, only allowing myself a furtive shake of my head.

"Aw, fancy that, he thinks he has a choice," Rawlson drawled. "You been taking it easy on your auggers, little lady?"

Sarah gave him a glare that wasn't quite as effective as her boot, but it got the point across well enough. Rawlson's smile became more forced, but he advanced on me with the neck manacle anyway.

Malakhai's hand on my shoulder kept me from stepping back. I knew I had to keep up the charade, but there was no part of me that wanted anything to do with being collared. "They've just never had cause to hurt their servants. Some people don't bring out violence in the Augmented like you, Deputy. Must be your charming personality."

Rawlson's grin disappeared, but he didn't dare shoot the Judge the scowl he was brewing. Instead, the junior lawman took it out on me, snapping the collar around my neck and catching skin. He was even less gentle forcing me into the leather harness. The battery for the collar rested between my shoulder blades, and Rawlson smirked as he cinched the getup tight before clicking a lock onto the back. Rawlson flicked a switch on the battery, and the collar sparked as it hummed to life. An ant swarm crawled over my neck, promising to bite if I did anything wrong. There was no doubt in my mind that the deputy could and would trigger the collar for any reason, and probably even without one.

"And one for you," Rawlson said, advancing toward Sarah with another collar and harness.

Malakhai held his hand out, blocking the deputy. "That's really not necessary, is it, Rawlson? The girl isn't a security risk, and she ain't going down to the fur any time soon."

For a moment it seemed like the redheaded teen would back down, but he scrunched up his face and stubbornness. "Rules are rules, Judge. Even for you. They aren't officially sanctioned, they have to be collared. No exceptions." He lowered his voice to a conspiratorial whisper. "Especially with the Talons and ... *him* ... here."

"Can't wait till *he* flies his happy ass away," Malakhai grumbled, but he relented and let the deputy do his job.

Sarah's elbow kept Rawlson's hands from wandering off the straps and collar, but I felt sick that she was learning to easily recognize a leer that she shouldn't have at her age. It might cost me a few shocks, but I resolved then and there to not leave her alone with the deputy.

Maggie was next to be shackled, and Malakhai added a pair of iron cuffs to her wrists and ankles as well. He was as gentle as he could be; after he was done he had Neshomne pick her up again. Waving off the Deputy, Malakhai took us by our elbows and escorted us from the processing area down the hallway.

The doors on each side bore a simple stamped nameplate under a flickering light. In addition to storerooms, there were also offices for Civil Engineering, Land Deeds, and other mundane rooms essential to running a city. But I didn't expect to find the Mayor's office snuggled up next to the Augmented Reclamation and the Punishment Bureau.

"Don't let it throw you, kid," Malakhai said. "Whether politicians or trash-pickers, they're all located here. Same thing, really. This serves as the de facto government center. The fact the citizens stay away is just an extra ace in the deck to the people running the show."

It took a longer walk than I'd expected and a dozen ignored junctions, but we eventually came to the end of the hallway. Although I was expecting to see the stairs going up, the ones going down surprised me a bit. There was an iron gate cutting off the stairwell, and Malakhai pulled a ring of keys from his pocket to unlock it.

If I'd thought the first hallway was grimy, it didn't hold a candle to the dank darkness we descended into. What little light there was came from the oldest electric lamps I'd ever laid eyes on. They sputtered with a buzzing noise that sounded like angry hornets, and the cobwebs strewn over the ceiling and walls couldn't hide stains that no one had ever bothered to try and clean up.

Barred cells lined the hall, the dark within them impenetrable and thick. There was furtive movement in the Stygian depths of a few, but there didn't seem to be many prisoners to keep. Something told me that Portland wasn't in the habit of letting captives languish, and that most sentencing went a single deadly direction: toward the gallows.

"We're not putting her in one of those," I said in a whisper that carried the weight of a shout behind it. Malakhai's scarlet eyes flashed in irritation, but I didn't care; I'd rather be caught out as a a fake Vocalator than leave Maggie in one of those stinking holes.

"You're right, we're not," he said, when he saw I was about to object again. "There's a set of rooms at the end, near the elevator the Talons use to access the labs in the basement. She'll be safe there until I can be sure she's well enough to be released."

"There's more floors below?" Sarah asked.

Malakhai gave an involuntary shiver and nodded. "I don't know how many, or what they use them all for. And I don't want to know. Neither do you."

It started to get a bit brighter, and we came into a section that was better maintained. The cell bars also changed in quality; instead of rusted pig iron, these were tempered steel. By the queasy feeling in my gut I could tell they were electrified, with enough juice running through them to send a furback reeling. Although there were six cells, only one was currently occupied. Its prisoner was a dirty man with weak shoulders and a hair lip, who sneered at Malakhai as we passed by.

"Bring me a playmate?" he asked with a rasp, coming as close as he could to the bars and leering at Maggie. Malakhai ignored him, but Neshomne raked his metal claws across the bars, sending an arc of electricity trailing sparks at the prisoner, who jumped back with a yelp.

Malakhai opened the cell farthest from the scumbag, using a small toggle on the outside to cut the current to the bars. Unlike the gate to upstairs, there were no keys here; a simple latch was all you needed when touching the cell door would shock you into unconsciousness. There was a bucket in the corner for doing business, and a thin straw mattress over the steel slats of the bolted-down cot.

Neshomne reached in with his long arm, carefully putting Maggie down on the prison bed without waking her. He stepped back, and the Judge closed and electrified the cell again. My face must've betrayed my apprehension; Malakhai clapped me on the shoulder and gave me a half-grin, his silver fangs flashing.

"Don't worry about her, kid. This is just a precaution. No one comes down here other than the Blood Judges and Rawlson. Ain't nobody that wants to remember the people stuck in the dirt jails we passed, and there's not a man in town that wants to tangle with someone put in the isolations. I'll log the three of you in with Rawlson to be on the safe side, but I doubt Tillman will give enough of a shit to check in on you, even if he does get back before me."

His assurances of safety didn't comfort me much, but we didn't have a lot of choices. Maggie's almost-shift had caught us by surprise, and as much as I wanted to protect Wardenclyffe I didn't have clue one on how to go about it. If the Advocates really were responsible for the telluric dead zone then I needed to talk to them. But since the nullification field they'd set up from their overlook on Mt. Hood was also protecting them from being eradicated by the Cabal, I doubted they'd shut it down voluntarily, even if we could find a way through the sickening disorientation effect. They probably knew they'd eventually lasso Menlo Station, and were looking forward to dropping it on Portland. The idea had a certain poetry to it. I might have gotten behind it too, if they hadn't roped in Wardenclyffe as well.

Neshomne put down the bundle of our possessions near the cell, tying the blanket tight so that nothing fell out. Malakhai pulled a table and a couple of chairs over to it. "Ya'll can wait here if you want. I've got a few other duties to attend to, but I'll check in later. I'll leave word with Rawlson to bring you down some grub when he feeds Staddard over there."

"And these?" Sarah's asked, pulling on her shock collar. "Somehow I don't trust him to not electrocute us as soon as you're gone."

"Fair enough," the Judge said. "Tell you what, I'll promise Rawlson that however he treats you young'uns is how I'll treat him. The moron's gullible for that kind of threat, like how Tillman has convinced him that me and Neshomne still go at it between the sheets so he keeps his back to the wall when we're around. As if anyone with an ounce of taste would want that hateful shit."

"Ick. I mean, not you, the situation—"

"I get it, kid. Appreciate the clarification. Even though we got used to folk treating us different a while back, it still stings," he said. Neshomne snorted in agreement. "That said, I don't mind using a fool's fear against him. I'll say 'boo' and jump out of the shadows if it keeps an idiot in line. Be back in a bit. Stay safe."

With that, the Blood Judge tipped his hat to us and headed out, trailed by his ironhide companion. We were left with the strange sounds of the Tombstone surrounding us. The prison bars and the shock collars gave off a low range buzzing in our ears, and the mutters and moans of the condemned in the darker cells merged into a murmur of despair that soaked into our bones. Even the leering prisoner quieted down, his own rambunctious desire for Maggie crumbling beneath the monolithic disdain emitted by the walls of the building. It was as if the Tombstone despised us in a primal, entropic fashion. It didn't put any particular effort into hating us. It just did, as surely as the sun burned in the sky and the waves crashed on the shore.

Careful to not touch the electrified bars, I straddled a chair in front of Maggie's cell. She slept fitfully on the thin mattress, tossing and turning, caught in some kind of nightmare. Her skin was flushed with a sheen of sweat. Her lips moved as she called out against whatever ghosts were after her.

Had I done the right thing? Going down to the fur forever wasn't something that Maggie and Sarah's people feared much. In truth, they looked forward to it, as it marked the end of their exile from family and friends, an end to the danger they represented to the other werewolves as a shifter. The Butler sisters had been trying to win me over to their point of view for the last few months, doing their damnedest to wean me off the Wardenclyffe teat and get me square with my fate.

But Maude didn't raise me to quit on nothing, and I sure as hell wasn't going to give up on being human quite that easy. Despite how Maggie and Sarah accepted it as a natural part of living, being infected, being a beast, wasn't the right state of humans. Although the permanent furbacks had figured out pack and family after a fashion, I liked being able to reason, read, invent, and love. While some folks didn't respect or hold to such things, I wasn't one of them. It was one of the reasons I despised ignorant scum like the Wallaces and Greene so much: they willingly gave up their minds and souls to feel superior. They didn't even have the excuse of the Wendigo infection robbing them of their faculties. They were afraid to use them, afraid to look at who they were head-on. And the longer they twisted in that dark pit the harder it was to believe they'd ever willingly climb out of it.

My ruminations were disrupted by a loud click from the leering man's cell. The screech of unoiled gears working against each other accompanied a rumbling vibration through the floor. I was half out of the chair, leaning over to see what was going on, when he screamed out.

"No! Not me, them, them! I'm just here for—"

His voice cut out with an incoherent shriek. I bolted from where I was, knocking over the chair with a clatter. I might not have appreciated his comments toward Maggie, but that didn't mean I was going to just ignore the cries of help from a fellow human being, no matter how tenuously he claimed that title.

A deeper darkness had enveloped the locked cell that Staddard was in. Through the iron bars I saw that the back wall had disappeared, and something had emerged to terrorize the trapped man.

I'd seen quite a few unnatural things in my life: werewolves, mad scientists wreathed in lightning, flying cities and trains, and now the vampiric Blood Judges. Hell, I'd even been witness to a man's torso being used as a portable alchemy lab for the Broken.

But nothing quite compared to the thing waiting for me in the screaming man's cell.

Chapter 15

THE CRITTER THAT EMERGED from the missing wall had once been able to lay claim to being a man, but that time was long gone. His lanky frame was contorted, bearing the half-changed shape of an infected who'd had enough electroshock treatments to keep from going full pelt into the wolf, but who'd failed to keep up the daily dose of lightning to stay human. Thin as a rail and near seven feet tall, he had elongated arms with long-fingered hands that hung near down to his knees. Despite his close call with the beast, he wasn't showing any fur; instead, the stranger had crusted red scabs in patches over his lily-white skin like a diseased snake's scales.

While his clawed feet were bare, the creature wore a pair of immaculate pinstriped pants and a sleeveless vest that covered much of his misshapen body. A multitude of brass tubes ran across his bare arms and into a contraption on his back that wheezed and chugged. Sores puckered on his arms and shoulders where the tubes had planted roots directly into the muscles, and the skin in those areas bulged and contracted in time to the contraption's rhythm. A bracer of brass and steel encased his left forearm, its face littered with a dizzy array of dials and switches. The telltale cadence of ticking and pops coming from the bracer spoke of intricate machinery dancing within its metal housing.

The stranger's face was as stretched as his limbs. Where a muzzle should have been there was instead an area that had been fused together, a solid mass of protruding flesh where mouth and nose had tried to form. Despite his contorted features, the man's eyes were the too-blue of a wolf's, alert and intelligent. The way he was staring at me made me shudder. A cluster of lenses sat on his sloped forehead, held tight by leather straps. He was a strange mishmash of monster and city slicker, but it was his neck that was truly disturbing.

Slit into the center of the man's throat was a ghastly mouth, held open by multiple tiny steel hooks and rods that worked the surrounding skin like a baker kneading dough.

That alone would have made me question the truth of my eyes, but inside the 'mouth' a set of human teeth had been implanted. The teeth clattered as the mouth sucked air, snapping shut and open rhythmically.

The creature raised its hand and wiggled its long fingers in greeting. The steel hooks pulled the throat-mouth into the caricature of a smile.

"Hello. Specimen."

Cold sweat broke out across my body, and I was suddenly very happy there was a locked cell door between us. It wasn't the rasping voice that spewed from his throat-mouth, but rather the eager implications buried in the words. He sounded like a kid at his birthday party. The spider-like fingers on his hands folded together, eagerly trembling at thoughts I did not want him to share.

An audible click came from the cell door separating us.

It had unlocked of its own accord.

I backed away a step as the cell door swung open, and the creature advanced the same toward me. The wall behind him had opened inward, revealing an unlit passage where he'd presumably dragged away the missing prisoner. My eyes betrayed me, looking anywhere but at the nightmare menacing me, instead focusing in on the multiple scratch marks along the walls of the passage. A freshly-ripped fingernail was stuck in the stonework, the blood marking where a desperate Staddard had been trying to avoid his fate in any way possible.

"Eli, get away from that thing!" Sarah shouted, catching sight of the advancing creature. She ran over to our belongings, struggling with the blanket's knot.

His attention turned to her, and the throat-mouth strained to smile wider, eliciting a trickle of blood from the abused flesh. I interspersed myself between the critter and Sarah, trying to give her the time she needed to get to the surge pack.

"Commendable. Loyalty. Vocalator. Come."

The creature raised his hand and spread his fingers. A thin metal spike slid out of the palm, and I nearly fainted then and there. My ruse had finally come home to roost; with the trouble he was having talking, the man-thing wanted to shove the spike into the fake neck and skull brace I was wearing. Apparently he was able to utilize the same way of talking as the ironhides, but there was one problem: without the surgery that let Vocalators interact with the spikes, he'd just be stabbing me in the brain. While killing might be preferable to what he had in mind, it still wasn't top of my list for a Saturday night.

He looked disappointed when I retreated farther, and the sigh of regret from his throat sounded sincere. The spike retracted back into his palm with a serpent's hiss. He raised his left forearm, and the fingers on his other hand danced across the dials and toggles covering it.

Electricity sliced through my body like a thousand razors, cutting into my nerve endings without mercy. The shock collar sent wave after wave of pain into me. I fell to my knees crying, all thoughts of keeping silent obliterated by a curtain of fiery agony.

"Um . . . Talon Thompson. Sir?"

Through the haze of pain, Rawlson's face slowly came into focus. He'd come down the hallway, carrying three tin plates with beans and burnt bacon. All the blood had drained from his face, and his eyes got big at seeing the secret passage that led from the prison cell into the recesses of the Tombstone.

The critter, the Talon, spun on him with a hiss of displeasure. He pointed a spindly finger back down the hall past the deputy.

"Go. Now."

The dinner plates hadn't even hit the floor before Rawlson disappeared, the reedy gasps as he ran echoing in the hall behind him. As the Talon turned back to me I tried to lunge forward, intending to hit him in that ugly-ass face with my weight behind me.

Electrocuted muscles betrayed me though, and I fell forward instead of lunging. The man-thing rasped its laughter again, and the shock collar lit me up from the inside out for what seemed like an eternity of pain.

There was no telling how long and how loud I screamed, but when the electricity finally let up my throat was bleeding raw and my muscles had fried themselves into place around my fused bones. The wolf in me moved sluggishly, and my wounds were slow to heal.

Tears streamed down Sarah's face as she fought and cussed the blanket's knot, calling out for me to hold on.

Thompson moved next to me, and reached down to my unprotected neck and spine. He ripped the mock Vocalator brace off of me, bringing up skin with the spirit gum.

"False," he rasped. He put the palm of his hand to the base of my skull, holding my head tight in his long fingers. Thin claws cut my cheeks and forehead, but the real threat pressed into the back of my neck. His palm-spike was cold against my skin, and I would've sworn the iron quivered in anticipation of skewering me.

Sarah finally got the knot undone, and our possessions spilled out onto the stone floor. She knocked aside clothes and tools as she dug out the surge pack, flipping the charging switches in the order I'd taught her.

The Talon hissed in fear as Sarah brought up the lightning rod. Hair across my body went straight out as she pushed the button that would release a lightning bolt into us.

There was a spark, a sad whine, and then the pack cycled down, going dark. Without an active telluric stream in the area, the surge pack had failed to charge like it would normally. There was no juice in it at all.

We all stood there for a moment, frozen in place.

Then Thompson started laughing.

It was a wheezing, clattering sound, unhealthy and evil. He shook me like a rag doll with his mirth. I couldn't say I enjoyed the joke.

Sarah's tear-streaked face grew red with fury. She threw down the lightning rod and rushed at the Talon, fists balled up and flailing.

The laughing Talon knocked her away with contemptuous ease. Sarah hit the wall with a terrible crack and slid down to the ground. Hopefully she'd just had the wind knocked out of her, but there was no way to tell.

Thompson held the false Vocalator brace in front of my face. His palm spike on the hand that held my head extended far enough to draw blood.

"Explain. This."

The position he was holding me in gave a good view of where Maggie slumbered in her cell. I realized he didn't know anything about us. He naturally assumed me and Sarah were there together, but there was no reason for him to tie Maggie to us unless I screwed up. Besides, there was someone else I could peg for us being there, and I owed him one. So I took a chance.

"We were sent to break out the man you just took," I lied. My voice was cracked and raw, which hopefully was enough to hide the fact I was terrible at fibbing.

The Talon jerked my head around, forcing me to stand upright as he turned me around to look at him.

"Staddard? Advocates? Impossible."

I cast around in my memories, desperately looking for any details I could give him to reinforce the lie. Then I remembered the quartering of the rebel wrong-wolf in the town square.

"Bloodrath!" I blurted out. "He sent us. Said that he needed Staddard for Sister Blister. We had orders to bring him back to Mt. Hood."

Thompson stared hard at me for a moment, lenses from his headpiece clacking down over one eye as he weighed my words. Choking laughter bubbled up from his throat-mouth, rattling his teeth.

"Liar."

The man-thing wrenched my head around, forcing my body to comply, and started dragging me toward the dark passage in the back of the prison cell. My body refused to fight back, and the world wouldn't stop spinning.

"Wait . . ." Sarah whispered, fighting to prop herself up. She couldn't quite get her limbs to work right. A bone was sticking out of her left forearm, sharp and bloody, but the right one didn't seem to be any better. "Don't . . ."

The Talon took a step back and grabbed her by the front of her shirt, hoisting her up with a grunt of effort. The teeth in his throat stilled, and a long tongue flicked out past them, licking Sarah's neck and face, leaving behind a thin trail of slime.

"Treat."

I aimed a kick right at his family jewels. But there was no force behind it, and the blow only elicited a mocking laugh from Thompson. He dragged us back into Staddard's cell by our heads, chortling at our feeble struggles.

Maggie muttered a few cells over, trapped in her nightmares. The Talon had no interest in her, at least for the time being. She was safe.

As the darkness of the secret passage swallowed us up, I found myself wishing the same was true for me and Sarah.

Chapter 16

THE ROUGH STONE OF the floor caught on the knees of my britches as we were dragged along, and my eyes struggled to adjust to the shadows. There was a dim glow coming from ahead, but the Talon's grip on my head kept me from craning my neck to see anything else.

A stench rose off the man-thing that made my gorge rise, a peculiar aroma between spoiled milk and rotten meat. The teeth in his throat chattered with excitement, but it was drowned out by a distant scream echoing off the walls ahead of us. Thompson quickened his pace, excitement writ large on his distorted features. We turned the bend and came to an open pit. Ropes stretched down from above, their length disappearing into the chasm. The Talon dropped us at his feet, grunting with effort as he stretched out and took hold of one of the ropes. His thin muscles stood out as he worked the line, hauling on it.

A wooden platform rose into view, the ropes attached to its corners to make a crude elevator. It swayed with the breeze that blew in from above, while being lit from below by whatever Hell Thompson was dragging us down to.

He tossed us into the center of the platform, making the whole thing sway toward the far wall. As the boards hit the stonework, I rolled on my back and saw stars peeking out from the night sky above. The elevator shaft ran from the roof of the Tombstone down to here, and beyond.

"Stay," the Talon rasped, clambering onto the wooden planks. The platform creaked under his weight, but held. Old bloodstains darkened the wood, and the faint scent of fresh red wafted up from below, accompanied by another scream.

As Thompson began working the hoist and lowering us down, I felt strength returning to my limbs. Unlike most infected folks, the lightning used against me was getting less and less effective. Even in the months leading up to discovering Portland, it had been taking more juice to keep me down each full moon. Best I could figure was that my mounting resistance to being shocked was a side-effect of what the Cabal did to my daddy back before I was a glimmer in his eye. But no matter why, the long and the short was that the Talon wouldn't be expecting difficulty from me this soon.

And I felt like being troublesome.

Sarah was still incapacitated, drifting in and out of consciousness. She'd be no help. But I didn't need it. At my violent thoughts the wolf in my blood surged forward. There was no lingering weakness from the shocks; in fact, I felt better than normal, stronger and faster than ever. Narrowing my eyes, I clenched hands into fists. The way out was above, and I sure as shit didn't want to find out what went on below. All I had to do was toss the bastard over the side and hoist us up. A quick stop to rescue Maggie, drop the elevator on Thompson's head once we were out, and call it a day.

Gathering my legs under, I watched for my opening. Lowering us down was taking all of the Talon's attention. He grunted in irritation as a snag in the counterweight rope made him stretch up to untangle it.

A surprised yelp escaped the man-thing as I charged forward, slamming my right shoulder up and under his outstretched arm, the one with the control bracer for the shock collars. There was a loud snap as his shoulder popped out of socket, and Thompson let out a screech.

The platform swung wildly as we tussled, him refusing to let go of the rope and me refusing to stop hitting him. The side of the elevator slammed into the stone wall, and a few of the planks splintered and fell free. The Talon desperately struggled to keep control of the ropes with his one good arm as I hit him again and again in the ribs, hearing satisfying cracks each time. Every snap made me grin wider, and it was getting harder and harder to see past the haze of red rising over my sight.

The wolf was surging in me now, urging me on to hurt this thing, this unnatural critter that had dared to lay a hand on me and mine. I roared incoherently with challenge and defiance that burned my throat with its savagery. Strength flowed through my body like searing lava, carried along by a viciousness that I welcomed. Thompson flailed at me ineffectually, trying to keep hold of the rope and fend me off at the same time. I sneered in disdain as I caught his injured limb.

I smiled with all my teeth and snapped the Talon's left arm in two, breaking the bone like a twig.

Sparks crackled across my body like water droplets, and for a second I paused in confusion. Was Thompson using some kind of gadget to fight back? No, he was barely holding on to the elevator hoist, and he flinched back as sparks leapt from my arms to shock him. The hair on my skin stood straight out like tiny lightning rods, sending galvanic energy into my enemy. Thompson wasn't doing anything but hollering in pain.

This bit of weird was all me.

"Eli!"

The weak cry of alarm caught my attention, and I turned around just in time to see Sarah sliding limply toward the damaged edge of the elevator platform. Although she'd been able to slur out my name, her arms were limp and useless as she tumbled toward a deadly fall. The ropes had gotten tangled with my attack on the Talon, and the platform lurched drunkenly at an angle.

I let go of Thompson and leapt forward for Sarah, trying to get to her before she slid over the edge. Horror chilled me as a werewolf's claw formed around my hand, a hollow shape outlined in lightning that crackled and popped with deadly energy.

"No!" I screamed, caught between saving Sarah and electrocuting her with the energy sparking off the phantom claw.

My terror at hurting Sarah chilled my guts. The ghost paw disappeared in the blink of an eye, leaving only my human hand, twitching and burnt.

The apparition had flickered in and out fast enough that I wasn't really sure I hadn't just imagined it. Somewhere inside me the wolf roared being denied prey.

I managed to get a hold of the leather harness for Sarah's shock collar battery as she went over the edge. Splinters dug into my belly, but I wasn't letting go. She wasn't that heavy, but one-arming it while desperately trying to hold onto the platform with my other hand didn't make for an easy pull. Whatever strength my inner beast had lent me was gone, and my arm felt like it was being pulled out of the socket as I struggled to hang on to her. Sarah's legs flailed uselessly over the chasm below, but she couldn't reach up to grab hold of my arm with hers. Her mouth worked just fine though; she was using every cuss word I'd ever accidentally taught her.

The elevator was still swinging with the momentum of the fight, so I timed my yank to coincide with the movement. I rolled on my back at the apex of the swing, using my weight to drag Sarah's lighter body up and over onto the platform as we swung back down. She managed to get one of her feet wedged into the wooden planks, keeping her from sliding back over.

A hiss of rage was all the warning I had before voltage suddenly shot through my body from my shock collar. The device smoked and whined for the length of time Thompson kept the current flowing, growing scorching hot against my neck as it tortured me. Somehow, I managed to push away from Sarah so she didn't get the same jolt, but after that my brain was too fried to think of anything else. There was no telling how long I writhed on the planks.

Thompson didn't stop until the battery was dry. The collar died with a sputtering whine as it put the last of its electricity into me. My nose was clogged with the scent of my own burnt hair and muscle, choking me with the sickly-sweet stench.

Somehow the electrocution hadn't knocked me out, and I cussed my brain for making me stay conscious.

The Talon gave a low reptilian snarl and kicked me with his clawed foot, breaking a couple of my ribs in payback. He took a deep breath and closed his eyes, apparently satisfied I was no longer a danger.

I was surprised I was still alive.

The sickening sound of bones ripping through muscle made me turn my head.

Thompson was straightening his broken arm, slowly and

deliberately. Sweat stood out on his twisted face as he worked the bone back into the right place, using fingers in his own wound to push it back to where it belonged. Blood poured out onto the planks of the elevator, dripping down to the abyss below.

With a yowl of agony he gave a sudden jerk of his shoulder, setting the bone. He pulled his fingers out of the bloody wound and flipped a switch on the control bracer. In response, the brass tubes covering his arms and back shuddered. One of them, weakened by my assault, broke open and spewed a sickly green ichor out. The Talon winced and grabbed it, shoving the jagged end straight into the open wound.

Green-blue smoke drifted out from his torn-open arm, accompanied by a smell like burnt leather. The broken arm's bone sizzled and fused together in an instant. Muscles and tendons started flowing across the exposed muscle like a spider spinning an impossibly fast web. Skin flowed in over the repaired flesh, hardening into a scabrous patch.

A moment later Thompson was able to flex the wounded arm without wincing. He stretched out a single long finger to point at me. Fury was blazing in his eyes.

"You. Pay."

I couldn't help but laugh. Although it didn't sound as defiant as I wanted, the fact I could do or say anything after the electrocution I'd just gotten made Thompson's eyes widen in surprise. I was right there with him; I knew better than most that I should be at the least unconscious, if not actually paralyzed or dead from the voltage my body had absorbed.

Thompson grumbled with his throat-mouth as he lowered us the rest of the way down the shaft, keeping a suspicious eye on me. He didn't know it, but the bastard had good reason to keep an eye on me: the feeling was already returning to my limbs. But there was no strength yet, and I couldn't risk Sarah again just for the sake of being contrary. There'd be a time and a place to kick the Talon's ass. But this wasn't it.

A blood-curdling shriek drifted up the elevator shaft; judging by the fact Staddard had been taken only moments before us, and how long it was taking us to descend, it wasn't a surprise when the platform came to a stop and I saw that Thompson wasn't acting alone.

His partner possessed quite a few of the same characteristics as the

Talon who had kidnapped us: lanky frame, scabby scales, brass tubes running across his reptilian body. Even a nasty throat-mouth. But instead of vest and britches, this one had on some kind of fancy robe, complete with hood. The fabric looked like silk, purple and shimmering, with gold thread embroidered in lightning and flame patterns across it.

The critter stood in the middle of a laboratory with a high ceiling, obviously built custom to accommodate the height of the Talons. Chemical apparatus lined the walls, some in use over burners, some not, and in the middle of the room were two steel frames with leather restraints sitting horizontal to the stained tile floor. Staddard was strapped into one at the moment, bawling like a babe. Steel spikes had been inserted into various parts of his face and torso, with wires leading back to a spherical device covered with glowing lights. The robed Talon was hard at work, industriously stabbing new spikes into Staddard at different spots, hissing with amusement at the noises he made.

Standing at attention next to him were two boys barely older than Sarah. Their clothes were rags, and whatever ember of life that had once danced in their eyes had been extinguished long ago. They were painfully skinny, and their emaciated frames shook under the weight of the tools they were holding. But it wasn't their burden nor their clothes that struck an ambivalent chord of pity and nausea within me.

The butchers that had operated on the two boys had removed the front half of their skulls.

But that wasn't the worst of it. Their brains had been cut into, with large sections of the front lobes removed. What remained had been left exposed in the open air.

The pinkish-beige brain remnants had been wired to a conglomeration of gears and metal boxes that took up the remaining space in their skulls. As the taller of the two boys turned to hand a small hammer to the robed Talon I saw he bore a Vocalator's neck brace as well.

Noticing us for the first time, the new Talon's throat-mouth pulled itself into a grin. He turned the boy around that had handed him the tool, extended his palm spike, and stabbed the child in the Vocalator's socket.

The boy's glassy eyes rolled back in his head. As the Talon turned his mouthpiece toward us, I noticed a life and spryness to the Vocalator's movements that unsettled me. I'd seen wrong-wolves use the Vocalators to talk before; the poor souls became stilted, jerky puppets, and their speech followed the same pattern. But this mutilated child acted differently with the spike in his head.

The boy moved as if infused with missing life, like a sleeper awakened. The Vocalator's face lit up with joy, even though his eyes remained dead and upturned, showing only the whites. The Talon's long fingers wrapped around from the back of the boy's head, the fingertips nearly meeting over the child's too-expressive face.

"More research subjects?" the boy exclaimed as the controlling Talon chattered his throat-teeth. "Excellent work, Dr. Thompson. We will have a viable candidate before week's end at this pace!"

The Talon who'd captured us bowed to the other's compliment. He reached down to pick up Sarah, who kicked weakly at him. Thompson easily batted her legs away and hoisted her up with a grunt. I was left lying on the elevator platform as he carried Sarah over to a set of chains and manacles attached to the nearby wall. Wrenching her broken arms up, he fastened her in securely, letting one finger linger on her cheek in a possessive gesture. The girl stood defiant, ignoring the bone sticking out of her forearm, channeling her pain into pure rage. She opened her mouth, and no words came out, only an angry hiss-growl that caused Thompson to recoil in surprise.

Anger flared in me. I should have waited for an opening, played possum for a bit longer while I regained my strength. But I was about done having every lowlife we met treat a child like a perverted toy that was only waiting to be unwrapped.

"C'mere and cuddle me like that, ugly," I slurred, lurching up to a sitting position. "I'll put that finger somewhere you'll never get it out from."

Thompson snarled and started forward, but the robed Talon put up his hand to stay the other's advance. The empty grin on the controlled Vocalator's face seeped with the malice that the robed Talon's warped mug was unable to show.

"Uppity, aren't we?" he asked with the child's voice. "I'd think the white man's blood in you would make you more civilized, but such is the result of mating with the savages. Oh, don't look so surprised. Of course I know you're mixed blood; can a breeder not identify the different lineages present when he sees a mutt?"

I wanted to grab hold of his head and tear it off, but my arms weren't responding yet. Neither were my legs. But my mouth worked just fine, even if the words slurred a bit. Luckily I was a master of quips, a veritable Mark Twain of insults, able to crush the spirits of my opponents with well-timed verbal jabs.

"You ain't exactly purebred yourself, handsome."

Amazingly, his spirit remained intact, and he didn't immediately fall prostrate begging for me to stop. I must've been losing my touch.

Rather than quail before my wit, the robed Talon instead strode over to me with a pair of manacles he produced from the folds of his robe. Instead of simple iron restraints, these were gleaming steel, with copper wiring wrapped around several posts that jutted out of the surface. There was a low-level hum from them that made the hair on my arms stand up. Thompson ripped off the sad remnants of my hot-suit jacket, and the other Talon snapped the mechanical manacles around my wrist. It came as no surprise to me when a painful jolt of electricity shot through me from the shackles.

He took hold of the restraints and dragged me off of the elevator and across the blood-stained floor to the wall. With no discernible effort he lifted me up by my wrists and fastened me into a neck clamp mounted on the wall. The manacles snapped into place above, leaving my feet barely touching the floor. I tried a weak kick to his balls in rebellion, but he easily avoided the clumsy strike. My weight rested painfully on arms and neck. But Sarah wasn't whining about her broken arms being shackled; I needed to show a fraction of her willpower.

"Yes, you will make a fine specimen," the robed Talon said, his throat-teeth making the disturbing chatter-laugh sound again. "Perhaps you will be the one, the subject that will allow us to finally deactivate Marie's execrable interference field. If you are a good little slave, I promise to reclaim what's left of you afterward and to rebuild you when we're able to return to Menlo Station. Wouldn't that be nice?"

"Better check with your bossman, handsome. Wouldn't want your all-mighty Edison to get angry at you for bringing home strays."

The Vocalator's face showed puzzlement, and the robed Talon tilted the boy's head in his confusion.

"You confuse me, specimen. Explain. Why would you think that Thomas Edison has any say in what I can or cannot do? I am beyond question, beyond reproach."

"He's your Dragon of Science, right?" I said, twisting my head and cracking my neck. Strength was flowing back fast, and I needed to keep the Talons talking long enough to catch them by surprise again. "I leafed through one of your Cabal flunky's notes back on Wardenclyffe, a mad doctor named Trent. He went on and on about kissing the ass of the Dragon of Science, and how he created the werewolf virus to wipe out us 'lesser' races. Didn't take a genius to figure out that your infatuation with the sub-par D/C transmission systems and using Menlo as your base of operation was due to Edison's influence."

There was a moment of surprised silence. It was broken by a sound I did not expect.

Laughter.

The Talons emitted the strange chattering laughter with their throat-teeth while the controlled Vocalator chortled hollowly. I wasn't sure which one unsettled me more.

"My dark friend, you are quite mistaken," the robed Talon managed to say through the laughing Vocalator. "Although it is true he once held the post, Edison is no longer the Dragon of Science. He attends to . . . other matters these days. We possess a new leader, one who dethroned the other Dragons of God and War, to become the sole head of our organization. Finally, we are free to shape the world according to the shining vision of Science!"

There was a sickly sheen of sweat on the Vocalator's face, a disturbing zealotry that promised violence was the tool of change in the Talon's mind.

"So who is this new head honcho that has you so fired up?" I asked, lacing my voice with mockery and scorn. It felt flat, but damned if I was going to show fear to this creature.

The Vocalator smiled wide, as did both the Talons' throat-mouths.

"Who else could it be?" the controlled boy said. "There is only one choice the Cabal could make after Edison's sacrifice. The man who authored this new world, who set in motion the downfall of the old, who swept away the decay of those who would supplant the natural balance for an artificial equality, the likes of which would obliterate the white race and replace it with the muddied waters of a sluggish river. The Cabal showed wisdom and elevated a worthy successor to the throne."

The robed Talon swept his hand out and performed a deep bow, as did the Vocalator he controlled.

"I am Dr. William H. Trent, savior of humanity and the ruling Dragon of the Cabal of Purity."

Chapter 17

S O YOU'RE THE BASTARD that ended the world."

Dr. Trent's teeth chattered in laughter at me.

"Yes, I'm sure to you the world seems a ruin," he said through the Vocalator. "But compared to what your kind was dragging us toward, this is a fresh start, a new day. One might even be tempted to call the premature release of the Wendigo strain as a Genesis event, setting the world back to a purer time. With the opposition to perfection obliterated, we will make America great again!"

"Bullshit," I said, spitting on the floor. "This is your ideal? Look around you, idiot. There's nothing left but wreckage, with a few poor souls picking over the salvage to try and survive. You're pissing on our heads and calling it rain, trying to make out like this was what you intended. But I read your journal, you demented freak. The Indians refused to just lay down and die to the disease. They turned your dog against you before you could teach it not to bite you."

Dr. Trent shook his head. "All too true, I'm afraid. As I said, this is a new age. Originally we wanted simply to restore civilization to the civilized, to save what evolution had built from you and your kind. But the red savages refused to go quietly into the night, and perverted our holy work with their so-called magic."

I cast a critical eye over the disfigured Dragon. Even with a robe on, Trent was an ugly cuss, too tall and thin to be human, with a face that a brick could only improve. "Seems like their hoodoo worked pretty good on your precious disease."

"Bah!" Trent responded, nearly ripping off his Vocalator's head with his vehemence. "They dabbled in forces they did not understand and named it magic. Any primitive will call that which they use but do not understand supernatural."

His ranting was a chilling reminder of how my friend Henry had regarded the Indian magics. It made me wonder, not for the first time, just how far apart the Cabal and Tellurian philosophies were, when you got right down to it.

Trent's Vocalator trembled, and the boy's body was bent almost in half by the Dragon's gestures. Visibly composing himself, the mad doctor took care to straighten the boy out, carefully standing him upright with a rueful chuckle.

"Ah, there I go again, letting my umbrage at their perversions of the work get the better of me. I really should learn to control my temper; it has cost me many a valuable slave. Then again, such small personal foibles also lead to valuable technological advances."

Dr. Trent suddenly yanked his arm down, snapping off his palm spike in the Vocalator's head.

"There, you see?" The Vocalator asked, still in the same speech cadence despite being disconnected from the Dragon. Trent showed me his palm; where I expected a torn wound or broken machinery, there was instead a small light flashing. He turned the enslaved boy around, revealing the detached spike also had a tiny light pulsing in sync.

"Braun should not have spurned our offer of kinship; we could have eliminated his little Marconi problem. Still, they are such wonderful tools, these radio waves he discovered," the boy said. "Not only do they allow the hive collars to operate without wired controls, they can also be adapted to more basic utilitarian purposes. With this, I am able to both speak and still operate on my test subjects. You see, halfbreed, that civilization has not fallen. No, it advances even now under our watchful eyes!"

Dr. Trent took a syringe full of milky yellowish fluid from the Talon who had been waiting in silence, and punctuated his proclamation of advancement by stabbing Staddard's right eye with its steel needle. The man screamed in agony as his eye popped with a wet sound. Blood and vitreous fluid streamed down from his eye socket in a tearful flow of gore. Trent slowly pushed the plunger, injecting the cloudy mixture into the man's brain.

"Why in God's name did you do that?" I blurted out, my belly roiling with revulsion.

"Not God, my dear halfbreed. We are authors of our own destiny here!" Trent said through the Vocalator. "Although Staddard is insufficient for the final treatment, he may prove useful in the distillation process. I do not expect your underdeveloped brain to be able to comprehend this, but if I can adjust the test subject's biological resonance frequency to the right wavelength he should be able to pass through Marie's negation field. With the right alterations I'm sure we will find our way forward. Of course it would be easier to go through his nostril cavity. But not half as fun."

Trent leaned in with a pair of small clamps and forced the remaining eye open, holding the lids completely out of the way with the tiny torture device. Staddard's naked eyeball spun wildly in its socket in time to his screaming. Thompson took a small pin out of his control bracer and handed it to Trent. Barely visible in the sputtering glow of the electric lights I could see a thin line of copper running back to the bracer. Careful to avoid the intact eyeball, Dr. Trent leaned in and pierced Staddard's tear duct with the pin, sliding the thin sliver behind the eye. Staddard shrieked and twisted his body, but the heavy leather straps kept his head still.

Trent nodded to Thompson, who began adjusting dials on his bracer. One of the lenses on the Dragon's headpiece dropped down over his malformed eye, and he focused in on his victim.

Staddard's guttural screams turned into a high-pitched keening that ebbed and flowed in time to the adjustments Thompson made with the dials. Puffs of smoke shot out of his ruined eye socket, burbling like a bloody volcano. Even from this distance I could feel the impossible voltage they were running into his head through the thin wire, cooking the man's brains from the inside out as Trent watched in rapt attention.

After what seemed like an eternity, Thompson finally stopped electrocuting Staddard. The man had gone limp, and a line of spittle dripped from his slack jaws. Trent gave a grunt of disappointment as his enslaved Vocalator brought him an empty syringe with a long needle.

He pulled the tiny pin free, and Thompson retracted it into his bracer. Without any hesitation Dr. Trent shoved the syringe into Staddard's remaining eye, bursting it like the other as he slammed the steel needle through bone into the man's brain.

Staddard uttered no sound. No matter the kind of man he might have been in life, I prayed that he was beyond pain when Dr. Trent pulled back on the plunger.

The Dragon withdrew the syringe from Staddard's eye socket with a wet sound. Cerebral liquid sloshed in a mass of cloudy yellow and beige inside the tube, the colors swirling together without merging. I realized it looked almost identical to the alchemical mixture Trent had originally injected into Staddard.

How many victims had the ghouls slain before today?

Trent detached the vial and held it up in the light, swishing it around. "Hopefully Staddard served some purpose. Dr. Thompson, if you would be so good as to analyze and catalog the results."

The Talon nodded his acquiescence, taking the vial from his superior and sliding it into an opening on his control bracer. He snapped his palm spike into the idle Vocalator, making his eyes light up with terrible life. With a yank he disconnected his spike, and the enslaved boy followed the Talon over to a large book that lay open on the corner of a counter that ran the length of the room.

"Sample One Hundred Twenty-Six," the Vocalator said as he scribbled in the book with a fountain pen. The Talon controlling him squinted down at his control bracer. "Purity level: Eighty-seven percent. No discernible gain from distillation process."

"Damn the man's mediocrity," Trent's Vocalator snarled. "Not even a single percent rise in potency? Ah well, I suppose we should be thankful that he didn't dilute its efficacy. I knew from the moment you brought him in that he was insufficient, even without a resonance test."

Thompson looked up from the readings on his bracer and shrugged. He pulled the vial of fluid free and placed it carefully in a rack on the counter.

"Unless we begin kidnapping citizens off the street, we are limited to what the Judges bring to the cells," his Vocalator said, turning from the ledger and mimicking the Talon's shrug. "I still say we abandon this experiment. What use do we have for this town and its Returned? Portland was not your vision . . . my Dragon."

Thompson's Vocalator had hastily added the last part when he saw the sharp look Dr. Trent had given him.

"Do you find your current form overly attractive?" Trent asked, dangerous sweetness dripping off the boy's falsetto voice. "I do not. Nor do I wish to mate with or beget children off such as we. While Edison was overly optimistic about the progress we'd make in this place, I believe the experiment has merit. We will reclaim the entirety of this land one day. For this we need to regain a smidgen of our humanity, at least enough for the brood sows to survive the copulation process. Do you not wish that fresh daisy in the corner to be at your beck and call for more nights than a single deadly, albeit entertaining, one?"

I barked a laugh, startling both of them.

"Good luck with that," I sneered. "She might not look like much after the shocks, but that girl will make sure the only thing getting bloodied is your ugly ass."

Rather than answer, Dr. Thompson picked up a fresh syringe. The steel needle he attached barely qualified as such; it was nearly a foot in length. It gleamed with deadly promise.

He advanced on me, and his controlled Vocalator smiled evilly behind him. "Do you imagine yourself as protecting her honor, boy? I will do as I wish, to whom I wish, when I wish. Such is the power promised to me by my master, the Dragon."

Trent chortled through his throat-teeth. "Ah, your bootlicking always amuses me, Thompson. But enough foreplay with the halfbreed; gather the sample. This one appears to have regained his strength far too soon. That holds promise."

I wanted to struggle, but the collar and manacles made the angle impossible. Thompson raised the syringe like a killer with his knife, and plunged it down at me. I winced, expecting the steel needle to slam into my eyeball, popping it like a frog on a griddle before being driven into my brain. Instead, it penetrated my neck at the base of my jugular, piercing down through my throat and beyond. I gagged as the cold needle sliced down through my windpipe and into my heart. The world went dark for a moment, and spasms wracked my body from the brutal invasion.

At least it wasn't my eyeball.

Lucky me.

Thompson pulled the plunger back, drawing blood and tissue straight from the core of my being. He pulled the syringe back out, relishing how I bucked and struggled against the restraints. There was no thought of revenge or resistance in me; only the pain of what he was doing existed.

When the foot-long needle was finally free of my body I sagged against the restraints. The wolf raced inside me to heal the mortal wound to my heart and throat before death could claim me. I retched blood up onto the floor, but my heart soldiered on, freshly mended by the disease.

"Fascinating," Trent murmured, accepting the sample proffered by the Talon. "He should be on death's door, if not actually dying. Staddard was in critical condition after the first sample. But look! The wound in his jugular has already healed; somehow this halfbreed possesses the healing abilities of a fully transformed lycanthrope while maintaining a human form."

"Could he be our answer?" Thompson asked, his excitement stretching the controlled Vocalator's face into the same rictus as his smiling throat-mouth. "Is he the secret we have been seeking for so long? I had given up hope . . ."

"We will see," Trent murmured, snapping the vial containing my essence into his own control bracer.

He made several excited clacking noises with his throat-teeth, and although his Vocalator remained eerily silent, the glazed look of joy that settled on the enslaved boy's face reeked of religious rapture.

"This sample . . . Dr. Thompson, bring me the logbook! I've seen a variation on this biological resonance before, I know it."

The excited Talon obeyed Trent, knocking his own Vocalator to the floor in his haste to fetch the leather-bound tome.

Dr. Trent used Staddard's cooling corpse as a book pedestal, quickly flipping through the encyclopedic pages. His clawed finger danced lightly over the paper, never tearing it, gentle and loving in a way he never showed his surgical subjects.

As he muttered and flipped pages, I felt my strength return once more. The wolf snarled down deep; there's only so many times you can kick a dog before he bites your foot off.

Sarah was groggy with pain from her arms, but she was fighting through it. She'd managed to form cuss words to go along with her hisses and grunts of defiance. Thompson looked over at her, but a single glance assured him that the chained-up little girl with two broken arms was no danger. If only he knew what Sarah would do if she could get loose. The Butler sisters were not fainting daisies, and I loved them for their strength and ferocity. Their mama would have been proud.

Thompson's gaze turned to me, and I sagged against the restraints, hoping to keep him from noticing my rapid recovery. I closed my eyes and forced my breathing ragged, like I was still struggling.

He didn't buy it.

Electricity shot through my body from the manacles, making me dance a crazy jig as my body spasmed. Thompson chortled from his throat, reducing the voltage enough that it wouldn't damage me, but leaving it high enough that a normal person would be in a constant state of pain.

I was not normal.

Sparks crawled along my skin from hair to hair, and I felt something I hadn't in a long while.

Healthy.

My skin and muscles were absorbing the low-level electricity, drinking it in like a sponge tossed in water. What should have been a constant source of pain was instead making me feel better, stronger. I could feel my muscles tensing not out of stress, but out of elation. The wolf inside me was lapping at the sparks, catching them in its jaws like fireflies and gobbling them down.

"I knew it!" Trent suddenly shouted, pointing a long finger at the tome. "This negro, one of the early experiments. The boy's father must have been Subject 23! There are simply too many similarities in their biological resonance."

He turned to me and noticed the sparks cracking over my skin.

"Imbecile!" Dr. Trent said, backhanding Thompson with a loud smack. "Are you trying to damage him? That halfbreed is the key to our cure. Turn it off!"

The electricity coursing through me petered out, and it was all I could do to not whine in disappointment. The sudden absence of energy shocking me made me feel like a drunk on Sunday: angry, sober, and hurting for the bottle.

"I'd always wondered," Trent murmured, turning toward me. "What became of that particular animal? Subject 23 was the only one we could never account for, that was never recovered in one fashion or another. Your father was a guest of mine, boy, many years ago. You, my dear halfbreed, are proof positive that not only did he survive, but that he raped a white woman. Unfortunate, but not unexpected given the proclivities of the lower races."

My head snapped up, all pretense at playing wounded burned away by rising rage.

"Shut your dirty mouth," I growled. "My mother loved my daddy; he didn't lay a hand on her that she didn't want. I'd let my grandma tell you the stories of their romance if she wanted, but likely as not Maude would just stomp your face into a fine paste."

Trent and Thompson chattered their throat-teeth at me in amusement.

"Listen to the pup bark," Thompson laughed. "Posture all you want, boy. You'll be trained in time."

The Talon cast a lascivious eye at Sarah, stroking the empty air between them like it was her skin.

"Both of you will be."

I snarled and surged forward, nearly breaking my neck in an attempt to get teeth into the deformed bastard's flesh. Thompson's chattering laughter hitched as he heard my restraints creak and groan, to the point of breaking. Sweat covered me as I pulled against the manacles and collar, trying to get within reach of him. I could feel the restraints starting to give way.

"Now, now," Trent admonished, flipping a switch on his bracer. "Be a good little puppy."

Lightning flashed through my body, more than I'd suspected the manacles were capable of producing. Faced with a flood of energy rather than a trickle, the wolf in my blood yelped and retreated, leaving me to endure a massive shock that stunned me.

"You are quite an intriguing specimen, boy," Trent said, retrieving the vial of vitreous fluid that had been drained from the dying Staddard from its resting place. He screwed the vial into the syringe as he approached me.

"Did your grandmother raise you on tales of daring-do? Did she regale you with dimestore novels and trash books detailing the honor and dignity of the west, of the heroes of old, of knights and kings? Or did she reach into the depths of the Bible, dredging up stories of virtue, parables of humility, faith, and strength? Where did these false concepts arise from? How did they find root in your tainted soil?"

I tried to raise my head, my hands, to punch him, to bite him, to resist at all. But the same electricity that had nourished the wolf in small doses had now overwhelmed it, leaving me defenseless as Trent closed in with the syringe.

"You see, my dear halfbreed, your grandmother lied to you. None of those stories are true. They're all things the weak tell themselves in the darkest of nights to comfort themselves until dawn. The hero falters, the damsel succumbs."

His fetid breath through the malformed muzzle made me dry heave as he leaned in, piercing my arm with the needle and shooting the vitreous mixture into me. The Vocalator's voice dropped to a whisper as molten fire spread through my veins.

"And the monster always win."

Chapter 18

W HAT THE FUCK IS wrong with you people?" I gasped, the pain racing from my arm to the rest of my body as the vitriol he'd injected me with made its way through blood and muscle.

"They're assholes, Eli," Sarah croaked from next to me. "Isn't that obvious?"

"No, I'm . . . I'm being serious here," I said. The arm Trent had injected was swelling up something fierce, and my veins were popping out in a disturbing yellow shade that didn't look too healthy against my brown skin. Itching crawled across my body like a wave of fire ants.

"I get the whole 'we want to rule everything' song and dance; little men with little peckers have chased that since time began. But this? Stabbing people in the eye with syringes, injecting me with God knows what? How do you justify any of that, even in your twisted vision of the world?"

Trent huffed through his distorted features, taken aback by my attitude. "What do you mean? Have I not been clear in our intentions and goals? Shall I gloat more specifically for your edification?"

The yellow veins had spread to my entire body, and the toxin was picking up speed. I felt my heart pounding like a stampede, and streaks of off-colors tainted my vision in a kaleidoscope of weird. It was getting more difficult to talk, to move, to do anything other than think about what the fluid was doing to my body.

"Do you actually believe you're doing something good, for anyone?" I gasped, trying to focus.

"Of course!" Trent replied, umbrage lacing his voice.

"And yet you acknowledge you're a monster."

The burning in my muscles had increased, and the itching was reaching a crescendo.

"I acknowledge that you see me as such, as would any lab animal who does not comprehend that their small sacrifice is for the greater good of the world. The weak always vilify the strong. But while it is true I despise the simplistic ideas of virtue and sin that the religious push upon the world, in the end it is the human race itself that I wish to advance . . . at any cost. I am truly sad you cannot see that, boy. I had hoped the white man's blood in you—"

"Enough!" I roared, my voice fed by the burning venom pulsing in my veins. "You really buy that load you're shoveling? Delusional don't even begin to cover it. You're flat-out insane."

Expressions were hard to read on the deformed muzzle-faces that the Cabal had, but the rage burning in Trent's eyes was unmistakable. He hissed through his chattering throat-teeth at me, and the Vocalator he was controlling started sweating profusely. Trent barked several quick commands to Thompson, who hastened to pull a pair of thick cables out of a large apparatus mounted on the wall. He fiddled with the knobs on it for a moment before sparks sputtered and spat out of the copper ends of the lines.

Numbness warred with fire in my muscles, a strange waltz of pain and nothingness. Each felt worse than the alternative as they mixed within me, and any sense of relief at one of them subsiding was smothered with panic as the other rose up.

"I should have known better than to try and reason with you," Dr. Trent growled, taking the cables from Thompson. "To argue with one without the wits to understand logic is an exercise in futility."

I smiled as he approached with the sparking leads.

"Took the words out of my mouth," I said.

The mad doctor's response was to place the ends of the live cables to my shoulders. My expectation was an agonizing death.

It tingled.

Trent laughed at my confusion.

"Don't look so surprised, my dear halfbreed. I said you were important, after all. By limiting the amount of voltage applied initially, I can force your enhanced physiology to absorb the larger infusion more rapidly."

"Just turn up the amps and get it over with."

Trent's throat-mouth pulled itself into an admiring grin.

"Color me impressed, boy. I assumed you knew nothing of how electricity works. Even in the times before New Genesis it was not common knowledge. Tell me, how did you acquire your surprising education?"

I remained stubbornly silent. The yellow veins from the alchemical mixture in my veins throbbed in time to the unsteady electrical current. All my hairs were standing on end, and the wolf was stirring. It howled inside me for more wattage, and I found myself pressing back against the cable ends, willing them to pump more energy into my body.

"Answer me, boy," Trent demanded, pulling the cables away. I almost whined at the loss of the shocks. The beast was closer to the surface than I thought. And it was hungry.

"Or what? You going to break your new toy out of spite?" I sneered, hoping to lure him in closer. I flexed my arms experimentally and heard the creak of the manacles resisting. I'd never felt this powerful before. It was as if the wolf was already burning in my muscles. The doctor had wanted to make me stronger, to enslave me to his bidding.

The bastard was going to get one of those wishes.

"Let us try a different encouragement," Trent said, dragging the cables over to Sarah. Tears streamed down her face from the pain of her broken arms, but she stayed defiantly silent. As tough as she was though, Sarah's eyes widened in alarm as the Dragon waved the sparking cables in her face. I tried to kick out at him, but there was enough space between me and Sarah that there was no way to reach them.

"Dr. Thompson, if you would be so kind as to increase the amperage. What say you, halfbreed? Five hundred milliamperes? I find that patients who die to lower amperage actually survive past a hundred milliamperes . . . although they often wish they did not. I suppose I should find the resulting smell of the burning flesh unpleasant, but I rather enjoy it."

Thompson leapt to obey his master, chattering his laughter as he spun a dial. My guts churned as I felt the energy being fed through the cables surge.

Sarah remained rebellious with a courage beyond her years as the Dragon put the cables right next to her face. She was willing to stand with me, to accept the pain and degradation Trent was threatening her with. The little girl wasn't going to give them an inch. She knew you didn't reason with evil. You didn't compromise for safety. Death was a better end than cooperation.

I wasn't as strong.

"Stop!" I shouted. I couldn't help it; there was a part of me that would not, could not stand by and watch a friend get tortured just to spite the Devil. I was willing to put my hide through the wringer for my own choices, but I'd be damned if I was going to let another suffer for my own defiance.

"Tell me, boy," Trent snarled.

"Fine," I said grudgingly, letting my shoulders sag in apparent defeat. "I am . . . I *was* a brakeman on a Thunder Train. My grandma's. She raised me up to know my way around the Double T, as well as what kept it airborne. At least as much as science could explain."

Trent's deformed face pinched in consternation. "It all has a logical solution. We merely need to quantify it."

"Whatever you say, handsome. How's that going? Figure out what makes the Indian magic tick yet?"

My taunting had the desired effect, and he stepped away from Sarah back toward me.

"As a matter of fact, we do have a working theory. The specifics are far too complicated for your primitive brain to comprehend, but the cellular structure of the infected shows the presence of an heretofore undiscovered physical phenomenon that we refer to as 'etheric energy.' This energy saturates the diseased cells, sustaining and mutating them. It responds to human willpower and imagination as if they were actual chemical processes . . . which can have volatile effects when an entire culture believes the same concept. The Ghost Dances the savages engaged in focused their thoughts on the same goal, which rippled across the biology of the disease. Suffice it to say that the 'magic' the Indians summoned to combat the virus mutated with their delusions.

They believed that the Wendigo was a man-eater, a beast, the rabid wolf in the night. And so when they were infected, they manifested their fears into flesh and blood via the etheric energy."

"So then . . . magic," Sarah interrupted. I silently cussed her for making the doctor look back. Her face was pale and covered with sweat from the pain in her arms, but she refused to give up.

"There is no such thing!" Trent's Vocalator was harsh and spitting the words.

"Uh-huh. And werewolves don't exist either."

"You're missing my point."

"Exactly," Sarah snorted.

"You admit you don't actually know how this etheric stuff works or where it comes from," I cut in, trying to draw his attention back to me. "The best you can do is guess what it does. Fancy words to cover your ignorance, slim."

The robed Dragon spun back toward me.

"Just because we cannot classify it yet does not mean we cannot manipulate it. Science is—"

"Not what you're doing," I sneered, earning a growl from him. "You're throwing shit against a wall and seeing what sticks. I've seen scientists before: they're called Tellurians, and as boring as they may be sometimes, at least they're methodical, accurate, and working against their own interests for the preservation of humankind. Truly, you are a disciple of Edison. The man didn't know his ass from a hole in the ground, just how to steal what real inventors came up with."

That'd done it. Although Edison might not be their Dragon anymore, there was no doubt that the Cabal still held him in some esteem. Even if they'd overthrown him, there was a difference between smacking around family and watching some stranger do the same thing. Especially when that stranger wasn't white and you were a racist asshole.

Trent was almost close enough now. While it was true that the insane doctor still held the pair of live cables, I had the element of surprise on my side. Just a few more inches, and I figured I could bust the manacles and get my hands around his neck before he knew what was happening. He had no idea how powerful his formula had made me, or that the restraints were giving way. I was going to use his arrogance to end him.

"Do your delusions and denials give you comfort in the face of my great works?" Trent's Vocalator purred, venom dripping off the words. "Evidence of my genius is all around you . . . and inside you. The Tellurians are inconsequential, as are their efforts. They cannot, they will not, shape the world as I have. As I will."

I lunged forward, snapping the manacles and collar like they were kindling. A savage grin split my face, the beast in my blood urging me to violence. Sparks sputtered and crawled along the upright hairs of my arms, and the ghostly werewolf claws began to envelop my hands.

Trent was ready for me.

The Dragon caught me square-on with the electrified cables, using the force of my charge against me. The jagged copper ends sliced into my chest, breaking right through my rib cage and into my lungs.

Any illusions I might have had about Trent holding back due to me being special were eradicated as he shoved the cables deeper into my chest. Lightning lit me up from the inside-out, and the beast got more than it bargained for as Thompson cranked the power up.

"You see, the energy within your cells responds to low-level shocks by becoming engorged and, paradoxically, ravenous," Trent shouted, seemingly from far away. The sound of my body frying like bacon filled my ears.

"But apply too much electricity, and the cells rupture," he continued, twisting the cables with a devilish throat-smile. "This causes the regeneration of the beast to accelerate to compensate, amplifying its effects as the Wendigo struggles to save the host's life, thus accelerating the change. Such is the secret of how both the Cabal and the Tellurians control our own infection. Although we do tend to allow it to progress further than the weak-willed Tesla followers to fully reap the beast's benefits, without care to maintaining the appearance of normalcy to our minions."

I fell to my knees, electricity coursing through my body in ever-increasing waves. The sweet relief of unconsciousness eluded me, forcing me to endure the pain. My pants and boots burned, crisping and falling off of my body as the skin underneath crackled with lightning.

Screams erupted out of me.

Trent just soldiered on, like I was whispering at his dinner party.

"I suspect your tolerance of the shocks is an inherited trait from your father, a result of the experiments I performed on him before you were even conceived. The vitreous solution I injected should enhance your cells' capacity to absorb and store electricity, essentially creating a slave capable of walking right through the Advocates' interference field without becoming fatally disoriented. You will be the tool I use to finally wipe out those misbegotten rebels!"

The words flowed over me without effect. Although I heard them through my tortured howling, they didn't exactly hold my attention like the hellish agony pulsing into my body. The sickly-sweet smell of my flesh cooking filled the room, making me gag.

I measured the universe in pulses, in the ebb and flow of the erratic current tearing through me. The beast within grew stronger before evaporating against the tidal wave of electricity. Then he rose again, like a phoenix made of rage and blood, even more powerful, before once more being beaten down into nothingness.

The tiny arcs that had sparked off of my arm hair earlier were nothing compared to the jagged bolts that shot out from my body now. It was as if a thousand voltaic devils shoved their pitchforks out from my skin in a roaring cheer for the beast's release.

And the wolf was responding.

Growls and snarls leapt from my lips as my brain fried, leaving only the beast to keep me alive. The only thoughts I could form were those of revenge, of bloodshed, of killing the man who dared to hurt me. The world narrowed, and the pain was forgotten as my vision focused in on Dr. Trent's mutated face. Hatred pushed the agony down, and purpose rose up to take control.

It was time for slaughter.

The lightning flashing from my skin began to form a massive coherent shape over me. Muscles woven of energy overlapped my tortured flesh in a galvanic phantasmal mass, with my real body floating like bones in the middle of a jellyfish.

A strange twinning sensation overtook my senses, and perception split between my physical eyes and the energy cocooning me. Lightning shrouded my real form with a hollow overlay of a werewolf's form, the electricity shooting from my skin forming the crackling ghost of a gigantic monster around me.

"Yes!" Trent shouted with crazed glee from his throat-mouth. The Dragon's excitement overloaded his poor Vocalator, who fell to the ground twitching and frothing at the mouth. "Thompson! More!"

Trent tried to hold the cables steady in me as his servant cranked the voltage up. The coruscating energy of the storm wolf threw him back, the ghostly chest that had formed over mine rejecting the mad doctor's invasion. Pain ceased to have meaning as my mind fled fully into the energy creature that had formed around my body.

The world was a beautiful echo of the physical realm. No longer was I constrained to the pathetic eyesight of a human. I saw the electromagnetic currents of the world overlaying it, flowing through it, the hidden lines of force and life that an engineer's blinder goggles could only hint at. Reality was overwhelming, and the sight stunned me for a moment with its incandescence.

Ever since Maggie had bitten me on Wardenclyffe I'd been pursued in my dreams by a beast of thunder and lightning, a nightmare of sweat and fear with sparking teeth that snapped at my heels. Countless nights I'd bolted awake gasping, terrified of the clouds in my sleep that hid the creature, the snarling voltaic beast that threatened to consume me.

Only now did I understand that I'd been running from myself the whole time. My true self, that part waiting to blossom, to consume . . . to ascend.

The twinning sensation faded as I embraced what I was, what I'd always been, what I'd always be.

With a crackle of effort, the new energy creature I'd become pulled free of the corporeal anchor of my flesh. I no longer feared the beast in the clouds. The luminescent being I'd seen in my nightmares was no stranger, no foreign creature stalking prey.

It was me.

The stormwolf was free.

And it was hungry.

Chapter 19

WHAT I DISTANTLY RECOGNIZED as my body fell away from the voltaic phantom of a werewolf that I'd become. I looked down at the twitching heap with disdain and welcomed the loss of my humanity. Almost imperceptible strands flowed from my new body to my old one, a ghostly web on the edge of my new-found vision.

"Success!" the Dragon shouted from where he'd landed, pulling himself out of a broken shelf with Thompson's help. Although Trent was sure of himself and his results, the stormwolf I'd become had senses beyond that of any other nightmare. I tasted Thompson's fear, his uncertainty, his suspicion that Trent had created something that no man could control.

I was about to show the Talon how right he was.

The two Cabalists were like ants trapped in molasses as I shot forward, teeth and claws arcing electricity out to caress the victims before my deadly arrival. There was murder on my mind, and the doctors were about to hear my thoughts on their professional conduct.

Trent saw me coming, but Thompson didn't. The Dragon of the Cabal showed his true colors by not warning his flunky, not even trying to save the Talon, but rather pushing him back toward me.

I was expecting to cut and bite, obeying my primal nature. But the galvanic creature I'd transformed into used other ways to kill. Thompson shrieked as my energy claws sank through his vest and into the brass tubes lining his body. The brass acted as a conduit for my rage; I could sense how the pipes ran through the Talon's body like blood veins. My jaws passed through his flesh with a sizzling sound as I took hold of the brass within.

My rage burned through the surgically-grafted tubes with the strength of living lightning. Dr. Thompson's flesh caught fire as he burned from the inside-out, and the scaled scabs burst into tiny flowers of fire under his vest and pants. Sparks shot from his skin as it blistered and peeled away from his body. I thought of how he'd handled Sarah, of the brazen hatred and evil I'd witnessed him display in just my short time of knowing the bastard. How many other innocents had fallen before his madness and his orders?

The sentence for his crimes: death by electrocution.

Slowly.

The smoldering corpse of what used to be Doctor Thompson eventually dropped to the ground, black flakes falling away from its cracked and crisped skin. Even the healing elixir running through his tubes had been unable to hold back the reaper. I'd managed to make Thompson's agony last a full minute, altering the current through his nervous system to keep him feeling it the whole time. Distantly the human part of me screamed that I shouldn't have done that; I was meant to kill with speed and not savor it. Or was that the beast protesting while the man inside was the one who'd exulted in the torture? Either way, the question seemed irrelevant, the concerns of the body I'd left behind on the floor. The ethereal strands that led back to the flesh of Elijah Kelly tugged at the doubts, irritating me. I snapped at them.

White-hot pain shot through the world, and my phantom body felt like it grew dimmer. The room spun, and my vision went black for a moment.

Apparently the stormwolf wasn't as independent from the constraints of flesh as I'd thought.

"Very interesting," Dr. Trent muttered through his Vocalator, glancing between my stormwolf form and the body I was tethered to. His spidery fingers danced over his control bracer. His confidence in the face of death offended me. I turned my phantom head to him and snarled. I'd almost forgotten about my real target, the son of a bitch responsible for destroying the world and endangering the ones I loved.

It was time to thank him for that.

Anger solidified my form, causing the stormwolf to glow brighter. I gave a bestial grin and surged at him.

Trent flipped a toggle on his bracer, but he was too late. My claws crashed down, seeking to pin him in place like Thompson for my jaws to finish off. I'd make it last even longer this time, hurt more. Both beast and human agreed with that.

A bright flash burst from my claws as they rebounded off Trent's purple robes harmlessly.

I roared in frustration, a screech like nails on slate, lashing out again and again, my attacks skittering across the Dragon's form like water off a duck's back.

"As I suspected," the smug bastard said with a chattering laugh from his throat. "You are quite a wondrous specimen, halfbreed. But even in this form you are constrained by the scientific laws that birthed you."

His words drove me into a frenzy, and the room was lit by more galvanic flashes as I railed ineffectually against his laughing face with teeth and claws. The tiny part of my mind that could still reason recognized he'd set up an interference field through his body that repelled the frequency of the stormwolf, but the beast didn't care. He wanted death. He wanted destruction.

Trent backhanded me across the muzzle. Despite the stormwolf's apparent size advantage it had no mass, and the sharp blow was enough to send my phantom body flying away from the doctor.

"That will be quite enough, halfbreed," he said. "While you have capacities I seek, do not doubt who is the master here. Thompson's loss is regrettable, but he is not the only Talon I arrived with. Consider his murder your treat for the day."

My snarls were electric crackles and pops like a frog frying in a pan, and frustration burned tight in my breast. The man who'd ended the world was literally within arm's reach, but I couldn't do a damn thing about it.

"Now let's see about putting a leash on you," Dr. Trent's Vocalator murmured. "If I adjust this a bit . . ."

Suddenly the electromagnetic field that protected the Dragon expanded, filling the room and knocking me back with an irresistible wave. I tried to fight it, but it was like kicking out at the ocean and expecting it to give way. The field continued to expand, forcing me through the shelves and the wall behind it like a ghost. My mind scattered as the stormwolf was driven back into the dark earth of the building's foundation. There was no light, no sound, nothing but soil scattering my form like dust in a storm. I could feel my coherency beginning to give way, and panicked.

Although invisible to normal sight, the eyes of the stormwolf could see the border of the electromagnetic field keeping me at bay. Scrabbling against the edge of the sphere, I climbed it, using its resistance to propel me upward through the oppressive earth.

My voltaic senses were confused, overwhelmed, but they cleared up as I flickered into a familiar corridor. In my desperation I'd come up at an angle, placing me squarely in the Tombstone's prison level. I saw the cells' iron bars as barely perceptible lines of force, and a thought suddenly took hold of me.

Maggie.

I had to see her, had to rescue her. It was difficult to think rationally, but there was a vague feeling that, somehow, we could fix all this together, rescue Sarah, kill Trent. If anyone could understand what had happened to me, could help me to wreak burning vengeance on the Cabal, it was her.

To the stormwolf's vision the dingy corridor was strangely clean, almost barren of electromagnetic energy. There was a distinct pull back toward the hidden laboratory below, as if a whirlpool swirled beneath my phantom paws. If I'd still had a physical stomach I would've been sick. The rational side that still existed within me called out the answer, and the stormwolf nodded its ghostly head.

The Telluric dead zone.

While the lab had enough juice running through it to counteract the lack of background energy, up here the absence of any electric activity was obvious. The human part of me begged us to find the source of the zone and destroy it, but the stormwolf put aside his petty concerns. Our mate was up here and in a cage.

That would not stand.

I drifted down the corridor with my legs making a striding motion out of habit without paws ever touching the ground. The world was like an ocean, and I could move in any direction at any speed I wished. Freedom was intoxicating. Maggie must join.

The electrified bars of her isolation cell were bright and crackling in comparison to the rest of the prison block, and my lips curved into a wolfish grin. What would have stopped man and beast was nothing to the stormwolf. Vaguely I sensed energy patterns moving behind the wall of the cell, but the sight of Maggie drove away all other thoughts.

She still lay in the same position on the cot we'd left her in, deep in the slumber of recovery. She possessed a new beauty to the galvanic beast I'd become. I'd always admired Maggie's defiant demeanor and slender frame, tall and strong like a willow tree. Her sharp features and freckles had become the definition of prettiness to me. Although she might be called pleasantly plain by the outside observer, any person who knew her heart could see a fiery beauty that eclipsed the sheath of skin and muscle that barely contained her soul.

To the stormwolf's gaze there had never been anything more stunning. The tiny lines of her nervous system laced through her body and face with their electric paths, making her skin seem translucent and glowing with life. I'd never seen anything quite like it before, and for a moment I stood in stunned silence, worshiping at the altar of the woman I loved.

Any hesitation, any second thoughts, any suspicion that my emotions were a product of the supernatural bond between us were dead and buried. I'd resisted long enough, fought hard enough to make sure the feelings were real. They were. And while the bond that resulted from her bite had reinforced and accelerated the bloom of affection, it was not the source of it.

I loved Maggie Butler.

And she was in a cage.

Although my mind had asserted control over the stormwolf, the primal thoughts of the beast still colored my world. The bars of her prison cell were an affront, an insult to my ladylove.

The stormwolf's phantom claws sparked as I took hold of the electrified bars. Although lacking a true physical presence, energy recognized energy, and I felt resistance beneath my new form's hands. Expecting a painful jolt by grabbing them, I was surprised to find something else rise up.

Hunger.

A ravenous emptiness overtook me, a starving void that felt like a newly-changed werewolf looking for his first meal. But it wasn't blood and muscle that I craved.

There was a distinct pop and crack from the bars as I pulled electricity from them into me. The stormwolf grew brighter as I drained energy from the prison, tapping deep into the circuit. I felt how it ran back to the D/C hubs, and from there to the different cranker stations where enslaved Augmented trudged along in disgrace and misery under the whips of the Cabal's flunkies. I pulled it in, drawing as much as I could stand, turning their forced labor into something that could murder their masters and break Portland open with its power.

The lights in the hallway flickered and then faded away as the Tombstone's power flowed into me, feeding the stormwolf, growing its strength. The beast's mind threatened to overtake mine again, but the sight of Maggie lying vulnerable past the bars kept me in control with an ironclad hand on the reins of the wolf.

Suddenly my feast disappeared.

I howled in protest, an electric shriek that sounded like nothing anything in nature could make. But it was to no avail. The prison bars were dead, as were the cables they connected to. There had been so much power left to drain, a smorgasbord that could have let me overcome any defenses Portland managed to summon. Someone had figured out something was wrong down the line and had thrown the switch to cut me off.

The sight of Maggie stirring in her sleep from my howls forced me silent. The last thing I wanted to do was to wake her when she was still healing from her ordeal. As her breathing quickened and her eyelids fluttered, I realized that ship had already sailed.

Lights had died across the Tombstone's prison level, but the stormwolf's galvanic body emitted its own glow, lighting Maggie's cell with an eerie blue incandescence. Even without that, though, I could still see the energy beneath her skin. In the dark she seemed like an angel alone in Hell, full of power and despair.

"What . . . where?" Maggie slurred, fighting against the grip of the sandman. She struggled upright, one hand gripping the wall and the other the bed frame to keep herself stable between the two.

I wanted to say something, to tell her how much I loved her, how much I understood now. She'd been trying to get her feelings through my thick head for months while I'd been an obstinate ass. Without the dam holding back my emotions I realized how difficult it must have been for her, feeling like this while I denied her at every turn. The wolf knew better than the human, and when we wore fur every full moon, he had no problems expressing his love physically. We'd both known what we did as werewolves, but I acted like not acknowledging it made it somehow go away. She'd just enjoyed the few hours each moon I wasn't stonewalling her.

The words of sorrow would not come from the stormwolf's maw. Hissing and crackling like static was all that I could produce.

Maggie's eyes focused on me. I'd expected her to scream at a ghostly abomination coruscating with electricity, but she just scooted back as far as she could on the prison bed. She cocked her head at an angle with an odd look.

"Elijah?"

Joy leapt in my heart at her recognition. I opened my maw to howl in reunion, but all that came out was a boom like distant thunder rolling.

"It is you," Maggie said with certainty. She put a hand to her forehead, massaging her temples. "Where are we? How did we get here? The last thing I remember is . . ."

I gave frustrated cracks and pops, but the words would not come. She held up her hand in response.

"Stop. It is obvious you are incapable of human speech in your current condition. Do you at least possess the capacity to understand me?"

The nod I gave her was enough.

"All right. Is Sarah safe?"

A hesitant nod, with a slight shake of my head.

"This is already becoming an irritating and inaccurate method of communication. Do you know how to restore your original form?"

The shrug I gave her was frustrating to both of us. I flickered through the bars, their iron determination nothing to the spectral beast I'd become. The need to be closer to her, to hold her in real hands again, was a lance through my heart.

She should have run from me, gotten clear of the deadly energy I was made of. Instead, she reached a hand out to me, ignoring the pain as a stray arc from my body seared her hand.

"Are you all right, Elijah?"

I shook my head in frustration. Panic threatened to overtake me. How was I going to get back into my body? Was this permanent? Was I going to lose my mind to the stormwolf and become a ghostly monster haunting the land, doomed to burn it and those I loved to a crisp by my mere presence?

Maggie saw my distress, felt it. Her eyes were filled with nothing but love as she took my phantom muzzle in her hands. I could see her skin blackening and crisping where she touched me, but I couldn't force myself to pull back. I'd not felt Thompson's body as I murdered him, nor the cell bars as I'd drained them, only a vague sense of resistance.

But I felt Maggie's touch.

"It will all be fine," she soothed, drawing my head closer. Finally coming to my senses, I yanked back before I could do any damage to her face. Her hands were scorched and bleeding, and the guilt written across my features made her give me a half grin.

"Calm yourself, please. I can feel the wolf near the surface of my skin; she will heal me before long. Whatever you did to stave off my transformation . . . I do not believe it worked. At least, not for long."

I crackled and screeched, grief stabbing my heart.

"Shh, Elijah. I told you: it will be all right. I will not leave you, even when my true form takes me. Do you understand?"

Silence was all I could give her, but she saw her answer in the lightning eyes of the stormwolf. I stood straighter, rising to the construct's full height, and bowed low.

"I suppose that means you will not leave me either," Maggie laughed, before her expression turned serious. "We need to find Sarah and depart this place. And somehow, someway, we must save Wardenclyffe as well. Otherwise you will never let me hear the end of it, even when we no longer possess the power of speech."

I lolled a wolf grin at her attempt at humor, but it died on my lips a moment later. A distinct click came from the far wall of her prison cell.

The hidden door swung open with a screech of gears, and Dr. Trent stepped through, his throat-mouth pulled into a ghoulish smile, trailed by his enslaved Vocalator. The field he used to protect himself from me was drawn back in, a tight invulnerable skin protecting the mad doctor and his proxy voice from me. His eyes roved over Maggie, who was momentarily stunned by the sudden appearance of the deformed Dragon.

"Hello there, young lady," the child he controlled said. "I'm afraid I must interrupt you two love birds, although I have enjoyed your attempts at conversation, in both a comedic and educational fashion. Quite instructional, really."

Trent turned his attention to me, and his throat chattered in horrible laughter. There was a dread promise buried in the sound that made even the stormwolf shiver.

"I believe I've found your leash, halfbreed."

Chapter 20

MY THOUGHTS AND FEARS raced each other to see what would take hold first.

Rationality won by a gnat's hair.

Trent thought the stormwolf was still in control of my mind. From what he'd seen, the voltaic beast acted just like a normal one, with no means of communication or thinking beyond a base animal level. He was focusing the lion's share of his attention right now on Maggie, as he knew that the field around him kept the doctor safe from the stormwolf's retribution. I decided to play dumb for the moment, watching for an opening.

"You will serve us well, my dear," Trent's Vocalator purred. The doctor reached out his spindly fingers and tried to caress Maggie's strawberry blond hair, but she batted it away with a glower. The prison cell rumbled with the crack of thunder as my rage flared in response.

Trent just pulled his throat-mouth into a smile. "Judging by his attachment to you, I assume you and the halfbreed are . . . intimate?"

Maggie, ever the conversationalist, spat in Trent's face.

"What I do with who is none of your business, abomination. Who do you think I am, to ask such a question as if you deserve an answer?" she asked, balling up her fists in anger.

"Why, his weakness, of course. Attachment to one's broodmares is a failing of lesser males in any species."

"A sad view you hold of womanhood to assume that I am a lever and nothing more," Maggie snarled. "In your world do females merely exist to be bartered and held hostage for favor? I see your game clearly, creature, and I will not play it."

Trent made the mistake of chattering his teeth in throat-laughter at Maggie, mocking the very concept of her words with its tone.

It was the last mistake those teeth ever made.

If I had blinked, I would have missed it. Maggie moved fast, faster than I'd ever seen. The recent brush with the permanent change to wolf had left behind vestiges of the beast's speed in her. Maggie's freckled fist slammed into Trent's throat-mouth, her knuckles breaking against the doctor's teeth like a tsunami into land.

Dr. Trent fell backward, his throat-mouth choking as Maggie drove forward again and again, punching his neck like a hydraulic press. The electromagnetic field that protected him from my attacks flared, and for a moment I felt him vulnerable.

But as I rushed forward to help her, Trent regained his bearings and knocked Maggie away with the back of his hand. The skinny woman was flung away from the towering abomination, her righteous fury no match for his larger frame. Although the lady's speed and ferocity had caught him off-guard, choking on his own teeth had brought the mad doctor back to his fighting senses.

My lightning claws flashed harmlessly off Trent as he stabilized the field protecting him. I'd been too impressed with Maggie's sudden assault to act quickly enough, and sparks rained from my ineffectual attacks as I took the frustration out on the doctor's impenetrable shield.

"That will be quite enough of that," Trent's Vocalator said. There was no chattering laughter from his wounded throat this time.

The cold rage that shot through the Vocalator's voice drew me up short. There was a meanness in the Dragon's warped eyes I didn't like. Bullies were never as dangerous as the moment after humiliation, and Dr. Trent had obviously never been manhandled by a woman before.

His gaze settled on Maggie, who'd withdrawn as far away as she could in the cell. Her knuckles were bloodied and she was panting, but there was plenty of fight left in her. My heart swelled with admiration that the woman I loved was willing and able to shove a boot up anyone's ass that dared to disrespect her.

"There is a price to be paid by any white woman who lies with the savages," Trent rasped.

Maggie barked a short, derisive laugh, but there was an undertone of uncertainty. She'd given her all fighting someone twice her size and weight, hurting and humiliating him. But there was little chance of her stopping the Dragon completely, or even managing another successful assault now that he was expecting it. And she knew it.

Although there was no real use to it, I put myself between Trent and Maggie, blocking the way with the stormwolf's hollow lightning-shrouded form. The Dragon could brush me away as easily as cobwebs with the field protecting him, but panic was rising and clouding my thoughts. I had to do something, anything, to help.

Rather than advancing and sweeping me from his path, Trent was fiddling with the controls on his bracer. An icy sensation ran up my ghostly spine that I refused to admit was naked fear.

"Ah yes," the doctor muttered as he spun a dial. "This should give me the privacy I need to punish in peace."

Cracks and pops shot out of my fanged maw as I snarled, but it was drowned out by the high-pitched keening as the electromagnetic barrier suddenly expanded from Trent, knocking me backward like a giant's hand. It kept growing, pushing me out of the cell.

I flailed uselessly against the field as it drove me before it like earth before a plow. Maggie saw me fall back before the invisible force, watching as the stormwolf's insubstantial body struggled helplessly against the tide. The wall of the Tombstone loomed at my back, and the field showed no sign of slowing its expansion.

"Do not let him use me against you," Maggie ordered, her voice hitching toward the end. She choked down whatever emotion threatened to overtake her, her emerald eyes growing hard as steel. "I mean it, Elijah Kelly. If you bend knee to this bastard because of me, I will turn my back on you. I love you, but do not dare let him use that love to break your will. It would be an insult to all we share and feel."

The field was pushing me through the wall of the building like a leaf in a windstorm. As the darkness of the Tombstone's foundation enveloped me, I heard Maggie's last words as if from the bottom of a deep well.

"You will not surrender. And neither will I . . . my love."

There was no sound or light as I fought against the irresistible force of Trent's field. I floated upward, propelled by rage and terror, trying to escape the crushing confines of the earth's embrace.

Morning light lanced through the stormwolf's body as I rose outside, my passage sizzling grass and soil as I struggled free of the ground. The Tombstone loomed huge before me, its concrete walls mocking my exile from the depths of its prisons.

Willing myself forward, I tried to move through the wall into the upper level of the Tombstone, seeking a weak spot in the field Trent had generated to protect him from me. But where before solid matter had given me no resistance, this time I bounced off the Tombstone's exterior as if I were still flesh and blood.

Placing my ghostly hand against the concrete wall allowed me to feel the pulse of the field, shaped and contained by the confines of the Tombstone. The cast iron rebar running through the concrete hummed with the energy of Trent's repulsion field. He'd managed to sync it up to the entirety of the Tombstone's structure.

There was no way I was getting back in.

With my real body trapped inside the Tombstone and the stormwolf denied entry, I was powerless to interfere, to even irritate, the damnable mad doctor that held Maggie prisoner.

It kindly pissed me off.

I sizzled around the building in a rage, a desperate phantasm flinging itself again and again at the energized building, seeking any way in. But it was useless. Bereft of hope, I allowed myself to drift upward in contemplation, past the resting form of the *Purity's Pride*, uselessly perched on the grounding trestle atop the Tombstone.

Portland had just begun to stir below. Its citizens would be starting whatever work they laid claim to, with the Augmented whipped to sweat at the hardest tasks. Between the people and the clogged sky of power lines carrying the current across the city, the stormwolf should have seen a beautiful, interlaced pattern of energy pulsing through the streets.

Instead, it was as if I floated over a desert, with nary a stray volt to be seen. What would have been my normal vision was a pale ghostly thing, a washed-out set of colors and shapes as Portland woke up. All of the components were there, but the telluric dead zone that had enveloped the land muted and drained away any and all energy that would have normally been freed into the world. Even the stormwolf's voltaic body dimmed outside of the confines of the Tombstone.

As I relinquished more and more control in my despair, floating higher and higher over the prison building, I became aware of an almost imperceptible pull, an undercurrent that crawled through the air around me. The stormwolf's body drifted into it, as if pushed by a small breeze, and the Cascade Mountains came into view.

If the rest of the world was a washed-out desert, then the mountains were a sickening ocean of discordant color. Electromagnetic energy swirled around Mt. Hood in the distance. Sixty miles and thick clouds couldn't obscure that the mountain itself was the source of the dead zone. Energy twisted across the peak like angry spirits around a graveyard, howling and screaming their wordless song as they fought the sluggish whirlpool that pulled them down to oblivion.

There was something very wrong with that mountain.

Nature abhorred the violation, her predetermined telluric flows ripped out of the gentle grasp of the earth and torn asunder. The stormwolf sensed the crime, snarled at it, even as its own unnatural form was pulled toward the mountains.

Beacons of etheric lightning burned across Mt. Hood, pinpricks of unbelievably bright energy. Although invisible to the naked eye, the stormwolf's gaze easily picked out the conflicting currents they set up, the shifting polarities that caused anyone in the mountain range to suffer from disorientation and sickness.

My interest caused the gentle pull toward the mountains to intensify, drawing the stormwolf along like a twig in a river toward the rapids. The body of the energy construct felt like it was nibbled at by thousands of tiny fish, tugged and twisted as I bobbed along. The burning beacons were a magnetic force, ripping apart the telluric currents even as they altered their natural flow. I turned to fight against it, to stay with Maggie. But it was no use.

An irresistible riptide grabbed hold of the stormwolf, dragging it toward Mt. Hood. In seconds I flashed across the intervening miles to the foot of the Cascades, where the wisps of the tortured telluric streams formed the invisible border of the disorientation field that enveloped the mountain range. As quickly as it had latched on, the riptide dissipated, leaving me howling in frustration.

Floating above, it was obvious that the telluric disruption beacons were connected by strands of power that ran deep under the mountain. Together they cast a web across Mt. Hood that protected it, that kept it safe from assault from both the ground and the air. I extended the stormwolf's senses, following the web's electromagnetic strands. There was a pattern, a mind behind the telluric dead zone and the disorientation field.

There was a central source to it all. A jagged scar ran across the side of Mt. Hood where trees still refused to grow, the devastating evidence of Carnegie City's impact. The eye of the disruption was buried down there somewhere, just out of sight.

All I had to do was to let go, to let the whirlpool sweep me up into its pull. The stormwolf snarled, and I joined in. Whoever had set all of this in motion was threatening to kill every man and woman in Wardenclyffe by crashing it into Portland. While I wanted to see the slavers' city burned to the ground as much as any other decent person, I didn't want the victory to come at the cost of ten thousand innocent lives. Lives that included my grandma, my best friend, and every person I'd ever known and loved.

Below me the tortured currents formed a thorn bush maze, full of twists and turns that would turn a man's stomach inside-out until he escaped. It saturated the air, but as I concentrated on it I could see gaps winding through it like a snake.

There was a trail.

The rage at being unable to rescue Maggie and Sarah coalesced into a new focus. I forced the stormwolf down through a weak spot in the miasma of conflicting energies, through trees that barely registered to the ethereal beast's senses, to a patch of nondescript ground. There was a lull here to the stormwolf's eyes, a place where the waves of the whirlpool flowed over and around each other. A clear path led off to the right, a twisting corridor that wound upward to the eye of the storm, a safe place where people could live and hide. It only made sense that the Advocates would leave a corridor for themselves to their haven, hidden to even blinder goggles. If the stormwolf hadn't been literally made of the same electricity it would have been impossible to see the tiny variations in the currents that led to safety up the mountainside.

Who had built the beacons, and how? The 'why' was blatantly obvious, but I doubted the Advocates that hid on the mountain had either the technical know-how or materials to alter the very fabric of nature herself. Although I'd never been privy to the secrets of the Tellurians, even the storm prophets had been unable to change the telluric streams that flowed through the world. As far as I'd known, it was impossible.

I had to see one of the disruption beacons in person. Otherwise I'd never be able to destroy the deadzone in time.

That need lent strength to my struggle as I bulled my way against the directed flows, like a man fighting the pull of a river. The currents tugged and snagged at the stormwolf's body, and what would have simply been unrelenting nausea to a flesh and blood man became an actual fight for the energy construct.

Flows closed behind me, and the pressure ahead became almost unbearable as the blazing beacon came into view. The resistance was unbelievable, unconquerable. As soon as I could clearly see the device though I understood how the Advocates had closed Mt. Hood to everyone else. The refugees who'd taken the mountain were experts at using what was on hand, salvaging that which others had thrown away, whether it be people or equipment. They'd managed to do something even the mighty storm prophets had been unable to accomplish, and in the process had taken the tragedy of the Cabal's power and turned it against those slaving bastards.

Towering from the tortured earth was a massive salvation city squall tube, a crackling beacon of hope and rebellion that stood defiant against the world.

Chapter 21

THE ANCHORING BEACON FOR the telluric dead zone rose thirty feet in the air. Overgrown vegetation pushed in until it was singed by its proximity to the crackling pylon, the lightning serving as both the god of life and death to the plants. The massive squall tube was a twin to the same gigantic lightning-lit devices that kept Wardenclyffe aloft. Deployed in clusters across the underside of the salvation cities, the oversized squall tubes had saved untold numbers of people from the werewolf apocalypse twenty years ago. And it was still saving folks now.

The Advocates were using the wreckage of Carnegie City to defend themselves from the very bastards that had brought the mighty city down.

Floating this close to the giant squall tube was wreaking havoc on the stormwolf's galvanic form. The conflicting electromagnetic flows were threatening to rip apart the energy construct like oil caught in the rapids. But as I was about to let the currents push me back to the safe spot where I'd landed, there was movement on the other side of the beacon.

Again, curiosity overrode my sense of self-preservation. I forced the stormwolf against the violent currents. As I fought through the flows, there was a howl of ragged agony. Urging the stormwolf onward, I rounded the corner of the squall tube.

Chained to the far side of the giant beacon was an Augmented werewolf. Like most of the Fixed the blond-furred ironhide had mechanical limbs replacing his real ones, with his torso and head left to its original flesh save for the spinal furnace. As he came into view a lightning bolt arced from the squall tube into his lupine head, illuminating his skull within the skin for a split second like a ghoulish jack o'lantern.

The electromagnetic backwash from the strike sent me spinning off into the underbrush, and for a moment it felt like the stormwolf was about to blow apart like leaves in the wind. I snarled and fought back, forcing the phantom form to stabilize.

The stormwolf floated to the ground, exhaustion running through its ghostly body. I could still see the Fixed chained to the squall tube through the leaves; he sagged against his bonds, somehow still alive. Smoking pits were all that remained of his eyes, and his flesh was burnt down to the bone in several places. Even now, though, the insanely-fast healing of werewolves was kicking in, mending his eyes and body.

The muzzle that all ironhides wore fell off of him like a stunned parasite, releasing the wrong-wolf's jaws from its grasp. He was still chained to the squall beacon though, easy pickings for another lightning bolt. But there was nothing I could do for him. The stormwolf's claws would pass through his bonds without breaking them, and I'd just found out how vulnerable I was to the effects of the giant squall tube's erratic pulses.

A motley trio moved out of the trees on the edge of the overgrowth surrounding the beacon. Two small forms stumbled through the bushes while the third larger shape crashed a path through. The huge one was another wrong-wolf, a female even larger than the chained one. Although possessing the metal limbs of the Fixed, this particular werewolf's hide was a patchwork amalgam of fur, differing in shade and texture from each other. The stitches that held her false coat together had the angry red of a nasty infection around them, as if the flesh beneath was rebelling against the skin it'd been forced to don.

The second figure was in her late teens, with light brown skin and a vacant expression. She'd been turned into a hunchback by a heavy contraption surgically attached to her back and spine. Someone had gotten ambitious when turning the girl into a Vocalator and just kept piling on the technology until she could barely stand.

Neither of them compared to the last member of the group though. The man leading them wore ragged garments reminiscent of a Blood Judge's getup, but without the hat and duster. His red leather gloves and boots were scuffed and worn with age, and the pistol he wore was an old ball and cap relic from a century ago. The cavalry saber strapped on the opposite side did nothing to dispel the notion that he was a creature of the past who'd risen from his grave to haunt the world. The stranger was hairless and painfully skinny, damn near skeletal; nowhere was that more evident than his macabre face.

The thin, translucent skin and muscles covering his features were drawn tight against his cranium. The man's nose had collapsed inward, and his ears had long ago abandoned their hold on his head, leaving his visage nothing more than a grinning skull picked clean by vultures. What blood vessels that remained pushed clear fluid through in a vain attempt at life, leaving his ghastly face devoid of color. But his mouth made it worse. The Blood Judges I'd seen were content to sport a pair of silver fangs to carry out their terrible duties, but the bony man had doubled down, and then some.

Instead of normal teeth there were silver inscribed fangs lining the stranger's upper and lower jaw. It was as if the Reaper took a gander in the mirror and figured he needed just a bit more horror in his grin.

"You've earned your place among us, *mon frère*," he hissed through his creepy choppers at the chained ironhide. "We honor Nox, we honor Cacophony, those of the Shadow Pack that have fallen. In their memories we rechristen you with your chosen name. Arise, Ragnarok, and make this mountain run red with our enemies' blood. Free yourself, as we will free all, whether they wish it or not!"

The light-furred wrong-wolf, Ragnarok, raised his head at the words. His ruined eyes were white orbs now. Pupils formed again, swirling around until they came to rest on the strange skeletal Judge before him.

With a roar that shook the leaves in the surrounding trees the wrong-wolf rose up, flexing against the chain fastening him to the squall beacon. The links snapped as if the steel held no strength, and Ragnarok leapt forward before another lightning bolt from the squall beacon's shifting frequencies hit where he'd been.

The female ironhide caught the smaller male with a gentleness I'd not expected. She rumbled in a comforting fashion as she helped the groggy Ragnarok to stand up straight with pride.

"Time to celebrate with a feast," the Reaper said with his horrifying smile. "Bruja, go fetch our picnic."

The big patchwork Augmented gave a wolfish grin and bounded back along the path she'd forged in the overgrowth, leaving Ragnarok to stand alone on shaky legs.

"Whisper," the skull-faced man said to the little girl. "Be a dear and remove Ragnarok's hive collar. The wiring for the kill switch should have been fried."

The Vocalator nodded and moved in front of Ragnarok. The ironhide grimaced at her approach; his ears went back, and he covered them with his metal palms. The Reaper followed suit. I'd expected the girl to wrest free the steel collar that all Augmented wore from Ragnarok's neck, but she made no move to grab it.

Instead, Whisper reached back to her artificial steel hump, her fingers dancing across the surface. Lights flared across the machinery in response and a whine like a generator overloading filled the air. The little girl opened her mouth and hissed at Ragnarok, the only sound left to any Vocalator after their brains had been hacked apart. Ragnarok closed his eyes and waited.

At first I didn't know what was going on. Then I saw the leaves of the bush I was hiding behind begin to shake. Normal vision and hearing were a hollow echo to the stormwolf's senses, but even so, a moment later I felt the deep thrum of Whisper's silent howl. It was less of a sound and more of a vibration of the world itself, as if she was screaming into the very fabric of reality. Even the stormwolf's phantom form shimmered in response to Whisper's howl as the hunchbacked girl amplified and warped what little sound she was able to make.

Ragnarok had it much worse. He howled in pain as blood seeped between his fingers from his ears. As he began to bleed from the eyes and nose the discordant sound changed suddenly into a metal shriek.

Ragnarok's hive collar flashed as if it'd been hit by a hammer, twisting around his neck like an angry serpent. It broke apart, shattered by its own thrashing. Whisper ceased her silent howl.

"Well done, *ma chérie*," the Reaper said, applauding. Whisper put a demure hand over her smile, replying with a quick curtsy to his praise.

Ragnarok gave a coughing growl. Whisper scrunched up her face for a moment, then gave a heavy sigh and turned her back to him. The iron spike in Ragnarok's palm slid out, and he stabbed it into the back of Whisper's neck, the connection point of the modified Vocalator's brace she wore. Whisper's eyes went unfocused, and her body sagged against the ironhide's grip as he took control of her.

"Hungry, Bloodrath. Feed me," Whisper demanded.

The stranger sneered, a hell of a feat for a guy with transparent skin. "Does that truly warrant taking control of my daughter in such a way, Ragnarok? We all hunger. Perpetually. Give Bruja a moment; our meal is notoriously difficult to wrangle. Now release my daughter, or I'll let Bruja gut you and add your miserable hide to her trophy coat."

Ragnarok released his hold on Whisper with an irritated huff, and the little girl swayed. The Reaper rushed forward to support his daughter's weight.

My thoughts were swirling. I'd heard tell a bit of Bloodrath down in Portland, some kind of leader in the Advocate movement. That he was also a father was unexpected, as was the visual evidence that he'd apparently been a Blood Judge before joining the Advocates.

Could these people help me free Maggie and Sarah? Would they? There was something unsettling about this Shadow Pack. Were there differing factions within the Advocates? And, if so, what kind of mentality and practices separated each? From Bruja's stitched hide and the offhand cruelty Ragnarok demonstrated by taking Whisper as his mouthpiece without warning I didn't imagine they were the kind and cuddly rebels.

A crashing noise distracted me from the suspicious thoughts as Bruja lumbered into sight from the dark forest. She was dragging a struggling bundle behind her in a burlap sack and being none too careful with it. The patchwork ironhide seemed to go out of her way to slam the sack into every root and tree trunk she could.

"Now, now, Bruja," Bloodrath chastised. "We can tenderize our own meat."

The Shadow Pack rumbled wolfish laughter, and Whisper even

hissed along with a grin. Bruja dragged the burlap sack forward and dumped its inhabitant out on the ground.

Judge Tillman, he of the artificial eye and terrible demeanor that had nearly caught us at the Grant farm, tumbled out. The pack jeered at their mortal enemy, making taunting sounds as Ragnarok and Bruja took turns kicking him in the ribs.

The elderly Blood Judge spit curses as he curled into a ball, trying to protect himself from the vicious blows. Even with the stormwolf's sub-par hearing I could make out the sound of ribs breaking with each kick. When they finally relented a little, Whisper squirmed her way in with a tree branch she'd stripped of its leaves and laid into him, her delicate face wrinkled into a mask of anger and vengeance.

Bloodrath let his pack beat the Blood Judge for a solid minute before he ordered them to back off. He drew his cavalry saber and cut the old man's hands free before grabbing hold of Tillman's duster. With a shake and a grunt of effort he wrested the elder judge's mantle of office from him. Bruja rebound their prisoner's hands with a length of rawhide, taking pleasure in wrenching his shoulders painfully behind him. Bloodrath made a fancy show of putting on the duster, relishing the look of impotent rage on Tillman's face.

"Well I'll be," Bloodrath gloated, turning this way and that to the bestial cheers of his pack. "It's a perfect fit. Pity about the old man smell though, *n'est-ce pas?*"

"Go to hell, you dirty augger-lover," Tillman spat. "When Adeline gets her claws on you, she'll make you wish you'd never turned from the righteous path."

Bloodrath chortled and kicked Tillman in his chest, sending him toppling backward. The most the other man could do was to spit curses and glare. Without their companion mounts the Judges were more vulnerable than most to being overpowered. Assuming you could lay hands on the speedy bastards in the first place. Tillman didn't look like he'd be sprinting anywhere anytime soon.

Even though Judge Tillman was a racist asshole, I felt bad for the bastard getting kicked around like that. Sure, he probably deserved worse, but he was in no condition to defend himself. I had a problem with the helpless getting beat on. Even when they so richly deserved it.

"All right, people, who's hungry?"

The pack roared in answer. Bloodrath smiled down at Judge Tillman, his bony face drawn into a horrible rictus of amusement.

"Those supplies you auggers stole were meant for a farm that hasn't done so well," Tillman said, spitting blood and dirt from his mouth. "Forgetting the debt you owe the hard-working white men who provided it, you're still taking food out of your own people's mouth."

A disturbing chuckle escaped Bloodrath, and he leaned in. "Oh, Tillman, you idiot bastard. That grain is destined for the other Advocates, to keep their misplaced morals off our backs for a while. No, we celebrate recruits into the Shadow Pack with a different feast. While the meat may be spoiled, the insult of the meal more than makes up for the taste."

Bloodrath drew the cavalry saber, making a show of inspecting its honed silver edge. The Pack rumbled with hungry anticipation.

So that's why I hadn't seen Bruja dragging up crates for their meal. No farm grew what these critters were after. They liked their prey struggling, bleeding, and cursing their name.

The Shadow Pack were going to eat Judge Tillman.

Chapter 22

I WASN'T INCLINED TO interfere.

Leaving aside the fact that Tillman set off every instinct in my head that told me to kill, I'd gathered from Malakhai and the Grant family that the old bastard was the shining example of the 'perfect Blood Judge.' He was everything that Trent and the rest of the Cabal wanted in an enhanced man, a creature of hate and spite that knew when to bend knee to his own masters. If he was guilty of half of what had been intimated, then his own judgment was long past due. There wasn't a chance in hell that I was going to jump in to save his sorry ass. If anything, I was more worried about how I was going to get by the ghoulish banquet without being spotted.

Bloodrath slashed his cavalry saber across Tillman's belly with a quick snap. The old man grunted in pain as blood fell in thick droplets to the ground. It wasn't enough to kill him immediately. The wrong-wolves wrinkled their noses at the smell of the fresh wound. A flick of the saber cleaned it of the Judge's blood, and it slid back into the sheath, job done.

"Ragnarok," Bloodrath said, his translucent skin spread into a bony smile. "As the guest of honor, you got the first bite. I know the flavor is ruined with the silver tang, but his screams will season it well enough to stomach."

"Choke on me, you dirty race-traitor," Judge Tillman spat, raising his head in defiance to stare Ragnarok in the eye. "The Talons were right to send you down to the chains with the augger filth. You might have been white in skin, but inside you were just another n—"

Ragnarok slammed a metal fist into the old Judge's face, sending teeth flying as Tillman's body twisted round and landed face-down in the wet earth. The Judge sputtered and spat, somehow righting himself back to his knees despite his bound hands. His face was a swollen mess, and it had shut him up pretty good. But the fire remained in his one good eye. Ragnarok huffed in amusement, doing his best to make a mock bow to his victim.

Tillman's courage would have been admirable if not for all the crimes he was guilty of. Still, I wished they'd take their dinner off the trail a bit. It's not that I objected to watching them end the cantankerous bastard, but there was far too much furry flesh between me and the other side of the squall beacon to make a run for it.

Although there was no chance the Shadow Pack could lay hands on me as the stormwolf, if they sent up an alarm the rest of the Advocates might have something unexpected that could hurt me. I'd already seen Trent modulate frequencies to block me out, and I had a burning need to shut off whatever the Advocates were using to generate the telluric deadzone. Wardenclyffe was only a couple of days off from crashing into Portland. There was no way Maude or anyone else could escape using the Double Ts. Henry had barely been able to use the *Bantam*, and now even it was surely grounded with the salvation city this close to the deadzone.

Ragnarok stalked around the helpless Tillman with an evil gleam in his eyes, flexing the gleaming blades that served as claws at the end of his mechanical arms. Gears clicked and pistons hissed, ready to lend their power to the ironhide's terrible work.

Something tickled the edge of the stormwolf's senses, a presence of flesh and metal lurking just within the edges of the clearing, safe from the electromagnetic maelstrom outside.

The bushes on the opposite side of the clearing erupted in leaves and twigs as a large silhouette burst out of them with a roar of challenge. The dark shape went flying through the air like a cannonball, hitting Ragnarok squarely in his midsection and sending both of them tumbling back in a confusing mass of fur and metal.

"Adeline!" Judge Tillman screamed in recognition, his face a mixture of horror and elation.

The two ironhides separated, with Ragnarok backing off and snarling. His right arm had been torn into, the metal slashed and gnarled into a sparking mess. The clawed hand on the end of the limb twitched like a suffocating fish, the bladed fingers spasming. But his opponent was much worse off.

The last time I'd seen Tillman's werewolf companion I hadn't taken particular note of her. She had just been another Fixed wolf, one more slave of the Cabal and its minions. The new ironhide was smaller than Ragnarok, which made her damn near dwarfed by the nearby Bruja. The stormwolf's eyes didn't handle normal sight well, but I could make out that Adeline was dark-furred with streaks of white around her eyes and paws. She had the mechanical limbs that all Fixed sported, although I was willing to bet hers had a few more upgrades given Tillman's status. Her teeth flashed with a metallic sheen as she clawed the earth, challenging Ragnarok. But no matter how many gadgets the Cabal had stuck in her, I wasn't sure Adeline was fit enough to fight a breeze right now, let alone a fellow abomination.

Scarlet welled up from new wounds from where Ragnarok had fought back. But that was nothing compared to the half-dried blood that already matted Adeline's fur. Wide swathes of coat were missing where she'd been savaged across her spinal furnace, and the pink flesh holding it in had barely stitched itself back together. From her injuries, it was easy enough to tell that Adeline had never stood a chance. She hadn't seen the first attack coming in the ambush where she'd lost her Judge. But she wasn't letting it stop her.

Despite her being a lap dog for Tillman and the Cabal I couldn't help but feel sorry for her. As far as I could tell, the swaying Adeline was only living with sheer force of will. Although the wounds to her back were the worst, she was cut up all across her body. The sum total of her infected regeneration seemed to be dedicated to simply keeping Adeline on her feet.

I shook my head in wonderment. What would possess an enslaved critter like her to fight so hard to keep living, to track her master through the surging currents of Mt. Hood only to commit obvious suicide by attacking the Shadow Pack in their home territory? Even if she'd been fit as a fiddle I doubted she'd have stood a chance against all of them at once.

The answer came to me as Adeline looked over to Tillman, tears in her eyes that had nothing to do with the savage injuries on her body. I felt like a fool; I'd forgotten something important that Malakhai had mentioned in passing when explaining the bond between Judge and companion. Adeline wasn't just Tillman's monstrous steed.

She was also his daughter.

Although the patched-hide Bruja circled nearby, neither she nor Bloodrath had made a move to interfere in the tussle between Ragnarok and Adeline. Whisper just sat on her heels at the edge of the clearing, content to let the situation play out without involvement.

"What's all this, Ragnarok?" Bloodrath asked, the tone in his voice carrying clear threat. He'd pulled his single-shot pistol free and was checking its load with a feigned sense of leisure. "I thought you finished the bitch off during the ambush. We took Tillman. All you had to do was kill her. The girl's blood, it was your price of entry to our ranks. She too much for you, *mon frère?*"

Ragnarok uttered a snarling whine in response, rattled by Adeline's appearance as much as the rest of his pack. Without Whisper's help he couldn't make a proper accounting of himself to the others, but it was clear enough that he'd thought the other ironhide dead. Judging by how the spark of life seemed to fade in and out of Adeline's ravaged body, I couldn't say I necessarily blamed him.

"Yes, yes, I'm sure you got the excuses," Bloodrath said, as if he'd understood the guttural noises from his subordinate. "But let's just put the little miss to bed for good, shall we? Cut her down, or you'll be taking Tillman's place for supper."

Ragnarok's ears flattened against his skull at the threat, and he growled at Bloodrath. Bruja turned her massive head toward him and snarled back. Whisper stood up ramrod straight, her eyes narrowed with fingers hovering over her modified Vocalator brace. A quick glance around at his pack mates put Ragnarok back in his place. He tucked his tail and let his challenging gaze drop from Bloodrath.

Adeline had taken advantage of the pissing contest to rest. The exchange had let her body heal from Ragnarok's reprisal, the flesh thickening with scarred muscle as it wove itself back together. It wasn't much, and she was still snuggled up to death's door; but it was enough. I realized with a start that she hadn't attacked Ragnarok blindly. She'd targeted bits the other wrong-wolf that couldn't heal back: the mechanical augmentations in his arm. She'd been trained well to fight her own kind. Although she still looked like hammered shit, Adeline was ready to throw down again. Her eyes focused on Ragnarok with a murderous fury.

As her target turned back to deal with the smaller beast, Adeline leapt forward, metal claws curved into terrible scythes. Surprised by the sudden attack from the wounded Augmented, Ragnarok fell back as Adeline slashed again and again at him. Her attacks were wild, desperate, but they managed to rake the bigger wrong-wolf across his abdomen with her wicked claws.

As he curled over in pain Adeline lunged forward, jaws wider than I'd have thought possible. There was a mechanical whine of servos, and I saw that she had hydraulic pistons connecting her jaw bones where tendons should have been.

Ragnarok caught Adeline's jaws as they began to close, trying to keep her from crushing his skull. Steel fought steel in a shrieking crescendo as Adeline desperately tried to finish off her enemy.

Whisper and Bruja glanced at Bloodrath as Ragnarok whined a desperate plea. The skull-faced man shook his head slowly, sadly.

"It's a sorrow, *mon frère*. We need more for the Shadow Pack. But you have the weakness in you. Couldn't kill her when the advantage was ours. Can't kill her now when she's nearly dead? Nothing for it."

Ragnarok howled in betrayed frustration as Adeline's gleaming fangs inched deeper toward his head. Despite his best efforts, Adeline was overpowering him. Every moment that passed she grew stronger, and Ragnarok lost more and more ground.

Ragnarok's damaged mechanical limb was sparking and smoking in protest at the struggle, gears shaking loose as pistons began to buckle under the strain of resisting the other wrong-wolf's jaws. His eyes went wide with terror as there was a sharp clang. Ragnarok's damaged arm suddenly went limp.

Adeline tore off his head in a spray of blood and oil with her hydraulic jaws. She gave a couple of determined chews on her prize while staring at Bloodrath meaningfully before spitting out the mangled mess of metal and flesh that had once been Ragnarok's skull.

"Well done, *chère*," Bloodrath said, clapping. He had not holstered his pistol. "It is better he dies now than when he guards our flank. We owe you a debt."

"Then let her go, Emanuel," Tillman pleaded through his ruined mouth. The old man's shoulders sagged with defeat; he already knew what I was just now realizing. Adeline swayed and collapsed to her knees. She'd fought past her limits to avenge herself and her father. But flesh and metal could only be pushed so far. Adeline had given all she had left to kill Ragnarok. There was nothing left for the other three.

"Afraid I can't do that, Tillman," Bloodrath said with a regretful shrug. "Not that your daughter would run anyway. Your dog has always been loyal."

Adeline rose up shakily, her anger kindling anew in her ravaged face. Ragnarok's claws had dug deep into her jaws, pulling several teeth out and slicing through her skin.

Bloodrath raised his archaic pistol, aiming at Adeline's head.

"No!" Tillman shrieked, trying to lunge from the ground at his skeletal tormentor. But with his hands still bound behind his back the impromptu charge was clumsy, predictable. Bloodrath easily sidestepped the other Judge. The old man went face-first into the dirt, struggling to flip over and try again.

"I believe the proper retort is: yes," Bloodrath taunted, waiting until Tillman had righted himself enough to witness the shot.

The sound of the pistol going off was louder than it had any right to be. The death of a daughter while her father looked on amplified the noise beyond rational thought.

A bloody hole blossomed in Adeline's forehead.

The light went out of Adeline's eyes, and she fell back to her knees. Despite the apparent power of the blast, there was no exit wound. I expected Adeline to topple over, the Augmented ironhide felled by a centuries-old weapon. To my amazement she stayed on her knees though, eyelids open, with a vacant look on her face.

Adeline still lived.

"Not like this, don't do this to her," Tillman wept, tears falling out of his one good eye as he collapsed in on himself. There was no thought of dignity; he was just a father begging for his daughter.

"Oh, so you remember my little trick?" Bloodrath said with a grin. He squatted next to the Judge and raised the older man's chin with the barrel of the smoking pistol. "But you were so fond of this game when you trained me. Such times we had! Where is the gratitude, then? Your darling daughter, she is still alive, no?"

Tillman's face hardened, and his voice was tight with rage.

"I know damn good and well she ain't. Not anymore. Not with what you've done."

Bloodrath laughed, prompting Bruja to join with her own wolfish chortles. Whisper squatted down, clutching her knees and watching.

"Fair enough," Bloodrath acknowledged. He stood up and holstered the pistol. "As we both know, I was quite adept at lobotomizing targets at distance when we hunted. With just the right amount of powder the ball lodges in the target's brain. There's just enough silver mixed in with the lead to keep their bodies from pushing it out. Makes them quite docile, yes?"

"Made them useless," Tillman growled. "Even after we dug out your round, any man or woman brought back from the fur after that were never quite the same. Memories, words, how to take a shit without help, all of it erased. The beast can regrow the brain back, but not what was in there."

Bloodrath laughed. "I know! But is that not what you intend anyway? Do they then not make the perfect slaves?"

"Deaf and dumb beasts that can't walk without help?" Tillman spat, his voice husky as he stared at Adeline. She hadn't moved, and barely breathed. "Ain't nothing that comes back from that. You were useless as a Judge; worse than that, even. Broke the ones we needed to rescue and spoiled the brains on the rest."

"Ah, but you still used me. At least until you had others survive the process," Bloodrath responded. There was a note of pain at the abandonment in his voice, almost covered by his sneering hatred of Tillman.

Bruja growled impatiently. The skull-faced man gave a heavy sigh and nodded.

"She is right, *mon ami*. Too much talking. Not enough eating. This is supposed to be a celebration! Although I suppose now it is a wake. Regardless, someone has to be starting the feast."

Realization struck me like a fist as Bruja lumbered over to Adeline. The smaller ironhide made no move to resist as Bruja picked her up by the scruff of her neck. Adeline's legs flailed helplessly for a moment before finding purchase, leaving Tillman's daughter standing, if only just. Bruja force-walked her over to where Bloodrath and Tillman were, keeping a firm hold on the smaller Augmented as she stumbled along.

"Please, God, no," Tillman wept. "Don't make her do this. If you have a decent bone left in your body, Emanuel, just stop."

"Ah, but what kind of papa are you then, Tillman? Do you wish your daughter to go hungry?"

Bruja rumbled with laughter as she wrenched Adeline's jaws open. Fresh blood from Ragnarok still coated the ironhide's steel teeth. Tillman stared into his daughter's maw, pleading, weeping, all to no avail as Bruja and Bloodrath laughed. Whisper watched it all with silent fascination.

I couldn't stand it any longer.

There was a line in the sand I wouldn't cross, even against someone like Tillman. A basic human decency that kept me fighting when the beast wanted to take hold. It was one thing to sit idly by while Tillman got what he deserved.

It was quite another to watch someone force his daughter to eat him alive.

The stormwolf's roar was a crack of thunder that shook the leaves as I charged out. I moved faster than any corporeal creature could, my target the patchwork fur of Bruja's head and neck. I'd killed Thompson the same way, and there was nothing the ironhide could do to keep me from ending her.

A flash of light and force hit me like a giant's fist, sending the stormwolf flying back when I tried to bite into Bruja's neck.

Leaves smoked and caught fire where I landed, righting myself as fast as thought. My ghostly jaws felt numb, the crackling outline of the white-blue energy distorted and surging. Where I'd bitten Bruja there was a burnt imprint of the stormwolf's teeth in her patched fur, but no damage otherwise.

Bruja shook her head, disoriented by the unexpected attack. Her eyes widened when she saw me, as did Bloodrath and his daughter's. Apparently a lightning-shrouded phantom werewolf floating above the ground was slightly out of their wheelhouse.

"*Mon dieu*, what are you?" Bloodrath murmured in wonderment.

In response I charged forward, my galvanic claws aiming for his skeletal face. He recoiled in fear, but another bright flash sent me tumbling backward as Bruja slashed downward to catch me. Her mismatched fur smoldered where it had touched me, but there was no other sign of damage or pain to her.

Bloodrath adjusted his stolen duster, trying to regain some measure of dignity. Bruja growled protectively, moving to put herself between Bloodrath and me.

All I could do was to hiss and pop back, the stormwolf's answer to her challenge. A smile crept over Bloodrath's ugly visage.

"No answer? Such is life. I see you were not expecting my friend to stop you," he said, patting Bruja's shoulder with pride. "You look to be one of her tall-tales. Perhaps your spirits are not so make-believe after all?"

Bruja rumbled a sound deep in her chest.

"Yes, yes. I owe you an apology. I'd only thought you justifying a fetish for skinning and wearing the pelts of your defeated foes. Little did I know."

The ironhide huffed in irritation.

"As I said, the apology is given. It appears your magic is real after all. It should not surprise me, given the time we live in."

My puzzlement must have shown on the stormwolf's face.

"Did you think no one could touch you, ghost?" Bloodrath laughed. "Or that your magic was the only that worked? Bruja was a powerful witch before she was bitten, and her power has grown in the years since the world ended. I'd merely thought her a cunning and powerful ally before today, if slightly delusional. Perhaps I should add more to my estimation, eh?"

Bruja rumbled her agreement. Her stance had eased, the surprise of my sudden appearance having passed. Whatever she had done to stitch the pelts of other werewolves onto her had somehow allowed her to repel me, to break my attacks without harm to herself. There was nothing I could do to stop her from forcing Adeline to consume her father, and she knew it.

Well. Almost nothing.

I bolted forward again, surging toward Bruja with an electric howl. Her tongue lolled out in a wolfish taunt, unconcerned about any threat. She released Adeline and stood ready, her claws eager to cut through my phantom form.

At the last moment I flashed around her swipe, changing my target.

I darted between Tillman and his daughter, thrusting an arm out to each of them. The Judge's eyes went wide as I shoved my lightning claw deep into his chest, grabbing his heart as I did the same to Adeline. I snarled with concentration as I sent every bit of energy I could summon coursing through Tillman and Adeline.

Smoke and sparks of flame lit their bodies from the inside out as I electrocuted them together.

"Th-thank you," Tillman managed to stutter as the lightning shot through him. For just a moment, I could've sworn I saw the same thanks mirrored in his daughter's dead gaze.

Bruja snarled in rage as she turned and tore through my phantom body with her claws.

The stormwolf's form flickered and distorted at the wolf-witch's attack. I fell back crackling a scream from Adeline and her father, pain searing my mind. Scuttling back as fast as the maimed energy construct could, I tried to get free of the deadly claws.

"*Fous-toi!*" Bloodrath snarled. He lunged to catch Tillman as the Judge fell face-forward. But he was already too late. The old man was smoking, his flesh seared and dead, a victorious smile frozen on his face. Adeline toppled to the side, her life snuffed out as well.

I'd given them the only mercy I could.

"Bruja! Bring me that ghost," Bloodrath ordered, his voice icy. "He owes us a debt."

The big Augmented rumbled in agreement as she advanced on me.

There was nothing I could do to escape her. The stormwolf's form had dimmed to almost nothing. The energy I'd used to electrocute the Tillmans had taken it out of me, and Bruja's claws had cut deep into my hollow form. I could feel the voltaic phantom I inhabited flickering, fading.

Bruja towered over me, her mechanical claws flexing with the mystical power her patchwork-hide granted them. She could touch me. She could gut me. She could end me.

The wolf-witch reached down, her claws coming for my life.

Brilliant white flashed, and the world ended.

Chapter 23

"WELCOME BACK, HALFBREED."

My eyelids ground open like rusted gears. Caked blood fell away when I rubbed at them. My skin felt see-through, translucent, as if the faint light in the room burned down past it to jellied bones inside. The headache that lived in my skull could give thunder lessons in loud, and my mouth tasted like I'd spent seven days and seven nights using an electrified rail as a candy cane.

Overall, it was not a pleasant experience.

As the world began to come into focus, I recognized the depressingly familiar walls of the Cabal's hidden laboratory under the Tombstone. My body, now the same old flesh and bone as everyone else, was laid across an operating table.

It didn't feel right, being me again. My skin was a foreign suit; its slick covering over muscles flecked with hair seemed obscene. The noisy processes of my guts growling for food and blood pumping through my veins made me nauseous at the awful sounds.

Of course, waking up to Trent's ugly face didn't help matters none either.

He'd donned a pair of black rubber gloves, and had a variety of evil-looking steel implements laid out neatly on a nearby tray. In his hands he held two sparking cables that had a huge wall-mounted contraption at the other end.

"I'm rather disappointed you came around so quickly," Trent sighed.

As before, it was the Vocalator's voice he used. It never ceased being creepy hearing a monster's thoughts from a child's mouth.

My own attempt to speak summoned forth a hoarse, rasping sound that hurt the bone-dry throat it cracked from. Trent grunted in irritation as he brought a glass of water up to my parched lips. I managed to get down a couple of gulps before a coughing fit seized me. The Dragon went ahead and splashed the rest in my face, worsening the situation. He peeled off his rubber gloves and motioned the Vocalator close.

"Experiment log seven, project name 'Thunderstrike,'" Trent's slave said into the bracer on the doctor's arm. "'Subject E seems to be drained of essential life energy after his unexpected manifestation of an energy construct form. Dissection should reveal more of the unique mechanisms utilized for the transformation. Log ends.'"

Trent grinned with his elongated face down at me. "A small joke, my dear boy."

"Liar," I managed to rasp out. "Wouldn't have put . . . in log if not serious. And those blades aren't . . . for tickling me."

Trent guffawed, unrolling a leather case into which he sorted and placed the various surgical tools. "True enough, halfbreed. You weren't responding to other stimuli, so I was preparing for the worst." He paused, examining the gleam of a scalpel in the lamplight. "This will become your future though if you continue to defy me."

The threat cut through the mental fog still clinging to my brain, and I looked around the room desperately.

There was no sign of Maggie or Sarah.

"Oh, you needn't worry," the Dragon said, as if reading my mind. He put the last blade in its place and deftly rolled the leather back up again before slipping it up the sleeve of his purple robe. "They are being taken care of. Siblings, yes? The familial resemblance is clear. The older sister certainly has spirit, I'll give her that. The younger one screamed when we set her arms. It took a while to get her to break her silence. But she warmed up to the idea. Eventually."

"If you—"

"Stop. I'd rather not endure an impotent threat from a boy so bedraggled as to barely form coherent thoughts. I will do as I wish, to whom I wish, when I wish. And there's not a thing you can do to stop me. But I am open to a trade, as it were."

I sat up and swung my legs over the edge of the table. A ragged shirt and pair of pants lay folded near my feet; I put them on in silence. There was a stubborn feeling taking hold of me. Maggie had told me not to let the Cabal use her against me. Although I was scared for her future, her advice had been sound.

"Will you not speak?" Trent sighed, shaking his head. "You only hurt yourself and those you love. What I ask is something that will benefit both of us. Wardenclyffe approaches; even those with human eyes can see it on the horizon now. How long until it crashes into Portland, killing both your people and mine? Two days? Three, at the most."

"The deadzone," I said, reluctantly breaking my silence. "I need it down to save my kin; you want it down to break the Advocates with your Augmented werewolf horde. That about the size of it?"

"Indeed. And before you make some absurd claim about not being able to bypass the disorientation field, I have received reports from several scouts that you were seen not only flying to Mt. Hood in that remarkable energy form, but actually landing there safely. Quite a feat, actually. You should be proud."

"Yeah, I'm all kinds of delighted," I muttered, shuffling around the table as if stretching my legs.

My eyes darted over everything in the room, but there was no sign of where he'd taken the Butler sisters. Briefly I considered the cells above us, but dismissed it as soon as I realized there was no way Trent was dumb enough to keep using a prison cell I could freely pass through as the stormwolf.

Thinking of the voltaic beast, I reached down, trying to find a spark of it. Maybe if I could control it a bit better I'd have a chance to take Trent out before he was able to reach his bracer and dial me out again. But whatever magic had manifested the critter was gone, drained dry by the vacation my mind had taken from my body. I wasn't sure it would come back, or even if it could come back if Trent wasn't electrocuting me half to death. Without its help I stood no chance against the Dragon.

I had to buy time for my body to recover. Play along with him, at least until I could come up with a way to kill him and get the sisters back safe.

"Let's entertain for a minute you make a lick of sense," I said, edging toward the elevator shaft. There was no sign of the platform. Someone had used it to ascend, likely with the sisters in tow. "Why would I work against the Advocates? Maybe I get up there, talk it through with them, and they can save Wardenclyffe without shutting down their field. It's possible. They put it up. They know how it works, they can alter it. You think holding Maggie and Sarah hostage will make me turn on people that want the Cabal to die as much as I do? What's the lives of two people compared to a whole passel of folks fighting a winning war against you pricks?"

Trent huffed out in disappointment. "Pretend all you wish, child. I've seen how you look at the older one, the Maggie girl. You'd bring down your own precious city for her."

"You don't know shit if you think that about me," I grunted.

Trent walked uncomfortably close to me, using one of his thin fingers to press a button next to the elevator shaft.

"You see us as the enemy. But you are wrong. We are your allies, as we have always been the ally of your kind. Without our guidance you poor wretches would have remained on the dark continent, content to kill each other without ever advancing your prospects or intellect. Why look at you! You're a brakeman on a Double T, well-spoken, and relatively clean. You're a credit to your race!"

The urge to punch him in the head until he stopped talking was strong, but I restrained it as the wooden elevator platform creaked into view. We stepped aboard, as did his Vocalator, and Trent began to hoist us up via the pulley. His exertions left little energy for talking through his puppet, and I didn't much feel like jawing anyway. Besides, we already knew what each other would say. We were just going round and round the same maypole without agreeing.

I expected us to stop at the prison level, but Trent just kept at it, raising the platform higher and higher. The afternoon cast sharp shadows on the elevator shaft as we rose. When we reached the roof the massive silhouette of the *Purity's Pride* and its grounding trestle blocked out a huge swath of sky. But that wasn't what Trent had brought us up here for.

Bells tolled in the distance from an unseen church, a somber and methodical clanging that held no joy. Trent beckoned me over to the edge of the Tombstone's roof. Leery of his intentions, I sidled over to see what he was pointing at.

A funeral procession was winding through Portland's main street just a block away. The shadow of the Tombstone reached out like a malevolent creature to envelop them as they came closer. The Returned humans in black mourning dress avoided the dark edge, but the Fixed wrong-wolf towing a wagon painted in black seemed impervious to fear. They passed close enough for me to read the white lettering on the side of the hearse: *Rose*. That had been my mother's name. It was just a coincidence, but for a moment I had a knot in my throat thinking about her.

"Do you know who resides within the coffins they carry?" Trent asked, pointing at the black wagon. When I refused to answer, he continued. "Victims. The poor wretches torn apart by the Advocates in a raid on an outlying farm, the Winston homestead. Most of them had been eaten; we barely found enough remains of the youngest child to warrant a matchbox for burial. One of our best Blood Judges died defending them."

"Tillman," I said with a nod, not thinking. At the odd look from Trent, I cleared my throat and shut up again.

"An excellent . . . guess," the Dragon replied. "And a correct one. Judge Tillman and his companion beast were missing in the aftermath of the battle. We can only hope they died on their feet, rather than being captured. Even I shudder to think of that possibility."

Marching in line behind the hearse were a half dozen Augmented, their claws and muzzles weighed down by heavy iron chains and their spinal furnaces burning low. These weren't the relatively well-maintained Fixed that I'd encountered serving the Cabal directly though. The slaves in tow were Broken, the sad half-failed experiments that served as the lowest echelon in Portland's slave society.

The crowd that had formed at the edge of the thoroughfare to watch the procession hissed and booed at the shackled ironhides, several throwing rocks and trash at them. The wrong-wolves endured the humiliation without lashing out or attempting to break their bonds. Their spirits were as maimed as their bodies.

"Members of the raiders?" I asked, puzzled. The sagging shoulders and downcast muzzles of the chained Broken didn't seem like Shadow Pack material.

"They might as well be. Those six are criminals, insubordinate auggers that need to be taught a lesson. That their punishment can help assuage the pain of the survivors is a fact we cannot, we will not, ignore."

Rather than ask what he meant, I settled back into a sullen silence. Given all that I'd seen from the Cabal, I wasn't really sure I wanted to know anyway.

With my bird's-eye view from the Tombstone roof I realized I could see nearly the entirety of the Portland downtown area. If I clambered over the Double T that rested on the roof I'd have an even better vantage point, but something about the pristine Thunder Train bothered me. The *Purity's Pride* was too clean, too immaculate, to be a decent hard-working machine. The sweat of slaves was what kept its steel panels gleaming.

The funeral procession made its way to the central square where we'd seen an Augmented get quartered the day before. The mourners spread out around the gallows platform while the pall bearers lifted six wooden coffins from the back of *Rose*. They handled the coffins too easily, as if they weighed almost nothing beyond the wood itself. The Shadow Pack hadn't left much of the bodies behind.

The coffins were placed upright in a semicircle around the edges of the gallows, leaning against the beams. The six shackled wrong-wolves were marched up none too gently and forced to kneel in front of each coffin, like furry supplicants begging forgiveness from angry gods.

"How fortunate that exactly the same number of Augmented broke your laws as people who died in the Advocate attack," I remarked with an arched eyebrow.

"Yes, the world does seem to enjoy balancing itself in such ways," Trent replied, with absolutely no hint that he saw anything wrong with the math.

Two mourners separated from the crowd and came forward. One

was a little boy, no more than five or six years old. The other was an old woman with a bent back.

"The remaining members of the Winston family," Trent murmured. "We will mitigate their loss. We will help them."

A Talon stepped forward from under the platform's shadow, a bullwhip clutched in his deformed hand. The crowd sank back reflexively at his appearance before crowding in closer. The Cabalist climbed the steps to where the Broken knelt, leading the old woman and the little boy like a shepherd with lambs. When they reached the muzzled prisoners, the Talon turned and offered the whip to the woman.

She didn't hesitate, taking the handle with a relish I could see even at this distance. The old woman shrieked something unintelligible at the shackled ironhides before drawing back the whip and then snapping it forward with a crack that drew a yelp of pain from the first Augmented. Fur flew away from his back as she laid into him again and again with the whip, flaying first the fur then the skin off his back, leaving it a bloody mass of pain. Throughout it all the Broken howled in agony, his high-pitched whines begging her to stop with each strike.

"Every time I think you bastards can't get any lower you never fail to prove me wrong," I grunted, my stomach churning at the spectacle. "This is what grieving looks like to you people?"

"In a manner of speaking, yes. By allowing the survivors to take out their pain on criminals similar to those that took their loved ones we can mitigate their grief. We're essentially killing two birds with one stone, and proving to any Advocate spies and sympathizers in the crowd that their rebellious ways punish the same creatures they claim to try and help. The auggers' torment thus serves not only to discipline them, but also to caution others against antisocial behavior while allowing victims' families to exact some measure of retribution. You must admit that there's as a certain elegance to the equation. Is this not a more civilized way to live?"

"That all depends on which side of the whip you're on."

Trent huffed, offended. But I didn't give a damn. No, that wasn't right. I enjoyed his taking offense. There were too many sins and crimes that the Dragon and his ilk held up as virtues and accomplishments. Slavery and degradation were his meat and potatoes. Pointing out he was a disgusting creature simply seemed to please him. That I'd finally managed to insult him was a precious achievement to me.

Once the old lady had tired herself out on the weeping wrong-wolf she tried to hand the whip over to the little boy. But the kid shook his head, staring hard at his shoes and refusing to take the weapon. His face was pinched and red.

The boy was crying.

The old woman gestured angrily, forcing the child to take the whip as she screamed at him. His movements were uncertain as he raised his arm, jerking it forward in a poor imitation of the woman's own whipping motion. The lash barely touched the second ironhide, not even parting his fur. The kid had a good heart and didn't understand the violence, didn't understand the pain he was supposed to inflict. Or maybe he did, and he was just too much of a human being to play their sick games.

The boy threw the whip down in disgust and fled from the gallows platform. The crowd had an ugly undertone to his defiance. When the child disappeared into their ranks I was concerned about his safety.

"Takes time to nurture hate and stupidity, eh? I like that kid. Got a good head on his shoulders." I smirked at Trent. The Dragon fumed, his face puckering like a load of lemons had hit him. But his Vocalator remained silent. He directed my attention back to the crowd.

The Returned humans in their nice linen suits were surging forward, fighting for the whip that the boy had discarded. The Talon was keeping order as best he could, and managed to line the mob up in a semi-orderly fashion. Each man and woman in their Sunday best took turns cracking the whip over the kneeling Augmented wolves, just like proper white folk. I couldn't stomach the spectacle; me and the Winston boy had that in common. Human decency just wouldn't let either of us tolerate the naked hate and cruelty.

Compared to the event below, the *Purity's Pride* took on an almost welcoming nature. I knew Thunder Trains, had grown up clambering all over them as a brakeman. Trent was too enraptured in the mob to care, so long as I didn't wander away.

The *Purity's Pride* was a Skybreaker like the *Heaven's Grace*, so theoretically I already knew every nook and cranny on it. But Maude had modified our train extensively. There was an academic curiosity about what was normal and what wasn't. I already knew about the dummy levers and dials she'd installed in the control cabin in her engine, which was one way she kept the big train out of complete Tellurian control. Anyone trying to pilot it other than her or me would quickly find the ground rushing up to meet them. In comparison, the engine controls for the *Purity's Pride* would be simplistic and boring. But as my hand ran over her gleaming steel hide, I noticed something odd about the boiler.

Although a secondary power system to the absorbed lightning, the boilers of the Double Ts served to get them through the dry spells between storms, running the enclosed wheels to power a turbine to keep the squall sparkers running. While the squall tubes on the *Purity's Pride* were dark and lifeless, there was some kind of secondary system that had been installed running from under the boiler to the tubes directly. There was no reason I could fathom for such a layout, and I lost myself in tracing the faint patterns running across the hull. Although the craftsmanship was impeccable, it was still something obviously added on after she rolled off the production line.

"Admiring our security system?" Trent purred in my ear.

I nearly jumped out of my skin and scuttled along the side of the engine to get clear of the abomination. He grinned and traced the same pattern I'd found with his thin fingers, making me uncomfortable on a primal level.

"Only a true man of the machine would have noticed such a subtle addition," the doctor praised. "Color me impressed, boy."

"It looks like a useless system." I was cautious, my words carefully chosen. I'd already seen my fair share of horror today, and didn't need any more shit added to the pile.

"The theft of the *Shrieking Sally* will not be a feat soon repeated. In the event of a criminal gaining control of a Cabal Thunder Train, a code will be sent from my control bracer to the security system, which activates the salt pumps retrofitted under the boiler. As a result, one pound of rock salt will be injected directly into the active squall tubes of the engine."

"You built a bomb into your train on purpose?" I was aghast. I'd seen a few squall tubes go up as a result of salt contamination. The resulting explosion made dynamite weep with how toothless it was.

"Can you think of a more effective deterrent to theft than knowing you'll detonate mid-air, without any way to stop it? Regardless, that is a distraction to the reason I brought you here. Now that you've seen the justice of our governance, the logical processes of it, you cannot help but understand the importance of working with us. You must help us defeat the Advocates once and for all."

"Have you lost your mind?" I asked, anger making my voice rise. "You've shown me torture, injustice, a system so corrupt and lopsided as to force a crying child to whip an innocent slave in the name of curing his grief! And all this after you kidnap my friends and threaten them with God knows what if I don't do what you say."

"Yes, yes," Doctor Trent said, waving his hand dismissively. "You've registered these complaints in one form or another before. But I grow tired of attempting to reason with you. So now we must return to the original threat. Do as I say, or the girls you cherish will suffer for it. Is that not a heroic enough reason to accomplish your mission?"

"Go lick a rail," I growled. "If Maggie found that I rolled over for you on her account she'd beat my ass from here to Judgment Day. Neither one of them ladies is soft, and they wouldn't want me to be on their account either. Try again, handsome."

"Wardenclyffe then. I don't care how you justify it to yourself, but you will do as ordered," Trent growled. "People will suffer no matter your decision. Remain recalcitrant and do nothing, and your city will crash into mine, killing tens of thousands of uninfected and Returned humans. There is no amount of refusal that will change that fact. Think what you may of the Cabal, but was that Winston boy deserving of being an orphan, of being forced to face this world alone? If you must use morals to tether you in this maelstrom, then use his face. Use his pain. But no matter your reasons . . . do as I say!"

Trent had let the anger he was feeling bleed through, and the frustration made him a terrible sight. But no matter how much I hated him and the Cabal, the bastard wasn't wrong. I'd hemmed and hawed long enough, and Wardenclyfffe didn't have time for me to pussyfoot around any longer. It was time to shit or get off the pot. There might be some innocents that got hurt on Mr. Hood, but there were even more that would die if I did nothing. It was the Devil's choice, and I had to make it.

I shook my head, refusing to let the tears fall. I didn't have the right to weep over this. That'd be saved for the victims after the deed was done.

"You win. I'll do it."

Chapter 24

"AHH! LOOK OUT! TREE!"

My warning was too late, but also unneeded. Neshomne dodged around the big cedar without hitting it, although he did slash his metal claws across the bark to mark his passing.

I clung to Malakhai's black duster like a child, trying not to fall off the back of the Blood Judge's companion. The exhaust pipes off Neshomne's hips glowed red with how hard he was pushing his rib-cage furnaces, and it was all I could do to not burn myself on the damn things.

The Fixed ran through the dense forest outside of Portland at a reckless speed as the last of the light disappeared from the sky. Neshomne alternated between all fours and his hind legs as he leapt over stumps and holes, occasionally using his arms to either grab hold of a tree to change our direction or, in one case, crossing them and smashing his way through a rotten trunk in our way. Wood and branches smacked me in the face until I took the Judge's example and leaned low with him across the ironhide's back. It was goddamned terrifying.

Malakhai just laughed though, one red leather-clad hand holding his hat on while the other gripped Neshomne's ruff as we barreled through the forest. The miles fell away as Neshomne's long stride and unique trailblazing cut a path that a simpleton could follow. I had to get back to Mt. Hood as fast as possible in my real body; there was a lot of work to do and not much time to do it.

Which is how I found myself clinging to a madman as his Fixed companion blasted through the woods . . . sometimes literally. Leaves and twigs were stuck in my clothes and hair, and a bug had decided to lodge itself in my teeth.

"How did the bastard convince you?" Malakhai called over his shoulder. I was about to answer, but then Neshomne vaulted over a wide ravine, sending the beans I'd been fed an hour earlier shaking in my guts. Neshomne barely made the other edge, scrabbling up the collapsing embankment.

After I'd regained my equilibrium and made sure the food was staying down, I gave him a concise explanation. City in danger, girls held hostage, me do good work and save everyone.

"Playing the hero, eh?" he bellowed without turning around. "That's a trap, young'un. Especially when the villain is the one convincing you to do it."

Neshomne dove low under a big branch that nearly took my head off. If I didn't know better, I'd have said the ironhide huffed in disappointment that I wasn't dead.

"Wait, aren't you supposed to be towing the line for the Cabal?" I asked.

"You going to tattle on me, Eli?" Malakhai was laughing, but there was an edge to it that had nothing to do with Neshomne's death-defying dash through the forest. "I know he figured out your weakness, kid, but that's no reason to go and start groveling at his boots."

"What else was I supposed to do?"

"Fight, Eli. Fight for all you're worth, and take a chunk out of the bastards on the way down."

I couldn't keep my mouth shut. "You mean like you did? Weren't you the man giving me a half dozen justifications for your own position in Portland?"

He stayed silent a minute, and I thought I'd gone too far. But his voice was gentle when he replied, carried on the wind rushing past us and laced with regret.

"I didn't say do as I do, kid. I said be better than me. It's hard . . . but worth the effort."

Neshomne must've heard the tone in his partner's voice, as he made a point of sprinting up a tree that had been blown halfway down, running up the forty-five-degree angle like a titanic crazed squirrel. I couldn't do anything else other than cling to Malakhai as Neshomne launched us off the log, the pistons in his mechanical legs firing and sending us shooting above the highest branches of the forest.

We crashed into a thick limb, and I thought we were done for. But Neshomne used it like a pole, swinging us around to the trunk of the tree and sliding down as his claws cut through the bark. We'd slowed enough by the time we hit the ground that he was able to take off again without hesitation.

There was nothing left of dinner in my stomach.

I'd said I needed to get to Mt. Hood fast, but I'd underestimated what that meant to Malakhai. The pace Neshomne set was unbelievable. His preternatural sense of where to put his paws in the forest combined with sheer brute force meant he was able to bull a path that a small army could follow.

And they would. I'd seen enough of Trent organizing Portland before we departed to know he was assembling a legion of the Augmented and their overseers. The ironhide force wouldn't be as fast as Neshomne, but with his marks and trailblazing they'd be able to catch up in a few hours. I'd wanted to kill the deadzone before Wardenclyffe arrived, but things felt like they were moving too quickly now, spiraling out of what little control I had over them.

The worst of it was, Malakhai wasn't wrong. I'd agreed to work with the worst devil of them all, the man who destroyed the world. How many millions of deaths, hell, tens of millions, could be laid at his feet? In comparison, the lives of those on Wardenclyffe paled, as did Maggie. But that arithmetic didn't stick. It wasn't making a gnat's ass of difference to my gut. I wouldn't, couldn't, let everyone I know die just to preserve some strangers.

No matter how many times I repeated it to myself though, doubts still plagued my thoughts.

We spent the rest of the trip in silence.

The foothills got higher and higher the closer we got to Mt. Hood, but the forest remained as dense as ever. The sick feeling from Neshomne's speed faded, only to be replaced with the disorienting effect of the deadzone's edge. The giant Augmented was more careful in picking his way now, and a couple of times he crushed saplings from drunkenly veering into them. Neshomne slowed as we approached the foot of the mountain, until finally he came to a dead stop.

"Time to speak up, kid," Malakhai said, pulling out a bit of tobacco and rolling papers. Maude would have killed the Judge to get hold of the cheroot he was so casually rolling. She hadn't had decent tobacco in ages. Malakhai stuck the end in his mouth and struck a match off the butt of one of his pistols.

"Where we going?"

My eyes widened. I'd thought Trent was just sending the pair to escort me to the start of the electromagnetic maze, but apparently they were planning on accompanying me up the trail. There'd be no chance to find some other way out of the terrible deal I'd made with the Cabal, no time to figure out how to save everyone. Any deviation from the plan might end up with a bullet in the back of my head. If Neshomne didn't get to me first.

That was, of course, assuming that Malakhai didn't have instructions to just gun down whoever we found on sight. The Blood Judge didn't like taking orders from the Cabal, but he still obeyed them. He might bitch and moan about every task, but in the end, he was their man, bought and paid for.

Regardless, I still had to find the way up the mountain. Closing my eyes, I sifted through the stormwolf's memories as best I could. Landmarks looked different on the ground, but soon I was able to work out what I figured was the start of the path, or at least close to. Neshomne followed my directions to an outcropping of rock that looked a bit like a wolf's head. Upon closer inspection I could see break points where someone had cleaved sections of the outcropping off to form the lupine shape.

My guts churned as we approached, then settled out. Neshomne's gait changed as well, becoming firmer and more sure of footing. Malakhai grimaced at the change, as if he missed the tug of the deadzone.

We hopped down from Neshomne's back; from here on out the climb would be too steep to be riding on the wrong-wolf's back. And if we were ambushed the giant ironhide needed to be able to respond with his own violence without worrying about passengers. Malakhai checked his twin revolvers, eyeing the incline ahead. Apparently satisfied, he spun them back into their holsters. There was no offer to loan me a gun or to even give me a knife. I was helpless in any fight that came our way. If the Shadow Pack attacked I'd have to rely on the duo to protect me.

All of that was assuming Malakhai didn't have orders that ended up with me in a shallow grave. There were a lot of unknowns, a lot of decisions hidden from me by others about my fate. I didn't take kindly to not being in control of my own future.

The path up Mt. Hood at first seemed to be unmarked, and several times when my memory was off we stepped right into the stomach-churning maelstrom of the invisible disorientation field that covered the area. The effect was more intense right outside the corridor than anywhere else, as if the deadzone was a strip of cloth that had been scrunched up on either side to make a stable way through in the middle.

As we ascended though, I began to notice claw marks in the rocks, similar to how Neshomne had marked the way the invading Portland army should march. It stood to reason that the Advocates would need to be able to get back and forth without having to walk blind each time, and the path was useless to anyone who didn't know where the starting point was. Still, it was unsettling to me how easily I could see the markers once I knew what to look out for. The rebels had relied on no one being able to find the start of their maze. Now that the secret was out, they were in deep shit. I didn't know how many fighters they could field outside of the Shadow Pack, and there wasn't much those three could do against the oncoming force. Bruja was the closest they had to a bruiser now. As good as Bloodrath and Whisper were against a single ironhide, they wouldn't have a chance against an entire horde of them.

With the help of the markers, we made excellent time up the side of Mt. Hood. In addition to providing shelter from the disorientation field, the path had been chosen for the easiest climb. Even so, it would still take hours to reach the eye of the disruption.

Malakhai was inclined to quiet, using all of his concentration for watching the surroundings for any sign of trouble. Although I wasn't wearing the fur like Neshomne, my recent excursion as the stormwolf had left a residual trace of the werewolf endurance in my body, allowing me to keep up with the big critter. He moved far too silently for something so big. It was frightening to think of what the ironhide could do to someone he'd snuck up on.

Despite his attempts to not hinder our speed, Malakhai didn't possess the same supernatural fortitude as his partner and me. Soon we found ourselves waiting for the Blood Judge as he struggled to climb rocks we'd easily traversed. The pale man was worse than a lunger, only able to go short distances before having to catch his breath. The experiments that had created him might have left Malakhai with superhuman speed and the ability to drain the virus off of folks, but it had robbed him of a normal man's endurance.

"Ready yet?" I asked at another one of his frequent stops. "I'm trying to be understanding and all, but we're on a clock. Maybe I should just go on ahead of you two. There's less chance someone will detect me anyway."

"No," Malakhai wheezed. He coughed a couple of times then spat. "I was told to stick with you. That's what I'm doing."

"We've lost at least two hours," I complained. "I know you can't keep up, so why not get back on Neshomne and ride the rest of the way?"

"If we get attacked—"

"The longer it takes to get to the center of the disruption, the worse the danger of us getting hit," I said, cutting him off. "We got a choice here: either you stop drag-assing and let your partner carry you, or we end up still climbing this blasted mountain when Wardenclyffe hits Portland. Even if we're ambushed, you just need a couple of seconds to slide off Neshomne's back. I'll trade those two seconds for the two days it'll take otherwise."

Malakhai grumbled, but he clambered back onto Neshomne. I just didn't understand the man. Most of the time he seemed like a reasonable sort, with a good head on his shoulders. So why the sudden change of attitude on the mountain? Was what the Dragon ordered him to do so awful that he'd waste every minute he could before it was necessary? Was there any chance at all that this mission didn't end with a bullet in the back of my head?

Didn't matter.

Wardenclyffe. Maggie. Sarah.

Suspicion and fear continued to gnaw at me as night fell. The stars above were clear and bright, and the moon that rose was about three quarters full. There was enough light to still see the marks, if only just. A faint glow backlit the trees in different directions from the squall beacons. But it wasn't the ancillary components I needed to smash. The eye of the storm, the nexus, had to be destroyed for my loved ones to live.

According to the stars it was about midnight when we ran across our first piece of debris from Carnegie City. A long I-beam with a jagged end had buried its nose deep in the side of Mt. Hood. Although it had barely been over a year since the salvation city went down, there was already a thick layer of rust over the steel support. Just like Wardenclyffe, the decomposition of Carnegie City had been sped up somehow. It had to be something to do with the constant electrical charge, but I was stumped as to how that could accelerate the corrosion.

We took our time, creeping up carefully now that we were deep in enemy territory. We already knew from the squall beacons that the Advocates had adapted salvaged technology from the wrecked city to defend themselves. It was natural that they'd have their central system somewhere deep in the ruins of Carnegie City. There was no telling what nasty surprises awaited us ahead.

Close to dawn Neshomne stopped, ears pricked up and armored muzzle trembling. He waved us back. Despite the Augmented process damaging his sense of smell, it was still a hundred times better than mine or Malakhai's. There were unseen sentries ahead.

It took another hour of shuffling at the edge of the invisible corridor to pass by the two human guards. We caught sight of them once, smoking and joking as they lay on their backs and watched the stars. The disorientation field had let them get lax. That was going to be their undoing.

Sunrise revealed a long wall ahead made of salvaged brick, metal, and wood. The ramshackle barrier curved around and out of sight both ways without signs of any way in. The first twenty feet or so from the walls had been cleared of trees and big shrubs, giving a clear kill-zone for anyone that didn't have themselves an invitation. There was a single Returned sentry yawning atop the wall, his rifle slung easy across his shoulder. But there was no telling how many more guards slumbered just beyond the wall, ready to bring their guns to bear.

"Damn, I was hoping the two we ran across earlier were the quality we could expect from the rest," I whispered to Malakhai. "With day coming on, I'm guessing there's a fresh set of eyes on the way to relieve our friend there too. So how do we get past the wall?"

The sound of one of Malakhai's guns cocking behind my ear made my heart skip a beat.

"I've got an idea about that, kid. But you ain't going to like it."

Chapter 25

"WHAT ARE YOU DOING?" I whispered.

"Laying my cards on the table," Malakhai answered, standing up. "Come on, get up. Hands in the sky and a smile on your face, young'un. You'll need both to survive in Libertas."

I rose, confused. The sentry still hadn't spotted us, so there was a chance we could get over the wall without him noticing.

Until Malakhai shouted at him.

"Hey, Bobby!" the Judge called out, waving. "Stop dreaming of your latest crush and pay attention!"

The guard's head whipped around. The rifle was off his shoulder and being readied before he saw who was shouting. Bobby relaxed, slinging the rifle back again. An easy smile spread across his face. Just what was Malakhai playing at?

"Mal, you bloody dog, how you been, mate?"

"Seen better days."

"Ain't we all?"

"Mind opening up the gate?" Malakhai asked. "Got a prisoner here that needs to talk to the sister."

"You got it," the guard said with a nod. He reached down and yanked a lever. A moment later there was the grind of heavy gears, and a twenty foot section of the wall broke open along what had looked like just another ragged crack in the ramshackle barrier. Hinges squealed in protest as the hidden gate swung outward.

"Better have Gretta get the oil can down here," Malakhai said to the guard as he marched me through the entrance.

"Sure enough, if I can get her awake at this hour. Neshomne," the man said, nodding in greeting to the ironhide, who returned the gesture.

"What the actual hell, Malakhai?" I whispered. His response was to shove me forward into the Advocate compound, the gun still aimed at my back.

Housed within the wall I'd expected to find a few broken-down attempts at buildings populated by a disheveled and miserable people living in squalor amid the ruins of the crashed city.

I couldn't have been more wrong.

The Advocates had managed to reclaim more of Carnegie City than I'd have ever thought possible. In addition to the mechanism for the wall, there were several wood and brick buildings that were twins of those on Wardenclyffe. There was also a huge structure at the end of the road, dwarfing the others, that reminded me of the giant Library that towered over Wardenclyffe's skyline. Excitement snagged hold of me; Carnegie City had carried the Library of Congress. Had they managed to recover the venerable tomes?

Cuddled up to what I hoped was the library was a decent-sized whitewashed church, complete with small steeple and belfry. Having such a blatant display of faith next to a repository of learning struck my Wardenclyffe-raised sensibilities as blasphemous.

Power cables ran between the buildings, providing electricity to at least twenty of them. Unlike Portland, they were utilizing an alternating system, and their sky wasn't choked with crisscrossing lines. I could feel the maelstrom of conflicting electrical currents just beyond the lines, but here at the eye of the storm it was a gentle tug instead of a slap in the face.

Most of the construction materials were a mix of salvaged wood and newly cut planks, interspersed with scavenged brick and metal. The sweet smell of cedar permeated the air from a half-built house near the main thoroughfare, and I noticed with surprise there was wiring running through the structure. The brick chimney looked expertly laid, and judging by its overall size there was a big family just itching to move in when it was done.

People were just waking up to start their day. It was barely six in the morning, but folks here seemed to be early risers. There were more than a few faces on rails and windows watching Malakhai march me through the middle of the compound.

There was a mixture of Returned humans and Augmented, sometimes together in the same house. Here I saw a small girl being cradled by a massive wrong-wolf that bared his teeth in warning at me, there a woman brushed an ironhide's pelt as it lapped a dish of water. It was a fairly even split between Returned, Fixed, and Vocalators. I'd guessed there would be people who depended on Bloodrath to keep them human in the Advocate settlement, but I hadn't figured there would be so many. The majority were black or native, with a couple of Chinese. But whites were present in a pretty substantial number too.

"I guess not everyone likes Trent's version of paradise." I smirked as we went up the main street.

"You can't begin to imagine," Malakhai said. "Some folk like the Grants play nice and blend in, riding the fence between Portland and Libertas. Others endure the scenic nature of the city to gather intelligence for the resistance. Mind you, I imagine a couple of rats have wormed their way into our ranks. But that's why the corridor through the disruption zone is only known to a select few."

"And you? Why do you bother pretending to side with the Cabal? It's pretty apparent now that you were stalling our climb, holding me back as best you could without tipping your hand. What's your place in all of this?"

"I'm a Blood Judge. These are good people, and they need me. Ain't nothing more to it than that."

"Bullshit," I said, shaking my head. There was an angry edge to Malakhai's words, a warning that I was straying into dangerous territory. "They got Bloodrath for those duties up here, right?"

Malakhai snorted. "I wouldn't trust that bastard to open a can of beans without killing somebody. He didn't get his little nickname 'cause he's bad at spelling. Emanuel earned it with carnage."

"The Advocates don't seem to mind their methods too much." As soon as the words escaped, I knew I'd gone too far.

Malakhai spun me around, sticking a red-gloved finger right in my face. There was wrath smoldering in his scarlet eyes. For the first time I actually felt scared of the Judge. "Watch your tongue, cloud jockey. There ain't a man or woman here that is the same as the goddamn Shadow Pack. People come to Libertas to be human again as best they can. The Pack embraces the very thing that the Cabal claims: that they're animals, not worthy of a place setting at the table of humanity. They act like curs, berserkers, killing without mercy, torturing without conscience. And worst of all, they're cannibals. They give in to the urge to consume human flesh while wearing the fur; shit, they exult in it. There ain't nothing decent about that. And there never will be."

His diatribe in the middle of the thoroughfare had attracted spectators. Faces with ugly expressions poked out of nearby windows. Many on the street nodded along with his words, their expressions hard as stone. There was a weight to their combined gaze, a pressure that told me I'd crossed an invisible line that was sacrosanct. I couldn't keep my peace though.

"You all take the supplies they give you, right?" I countered, turning to meet the onlookers right in the eyes. "You don't approve of their means, but you're happy enough to eat what they steal and rely on them to guard your asses? That's some high-grade hypocrisy right there."

Malakhai cuffed me across the ear, sending me stumbling. My face reddened with a mix of anger and embarrassment, and I stopped just short of taking a swing at him.

"Don't you do that," the Judge snarled. He looked around at the folks circling us, poking a couple in the chest to force them to meet his fiery gaze. "And don't you let him do that to you. He ain't been here. None of his kind ever seen the dirt as anything other than a place to plunder. The city slickers got no idea what it was like, how hard you had to fight and bleed to get what you got today. How bad it is for those still under the lash down in Portland."

Malakhai turned back to me, and for a moment I thought he was going to shoot me right between the eyes.

"Don't you ever let the sky-huggers talk down to you. Not ever. Him and his kind ain't better than you. They're cowards that washed their hands of the rest of us a long time ago."

His words got my back up, and the temptation to attack the Judge was almost irresistible, even with Neshomne towering behind him protectively. I opened my mouth to retort, but a gentle voice interrupted me.

"Please, Brother Malakhai. This is a place of peace and understanding, even for the refugees of the salvation cities."

There was a calm to the voice that doused some of the coals in my furnace. I turned around to see who it was that jumped in our argument. What I saw wiped the words out of my mind like an eraser on chalkboard.

The lady that had spoken was dressed like a Catholic nun. She had a black and white habit, bone-beaded rosary hanging around her neck, and a general feeling to her that fit every gentle bit of the Bible I'd ever read.

But the bandages that covered her hands and arms were stained with blood and pus. Her face was swaddled in the cloth as well, although there were allowances made for sight and speech. Her eyes sparkled green like emeralds, but the pustules and sores that seeped from her forehead and nose threw off any impression of beauty. The nun's lips were pocked and blistered, and every word made her wince in pain.

There was an unpleasant smell of rot and sickness coming from her that the woman had not attempted to mask with perfume. Given how strong the putrescent odor was, any attempt to mask it would have just made it worse, like laying a flower on a pile of crap. Even so, she bore the stink with an air of suffering patience, and something told me she wouldn't take offense to folks holding their noses around her. She was just that kind of person. But the thought of doing so would shame anyone that tried. There wasn't any doubt in my mind who she was; she fit the moniker to a tee.

"Sister Blister," I murmured, enraptured by the walking conflict in front of me. Every bit of her flesh screamed corruption, but she shone like a beacon of light from within. I'd never known that such a soul could be housed in such a body.

"Please," she said demurely, bobbing her head in greeting to me. "I prefer my given name of Marie Teresa Trent. But you may call me Sister Marie, if you so desire."

So fascinated was I by the lovely voice coming out of such a ravaged frame that it took me a moment to fully comprehend what she'd said and its implications.

"You're . . . you're . . ."

She nodded with sadness. "Yes. I am."

Sister Marie, the leader of the Advocate rebellion and one of the first victims of the Cabal's mad experiments, was none other than Dr. Trent's own daughter.

Chapter 26

"BUT I THOUGHT YOU were—"

"Dead?" She asked. "That was not my fate. No matter how my father had wished it was."

My brain raced, dredging up everything I could about her from the depths of my memories. I'd run across Trent's horrific medical journal on Wardenclyffe, where the Tellurians kept it secreted as a forbidden historical document. Trent and the Cabal had experimented on hundreds, maybe thousands, of unlucky folks, most of them blacks and Indians. They'd been trying to perfect a race-specific virus, capable of murdering millions of people they deemed 'inferior.'

They'd captured both my Pa, Thomas Kelly, and the eventual savior of mankind, Nikola Tesla, after the work crew they were part of had gotten infected by an early form of the Wendigo virus. Cut on and poisoned for months and months, they were the guinea pigs that Trent used to make the infection even more virulent. The crazed doctor might have even succeeded in finishing his bigoted disease if his daughter hadn't interfered. The journal had been sketchy on the details, but Marie had been instrumental in helping to free the survivors of the experiments, including both Tesla and Pa.

It had, however, gone on to detail in excruciatingly precise terms how Trent turned on his own daughter as a result, subjecting her to the modified Wendigo strain and forcing her to be a replacement for the escaped prisoners. I didn't know if he'd specified anything else in the journal, because I couldn't force myself to read it past that. I'd figured

Trent had tortured her to death with the experiments. Truth be told, I didn't have the stomach to sit through a telling of her final days.

But here she stood, hale and hearty.

Well.

She was still alive, at least.

As I stared, mouth agape, I saw a quiver under her left shoulder bandage, a small bulge that could only be some sort of growth. A mixture of pain and rapture passed over Marie's visage. She leaned her head to the left, closing her eyes.

The unseen blister ruptured beneath the bandage, soaking the cloth with blood and pus. An unholy stench escaped the bandages, like a corpse long past its bury date had come a'calling. For just a moment I could've sworn I heard something that sounded like garbled moans from the burst pustule.

Marie gave a sigh of contentment and a wince of pain, an ambivalent response that confused me more.

"And you," she said, eyes opening and staring at me. "Are Elijah Aloysius Kelly, although your friends call you Eli. All save for the woman that loves you, who even now suffers under the attentions of my wicked father; the very woman, in fact, who infected you in the first place. You are also the stormwolf, an entity never before seen, a creature that might tip the balance of power between the warring Cabal and Tellurians in either direction. Despite being exiled from your beloved salvation city by the very people you are trying to preserve, you still place Wardenclyffe's safety above that of your own. A noble sentiment, if I may say."

I'm pretty sure a gnat flew into my open mouth as I gaped at Marie.

"You'll get used to it," Malakhai muttered. "Well, not so much used to it as able to hide your surprise better."

"What? How?" That was pretty much the extent of the intelligent questions I could muster.

Marie gave a shy smile. Despite the plague ravaging her face, she managed to look almost cute doing it.

"God speaks to each of us. We need only to listen."

I looked over to Malakhai, more confused than ever.

"She thinks that when her pustules pop, they whisper secrets of the universe to her," the Judge explained through gritted teeth.

"I take it you don't believe her?"

Malakhai gave Sister Marie a long look. "I think she's crazier than a shithouse rat. Miss Trent here is hanging her abilities on some imaginary and invisible father-figure because she's too damn humble to take credit for her own powers. Besides, I figure if God wanted to chat with someone, he might have easier ways to do it."

The small smile never faltered on Marie's lips. "You mean like a burning bush? Or dreams and visions? Mysterious ways are his preferred form of communication, after all."

"Bah!" the Blood Judge said, waving his hat at her like he was trying to fend off the crazy. "I saw enough preacher tents during the Panic to know where that talk ends up. They were the easiest meat for the furbacks and laid the groundwork for the damned Brimstone Riots of '99. Keep giving the all-mighty credit for your own accomplishments and you'll underestimate yourself every time. That can get a body killed."

"But what about her knowing all that stuff about me?" I interjected.

"Oh, I ain't saying she ain't got talents," Malakhai said, putting his hat back on. "Trent didn't just subject her to the Wendigo; she had enough crap run through her system to make what happened to me and the other Judges seem like a cleansing bath in comparison. Ain't no telling how long she's got left to her, or even how sane it left her. Either way, thinking God talks to you when your blisters bust is just too far down the tracks for me to follow."

"Then we will wait for you to find your way," Marie said, bowing her head slightly.

Malakhai threw his hands in the air, exasperated. "See? This is why I hate talking to you about this. Nothing but platitudes and runaround speak! Can't get a straight debate out of any religious types that make a lick of sense."

Neshomne had his tongue lolling out, a doggy grin on his face saying this was a normal feud for the pair.

"Now that we have established your distaste for others' faiths, perhaps we should retire to a less public venue to continue our conversation?" Despite the softness of Marie's tone, there was a steel-hard order behind the words. Malakhai narrowed his eyes and pursed his lips, his pale skin going red with a combination of anger and embarrassment.

But he was smart enough to hold his peace for now.

Sister Marie led us off of the thoroughfare. I managed to hide my sigh of disappointment that we weren't heading for the big library as we traveled uphill. At the end of a small path a steel and wood building squatted like an irksome child determined to sit in the dark away from Libertas. Although it'd been hollowed out and its boiler broken open, it was still easy to tell that the shell of the makeshift house was the wrecked hull of a Thunder Train.

But it wasn't like any Double T I'd ever seen before. Even with the modifications that had been done to convert it into a dwelling, I could tell that its squall tubes and control assembly had been mounted in the strangest fashion when it was still running, at the rear of the train. With that setup any engineer trying to pilot the thing would barely be able to point it in the right direction. Landing would be impossible, as would nearly any kind of real maneuvers mid-air.

The face of the train, which normally housed the sparker assembly, had instead been festooned with heavy iron plates crudely welded into a wedge shape. An opening was cut into one of the plates, in which sat a reddish cedar door.

There were badly-weathered letters across the side of the hull where the train names were generally painted. I didn't need the wolf's nose to recognize the dried brown-black smudges.

This Thunder Train's name had been written in blood.

I hesitated as Marie opened the door and stepped inside, but a gentle nudge from Neshomne propelled me forward into the hollowed-out Double T.

Inside I was amazed to see that light streamed in from skylights above, turning what I'd thought would be a Stygian abyss into a well-lit and homey living space. Marie had hung several brightly-woven carpets around the inside to hide the iron husk of the train's engine. A pang of memory hurt my heart as I remembered how Maude had done the same for the caboose of the *Heaven's Grace*, our home for most of my life. I'd been forced to cut the car free during an ill-fated flight when Omega

Cornelius had pulled a stupid trick that nearly killed us all. A part of me I'd thought long-gone suddenly ached for all the memories lost with that caboose.

The room was too small for Neshomne to enter, so he squatted outside the open door, his big head level with ours. There was a short cot in the corner, barely long enough for Marie to sleep in with some blankets on it, a rickety bookshelf with dog-eared novels stacked within, and a small iron stove where the boiler used to be with a line of cracked dishes stacked neatly on a shelf to the side. The only seat was a stained wooden rocking chair nestled near the stove. The space was tiny and claustrophobic, barely large enough for the three of us to not elbow each other in the face. Warmth emanated from the stove, making it a bit too hot for comfort. Sweat immediately beaded on my forehead.

"My apologies for the temperature," the Sister said, ducking her head and motioning at a pile of blankets in the corner. "I catch chill easier than most. We can leave the door open to bring a breeze for you both. Please, sit wherever you wish. The blankets are comfortable enough, for a while at least."

Marie sat down in the rocking chair, giving a sigh of relief as she did. Malakhai squatted down, not bothering to let his ass rest. The man looked ready to spring forward at a moment's notice, and his demeanor made me uneasy. As for me, the thick blankets of Marie's bed made a decent cushion for my ass as I plopped down.

"Why?" I asked, gesturing around us. "You're the leader of the Advocates; there's got to be better homes than this. Why do you isolate yourself in this thing, up here?"

"All in due time," Marie said. I suddenly realized that all traces of kindness had fled from her tone. The Sister's eyes were too clear, too penetrating. "First, let us discuss your presence in Libertas: you are here to betray us, yes? Father wishes us dead, and seeks to use you as his tool."

"What?" I said, startled. "Uh, no, that's not—"

"Perhaps 'betray' was too strong a word for your tastes," Marie replied with her small smile. It did nothing to dismiss the coldness in her eyes. "To become a traitor, you must first ally yourself with the cause you turn on. I presume too much, it seems."

The woman was good. She'd managed to fluster me with her

directness. There was a forgiving way about her words that made me ashamed without having sinned. The nun habit she wore suited her.

"Look, lady," I replied, trying to gain some verbal footing. "It ain't like I don't agree with you folks up here. But you're putting a hell of a lot of people in danger to stay safe. Even leaving aside my grandma and all my friends being on Wardenclyffe, your little defense system here is going to trade a couple hundred lives for over ten thousand. Those numbers just don't track, no matter how you add them up."

I braced myself for the inevitable rebuke, the argument that it was God's will to save His chosen people in Libertas. I'd been around enough hallelujah-slingers to know what they're whip out of their holsters when their feet were put to the fire.

Marie surprised me by nodding in agreement. "You are correct, Elijah. That would be a selfish and sinful action on our part to trade the lives of thousands for our own safety."

"Wait . . . you're not going to try and justify killing me and watching the cities burn?"

Despite being covered in rancid blisters, Sister Marie was still able to look sickened by my accusation. "What must you think of us? Who could ever accept the murder of so many with any kind of conscience?"

I didn't have any kind of answer. She'd caught me off-guard by agreeing with me.

"It don't seem too dandy to me," Malakhai growled, staring me down. He'd shifted his weight, and I could swear his was about to spring at me. "I ain't about to let the good people on this mountain perish for some strangers that went and hid in the clouds when Lucifer came calling. We've fought and bled for our freedom, for our lives. We've damn near sold our souls to survive. And you want us just to roll over and die because your precious technology backfired?"

I shook my head in surprise. I'd expected to have to argue with Sister Marie, plead with her to turn off whatever she was using to generate the telluric deadzone. And I'd hoped that Malakhai would back me, seeing as he knew not all the people in Portland were assholes, that there were some that hated and worked against the Cabal's rule. The reversal of friend and foe threw a wrench into my mental gears.

"All we got to do is grab who we can from the city and head for the hills," Malakhai continued, as if in answer to my thoughts. His eyes were scarlet and hard, like deadly rubies. "You and the Returned Portland bastards can figure out the rest in fire and pain. Ya'll deserve each other."

"It is not that simple, Malakhai," Marie chastised. She rose, touching the Blood Judge's shoulder lightly before turning to the iron stove. Her brief contact settled him back, but he still had a mean look in his eyes. Marie opened the stove's door, stoking the embers glowing within. Placing a kettle on top, she set out four cups, spooning tea leaves into each before returning to her rocking chair.

"Hell it ain't," the Blood Judge said, waiting until Marie had situated herself again. "Those worthless sky jockeys ain't done nothing but take from the ground since they ran off. I don't got any sympathies for those who don't fight."

"You think it's been easy up there?" I asked incredulously. "We've been living by the skin of our teeth for nearly twenty years! No one even knew there was anyone still alive down here that wasn't wearing fur and howling at the moon, hungry for our flesh and ready to kill us all."

Even as I said it, I realized it was a lie.

When it came to contact with the outside world, there were only two ways it happened for any salvation city. The first was the lightning-quick runs to the supply depots by the Thunder Trains, occasionally supplemented by desperate raiders using homemade balloons and airships to harvest any overgrown crops they could find before the city left them behind. The other was the telepulse, a communication system controlled by the Tellurians that used variations in a salvation city's squall tubes to send code to other cities like telegraphs.

No one was exactly trying to be friendly when the supply runs happened; we had to get in and get out before the werewolves found us. But the messages received via telepulse weren't rushed, weren't under any kind of threat or time limit. The storm prophets monitored the system constantly, which was how we'd known Carnegie City went silent over a year ago. And building a device to surge the tiny variations across the telluric currents wasn't hard; the know-how for it was widespread long before the first salvation city ever lifted off.

"The Tellurians knew," I whispered, the magnitude of the

realization rolling over me like a freight car. "The ground wasn't silent like they told us. There were folks shouting out for help. They knew there were survivors, crying out in the dark. And they ignored them."

Malakhai nodded. "Cowards, the lot of you. The so-called 'Society of Truth' left the world to die. But it took a lot longer than they figured it would. Hell, there were still enclaves of uninfected people around as recent as five years ago, hanging on to life by their fingernails. But even the ones that managed to cobble together a telepulse machine got no answer. The gods of science had abandoned them, left them to get picked off. Until there was truly no one left. Your beloved storm prophets made sure their predictions of doom came true for us down here."

In my mind's eye I could see them. Groups of folks fighting the wolves, making the hard choices as one by one they fell to tooth and claw. How many had killed loved ones infected by the furbacks to keep their dying communities alive, hoping that their sacrifice wouldn't be in vain, that the Tellurians would finally return and save the world? Me and Maude had barely made it off the ground by salvaging the *Heaven's Grace*, and in the process hundreds of people who worked on us with it lost their lives as we fought and protected it. Others hadn't been as lucky. They'd had no hope, no way to get clear of the death that stalked them.

I'd known people hated those that escaped on the salvation cities; it was an inevitable consequence of having to choose some to live and some to die. Maggie and Sarah hadn't bothered to hide their disdain for Wardenclyffe and its residents. But cold logic said it was better to save some than to have all die. The salvation cities couldn't support everyone. There was no amount of hemming and hawing that would change the numbers. Each person ate a certain amount, drank a certain amount, took up a certain amount of space. It had been a necessary evil to leave some behind to save the rest.

Hadn't it?

Finding out that civilization kept stumbling along so many years after the salvation cities lifted off shook me to the core. There was an unspoken accusation in Malakhai's words. Could the Tellurians, or Tesla, or Edison, or anyone, have figured out a cure or a way to stop the disease if the entire scientific community hadn't just packed its bags and soared away? The inhabitants of the cities had stolen the lifeboats, let on they deemed worthy, then kicked away from the sinking ship and watched their fellow humans die. If instead of everyone looking after their own asses we had banded together, could the entire apocalypse have been averted?

"There it is," Malakhai said with a nod. "That look. That awful kick in the gut. Real truth is a cruel bitch, kid. She don't care what excuses you got."

I shook my head, trying to get my footing. There was something off about what the Blood Judge had said, a venom in his words that reeked of hatred and loathing that had nothing to do with the salvation cities.

"How do you know?" I asked.

"What?"

"That last group of uninfected you mentioned. How do you know they'd been calling for help? How do you know when the last survivors went down to the wolves?"

Malakhai lost the hardness in his eyes and stared down at his crimson boots.

"Answer him, Brother." Marie's words were kind in tone, but there was an unrelenting steel to them. The stuffiness of the small room seemed to increase, a smothering wave of heat as Malakhai ducked his head in shame.

The Blood Judge sighed and looked up. "Fine. I know exactly where and when the last of the holdouts were finished off . . . because I was one of the bastards that took them down."

Malakhai jutted his chin out and stared me down, as if daring me to take a swing at his grizzled face. "We captured who we could. It was fast and brutal. The Cabal killed the survivors who resisted. I killed them. We did. Doesn't matter. My hands are as bloody as Tillman's, as Trent's. More than them, because I knew it was wrong. But I went along with it."

"Why?" My voice was laced with revulsion, with condemnation. But, perhaps worst of all, there was something else that cut him like a blade: pity.

"Does it matter? Every man has his breaking point, the spot where he starts compromising his values. Your life, the life of someone you love, an ideal. It's all the same, in the end. An excuse. Once you cross that line, for any reason, it gets easier to go back and forth. You tell yourself that it's for the greater good. But you know you're lying. You can feel it. In your bones. In your soul."

"And you went along with it. Cleaned out the rest of humanity to keep your own ass safe?" The words felt like hammer-strikes as I said them.

"Not just mine," Malakhai whispered. He looked out the door to Neshomne. My heart dropped, and I couldn't help but forgive the broke-down man. He'd committed terrible, unforgivable crimes to keep the person he loved safe.

And I was headed down that same road.

Chapter 27

WARDENCLYFFE AND MAGGIE'S FATE warred against decency in my head.

"But how are they doing it?" I asked, shuddering with dread. "Menlo Station downed the other salvation cities; sure, I'll buy that. The Cabal is a gigantic sack of festering assholes that were running out of test subjects, so them turning on the human race doesn't surprise me. The method, though—"

"Is rather obvious," Marie said. "You've already experienced one Thunder Train smashing into your city."

"The *Shrieking Sally*," I replied, nodding. "Maggie escaped Menlo Station by stealing the Double T with some other prisoners. She didn't want to talk much about her time there, but I got the feeling it was only luck that didn't see her cut on and Broken."

"She has no idea. Now imagine if, rather than a few infected refugees, the *Shrieking Sally* had instead carried a hundred Augmented werewolves in freight cars behind it."

I shook my head. "That doesn't make any kind of sense. Malakhai said they needed uninfected people for their experiments. What use is letting loose a bunch of ironhides on the populace?"

The whistle for the kettle began to shriek. Marie rose and poured the boiling water into the cups. She motioned to the patiently-waiting Neshomne. He was still squatting outside, eyes half-lidded as if fighting off a nap. "Brother Neshomne, be a dear and remind our new friend of the defining characteristics of the so-called 'Fixed' werewolves?"

Leisurely, the gigantic ironhide stretched his mechanical arm into the cramped room. The steel claws on the end of it were like short swords in front of my face. I shrank back against the wall, panic blossoming at the possibility of bladed murder. But Neshomne's limb wasn't threatening me. He was merely reaching out to take the cracked teacup that Marie offered him. He delicately gripped the cup between thumb and forefinger claws.

"Do you see now?" Marie asked, smiling as Neshomne withdrew his massive arm, careful to avoid spilling his tea. "The Cabal may be evil, but they are not stupid. The Augmented are modified in this fashion for multiple reasons, not the least of which is keeping them from spreading the disease. Those that are slammed into a salvation city have their muzzles locked shut for the duration of the assault as well. Outside of direct blood contact on open wounds the Hellions are able to neutralize any defenses without fear of contamination, leaving its population vulnerable to the harvest."

Seeing my confused look, Malakhai clarified. "It's what the Cabal call their shock troopers."

Marie gestured at her cramped home. "And the Thunder Trains they modify, such as this one, they dub 'Hellhammers.' Only they would joke in such a way about murdering the salvation cities."

"The overseers even make it into their own cute little ritual," Malakhai said, nodding. "The Cabal bleeds the Hellion soldiers for the ascension fluid used in the Hellhammers' squall tubes. The final touch is renaming the Double T into something sinister. This house here was once known as the *Devil's Deal*; it was the spear that pierced Carnegie City's heart and brought it down. Not that the ironhides care about any of the rituals, one way or the other. The Talons crank the Hellions' adrenal levels through the roof with the hive collars, sending them into a psychotic rage before they hit the city."

A sharp bark drew my attention to where Neshomne squatted, and with his free arm the wrong-wolf parted his furry ruff. Encircling his neck was a thick band of steel and gears; judging by the irritated flesh puffed up around it, the collar had surgical roots down deep into him.

"Yep, those," Malakhai said with a nod. "Hive collars are the other half of the equation those bastards used to build Portland. Judges keep the white folk Returned, and the collar keeps everyone else enslaved."

"But I saw those on other Augmented when we were walking up here," I said. "The Advocates use the same slavery they vilify?"

"The hive collars are more than simple control mechanisms," Marie corrected. "They hold a supply of silver nitrate that is distributed in minuscule amounts via shunts into certain brain sections, controlling aggression and independent thought. This destroys the area and represses the regenerative effects of the disease, making the Augmented more docile. However, by altering the parameters of the system I've been able to direct the diluted solution in ways that allow the subjects to experience a mind state similar to what they enjoyed before infection, while still suppressing the rage that comes bundled with the disease."

I stared at Marie in amazement. She smiled shyly and bobbed her head in acknowledgment of the unspoken compliment.

"I am, after all, the daughter of the scientist who invented the devices," she said with a regretful shrug. "My father is an evil man, driven by unholy desires, but he cannot help but feel the urge to teach and explain himself to his favorite test subject. I felt the sting of the hive collar long before it rested upon any Augmented neck, thus becoming all too familiar with its effects. While I no longer wear mine, I know more about them than anyone ever wished to. I've had twenty years to learn how to sabotage his goals."

In the uncomfortable silence that followed, she finished pouring the tea and distributed the cups among us. Malakhai grimaced at the bitter brew, but he still sipped it. I was used to horse-piss coffee triple-run through old grounds from the rail yards, so anything fresh-brewed was a rare joy for me.

"The hive collars have a variety of capabilities, even though the Cabal utilizes only the worst," Marie continued, sipping at her tea. "The discovery of Hertzian waves had stimulated scientific research for decades before the apocalypse. Although my father had no interest in such principles of physics, he and the Cabal recognized the potential. They forced an Italian by the name of Marconi into their service before the Blood Panic truly dismantled society; he proved instrumental in developing the hive collars. Marconi discovered a way to manipulate what he came to call radio waves in a fashion that gave remote dominion over the collars to the Cabal."

"The control bracers they wear!" I guessed, blurting out the interruption in my excitement. "That's why the ironhides don't revolt!"

Marie nodded. "Precisely. For any Augmented that does not obey, the hive collars have a kill switch built into them. At any Talon's discretion it immediately injects the entire month's supply of silver nitrate into the werewolf's brain. The result is quite . . . explosive."

My eyes darted to Neshomne in worry. Marie smiled sadly.

"Yes. His kill-switch is still active. Although I've been able to deactivate it for the Augmented residents of Libertas, Neshomne's work with Malakhai means he is subject to frequent scrutiny by Cabal scientists. They would notice the tampering. Nor are we able to bestow the gift of freedom to those Augmented dwelling in Portland. The process for disabling the kill-switch is not a rapid or unobtrusive one."

"We're as useless as tits on a frog," Malakhai grumbled. "Can't save the folks we're supposed to. Get, what, a few free a month? Out of thousands, a number growing steadily each day. They convert them faster than we can liberate them."

Marie sighed with heavy resignation. "We have had this discussion, Brother Malakhai. We must be patient and trust in God's—"

"There's two days left for your miracle to appear before the kid's city visits hell on Portland," Malakhai snapped, cutting her off. "God ain't got the time to sit on his ass anymore."

Sister Marie bit her tongue, masking her irritation with a sip from her tea. With a slight nod of her head she pulled me back into their conversation. "Perhaps he has already sent us the boon we require."

Malakhai snorted in derision. "The young'un? No offense, Eli, but you ain't exactly the Jesus-type we been expecting."

"There's no need to be rude," she chastised.

"Truth might be rude, but that don't make it less true," he snarled, flicking the tea in his cup out the open door and making Neshomne jump back with a grumble. He placed the teacup gently back on her shelf, but there was nothing but iron in his voice when he turned back to us.

"There's hard choices on the horizon, darlin'. You can quote scripture and forgiveness all you like, but there's a reckoning coming. There's no good way through it; best we can do is try to preserve our own. Don't forget: thanks to your would-be savior there, the dogs are marching on the mountain right now. You let him take down the deadzone, and you're just trading the city folks' lives for our own."

With that the Judge nodded curtly, tugging down on the brim of his hat at Marie. He stalked out of the cramped confines of her home. Neshomne huffed a snort of irritation at his partner before sighing and downing his hot drink all in one gulp. The big wrong-wolf placed the chipped teacup down at the doorway and loped off after Malakhai.

An uncomfortable silence stretched between me and Marie, which both of us tried to cover by sipping the tea. After a couple of minutes, I couldn't bear the weight of staying quiet anymore.

"I'm sorry," I blurted out. The bandaged woman just watched me silently, waiting. I screwed up my courage and forged on. "I know it's going to be bad for you folks, but the barrier has to come down. But I'll stay here, with you, for when the Cabal attacks. Malakhai's right about one thing; asking you to trade your lives for strangers ain't right. If me going down with your people to the ironhides can balance the scales a bit, then it's the least I can do."

Marie shook her head. "I will ask no such sacrifice of you, Eli. This is not a situation of your making. Malakhai's attempts to draw you down to the depths of his rage and depression are an artifact of his own guilt. He wants Portland to die in fire and pain; I have no doubt that our tortured friend would arrange to be caught in the destruction as an act of penance for his past. Hating yourself is a virtuous poison. The martyr dies the easiest death."

"So . . . you'll kill the deadzone then?" I probed. "Much as I want you and the Judge to feel good about yourselves, we got concerns a bit bigger than any one person's feelings. Hell, I'd let Malakhai gun me down if it meant getting this done."

Marie finished off her tea without answering, staring down into the damp leaves at the bottom of her cup. Something about how she was acting had my back up, so her answer wasn't entirely unexpected.

"No, Eli. I cannot bring down the telluric deadzone."

It was everything I could do to keep from exploding. My face was hot, and the stormwolf raised its head inside me, a growl on its hollow lips.

"After all that talk, you're just going to—"

"Please," she said, holding a hand up to stop me. Given the dark thoughts running through me right then, that was probably for the best. "Understand me, Eli. I was not saying I do not wish to do as you ask. I literally can not.

"We're not the ones that put up the deadzone, nor can we disable it."

Her admission took the wind out of my sails. I sank back into the blankets with a confused look on my face.

"But it keeps you safe," I protested.

"At most, we do basic maintenance," she clarified. "And yes, it does shield us from the wrath of Portland. Admittedly, we modified the scattered squall tubes from the city to turn them into the protective network as per our instructions. But we didn't know what it would mean, that it could potentially cause so much harm. We were desperate, so we listened to him."

"Who? God? Did one of your blisters pop and whisper some schematics to you? Well ain't that convenient, all that responsibility just bleeding away."

"Please, Eli. I am not stringing you along. And while you may not hold my faith, I ask that while you are in my home you show at least a modicum of respect. Malakhai has earned the freedom of his tongue with sacrifice; you have not."

I lurched up off her bed, and Marie shrank back as if I intended harm to her. Shaking my head in disappointment at her reaction, I instead took three steps to my right, thus leaving the husk of the Double T she called home. There was no sign of Malakhai nor Neshomne outside. Although the Judge didn't agree with Marie most of the time, he'd likely lay me out for what I was about to say to the blighted nun.

"So," I said, turning around and peering into the confines of the Hellhammer. "You want to try again? Do I need to telegraph one of your pustules asking it to take the deadzone down, or is there a flesh and blood scientist to talk to?"

"Neither," Marie replied, rising with a resigned sigh.

"What?"

"It's easier if I show you," she said, stepping out into the summer air. Despite the warmth of the day, she pulled a shawl close as if chilly.

We walked in silence as she led the way up past her home. There was a well-used trail in the woods that led farther up the mountain, toward what me and the girls had figured out from the map was the crash site of Carnegie City. I couldn't see the wreckage from here due to the forest, but when I'd been the stormwolf, the scar the impact had left on the side of Mt. Hood had been unmistakable.

After about a quarter mile of climbing Marie's breathing became labored. Belatedly I realized that being full of disease hadn't granted her the werewolf's stamina; she was just as sick and weak as any other plague victim. I offered my hand and arm for her to lean on.

She took them with a grateful sound. My nose wrinkled at the fetid stench coming from her bloody bandages, but I kept my mouth shut. What happened to Marie wasn't any of her fault. I'd be damned if I'd make a victim feel bad about what her torturer did to her. The clean white bandages were becoming bloodier as we hiked. It was obvious that she wasn't used to such exertion. After a mile, every movement seemed to hurt her, and I heard whispers from the bandages as blisters burst and ran putrescence from her effort.

My stomach was churning, and it wasn't from the rank smell from my guide. I'd vacillated between wanting to throw up and being fine my entire time on Mt. Hood due to the effects of the telluric violation on the wolf infection. But it'd never been this bad before. The very air seethed with rancid energy. Even the forest showed signs, with blackened tree trunks and leafless branches interspersed with the deep green and brown of life. It was as if the mountain itself couldn't decide whether to live or die.

I was just about to suggest that we turn back when we came upon a clearing. What trees that remained were crookeder than a bought politician, all angled sharply away from where Carnegie City had crashed into the mountain.

Someone had cleaned up the loose wreckage of the salvation city, carting it down to build Libertas. But there was plenty of the steel superstructure left that had simply been too big to move, rooted deep into the ground like skeletal weeds that refused to be uprooted. At the center of the broken metal web was one of the giant squall tube clusters that kept salvation cities aloft. The smaller tubes on the sides had been smashed open by the impact, but the center tube, the big one, was still intact. It rose nearly fifty feet in the air, and at least that much had been buried in the mountainside by the crash. Cables attached at various points to the gigantic squall tube and ran off in the direction of Libertas.

It was the center of the squall network I'd seen from the sky, shrouded in electricity and glowing bright blue light from the fluid inside. Fulgurites, sand blasted into jagged glass by lightning strikes, spread from the base of the squall tube like a petrified root system, evidence of the danger of approaching too close.

My stomach roiled from being at the heart of the disruption. The ravaged energy that the deadzone was sucking from the telluric streams thrummed underfoot. I'd known there was no way to destroy the energy of the telluric streams, but I hadn't been able to piece together where it was going until now. The answer had been as plain as the nose on my face, or, more accurately, a rock in my boot. The electromagnetic energy had been sucked in and contained in the biggest storage shed anyone had ever conceived of.

Mount Hood itself was being used as a battery to store the violated telluric energies.

I didn't need Marie to explain why she couldn't shut the deadzone off. The Advocates had used cranker generators to feed energy into the main squall tube, lighting it up and allow it to power the makeshift network they'd set up through the modified tubes scattered across the mountain. After it'd sucked in a certain amount of energy though the process had become essentially self-sustaining. There was no way for Libertas to shut it off because they weren't supplying the power anymore. Worse, it wasn't like that energy was just local. The telluric streams connected to each other throughout Earth, pulsing and flowing with the life force of the entire planet.

It was a terrifying abomination. The network would continue draining the world's telluric energy until the mountain was full to bursting . . . and then there'd be nowhere for all that energy to go but out. The resulting explosion would be incomprehensible. If the boom didn't crack the planet in half it would still likely wipe out every living thing on Earth with the shockwave from the detonation.

"Why would you do this?" I whispered, the enormity of the danger washing over me.

"We did not know," Marie replied, eyes downcast. "We were desperate, under siege. The Cabal were breathing down our necks, and a solution was proposed. No one understood what it would mean, or the inevitability of the science behind it."

"Who?" I asked, tearing my eyes away from the brightly glowing squall tube. "Who did this? You lot don't got the know-how, and there's no Tellurians in your ranks. Who figured out how to do this?"

"A man with . . . intimate knowledge of the machinery. The person who I brought you to see."

"Who?" I demanded again, resisting the urge to shake the answer out of her. My brain was still unfolding all the possible devastation that could come of this jury-rigged apocalypse. It was steadily terrifying me more and more.

Marie endured my tone without flinching, as if she felt she deserved my wrath. She raised one bandaged hand, pointing to the giant squall tube that would eventually explode and take the whole world with it.

"Him."

I turned back to the column of encased light, confused. Hesitantly I approached it, peering into the glowing depths, trying to see what Marie was pointing at. Electricity crackled around me as I drew nearer, striking the scarred dirt I walked over. The fused glass of the fulgurites cracked under my weight, threatening to slice me up if I fell into the petrified lightning.

Something moved within the depths of the squall tube.

Fascinated, I pressed on into the glowing death. Tiny sparks jumped off me as lightning arced to me, burning flesh and hair. But electrocution didn't matter. There was no pain, no world of physical agony or the smell of my own skin frying. All that mattered was the thing moving within the squall tube. It was impossible. There couldn't be anything living in there, let alone . . .

The human hand I'd seen before pressed against the inside of squall tube, as if beckoning me closer.

The glowing liquid within the tube hid the hand's owner. I pushed closer through the surrounding energy field. Lightning played across my skin, leaving scorch marks even as the energy burned my bones and organs. Still I felt no pain. I had to see. I had to know.

A man's face slowly appeared from the swirling blue liquid, its contours gaunt. It was twisted into permanent agony, and the eyes had long ago burnt out of their sockets. But somehow I knew he could see me. He knew I was there.

And he was screaming for help.

Thunder boomed as the mother of all lightning bolts struck right in front of my feet, throwing me back from the squall tube with the force of a giant's punch. I landed in a smoking heap twenty feet away. Marie rushed over, concern writ large across her face.

"Who . . . who was that?" I gasped out through cracked and bloody lips.

Marie looked up to where the man had been. There was no sign of a hand or face now. But she'd seen it too.

"That was Andrew Carnegie, the Alpha of Carnegie City."

Chapter 28

"ELI, STAY STILL," SISTER Marie said as she tended to my smoking wounds. "If you move you'll . . . wait, what's going on?"

I felt the stormwolf in my blood, re-energized by the lightning strike I'd just endured. The ethereal creature rushed through my veins, mending the blistered flesh.

"I'm a werewolf, remember?" I muttered. My attention was still focused on the giant squall tube. "Is Carnegie still alive in there? He can't be, can he?"

"No infected retain their regenerative properties in human form," Marie replied matter-of-factly. "My father went to extreme lengths to attempt to bridge that gap once he realized white men could be affected by the Wendigo virus. And yes, to answer your question. Andrew Carnegie thrashes within a prison of his own making, caught within a never-ending nightmare."

I shook my head, trying to understand. The discovery that Tellurians used their own blood to craft the ascension fluid used in squall tubes had been a startling revelation, but this was beyond the pale.

"Is he trapped in there?"

"Yes," she answered. "Based on what I've been able to piece together, there is an Alpha sealed inside the primary squall tube of every salvation city. They martyr themselves for the good of all. It is the reason that the Tellurians given custodianship of the regulation of the cities are, at most, Betas. Of course, the original hierarchy of the storm prophets was set forth by the first Alpha of their order: Nikola Tesla."

It only made sense that Tesla, the founder of the Telluric Society of Truth and genius behind most of their inventions, would serve as its first Alpha. The Serbian had been dedicated to science and mankind in a fashion seen once in a generation, if that. Sacrificing everything from personal health to monetary gain, the man had burned bright toward an enlightened age of humanity. But he'd gone missing before the launch of the first salvation cities, right when . . .

"Tesla was the first Alpha," I repeated, finally comprehending all of the implications. "He imprisoned himself in the main squall tube for Wardenclyffe. To save us."

Marie nodded. "That would make sense. I suspected as much once I learned the truth behind the Alphas. But God does not always provide the clearest explanations. The revelations sent to me were more of how to re-purpose the squall tubes. Ancillary facts were often missing."

"God told you to do this?" I said, waving to where Carnegie's glass cylinder had been connected to the power network. "He wanted you to create a bomb that could blow a hole in the world?"

Marie shifted her shoulders, as if trying to wriggle out of a bear trap. "We do not always understand His plans."

I pursed my lips and raised my eyebrows in disbelief. It was becoming obvious why Malakhai held her faith in such scorn. Disaster or blessing, to the faithful every outcome could be justified by the easy mystery of the divine. In the end, the believer gained nothing other than comfort from such explanations. For some, that was enough.

But not for me.

"So if God told you how to build the deadzone, why doesn't he go ahead and use your blisters to tell you how to disable it?"

Marie's eyes darted back and forth, distraught. I felt like an ass pressing her, but it was a fair question. Her faith had led her into a dead-end alley.

"And let me guess," I continued. "The lightning bolts from Carnegie's squall tube are still a danger to you. So no one can get close enough to disarm the system, even if you knew how to."

"We tried breaking the glass by shooting at it . . ."

I barked a laugh. What most groundhogs didn't realize was that the glass of squall tubes became harder than steel once it had a current running through it. When I'd been a brakeman aboard the *Heaven's Grace* the majority of my job had been clambering around on the outside of the Double T chipping the black salt deposits from the tubes with a pick and hammer. The crust was a natural result of the ascension fluid being energized, like condensation from a cold glass on a hot summer's day. Without in-flight maintenance the residue would build up, eventually covering the squall tube and preventing the lightning from striking the fluid within. Although true salt would cause an explosive reaction if it came in contact with an active tube, the blackened crust produced by the tubes was nonreactive, a perfect insulator that would cause a Thunder Train with lazy brakemen to fall out of the sky.

"Where is it?" I asked, realizing I'd just stumbled on the solution. At Marie's confused look, I gestured to the patch of fulgurite-strewn earth around Carnegie's prison. "The black salt? If we can get hold of enough of it, we can break the feedback reaction going on with the lightning."

"Alpha clusters don't generate the deposits you're referring to."

It was my turn to look confused.

"At such a size, the salt would become unmanageable," Marie explained. "No salvation city in the world could stay aloft if they went through the same physical processes as their smaller cousins."

She was right, of course. The squall tubes Thunder Trains used were about the size of my thigh, but Carnegie's tube was the size of the *Heaven's Grace* itself. If there had been accumulation it would have taken a team of brakemen working nonstop to keep it functioning.

"So how does this work then?" I gestured at the Alpha squall. "It doesn't matter how inconvenient facts are; a stronger reaction should produce a stronger effect. Just because we don't want it to doesn't mean physics stops working."

"As I said, God does not explain his ways," Marie said. She raised a hand to forestall any response from me. "However, I am not claiming the Alpha tubes as miracles. I've had several months to observe and theorize. I believe that the squall tubes function much as living organs. Without fresh blood or, in this case, ascension fluid, the arteries clot and clog. I imagine that is the source of the black salt that condenses on the tubes. There's one way to avoid that in biology, and I imagine the Tellurians employed a similar principle."

"There has to be a fresh supply," I breathed, understanding what she was getting at.

In my mind's eye I could almost see the schematics of how the prophets had accomplished it. To keep unspoiled fluid in the gigantic tubes, the only choice was to use a living subject. An infected human, their arteries sliced open from bow to stern to keep the blood circulating. The chemicals of the bath would be the same that the Tellurians used to formulate the finished ascension fluid. Likely the victim's veins were held open in perpetuity by surgical shunts so that there would be free fluid exchange between his body and the chemicals within the tube. If there was a shred of humanity in the engineers, the man inside would be anesthetized by the formula. They'd be trapped in a waking dream for the rest of their lives.

Or a nightmare.

I shuddered to think of Carnegie, of Tesla, caught in such a tortured half-existence, floating within a vat of their own chemically-altered blood for eternity. What kind of man would volunteer for such a procedure? I didn't know if I would've had the guts, even knowing how many lives it would save. The people who became Alphas deserved the adoration and worship the Tellurians showered them with. They were the closest thing to saints that scientists would ever have.

But it still left the problem of how to shut off the deadzone.

"A telepulse signal?" I mused out loud. "No, that won't work. He's not conscious. It'd be like whispering to a comatose patient."

Carnegie wasn't consciously controlling the field. The poor bastard probably didn't even realize what was going on, or how he was being used.

"Precisely," Marie said. "And there's no way to know how his mind would interpret it even if you could. For all we know, it could worsen the problem and accelerate the degradation of the telluric streams."

There was nothing else for it, then.

"We have to crack open the Alpha's squall tube."

"That's impossible!" Marie objected. "Eli, as tough as you think the glass is from the energizing process, it is exponentially worse than that.

I've spent the last few weeks working out the calculations. As the size increases, so, too, does the modified strength of the tube. There's not enough dynamite in Portland and Libertas combined to crack that glass."

Marie shrank back from the savage grin I gave her.

"Sister, we got something a lot more dangerous than TNT. And it's just itching to be let loose."

Within my skin I could feel the beast rumbling. The shocks I'd received from Carnegie's tube had resurrected the stormwolf; it snuffled around in my mind like a dog that smelled steak.

Sister Marie backed away, but it wasn't out of fear. Her eyes were unfocused, as if she saw something far away. A whiff of rancid air carried from her, and her shoulder bandage grew wet with blood and pus. She shook her head, muttering something.

"What's wrong?" I asked, but she couldn't hear me. Whatever revelation she was receiving had trapped her attention.

"All dead . . . all . . ." she whispered. I couldn't tell whether she was trapped within a vision, or if she was trying to warn me.

"Well, that's encouraging," I grunted. "Doesn't matter what your pustule just told you; if I don't do this, there'll be a lot more corpses around than just ours. Your God can kick up a hissy if He wants, but unless He gets off His ass real quick-like we're out of options."

Taking hold of the wolf in my mind, I stepped forward again. There was no use hesitating. If I didn't jump right in, it would just get harder to take the leap.

The crunching of the fulgurites sounded like the drum-roll of an executioner as I approached Carnegie's squall tube. There was no sign of the man in the glowing liquid within. Tangled cables led to the base of his prison, the abandoned artifacts of the original Libertas effort to harness his power to defend themselves.

I picked up the ends of the cables and gritted my teeth.

This was going to hurt. A lot.

Before common sense could stop me I sprang forward, yanking on the cables to slingshot myself into the side of the squall tube.

Lightning crackled around me with a blazing intensity, as if angry at the few feet I'd stolen. Bolts of blue-white light arced out from the glowing tube, whipping me again and again for my hubris. There was a thunderous boom, and the full brunt of a colossal lightning strike lit me up from the inside out. I writhed and screamed, blood sizzling in my veins. The shockwave blew out my eardrums as the force of the hit sent me tumbling back.

Then, suddenly, the pain disappeared.

The stormwolf roared as it rose up.

My senses twinned, caught between the anchor of my body and the energy construct that was trying to wrest itself free of the confines of skin. This was nothing like when Trent had forced me into the stormwolf the first time. Without the alchemical cocktail he'd injected into me, the body was refusing to let go of the spirit. I'd been betting that there were traces of the drugs still in my system, that I could force the voltaic critter out again by shocking myself enough.

The gamble had failed.

It felt as if my mind was being ripped in two, one part anchored in the physical world while the other tried to escape to the ethereal.

Looking down with the stormwolf's eyes I saw my flesh and blood body writhing in an agony that the ghostly form could not feel. The stormwolf's torso was rooted to my body's chest by smoking tendrils. My galvanic form crackled and roared as it tried to pull free. Frustration lanced through me as I struggled; Carnegie's squall tube wasn't ten feet away. Sporadic energies struck the shaking form of my physical body from the charged tube, but the electricity wasn't enough to fully energize the stormwolf. Whether because I didn't have the Cabal chemicals running through my veins or it just hadn't been enough time since the beast was last free, the result was the same.

I was stuck.

A high-pitched keening made the stormwolf's ears prick up. Although I managed well enough to see and hear within the energy construct, there was a range of sight and sound available to the beast that no living thing had access to. As I ceased trying to pull free of my real body and focused in on the frequency, the keening clarified.

It was a man weeping.

The crying was coming from Carnegie's squall tube. To the stormwolf's eyes the glowing blue fluid within was translucent. Instead of a mass of blinding light, there were waves and currents of electromagnetic energy forking out from the body within. Carnegie served as both the source and terminus of the arcs. He thrashed within his prison, screaming, howling, the same as he had for the last twenty years. The old robber baron was in a personal hell, his mind fractured and lashed by the lightning. As I listened to his keening, I realized the truth with a growing sense of horror. Carnegie wasn't trapped in a nightmare.

He was awake.

The electricity would not let him rest, denying him sleep from the moment he'd entered the fluid nearly two decades ago. Worse yet, floating in the brine of ascension chemicals had extended his senses beyond the limits of his body. His cries rippled through the stormwolf's form with terrible knowledge. The squall tube was more than his prison now, more than a container into which his life had been poured. It was as much his body as his flesh. He had become one with the city that he'd sacrificed so much for. Carnegie's mind raced through the ascension fluid, through the steel, through the glass.

When the Cabal destroyed Carnegie City, he'd lost the last shreds of his sanity in the agony. It was as if his body had been torn apart, mangled, and scattered across the mountainside.

And he'd felt every bit of it.

The stormwolf could hear him, could sense his pain. Pleading, begging, weeping.

Crying out for the mercy of death.

Snarling with popping sparks, I forced more of my soul into the energy construct, putting an iron will behind it that I didn't know I possessed. The twinning of senses faded as I became the stormwolf completely, giving myself over to the creature. I reached out toward the squall tube with crackling claws, straining. I would not, could not, surrender. Carnegie deserved better.

With a sickening lurch I felt my physical body's suction give way.

The stormwolf surged forward, exhilarated by the sudden freedom. But the ethereal cords that still connected the phantom beast to my normal body were thicker this time, more visible. They pulsed with magnetic attraction, threatening to pull the stormwolf back down to the fleshy depths.

Taking control of the beast's mind, I focused on one goal, narrowing my world down.

With a growl that caught Carnegie's fragmented attention, the stormwolf flew at the gigantic squall tube.

Relief washed through the man's keening despair as the voltaic beast penetrated the barrier glass, modulating itself to pass through the wall. Carnegie concentrated his mind back into his floating body, his arms raised in supplication as the stormwolf drew back its ghostly claw for the killing stroke.

The world flashed white.

"Eli? Eli!"

My vision spun, bleeding colors into each other while an earthquake rumbled through my mind. The touch of Marie as she shook me felt alien, unnatural, as if my skin was a crusted cocoon of filth. I tried to answer her, but the words slurred together.

Reality started to settle down, with discernible shapes and sounds that didn't taste like pain.

The ascension fluid within Carnegie's tube had gone black, turning from a glowing blue to a murky abyss. Lightning sputtered wildly around the clearing, arcing miles into the air, flashing bright across the underside of darkening clouds. An ominous boom thundered from the sky as it answered.

Deep within my body, the stormwolf ducked its head in fear.

The ground trembled, sending pebbles and underbrush scattering across the slope. With a snapping sound, the fulgurites around Carnegie's tube shattered all at once, spraying glass in every direction.

Marie shielded me from the cloud of shrapnel with her body. A fetid smell escaped the bandages on her back, and she grimaced as she hooked one of my arms under her shoulder.

"You should . . . run," I whispered. It was all I could muster. The stormwolf had sapped my energy; just staying conscious was a struggle.

A wave of telluric energy arced away from the earth, causing my insides to flop around like a dying fish. It reared up like a wild horse, bucking out of the ground, violently released by its jailer's passing. The land screamed at me as the other telluric flows followed suit, surging past their broken bonds. The sky glittered strange colors, and animals across Mt. Hood screeched in terror.

My eyes rolled back in my head and I spasmed when the wave passed through me. Marie collapsed under my weight, her legs buckling as she felt the passing of the dampening field. The world hollered out in protest as the mountain let go of the vital energies imprisoned within. Blessed darkness smothered me before the screaming could shatter my throat.

There was no telling how long had passed before the waking world intruded. Marie was calling my name with panic in her voice, shaking me. When my eyes could focus I saw she was covered in dirt and twigs, her bandages grimed up by her own bout of seizures. I'd lay odds there wasn't a living thing within a hundred miles that hadn't broke down and frothed at the mouth with the release of the telluric streams.

The church bell down in Libertas began ringing frantically. I didn't need to hear the shouts and curses from town to know the reason for their panic. Although the world had been incapacitated briefly by the release of the earthen forces, events were unfolding now with a dread inevitability.

Without the telluric deadzone, the army of Cabal ironhides waiting at the foot of the mountain would be swarming up the slope toward Libertas.

The war had begun.

Chapter 29

CRASHING SOUNDS CAME FROM the forest.

"They can't be here already," I said, the grogginess making my head feel numb and heavy. "The feedback pulse didn't knock us out for that long. Did it?"

Marie struggled to answer. The blighted sister had been hit hard by the telluric backlash. Although I wasn't in much shape to do any protecting, I limped over to put my body between the leader of Libertas and whatever was crashing through the forest toward us. The wounds from my suicidal run into Carnegie's tube had mostly mended, although I'd likely have some nasty scars from it. Still, I was thankful for what healing the stormwolf had left behind.

The closest tree exploded as the huge figure of an ironhide slammed through it.

"Damn it, Neshomne!" Malakhai hollered from the Fixed's back. He had a leather-clad arm up to protect him from the shattered wood slivers and was spitting out leaves. "I told you to watch where you're going!"

The gigantic wrong-wolf swayed drunkenly, nearly falling over. Neshomne's ears folded back as he forced himself to stop before barreling into us.

Malakhai slid down from his partner's back with a reassuring pat. "Sorry, furball. I know you're doing the best you can."

Neshomne grunted in acknowledgment, tongue lolling out of his lupine head. The Fixed stumbled in place, as if he was trapped on the deck of a storm-tossed boat. I felt sorry for the big critter; the backlash from breaking the deadzone was affecting him far worse than us.

"What the blazes did you do, kid?" Malakhai growled, his scarlet eyes glittering with anger. "The whole town went deader than a whorehouse on Sunday. Scared the living shit out of me."

Marie shook her head with confusion at the Judge's immunity to the backlash, but I figured it out pretty quick. "He's not infected like the rest of us," I explained.

Marie's eyes were starting to focus better, and she managed to nod in understanding. "It would appear that the closer a subject is to being fully transformed the greater the effect from the electromagnetic back-blast that resulted from shutting off the field."

"Shutting down . . . shit, kid, please don't tell me . . ." Malakhai trailed off, catching sight Carnegie's dead squall tube behind us. Although it still sparked with errant lightning, the fluid in the glass prison was losing the last of its sputtering light. The opaque fluid hid the dead body floating inside.

Andrew Carnegie was finally free of the nightmares.

"How dare you?" Malakhai bellowed, pulling his twin revolvers and leveling them at me. "You stupid, arrogant, self-righteous—"

"Put those away," Marie interrupted, adjusting her nun's habit and standing up straight. Although the blood and pus from her recent revelations had yet to dry and she reeked of rot, there was still a commanding elegance to her demeanor. "Elijah did as he thought was right. And I happen to agree with him."

"But Libertas—"

"Will survive," she said, cutting him off again. "We at least have a fighting chance, which is more than what Wardenclyffe would have had were Elijah to heed you. Regardless, what's done is done. We must focus on the here and now."

The Blood Judge shook his head, but he had an air of resignation. He'd fought against me ending the deadzone, but I half suspected it was more out of a habit of being cantankerous than because he really believed it was the right thing. As much as he'd argued for letting Wardenclyffe die, I didn't think the man could have lived with himself if I'd listened.

"Fair enough, Sister," Malakhai said, holstering his weapons. "You two got any kind of plan, or are we just praying for mercy until the ironhides get here and end us?"

Marie and I shared an uneasy shrug.

"Figures," the Judge sighed, swinging back up on to Neshomne's back. He held out a gloved hand to us. "Well? Grab your asses and get on! We got to get down to the town hall. There's a few ideas wandering round there. Including the ravine charges."

"No!" Marie objected as she accepted his help up on to the wrong-wolf's back. "We will not condemn them to such a fate."

"Better them than us," Malakhai grunted as I hopped up behind Marie. "Hang on; the furball is a bit unsteady still after the pulse."

Neshomne snuffle-barked in irritation.

"What?" The Judge said with an affectionate silver-fanged smile. "Drunk rattlesnakes slither straighter than you."

The big Fixed ignored his partner's jibe and took off down the slope. The breathtaking pace worried me until I realized Neshomne was being as careful as he could on our descent. There were still a few oak trees that didn't fare too well, but the ironhide managed to keep from flipping over and smashing us into the ground.

Libertas wasn't doing much better. There were more than a few wrong-wolves dry-heaving and swaying too much to stand upright. The Vocalators tending them were steadier, but they still staggered every once in a while. Even the Returned humans were lurching around like sailors on shore leave. The backlash had caught the town unawares. Could the Augmented at the foot of the mountain recover quicker with the Talons tending to them? Were they even now smashing their way up here?

"How long will it take them to get here?" I asked as Neshomne skidded to a stop in front of the church. I looked longingly at the library, but the town's Returned seemed to be congregating in the house of worship. "The enemy, I mean. Your bosses."

"Never going to get off that horse, eh, Eli?" Malakhai drawled, sliding down from Neshomne's back.

He reached up and grabbed Marie by the waist, gently setting her down on the ground. He went to help me down the same way, but I waved him off and dropped to the ground. The stormwolf had absorbed part of the escaping energies, and I'd wager I was feeling better than pretty much anyone outside of the Blood Judge himself.

It wasn't fair to keep riding Malakhai about his sins. He'd done the best he could with what he had; his greatest crime was losing hope and giving in. Anyone could make that mistake. As for the army of the damned coming for us, I knew better than most that the Cabal's army of Augmented were slaves, kept in line by more than just lash and fear. As long as they wore the hive collars, there was no possibility of revolt. It was a death sentence to try.

"If we could just talk to the Augmented, reason with them, maybe we could get them to drag ass like you did," I said.

It was Marie's turn to shake her head at me.

"You're making a basic mistake, Eli," she said. "They're not just motivated by the Talons' control bracers; they have had their mental chemistry altered. It's a natural consequence of my father's experiments on restraining their impulses. The hive collars operate on a theory of limited brain damage. All they have to do is to reduce the flow of diluted silver nitrate to the sections of Augmented brains that controls aggression, allowing the werewolves' natural healing to take over. As they climb the mountain, the Augmented become less and less controllable. More feral and wild."

"You sound like the Cabal," I said, restraining my temper. I held the door to the big building open for her by habit, but what I said next made her hesitate accepting the courtesy. "Anybody that ain't white is dangerous, right? More prone to going savage and primal?"

"It's not that," Marie objected. "It's the nature of the disease and its progression, not the people who have been infected."

I turned my back on her and went into the town hall ahead of her. What she said made sense, but it hit a sore nerve. I'd seen too much justified even on Wardenclyffe with similar arguments. Folks like the Wallaces worked to instill the idea into other people that anyone that wasn't lily-white was just a beast in human skin, waiting to break free the moment the good pasty folk took their eyes off of them. That the Cabal had used mad science to make people fit that mold pissed me off as much as anything else. It didn't count as being right if you forced your victim to conform to the prejudices you used to justify stripping them of their humanity in the first place.

Walking into a church, seeing the cross on the wall and the pews, was a strange experience. Wardenclyffe didn't have any churches left, not after the Brimstone Riots of 1899 that brought down so many of the other salvation cities in righteous suicidal frenzy. The houses of the holy on the salvation city mostly used their bells for alerts and their pews for storage these days. While there were still quite a few religious people aboard, they mostly kept to small groups in their cramped homes. No one particularly bothered them, as long as they weren't trying to throw other folk off of the flying city.

I'd never felt the pull to God myself, but there was something about the simple Libertas church that made me want to speak in a hushed voice and tamp down the temper that was rising in me. Realizing that just made me set my jaw tighter though and hold on to the anger. Maude didn't raise me to be anything other than stubborn and independent. Damned if I was going to let whitewashed walls and a cross control how I felt. The fact it was trying to seep into me was enough to raise my hackles at the taste of God that permeated the church.

The pews had been pulled into a semi-circle around a big map tacked up on the wall, with the pulpit pulled off to the side like an abandoned professor's lectern. As Marie entered, the Returned filling the seats murmured among themselves with a hopeful buzz. Wrong-wolves squatted on mechanical limbs alongside the pews and outside, and several Vocalators had already given themselves over to allow the lupine monstrosities voices. More than one of the faithful had a Catholic rosary, kissing the baubles as Sister Blister walked down the center. Despite the reverence they showed her, the benedictions she whispered on each as she passed were heartfelt, private words that only reached the ears of those that needed it most.

Letting the anger at religion fester in me, shield me, I shouldered my way up the side, earning several hard stares from the people I jostled on my way. I didn't want anything to do with their belief, so I refused to follow in Marie's footsteps. Their faith wasn't mine. It was hard to trust a believer. There was no telling when fiery rhetoric might make them abandon all sense and ethics. They were acting all peaceful now, but give them a target and God's permission and atrocities were inevitable. They'd do near anything if a bible was smacked when the order was given.

Like burying immortal creatures in an avalanche.

There wasn't anything I'd ever encountered to indicate that starvation, thirst, or suffocation could put down a furback. By wanting to lead the enemy Augmented into a ravine and collapse it on them, Malakhai would consign them to never-ending torture. I had to give Marie credit though; at least she stood firm against the plan.

But from what I was seeing drawn out on the map, pragmatism might have a head start against the sister's morality. Red marks indicated the location of the Cabal army that had gathered down slope, with estimated numbers from scouts printed next to them. The number took me aback.

"A thousand Augmented?"

"Worse than that, Eli," Malakhai drawled, pushing through the townsfolk to the map. "That's just the first wave, the Fixed. Trent sent the order out for all the farms and cranker mills to send their slaves along. Even with some of the less enthusiastic citizens like the Grants holding back, there's at least another thousand or so Broken heading here as reinforcements. Likely more. That ain't even counting the ones too busted-up to fight on the front lines that can still be lashed into a frenzy as a last ditch attack."

Marie took a sheet of paper from a mousy lady with downcast eyes. The sister cursed softly, her eyes narrowed.

"How many?" Malakhai asked her, resignation lacing his voice.

"Twenty-seven."

"Twenty-seven what?" I asked. "What are you two discussing?"

Malakhai picked up a blue pencil. "Twenty-seven Augmented fighting on our side." He made several notes on the map around the Libertas border. "The rest of them are unfit for one reason or the other. Machinery broken, injured on supply raids, and a couple who just plain ain't got the guts to tussle with their kin. Most of the Vocalators and Returned are willing to take up arms, but there's only a handful of rifles and pistols between them. This goes the way we're thinking it will, there'll be men and women with pitchforks fighting Augmented werewolves outnumbering them ten to one. Those ain't just bad odds; that's a few miles out into impossible."

The Blood Judge turned back to me, his face as stony and impenetrable as the mountain we stood on. "Too bad we didn't have more time to prepare. Might have gone a bit better for us if we'd known you were going to obey the Cabal and bring down the only protection this place had."

My face grew flushed, but I shook my head. "Just because I had the guts to make the call you couldn't don't mean you're better than me, Malakhai. If you ain't got another way it could have gone that didn't end with Wardenclyffe in flames, I don't got to listen to a blessed thing you say. So shut your fanged mouth. I'll be damned if I stand here and let a coward lip off to me when his spine took to the hills long ago."

My Southern had come blazing through. I knew full well the magnitude of the danger I'd put Libertas in. But I'd had a choice. And I made it.

There was an ugly air in the room as my words soured in townsfolk ears. The realization was rolling through the gathered folk like a putrid cloud: I was the one. I'd killed Libertas. And now they all knew it.

The crowd teetered on the edge of violence, with several of the wrong-wolves growling. One had raised half up off his hindquarters, and there was no mistaking the rumble from Neshomne outside. Given I'd just taken his beloved partner to task, I wouldn't lay odds on him being none too friendly to me.

A slow and steady sound broke through the rising murmur of anger.

Applause, from a single set of leather-clad hands.

"Bravo," Bloodrath said, stepping through the doorway into the church. "I could not have said it better myself."

Whisper followed her father in, as did the patched-fur figure of Bruja. The witch-wolf crinkled her snout at me, as if catching a whiff of something foul. She placed a metal-clawed hand on Bloodrath's shoulder, grabbing his attention.

"Something bothering you, *chère?*" he asked, his skeletal face turned up to her quizzically. Bruja nodded at me, rumbling a deep thrum of a growl.

"Interesting," Bloodrath said, cocking his head at me. "She appears to recognize you, child. I must admit, there is a particular rat scratching the back of my neck when I look your way. May I have the pleasure?"

"It don't matter who he is," Malakhai interrupted, stepping in front of me with a hand on one of his revolvers. "You ain't got no business here, Reaper. Move on back to the shadows, where you and yours belong."

Bloodrath sighed, clucking his tongue in reproach against his death's-head teeth. "Now, now, is that any way to treat a fellow acolyte of the blood? Libertas is our town as well. We feed it, as we in turn feed on it. Of course we would come to you in your hour of need."

Marie laid a bandaged hand on Malakhai when he tried to pull his pistol. The Blood Judge's jaw worked as if he was trying to chew old jerky, before turning away with a frown, weapon still holstered.

"You do have impeccable timing, Emanuel," Marie said smoothly, covering the grunt of displeasure from Malakhai.

"Ah, my thanks, mistress," Bloodrath said with a bow. "It is always nice to see your father's training in logic supersede his example of emotion."

Marie gave a humorless smile, gesturing for the crowd to make way for Bloodrath and Whisper. Bruja settled down at the door, trading murderous glances with Neshomne.

Although I'd expected the outcast Judge to get a cold reception, there was a peculiar feeling of relief permeating the crowd. If there were monsters to be fought it helped to be reminded you had a walking atrocity on your side.

"So this is the end, n'est–ce pas?" The skeletal man peered at the map with eyeballs naked of both lids and humanity. Bloodrath turned to Malakhai with an accusatory glare. "Why are you still here then? Do you not have an army to lead to oblivion?"

"They don't want to blow the ravine," the other Judge replied, his distaste at being allied with Bloodrath writ clear on his face.

Bruja barked a derisive laugh from the doorway.

"She has the right to it," Bloodrath said. "Are you back to the silly notion of their lives being equal to ours, Sister? Surely you have abandoned such whimsy by now?"

"Marie's not the only one holding on to a shred of her humanity," I said, jutting my chin out. "She don't stand alone in trying to be decent."

If he'd had eyebrows Bloodrath would have raised them. "And who are you, that your word and morality should stand in consideration against our lives, child?"

"I'm the man who brought down your deadzone," I replied, gritting my teeth at the wave of hostility that surged from the townsfolk in the church. I could nearly see them tying the rope into a noose. "Elijah Aloysius Kelly. I've met the Cabal monsters in their den and spit in their faces, seen what you're facing in person. I've also seen your crimes, Reaper. There ain't that much difference between you and Trent. Neither one of you got the first clue of what it means to be decent. So who are you to question anyone's ethics?"

Bloodrath grabbed Whisper's arm as she lunged for me, spinning her around into a fatherly hug that also pinned the girl's arms firmly to her side. His gentle voice was at odds with his appearance, but there was a dangerous edge to his words that made Bruja's ears perk up.

"I do not recognize you, child. So how is it that you can render judgment upon me and mine with such certainty?"

It was my turn to smile and give a mocking bow.

"I'm the one that interrupted your feast and killed Judge Tillman. I am the stormwolf. And he's just itching to meet you again."

Bloodrath stood silent for a moment before doing something surprising.

He laughed.

The townsfolk in the pews looked at each other with uncertainty, their shared malice toward me broken by the Judge's strange behavior. Bloodrath released his daughter, who stood by him protectively, her hand firm on the modified Vocalator brace that would release her devastating voice.

"You are a treat, *mon frère*," Bloodrath said, clapping me on the shoulder hard enough to make me wince, still chortling. "It is good to see Marie fit with a companion as delusional as she! Still, we will play by your rules until you realize how useless your honor is. Not that we'll win either way, of course."

The tension in the air drained away somewhat, only to be replaced with dread from the assembled crowd. Bloodrath didn't care what stipulations we were holding to; he'd already accepted Libertas and the lives of all the Advocates were lost. If anything, he seemed to revel in the idea, as if dying were the crescendo of a symphony he'd enjoyed for too long.

Bloodrath turned to the map showing our hopeless situation and held up his hand as if toasting it.

"Shall we go meet the glorious doom awaiting us all, then? Death is a jealous mistress, and it is impolite to keep her waiting!"

Chapter 30

THE SKY WAS ON fire.

Sheets of greenish light raced across the sky, flickering like a bonfire in a tornado as they danced between the dark clouds.

Malakhai whistled in appreciation. "Well, ain't that something? Haven't seen one of those since I was up north-ways a few years ago."

"What is it?" I asked, entranced by the shimmering curtains of light that fought the sunlight for dominance.

"Aurora borealis, if I remember it right," Malakhai said. "Never thought I'd see it this far south. It'll make for a pretty sight come dark, assuming it stays around that long. The light show has something to do with magnetic fields and the like. Must be from you breaking the deadzone."

I winced, his jibe hitting its target. If the ethereal effect was created by an electromagnetic phenomenon, then it had to be a result of letting the telluric streams loose from Carnegie's hold on them. Although I hoped the fireworks show above was the worst result of my actions, I'd begun to suspect something else was wrong as well. My guts were churning like a storm was already raging, but the thick clouds from the backlash hung heavy in the sky without rain or lightning. The only thing that moved in the still air was the dancing emerald of the aurora.

Standing atop the ramshackle wall that encircled Libertas, we were able to get a good vantage point across most of the side of the mountain. There were guards with pistols and rifles posted every thirty feet, and the twenty-seven Augmented that were battle-ready milled behind us on the ground, awaiting orders. It would have been an inspiring sight if I hadn't known what was climbing the mountain toward us. The futility of the situation was finally settling in, tightening my stomach with fear.

Malakhai had taken the reins of the ramshackle army, enlisting me as his second in a bid to keep me safe from the irate townsfolk. I wouldn't have blamed them if they'd lynched me on the spot, but with Marie and both the Blood Judges backing me the residents kept their hostility confined to angry glares and mutters.

Bloodrath and Whisper stood sentry next to me and Malakhai, with Bruja patrolling outside the wall. Even though the citizens of Libertas appeared to tolerate and, in some cases, idolize them, the Shadow Pack was content to keep their distance. I wasn't sure if it was some kind of deal the Judges had hammered out between them, or just a different way of thinking that made the Pack seek isolation, but I was glad of it. Although Libertas had benefited from the Pack's savagery, I was pretty damn sure they'd have recoiled in horror had they seen the spectacle with Tillman. There was little doubt in my mind that the Shadow Pack had committed other crimes just as bad. A body don't glorify in cannibalism and torture unless they been down to the abyss and shook hands with the worst in them.

"Yes, yes, the lights are very pretty," Bloodrath said, waving a dismissive hand at the beauty lacing the sky. He then pointed at the shape of Wardenclyffe where it floated on the horizon. "But the question remains, child: will your precious city send anyone to help us?"

I pinched my eyes closed in frustration. "Look, I told you before. Even if they wanted to, the telluric streams are still too volatile for anything to fly. I'd lay odds they'll try, but don't count on anything any time soon."

"Try, eh?" Bloodrath sniffed dismissively through the cavity that had once been a nose. "*Mon dieu*, child, is that the spirit of creativity and fortitude that has kept your kind in the clouds for twenty years? As fond as I am of watching the end of the charade of life, I rather enjoy kicking at death as she approaches. Without your Tellurians we might as well salt our hides now so the meat goes down easier for the beasts."

"There won't be any help coming from the cloud jockeys,"

Malakhai muttered. "Ain't either of you noticed? The city's changed course. They're running from the fight."

I shook my head in instant denial, but Wardenclyffe did seem a bit smaller than it had before, as if the city was receding.

"It's physically impossible for them to flee back the way they came," I objected, as much to myself as to the Judge. "If a salvation city tried to backtrack on its telluric stream the feedback would break it apart like balsa wood in an earthquake."

"That's as may be," Malakhai said. "But what about switching streams? I didn't say that they were going backwards. Just that they ain't getting any closer."

Again, I grunted in denial. "There weren't any tributaries that could have supported a city. It was pretty much a straight shot here along the only course available."

"You are right, child. There *was* only one course before." Bloodrath cast his lidless eyes to the aurora over us meaningfully.

I caught myself before flat-out telling him it was impossible. There weren't any Tellurians around to say one way or the other, and all my knowledge was based on hearsay and hands-on experience. Was it possible I'd somehow altered the flows around Mount Hood and Portland? Since I hadn't been present before the deadzone went up, there was no way to know.

"Well," I replied, crestfallen. "Huh. Shit."

"An accurate summation of the situation," Bloodrath said, nodding.

Malakhai scratched at his muttonchops. "Well, that tears it then. No choice left. We blow the ravine."

He cut me off as soon as I opened my mouth to object.

"I don't care what Marie thinks," he said. "Our backs are against the wall, and I'll be damned if I let her squeamishness take Libertas down without a fight. If it makes you feel any better, I won't be making it out alive either."

"Stop trying to kill yourself," I replied, my frustration mounting. "Just because you want to make up for—"

"Shut it, kid. That ain't what it is. My past got nothing to do with having to bury the trigger lines to the dynamite deep so the squall network wouldn't set it off."

Bloodrath nodded. "Indeed. We discovered the folly of bringing uninsulated explosives to Mt. Hood the first week the field was live. One stray spark and boom. It took us nearly two weeks to find poor Bruja a replacement arm."

"So how do we set it off then?" I asked.

"There's no 'we' to it, kid. The dynamo box with its plunger is at the top end of the ravine. I'll lead what wolves I can into the trap. Hopefully enough to turn the tide."

"No," I said, shaking my head.

"*Mon dieu*," the skeletal Judge said angrily. "Do you not understand—"

"Malakhai won't be the one to trigger the charges," I interrupted. "I will."

My assertion brought the Blood Judges to a sudden confused halt.

"I'm not a fool," I explained. "Nor am I a selfish prick. Libertas is in danger because of my choice, because of my love for my kin and friends. I'd hoped Wardenclyffe could help out, but that don't look like it's going to happen. That don't leave us much wiggle room."

"You'd cross Marie without a second thought?" Malakhai asked, a sneer of disdain creeping across his pale face.

"I suspect not, *mon frère*. Hear him out."

"She wants to defend folk, to carve out a spot for hers using love and tolerance," I explained. "But sometimes you got to have a good man do a bad thing to clear the way. I wanted to keep it above the board, but Wardenclyffe changing directions breaks our hope. The ravine is the only way now."

"A compelling reason to ignore Sister Blister's wishes," Bloodrath said with a skeptical tone. "But why volunteer to do the betraying yourself?"

"I don't know how many ways I got to say it before you hear: this is my fault. I'm the one that pulled the trigger. I'm the one that gets to try and fix it with my blood. If there's a stain to be borne for treason, it's mine to bear."

Bloodrath bowed to me as if at court, accepting my explanation. But Malakhai still looked like he didn't trust me.

"Do not fret," Bloodrath said, clapping Malakhai's shoulder

jovially. The other Judge looked like he'd rather be bit by a leprous rattler. "I and mine will accompany our young prince here on his noble quest."

He put a single red-gloved finger under my chin and turned my head to meet his gaze full on. The crimson irises glittered, and a worm of fear slithered in my belly.

"And we will kill him if he shirks the duty he has taken on."

I jerked my head away, but the gaze lingered on in my soul.

Malakhai's jaw worked as if chewing old leather. "This all right with you, Eli?"

I heard the real question in Malakhai's voice. He didn't trust Bloodrath, and despite his anger at my choices, he wasn't about to hand me over to the cannibals without getting my word on it.

"It's fine," I said, steeling my voice to keep the quaver away. The Shadow Pack could hound me if they wanted; I wasn't going to try and squirrel out of the deal.

If I was lucky, they'd be stupid enough to hang around for the explosion. There were more than a few demons I could bury in the dynamite's landslide.

Malakhai stared hard at me for a moment before slowly nodding. "As you say, then. Neshomne and me will ride hard for the Cabal army front. There'll probably be a Talon leading it, but those lab-bound bastards know nothing about tactics. I should be able to convince him I've been scouting the way. You remember where the ravine was on the map? Good. I'd be obliged if you gave some sort of signal before you bring the mountain crashing in, but if it comes down to it, you bury us right along with the Cabal troops. You got that?"

Not trusting my voice, I nodded. Malakhai gave a long warning look to Bloodrath and Whisper, which they studiously ignored, before letting loose a heavy sigh. He called Neshomne over and vaulted to the big wrong-wolf's back. He rode down the line of the wall calling out final instructions for the defenders. After one last backward glance the Blood Judge and his mount plunged into the forest on the other side of the clearing, riding hard to meet up with the army he intended to betray.

"Toodles," Bloodrath called out, waving a dirty handkerchief in mockery. He turned to me, dabbing it to the corners of his lipless smile.

"Well, now that dear papa has ridden off to the war, shall we go play with high explosives?"

I didn't bother answering, instead sliding down the ladder to the ground. Bruja appeared at the edge of the forest, gazing at me intently through the open gate.

"I'm afraid she is rather particular about who she allows to mount her," Bloodrath said with a disturbing giggle, motioning the witch-wolf to him. She bounded to a stop in front of us, her eyes locked on mine with clear hostility.

"You do have the stamina to make it, do you not?" The skeletal Judge asked me as he lifted Whisper up on Bruja's back. The girl took hold of the patched fur as her father swung up behind her.

Bruja took off in the direction of the ravine.

"Come, Eli, run, run!" Bloodrath called out from ahead. "You wouldn't want people to think you were going back on your word, would you?"

I broke into a jog toward the woods, watching my step as I hit the underbrush. The last thing I needed was to sprain an ankle or break a leg. Something told me that Bloodrath would gleefully put me down like a lame horse.

It felt good to run again. Without the deadzone gutting my senses, I was able to stretch out my mind as well as my legs. The forest was easier to navigate than I'd thought. I could feel the stormwolf energizing me, running through my legs and eyes as I picked my way across the landscape like a mountain goat. Bloodrath tried to engage me in conversation several times as Bruja loped ahead, but I concentrated on my breathing and my footing, ignoring him.

We made good time, and it only took a couple of hours to reach the ravine, even with having to double back due to the terrain. Heavy overgrowth and rockslides blocked any access except by coming in from below, a box canyon on a smaller scale. But that just made it a more effective trap for the enemy. Bruja wasn't even breathing hard under her stitched hide, and neither Bloodrath nor Whisper showed any signs of discomfort from their ride.

I, on the other hand, was panting like a dog in an Alabama summer. Although the beast within had lent me his senses and a portion of his stamina, it had been a couple of days since I'd gotten any shuteye, and my belly was rumbling for food and water. The tea I'd spurned back at Marie's seemed awfully tempting now, and I wouldn't have turned my nose up at a cracker or two.

Bloodrath tossed me a canteen from his belt.

"Inside, you will find the courage you need," he laughed.

When I unscrewed the top whiskey fumes hit me like a prizefighter. The wolf inside wrinkled its muzzle in disgust, but the burn as it went down felt good. My empty belly roiled as the liquor hit, but I refused to retch it up.

"Ah, you drink like a man, *mon frère!*" Bloodrath said, catching the canteen after I threw it back. He saluted me with it before taking a pull off it himself. Through translucent skin and muscle I could see the brown liquid slosh down his throat; it was nearly enough to bring what I'd drank back up of its own accord.

"There lies your path to glory," he said, motioning up the ravine. "About a half mile up is a small overhang, under which sits a tree as gnarled and dead as the Dragon's soul. Nestled within its roots is the dynamo box that will set off the fireworks."

"You're not going in with me?" I asked, caught between disappointment and relief.

"Sadly no," Bloodrath replied, swinging back up on Bruja's back. "We have our own engagement. *Monsieur* Malakhai will need assistance to herd his flock into the jaws of Mother Earth. We will serve as bait for those who rush to the trap, and a final mercy to those who do not."

"You'll be outnumbered a hundred to one," I said. "Even if half the army is trapped by the ravine, there'll be more than enough left to kill you."

Bloodrath shrugged, as if I'd told him that rain was due tomorrow. "Such is life, child. If our time is done, so be it!"

"What is it about you damned Blood Judges and trying to get yourselves killed?" I asked, scorn lacing my words. "Don't you think Whisper would like her daddy to live? Or, hey, maybe even herself?"

I'd expected another chilling laugh or joke, but Bloodrath was deadly calm.

"Lives of service, even ones as twisted as ours, end the same way for the true believers. The will that keeps a body alive through the transformation process is one that inevitably turns in on itself. And if you think I would leave Whisper to face this world without her father then you are more of a fool than I'd suspected."

The Shadow Pack considered themselves already dead; they were just waiting for the killing blow to catch up with them. In a strange sense, it made them free from worry. They were able to do anything to anyone without conscience, knowing that their judgment day was already writ in blood. Apathy to their own existence made them strong, if only for a moment in time.

"I won't wish you good luck then," I said. "Just make sure the tally makes Satan howl before you're done."

"And you, *Monsieur* Kelly!" Bloodrath shouted as Bruja reared up, roaring. "Bury their dreams of massacre with their bodies!"

Waving with mad abandon, the skeletal Judge and his family of killers rode off into the trees. Despite their bravado and apparent trust in me, I felt the Shadow Pack's unseen eyes on my back as I turned to climb the ravine. The feeling didn't fade until I was several hundred feet in, well beyond sight of the forest.

The cloudy sunlight didn't filter too well down into the deep shadows of the crevasse, and what rays that did penetrate were tinged with an infernal tone by the flickering green aurora high above. The bushes were gnarled and twisted things that fought each other for what warmth the day held. To my right, the natural earthen wall rose up over forty feet. It was a hundred feet to the other side, and the opposite wall was even higher. Damp soil made a muddy slush of the ground as I tore it up with my boots. The sides of the ravine felt like they were ready to fall in at any moment without the help of the explosives hidden in their depths. Loose dirt and rocks were barely held back by a tangled network of exposed tree roots, slimy and slick with moisture.

Time didn't seem to have meaning in the twilight of the ravine, and it was difficult to tell how long the trip was taking. Panic started to nip at my heels as I fought through the muck. How long until the Cabal army caught up? The wrong-wolves moved much faster than me over the land, and Bruja's reluctance to give me a lift had cost precious time. Something told me that was exactly what Bloodrath had counted on. It meant less time sitting on my hands and second-guessing the promise to martyr myself.

I was exhausted when the broken form of the dead tree rose up before me. I'd taken to trudging with my eyes downcast to catch sly roots before they could trip me, and nearly ran into the gray goliath. The tree's hide was scarred by lightning strikes like lashes on a slave's back, and it had taken a section of earth with it out of spite when the land above had given out. Although it was long dead, the arboreal husk seemed to emanate an aura of malevolence.

It felt like a morbid violation as my hands groped around under the tree's tangled roots, as if I was trying to get under a ghoul's skirt. Soon enough I found cables that led to a bundle, wrapped in oilcloth and nestled in a dry spot under the dead roots. Dirt and squirming beetles clung to it as I pulled the package out.

Unwrapping it revealed an old wooden dynamo box, with the detonation wires coiled round like a serpent. It was heavier than I'd expected. The wires hadn't been put on the leads yet, but it was a simple task to strip the ends and twist the exposed copper around them. The plunger was flush with the box; I'd want to leave it in place until the time came to detonate the dynamite hidden in the ravine walls. Settling back as best I could, I let the tangled roots of the dead tree hold me close.

There wasn't anything to do now but wait.

After the first hour, I started feeling like a damn fool. Here I was worried I wouldn't beat the Cabal army to the ravine, and yet there was no sign of them yet. I'd not counted on how long it would take Malakhai to make it to them and convince them, nor the travel time back up the mountain. Or was it worse than that?

What if they didn't believe him? What if they'd just killed him out of hand, and even as I huddled here in the shadows Libertas was being torn apart by the mechanical monsters?

Doubts and fears plagued me, and was almost a relief at the end of the second hour when I heard the first of the hunting howls. They had a metallic reverberation, and soon a mighty chorus of them filled the ravine. The echoes were otherworldly, haunting, raising a chill up my spine.

I pulled the plunger of the dynamo up with a rattle, ready to slam it down as soon as I saw the first of the Augmented. They'd be on me in seconds. The time for fear was almost over, and there was a strange sort of liberty to the feeling. No more running. No more hiding. No more guilt.

The end to all my problems was coming in fast.

Chapter 31

ALTHOUGH MAUDE HAD NEVER taught me much about religion, I knew enough that when the end was in sight, you had some mumbling to God to do. I didn't rightly know any prayers, but a good cussing-out for the divine bastard that had let loose the furbacks on the world seemed a bit more appropriate than any pleas for final mercy. If I was to come face to face with the Almighty, he had some explaining to do.

Looking toward the shimmering heavens for the final prayer of heresy, I saw something I hadn't expected.

Hope.

There was a familiar comet of lightning and flame streaking across the aurora-filled sky. The object changed course erratically, buzzing low over the tree line before arcing up at the last minute to avoid a crash. I didn't need to see the man clinging to the back of the contraption to know who he was looking for.

Me.

The *Bantam* jerked across the sky like a catfish wrestling on the line as Henry maneuvered it across the chaotic telluric streams. He'd probably figured out I'd been successful at bringing down the deadzone, although he had no way of knowing the specifics. Hell, seeing Portland, a thriving city with apparent humans and mechanical werewolves serving them should have made him second-guess his eyes. He'd have been drawn to the mountain, figuring it as the center of the telluric disruption I'd been fighting. It was a shot in the dark, a desperate attempt to find me before Wardenclyffe flew out of the *Bantam*'s limited range. Maybe he thought he'd pick me up, bring me back to the city. Maybe he just plain wanted to see my ugly mug again.

Either way, there was no chance he'd discover me down here in the ravine. It was for the best, anyway. I didn't want the temptation of safety when I'd promised so many folks I'd die for endangering them. Just didn't seem right to covet hope when I'd stolen it from others. But then another thought hit me.

Maggie and Sarah.

If I could somehow get Henry's attention, pull him down to me, I could try and convince him to go rescue the Butler sisters. Although Maggie would lay me out for thinking of her as a damsel in distress, the girls still needed help. No matter how strong a person was, once in a while everyone stumbled and needed a hand. There was no telling what condition Maggie was in now, whether Malakhai's treatment had managed to stave off the final werewolf transformation or not. Even if it had, there was no chance Trent had the common decency to continue letting Blood Judges attend to the infection. No doubt he'd use Maggie to draw me back in to enslave the stormwolf.

I closed my eyes, reaching down to the voltaic beast inside.

The stormwolf was drained, exhausted. But there was still power there. Unlike the other infected in the world, my curse refused to leave me in peace when the moon was hidden. So, I might as well use the blasted thing.

With my eyes shut, the stormwolf's senses strained to take over. The black nothingness of my sight had energy patterns streak across it, twisting and surging with the electromagnetic currents of the earth. The more I let the wolf rise, the stronger the false-light became, until the world seemed as vibrant and alive as a Tesla coil. The forest and mountain became ghostly shadows while the electricity of the world flashed brighter and brighter. I didn't need blinder goggles anymore: the beast had that covered.

Under the stormwolf's ethereal sight the trail of the *Bantam* in the sky became as solid as rails. The machine itself felt strange and foreign. Man's machines might measure and use the telluric streams, but they were as out of place as an oil slick on water. As I focused in on Henry and his experimental mount, I noticed something else. Something wrong.

The *Bantam* was injured.

Henry was fighting desperately to keep his invention airborne. It rolled over before he could right it, nearly throwing him off as it bucked and fought him.

I probed deeper, reaching out with the stormwolf's senses for the machine, and found the problem. Two of the *Bantam*'s squall tubes had been damaged. The steel-hard glass was fractured and leaking ascension fluid. But there was another injury, one done to man and not machine.

Henry had been shot.

I felt the disruption in his energy pattern as he held one arm tight to his side, stemming the bleeding as best he could. But his life force was draining, the pattern of the wound becoming more chaotic by the moment as he strained and fought. It was only a matter of time before my friend bled out while looking for me.

The wolf inside me rose groggily as I whipped it, my desperation and love for Henry giving me control I'd not known I possessed. The voltaic phantom resisted, but I took hold of the stormwolf's ruff with my mind, shaking the bastard until it did as it was told.

A moment of clarity seized me, an omniscient view of Mt. Hood and all the living things clinging to it. For a split second I could see how far out the Augmented Cabal army was, the Libertas defenders huddled behind their wall awaiting death, and the speed and course of the *Bantam*. And I felt fear.

Henry was going to smash into the side of the mountain.

Desperation fueled my will as I forced a portion of the stormwolf's essence out, manipulating the invisible energies of the world. The telluric currents in the area were still malleable, like wet cement, and although it was drying fast it could still be changed.

I screamed, both in the real world and the one I envisioned in my head, as I forced the stormwolf out into reality.

Darkness threatened to claim me as the world flickered. But I'd done it: I'd changed the course of the *Bantam*. I opened my eyes, tired beyond reason. The world of the telluric streams faded from my vision, replaced by a pounding headache and drab reality. The ravine pressed in, echoing the howls of the ironhides headed into the trap. I barely had the energy to check if I'd really changed the *Bantam*'s trajectory, rather than hallucinating it. There was mixed relief and dread when I understood just how successful I'd been.

The *Bantam* was headed straight for me.

The stormwolf snuffled in annoyance within my flesh, burrowing deeper to avoid my desperate grasp. He'd be no help now. I'd asked one too many tasks of him, and the galvanic ghost was done with me. I was empty, the bullets shot, the coal burnt away. There was nothing left.

Henry fought the controls of the *Bantam*, weaving back and forth over the course I'd set him on. Two pieces of the vehicle broke free and spun away before detonating with devastating explosions. Henry must've been able to wrench away the damaged squall tubes. But would it be enough to give him back the lost control?

In the scant seconds left to me as the *Bantam* bore down on my position, I realized with horror that I was still holding the primed dynamo in my hands. It was too soon. If the residual electricity from the *Bantam* struck it, there'd be no need for the plunger; the TNT across the entire ravine would detonate immediately, burying both of us and only catching a few of the incoming Cabal army.

I yanked the leads away from the dynamo's box, wrapping them back up in the oilcloth and shoving them under the roots of the tree. There was no way to know if that was enough insulation, but it'd have to do.

Henry managed to put the *Bantam* into a nosedive toward the ravine about a hundred feet down the slope. The lightning-shrouded comet slammed into the ground with a hideous crunching sound, sending up a sheet of earth and underbrush. It bounced off the earth like a stone skipping water, crashing back down only twenty feet away. The next skip was shorter, as was the electricity arcing off the machine.

I threw myself to the ground as the *Bantam* flew over my head by scant inches, smashing into the dead tree behind me. The ancient oak caught the vehicle with all the gentleness of a sledgehammer as the comet blasted apart the deadwood with the sound of a tidal wave crashing onto shore.

The force of the crash landing sent me tumbling, pelted with the splintered remnants of the ruined tree. My head was spinning, and blood clotted my vision as I struggled upright. Small fires littered the ravine. The *Bantam* had come to rest in the middle of the destroyed tree.

Henry wasn't moving.

I fought to keep my balance as I got up and headed for my friend. He was slumped over the machine's controls, the back of his bald head an unhealthy pale shade. I couldn't see much more of him than that, as he was wearing the Tesla coil-laden generator on his back that Tellurians donned when they expected a fight and needed to power their arc bracers. The coils sputtered as I approached, leading me to wonder if the generator had been damaged in the crash.

"Wake up!" I slurred, reaching out to shake him. "Damn it, Henry, get your ass moving! Don't do this to me!"

A low moan escaped his respirator when I pulled him back from the controls into my arms. I damn near wept in relief. Pulling the mask off revealed the tell-tale signs of werewolf infection that all storm prophets hid, the hideously mutated mouth full of razor-sharp teeth. I yanked his blinder goggles off as well, exposing his too-blue wolf eyes to the meager sunlight filtering down into the ravine.

"Ow," he muttered, weakly trying to pull the goggles back down. "Lemme lone. Tired."

Ignoring his protestations, I forced him upright as best I could, slapping his cheeks.

"Get up, you lazy bastard," I said, shaking him. "We got to get you out of here before the ironhides overrun us."

As if in answer to my fear, the metallic howls of the Cabal army rang across the ravine. They were close, well within the trap now. This was a dead end, in more ways than one. Malakhai and Bloodrath had chosen their battlefield well; even Augmented couldn't leap free of the ravine.

Henry was still incoherent, muttering gibberish while swaying back and forth drunkenly in my grip. What sense he'd possessed had been knocked loose by the crash.

The *Bantam* still sputtered, electricity sparking over its dented frame. Despite the force of the impact, the electromagnetic field surrounding it had blunted the damage. About half the squall tubes were still lit, but the vehicle's batteries were broken open and leaking acid out the front. There was no way of getting it airborne under its own power.

An idea grabbed hold.

With the howls of death at my back, I fell to stripping the Tellurian weapon's cabling off of Henry like a starving man at a feast. My hands flew over the restraining bolts and wiring, relying on my innate skill at mechanics to enact the half-formed plan in my head.

It only took a couple of minutes to wire the Tellurian arc generator into the *Bantam*'s system, but it felt like an eternity. The sound of the approaching Augmented had become deafening in the confines of the ravine.

Henry was still insensible, so I had to grab the controls of the *Bantam* around his limp body, nestling up close to the live coils. The hair all over my body stood straight out from nuzzling the generator pack, but there wasn't anything to be done about it. The shocks were going to hurt. A lot.

"We ain't going steady or nothing," I whispered to Henry, fighting back the urge to giggle maniacally.

It was hard to see the controls proper around his body, and I only half-remembered watching him pilot the vehicle from before. After a couple of false starts, I managed to get the *Bantam* to shudder to life, groaning as it tried to wrench itself free from the dead tree. Balancing the thrust from the remaining squall tubes was like playing the piano with my hands greased up.

"This way, men! We'll get those bastards yet!"

Malakhai's voice carried over the barks and snarls of his Augmented army, a note of desperation in it. The Blood Judge knew how long the ravine was, and exactly what was waiting at the end. I hadn't given him any kind of signal, and he likely figured I'd abandoned my post, leaving the suicidal detonation of the dynamite to him.

But I couldn't just let Henry die.

Maggie and Sarah's predicament had never been far from my mind either. Having the telluric streams flowing again meant it was only a matter of time before the *Purity's Pride* launched from the Tombstone's grounding trestle. Even though I'd held up my end of the bargain, I held no illusion about Trent being a man of his word. Promises were easy to say and even easier to break for that kind of lowlife.

A deafening roar behind me sent chills up my spine. I twisted in the saddle to look my death in its eyes.

It was Neshomne.

The giant, white-furred Augmented and his partner had pulled ahead of the army, leading them from the front. Malakhai clung tight to the back of his ironhide as they rounded the corner. The Judge's eyes widened in surprise at seeing me.

"Hurry up!" I shouted at him, waving him closer. "I think this thing has enough juice, and I've mostly figured out the controls, but you got to move your ass!"

Malakhai put heels into Neshomne's side, encouraging the Augmented to run as hard as he could. All the while the Blood Judge hollered back to the army dogging the pair, encouraging them onward to their doom.

The *Bantam* whined in protest as I energized the squall tubes with more power from the jury-rigged generator pack. Painful shocks snapped across my cheeks from how close my face was to Henry's back, but I held on tight. The vehicle shuddered and shook as I wrenched the controls back and forth, trying to free it from the dead tree.

"What the hairy hell is this thing?" Malakhai wheezed as Neshomne slid to a stop below. "Actually, no, screw that. Where's the dynamo box? I didn't figure on getting out of this alive, but I'll be damned if I let the whole plan go to shit just because you lost your balls."

If my hands hadn't been so busy working the controls of the *Bantam* I would have smacked myself. I'd been so preoccupied by the appearance of hope that it'd blown all my other thoughts off course.

"Down there," I nodded to the tree, "under the roots. But forget the blast-box; just grab the wires. We got something better than a plunger."

Confusion warred with anger in Malakhai, but fear came from behind to win by a nose as the first of the Augmented Cabal army rounded the ravine's corner. Slavering and full of blood lust, the mechanically-enhanced werewolf crashed forward, wild-eyed and savage, a mass of teeth and claws behind him as the others followed. The

Blood Judge burrowed desperately in the roots of the destroyed tree, looking for the detonation wires.

"Grab him, grab this thing, and hang on!" I shouted to Neshomne as I yanked the controls of the *Bantam* back.

The giant ironhide barely had time to latch a claw on the *Bantam*'s hull before the vehicle burst free of the wooden tomb of the tree, blowing apart what was left of the poor oak. Neshomne's other claw snagged hold of Malakhai's black duster. The wide-eyed Judge held the detonation wires with a flabbergasted look on his face as he was yanked off the ground by his mantle.

The squall tubes studding the *Bantam* screamed in protest as electricity surged through them. Neshomne and Malakhai's weight were far too much for it, but I shoved more and more energy into the tubes. I danced a fine line between overload and life as the vehicle strained to lift us all. One volt too much and it'd set off a chain reaction in the squall tubes, blowing us all to kingdom come.

A stray bolt arced from the *Bantam*'s squall tubes and caught the exposed copper of the wires in Malakhai's hand, sending a spark through the detonation lines into the dynamite lining the ravine.

Hollow thunder boomed from the root-encased earthen sides of the crevasse, deep and resounding as if unseen giants battled. Dirt and fire sprayed out as the buried charges exploded down the line.

Howls of fury and pain were buried along with the jaws that uttered them as the *Bantam* rose shakily above the chaos, the avalanche nearly taking Malakhai's boots with it as the earth slammed closed below us.

Almost as soon as it had begun, it ended.

The unstable ravine had collapsed inward, burying the Augmented army trapped within. Other than torn-up trees and disturbed dirt there was no sign of the five hundred souls who'd been enslaved by the twisted technology of the Cabal.

Howls of rage farther down slope reminded me there was still plenty of death to come though.

Neshomne let go of the struggling *Bantam*, pulling Malakhai up into a cradle as he dropped down the twenty feet to the turned earth.

Without the wrong-wolf's weight the vehicle shot up, and I struggled to bring the damaged machine under control.

Descending as safely as I could, I put the craft down close to Malakhai and his partner. Battery acid from the front sizzled to the ground. The steel frame was blackened and twisted.

But it could still fly.

"We don't got time," I snarled to the dazed Malakhai as he tried to formulate questions.

His proximity to the explosions had left the man shaky, but the Judge seemed to understand me well enough. I stripped Henry out of the Tellurian arc pack he wore, my fingers flying over the buckles.

"Here, take him," I ordered Neshomne, muscling Henry out of the *Bantam*'s saddle. "Gently! This man is my oldest and dearest friend. I'll be deathly peeved if anything happens to him."

Neshomne's furry eyebrows raised in bemusement, but he treated Henry gentle as I passed my scatterbrained friend over.

"Where you think you're going?" Malakhai asked as I shrugged into the Tellurian arc pack. Minor shocks from it made my skin tingle, but I needed the portable generator to run the *Bantam*.

"To keep another promise," I growled. "Keep your sermonizing to yourself. I did what I said I would. Other than shooting a pistol badly, there's not much left here for me. And I have the chance to save the girls now."

Malakhai nodded, understanding my meaning. "Well, good luck to you then, kid," he said, voice louder than it needed to be, his ears still ringing from the explosion. "We got too much on our plate to chip in, but bring your ladies by afterward if you want. If we live, that is."

Howls from down slope punctuated his words. Libertas still had a hell of a battle ahead. Outnumbered badly, there was little chance I'd ever see the Blood Judge or the townsfolk again.

But I'd evened my debt as best I could, and there were other friends that needed me more.

The *Bantam* whined in protest as I forced the squall tubes to life. The battered machine wobbled up into the air, far more sparks shooting from it than was healthy.

Turning the abused nose toward Portland, I prayed that the vehicle would hold together for the trip. I had a place to be, a promise to keep.

And a Dragon to slay.

Chapter 32

SHOCKS JOLTED MY LEGS and crotch as the *Bantam* hobbled along. Treetops scratched at the battered hull, trying to bring down the wounded contraption. Behind me, a trail of smoking branches showed where the vehicle had dipped down too low and nearly paid the final price for it.

Every shudder, every rattle, made me think the whole thing was about to blow up. The squall tubes kept going dark before flaring to life again, and the varying thrust made it hard to fly even in the general direction of Portland.

The scar of the collapsed ravine ran down the mountain off to the left. I'd seen a couple of monstrous mechanical limbs sticking out of the ground twitching, and once a lupine head buried neck-down whined pitifully as I flew by. I tried to put aside the thought of the hundreds of enslaved Augmented buried under that dirt. But my guilt wouldn't let me.

An inhuman scream sounded from down slope.

Something big and mean was dying painfully nearby. There were still hundreds of the Cabal Augmented roaming the side of Mt. Hood. But without Malakhai they lacked a leader . . . or did they? The Judge had implied the army would have a controller, probably a Talon. Was the Cabal lackey able to rally the troops and take them against Libertas? Even if he lacked any kind of tactical mind, it didn't take a military genius to overrun an ill-defended town when you outnumbered them ten to one and didn't give a single shit about your troops' lives.

"Can't worry about that now," I mumbled to myself, fighting to keep the *Bantam* from veering into the ground.

It wasn't that easy though to brush aside the whispers of guilt. I wanted to rescue Maggie and Sarah, sure. But despite telling Malakhai I'd discharged my duty, the responsibility of leaving Libertas to fend for itself still weighed on me. The sounds of fighting as I traveled toward Portland just reminded me that I was choosing me and mine once again over the lives of the innocent.

Wait. Fighting?

Curiosity allied with guilt finally overcame the burning desire to rescue my beloved and her sister. I turned the scarred machine against the telluric stream I was following, cutting across the flow and in the process nearly shaking the thing apart. There shouldn't be any battle this far from Libertas. Assuming that the leading edge of the army was gone, we'd bought the refugee town at least a couple of hours or more. So, who was making all the racket?

The answer became bloodily clear as I crested the treeline on the other side of the mountain's scar.

I'd forgotten about the Shadow Pack.

The scene was one of brutality and cannibalism, turning my stomach before the smell hit. Bruja raised a bloodied maw from the corpse of the Augmented wrong-wolf she'd brought down, howling in victory. There were four, maybe five bodies littered around the battle site. They'd been so savagely torn apart that it was hard to tell.

Whisper playfully threw a bloodied hunk of meat at her skeletal father, who laughed in a carefree manner as he caught it and tore a bite off with his silver fangs. The trio looked up at the sound of the *Bantam* clipping a treetop. Fear laced my heart at the wild scene, and for a moment I couldn't breathe as I felt their eyes lock on me.

The Pack waved jovially at me, as if greeting an old friend returned from a trip.

Reflexively I raised a hand, more out of self-preservation than camaraderie. My guts churned as they motioned for me to land, to join in their terrible feast.

I revved the charge to the squall tubes, sending a dangerous number of volts surging through the damaged machine. The *Bantam* shot away from the grisly picnic as I clung to the saddle. It wasn't just the gore I'd witnessed that turned my stomach. The Shadow Pack considered me a friend.

That thought haunted me as the sputtering *Bantam* shot downhill at a dangerous pace. A man could be judged by the company he kept, by the allies that stood beside him.

What sort of monster did that make me?

Ignoring the doubts that plagued me, I twisted in the saddle to avoid an unexpected lunge from a hidden Cabal Augmented that shot out of the trees toward me. The surprise attack was a relief, a respite from the fear of being counted a friend of the Pack. As were the three subsequent attacks that I managed to swerve the *Bantam* around.

The Cabal army still infested Mt. Hood, but soon enough I was beyond their stomping grounds. As much as I hated the thought of the Shadow Pack, at least I could count on Bloodrath and his allies to strike at the flanks of the disorganized ironhides heading for Libertas. It was cold comfort, no more than a delaying tactic. But it was better than nothing.

Steeling myself, I gunned the *Bantam* into the thickest telluric stream I could sense. The vehicle settled down like a horse into a well-trod path, evening out. Acid from the broken batteries in the front sizzled across the steel hide, and my shins burned from where it had spattered in my maneuvers. But it still flew. Like me, the machine was holding together, if just barely.

The damage it had sustained kept the *Bantam* from achieving any true speed. It took two hours to cover the distance from the ravine to Portland, giving me more than enough time to focus dread and fear into a knot in my belly. My imagination ran wild, dreaming of all the horrors that Trent and his insane scientists could visit on the Butler sisters. For once, I wished the girls were weaker than they were; death would be a blessing compared to what the Cabal would put them through.

Portland loomed ahead, full of menace and evil. The outskirts were deserted, as I'd expected them to be. Every ironhide slave they could muster was currently assaulting the mountain. The good white folks that made up the so-called master race were huddled in their homes, letting their servants do their fighting for them. Still though, I encouraged the

Bantam to gain a little altitude. I wanted to see any attacks coming ahead of time.

The Tombstone squatted on its hilltop in the center of the deserted town like a bloated tick, daring me to come closer. From this height it looked like the building was indeed a grave marker that had been knocked onto its face, a squat and ugly stone mass marring the terrain. The grounding trestle curved around the roof, dominating the top of the Tombstone like a madman's roller coaster. Perched upon the rails like an iron buzzard the *Purity's Pride* lay gleaming in the afternoon sun.

I didn't need my guts churning to tell me it was ready to launch.

Sparks crawled along the rails of the charged grounding trestle as the Thunder Train lurched into motion. The Double T screeched and screamed like a vampire burning in the sun as its steel wheels spun and caught hold of the rails. The enclosed boiler system had been stoked by an unseen engineer until the air smoked around the engine. Between the charge from the trestle and the turbines attached to its trucks, the *Purity's Pride* was building the charge it needed to energize the squall tubes lining its hull and take to the sky.

And I wasn't going to reach the Tombstone in time to stop it.

I hollered to the uncaring sky as I fed every bit of power I could from the Tellurian generator pack into the *Bantam*. The tubes across its scarred hull flashed bright, brighter than they should. With a strangled cry I brought my boot up and slammed it down on the brightest, smashing its mooring bolts and sending it spinning off as the *Bantam* shot forward. The overloaded tube detonated in the vehicle's wake, sending a wash of fire and shrapnel over me.

The *Bantam* bucked as I desperately tried to regain control. Another tube flared white-bright, but my boot was too slow this time. I barely managed to kick the overloaded tube free before it exploded.

Pain shot up my leg as the explosion took my foot with it.

Fighting to stay conscious, I clung to the saddle of the *Bantam* as it spun through the air from the force of the detonation. Blood sprayed from my smoking ankle in the air in concentric circles, strangely beautiful to my dazed mind. A deep thought, bordering on instinct, forced my leg to slam the ruined ankle into the burning underside of the

Bantam. Flesh sizzled on steel as the flames licked over the wound and cauterized it.

I screamed in agony, unable to break my mind free of my body. Never had I wished so hard for the stormwolf to answer and lift me away from my body. But there was no answer from the voltaic phantom hidden deep within.

The world spun, but somehow I managed to regain control of the *Bantam*, leveling it off by playing piano with its thrust system. Flames licked the hull in multiple places, and the very bolts holding the saddle on rattled as if about to let go.

My groggy attention snapped back to the *Purity's Pride* as it shrieked around the grounding trestle, gaining speed at an incredible rate. The attempt to force the *Bantam* faster had crippled it, cutting its pace to half of what it had been. What hope I'd had of reaching the enemy Double T in time had been destroyed by my impatience.

The *Purity's Pride* hit the launch ramp of the grounding trestle, bulling its way into the air like a middle finger to God. With only the fuel car attached, the Double T was quick off the launch, rattling clear of gravity's embrace into the realm of the impossible. Its squall tubes glowed bright and steady, suffering none of the imperfections plaguing my own little vehicle's propulsion. But the Devil is never satisfied with killing a man's hope; old Scratch has to shit in your face to rob you of the last shreds of dignity as well.

The door to the engine cabin of the *Purity's Pride* slid open, and Dr. Trent leaned out. His twisted face was full of glee, a triumphant joy that made me want to leap the hundreds of feet between us and smash it with a sledgehammer.

The *Purity's Pride* circled above the sputtering *Bantam*, flying in a wide, lazy arc. Trent could have simply flown off into the clouds without a care in the world. But the Dragon's ego would not let him escape so easily.

The wind stole whatever taunting words he threw to me as Trent's eyes locked with mine. But I didn't need to hear him to understand him. The meaning was clear.

He'd won.

Snarling in defiance, I angled the *Bantam* upward and dared to surge the tubes again. The poor broken vehicle tried to climb, a valiantly useless struggle that ignited more fires and smoke along its mortally-wounded body.

Trent laughed mockingly, reaching behind to pull forward his final insult.

Maggie and Sarah.

He held both the girls by their hair, leaning them out of the door. Sarah's broken arms had been bandaged with splints, and the rough treatment made the child cry out. Trent tossed her back into the depths of the cabin contemptuously. It was a mistake.

With her sister in harm's way, Maggie had held her temper. But now my love struggled against her captor, spitting and clawing at the Dragon. Trent's mutated strength was too much for her human form though, and while several of Maggie's punches landed solid on him the mad doctor was too enthralled with his victory to care.

Suddenly something changed in the air. The stormwolf stirred within and raised its head. There was a familiar taste, a feeling shared between Maggie and me. An old bond, the start of our infatuation with each other, pulsed like the ocean under a sheet of ice. I'd spent so long trying to ignore the bond, to see if I loved Maggie without it, that its awakening caught me by surprise. The feeling pulsing along it was familiar and dangerous. I'd sensed it before in the streets of Portland, weeks before it was supposed to rear its head. And this time there was no Blood Judge around to stop it.

The werewolf was breaking free of Maggie's flesh.

As Trent gloated, Maggie stopped struggling against his grip. The wolf in me answered my mate, sharpening my vision, cutting through the distance like a lightning bolt to where I could see every hair on her head, every freckle on her sharp cheekbones. Maggie's irises had disappeared, swallowed as her pupils grew to consume the rest of her eyes. Red light flickered within the depths like hot coals as the beast in her rose up, eager to claim her body as its own in the final transformation. Distantly I felt Trent's hands on her; clammy, painful, and desperate to claim ownership.

But Maggie wasn't no one's property.

The Dragon awoke to the danger a second too late, realizing the doe he'd kidnapped was a rattlesnake in his grasp. He tried to thrust Maggie away, but she was having none of it. Where before she'd fought against him, now she clung to the Cabal leader, slashing at him as her fingers elongated with snapping sounds. The werewolf's claws burst through her own bones, slashing into Trent as he fought to reach his control bracer.

I forced the *Bantam* upward, aching to join the fight. At that moment I would've sacrificed Libertas, the Advocates, hell, even Wardenclyffe itself to reach my lady as she fought.

But she didn't need any help.

Trent hollered for help from his lackeys as Maggie ripped into him, slashing his skin to ribbons. Her jaw dislocated, stretching wide like a serpent's, and the werewolf's teeth pushed out. Maggie's flesh rippled and contracted, fat and muscle burning as the transformation took hold fully, the beast howling in rage and pain as it molded her human form into something far deadlier.

Other hands, long-fingered and inhuman like Trent's, reached out of the Double T's cabin and took hold of Maggie's head and shoulders. She thrashed against them, tearing into the Dragon as Trent hung half in and half out of the open door. There was no more gloating from him as the *Purity's Pride* flew in circles above me. Only desperation and pain.

Trent managed to get to his control bracer, his spider-leg fingers dancing over the switches and dials. Lightning arced out of the Double T's frame, striking Maggie. But her grip on the Dragon grounded her, sharing the painful jolt with her would-be captor as energy coursed through them both.

Doctor Trent screaming was a sweet, sweet sound.

Despite the stunning effect from being electrocuted, the beast in Maggie's skin refused to be denied. She roared in pain and elation, and bit down on the Dragon's left shoulder. Muscle and bone tore away from his arm with a sickening ripping sound when she yanked her head back. Maggie greedily gulped the warm meat down, fueling her final transformation into beast.

Trent screamed in pain, bludgeoning Maggie's head with his one good arm as his other dangled by shreds. But now that the beast had tasted blood, there was no stopping it.

Maggie bit down on the wounded shoulder again. This time when her head came away, so did the arm.

The Dragon's left arm spun away from his body and the *Purity's Pride* as he looked on. Blood trailed from it as it flipped end over end.

My cheers were swallowed by the wind. But in the midst of yelling my support, I realized something critical.

Trent's severed arm still had the control bracer on it.

Inspiration grabbed hold of my brain and wouldn't let go. The desperate Dragon had accessed his controls, unlocking them to try and fight off the rabid werewolf Maggie was transforming into. His bracer, imbued with command above all others, could claim dominance over any Cabal machinery.

With it, I could free the Augmented.

Time seemed to slow down as I watched Trent's arm falling.

Bolts of lightning struck Maggie again and again, horrifically bright as she lit up from the inside out. Trent's minions were shocking her into submission, forcing the werewolf to unconsciousness. Maggie let go of Trent's bleeding body, falling backward into the cabin of the *Purity's Pride* as she finally succumbed to the pain.

The wounded Dragon was pulled back into the Double T, hatred and pain etched across his distorted features. There was a promise of torment for Maggie and Sarah burned into Trent's face, one that turned my stomach.

His severed arm fell past the *Bantam*.

In my mind's eye, two futures stretched away to the horizon. One tomorrow saw me send the *Bantam* into a suicidal plunge after the amputated limb. If I dived now, I might be able to grab the functioning control bracer before it hit the ground and turn the tide of the Libertas war, saving the lives of thousands of strangers. If I kept climbing though, I could reach the *Purity's Pride* as it circled, smashing into them before they realized the danger. I could save Maggie and Sarah. Could be their hero, the man who . . .

The man who abandoned everyone else to follow his own desires.

For a split second I stood on the knife's edge, that place between one future and the next.

Then I made my choice.

Chapter 33

I NOSED THE *BANTAM* into a screaming dive, turning my back on Maggie and Sarah.

"Trent won't kill them," I growled to myself to assuage my conscience. "He'll torture them, he'll experiment on them. But he won't kill them. And if I'm fast enough I can stop him from doing any of those things."

Doubts and fears cackled at my justifications, but I pushed them away. I'd spent the last few days making choices to save those that I loved, holding their lives above those of other innocents.

I had to balance the scales.

Although the Dragon would likely keep the Butler sisters alive to slake his revenge, there was no way Libertas was going to survive without help. I weighed certain torture against certain death and decided that it was better for some to suffer and live than for all to die.

It was cold comfort though.

The ground rushed up quickly as I pushed the *Bantam*'s squall tubes beyond breaking. Spiderwebs of cracks snapped across the steel-hard glass surfaces, with daggers of bright-white light shining through.

Trent's arm tumbled end over end, the control bracer vulnerable to impact. I shot toward it and the ground beyond like a bullet, burning the *Bantam*'s life away in a blaze of glorious speed.

Timing it as best I could, I leapt free of the *Bantam* as it rocketed past the falling arm, pushing off with my one remaining foot to try and get clear. The severed end of Trent's arm slapped me in the face like a spurned lover as I grabbed hold of it.

Bereft of any controlling influence, the *Bantam* spun drunkenly through the air at an angle away from me, heading right for the Tombstone.

The flaming steel comet of the *Bantam* slammed into the concrete roof of the Tombstone, smashing through the grounding trestle down into its guts. Explosions shook the building as the squall tubes shattered from the crash, sending waves of flame and force cascading through its innards and obliterating stone and man. The walls blew out as the roof collapsed in, burying those that dwelt inside.

The Tombstone burned bright as it died, fire and blood cleansing it of the crimes of its masters.

I curled around the Dragon's arm, trying to protect the control bracer with my body. The unforgiving earth rushed up faster than I'd expected, and I slammed into the ground like a cannonball.

Bones throughout my body shattered with the force of the impact, and it felt like flesh and blood wanted to keep going. The pressure was incredible, the pain unbearable, and I nearly blacked out from it.

I fought to keep conscious, to collect all the scattered marbles that had spilled out of my head. If I passed out, if the Cabal found me here vulnerable, clutching the key to undoing all of their plans, I was doomed.

As if from a great distance, I heard yelling, shouting, followed by the howls of servants. I was having trouble focusing, but the sounds grew closer.

Agony laced my every move. There was no telling how many bones I'd pulverized from hitting the ground at the speed I did, but there was no doubt that it was only by the grace of the beast within that I wasn't dead. Since I could still move my arms and head, my spine was still intact. But there was precious little beyond that I could count on. My legs refused to obey, and the right one was twisted at a terrible angle, with the kneecap on the wrong side.

"Here! Over here!" came a cry from the direction of the burning Tombstone.

There were only seconds left, minutes at most, before the Cabalites in the city discovered me. Trent's severed arm flopped around like a comical fish as I righted the control bracer. Lights flickered across it, indicating it still retained life.

None of the dials or switches were labeled. There was no glowing sign pointing to the lever I needed to manipulate to free the Augmented. It was a mystery, opaque and indecipherable.

I had failed.

No.

There was a logic to everything, a way of operating inherent to the world itself. That was the basis of science, and despite the terrible monstrosities they'd birthed, the Cabal were still beholden to those concepts.

I focused, shutting the pain from my broken body off as I traced the reasoned patterns of thought behind the control bracers. This went here, that would control those, and these would be grouped together out of necessity. The mechanical inspiration that had guided my hands throughout my life was simply a hidden intelligence, a working of clockwork gears in my unconscious mind. And it was well past time I threw back the curtain and viewed the calculations in all their glory.

In the end, the answer was ludicrously simple.

"Found him!"

I strained to focus on the speaker, a red-headed, gangly young man. It was Rawlson, the churlish deputy who'd tried to impede Malakhai saving Maggie. The deputy had a leer on his face, the look of a violent child well on its way to becoming a lifetime bully, encouraged by its parents to eat or be eaten by the world. He'd bought into the Cabal's religion of superiority hook, line, and sinker.

Flanking him were two Broken ironhide slaves, their jaws forever sealed shut by iron muzzles. One had an arm missing, and the other walked with a distinct limp with the gears in his artificial leg visible and clicking loudly. Accompanying them were three Vocalators, bearing a variety of farm implements that they brandished as weapons. Their eyes were dazed, as if asleep, and the movements of the slaves were all jerky. They were fully under the sway of their hive collars.

My impromptu suicide run on the Tombstone had obviously interrupted the Cabal's efforts at organizing a second wave of Augmented to assault Libertas. It was only a matter of time before more troops converged on our location. How many ironhides wandered Portland's streets, preparing to bring death to the very Advocates that wished to save them?

"Looks like we get to have some fun after all," Rawlson gloated, recognizing me. He wore a gun belt that had been cinched tight around his skinny hips, and his thumb stroked the hammer of the holstered pistol like he was trying to make it moan.

"You!" Rawlson said, pointing to the one-armed Broken. "It's not right he's got both his limbs and you're a cripple. Go ahead and rip off one of his. Call it a gift."

The wrong-wolf rumbled a growl low in its chest, taking a step forward and reaching out toward me with its bladed claws.

I flipped the switch on the control bracer that neutralized the Cabal's control over the Augmented.

Several breaths of anticipation went by.

Nothing happened.

The Vocalators encircled me, pitchforks and hammers at the ready to fence me in so that I couldn't escape the ironhide advancing on me.

"You don't have to do this," I croaked. It was all I could manage, and even those few words exhausted me. I was so tired. I wanted nothing more than to fall into the arms of the blackest nothingness, of the final slumber.

"Of course they do!" Rawlson said, laughing at my pitiful objection. "They are the slaves. We are their masters!"

"Not ... anymore ..."

The Vocalators looked at each other in confusion. Realization slowly dawned on them, and one threw her pitchfork to the ground experimentally. The others grinned at her success.

Rawlson looked confused, but not as much as the one-armed Broken next to him. The wrong-wolf raised his claws, flexing his fingers in wonderment at having control of them. Carefully, almost daintily, he reached out to Rawlson's face and flicked a bladed finger.

Blood welled up from a small cut on the freckled man's cheek.

Horror dawned on Rawlson's face as the other Augmented turned to him, their faces hardening. The Broken growled low and steady, memories of beatings and punishment rolling through their heads. The slaves remembered all that the masters had done. Crimes were never forgotten by the victims.

The Vocalators around me turned their backs to my vulnerable form, shifting from aggressors to protectors in an instant. But they needn't have bothered. I was in no danger from the ironhides anymore.

The Augmented werewolves were entirely focused on Rawlson.

As blessed darkness claimed me, Deputy Rawlson's dying screams were a lullaby that sang me to sleep.

Chapter 34

A FAMILIAR MELODY PENETRATED the darkness. The hymn was wordless, off-key, but hummed and murmured with a devotion that vibrated down in my broken bones.

As if awakening to the thought of them, shooting pain ran up and down my skeleton.

"Ouch."

It was the best I could do. The hymn paused, and false teeth clacked around the stem of a pipe. Soft rain pattered off of a metal roof. Warmth surrounded me, almost stifling, but still comforting.

My nose twitched at the scent of tobacco, prompting me to try and open my eyes. Crusted tears broke free as I forced them open, letting in the searing light from a sputtering candle. The night roiled above with storm clouds though the skylights.

"Ouch."

"You keep saying that," an old woman's voice said. "Stop milking it, boy. Get up. We got work to do."

Thoughts swirled around, suffused with hope like light through the cracks of molten lava. I hadn't heard that voice in months, had thought to never hear it again.

"Grandma?"

"That ain't my name, idiot," Maude murmured. "We never stood on that formality."

I tried to crack a smile, but it hurt.

Everything hurt.

The world was full of indistinct shapes. But it was warm, comforting. And my granny was there.

Slowly my vision brought into focus the inside of Sister Marie's makeshift house. The curved iron walls of the modified Double T boiler stretched above, and rain fell steadily on the outside. I was bundled up in blankets on Marie's bed while Maude's sturdy silhouette rocked near the stove. Her blind eyes were untroubled by the darkness of the stuffy room, lit only by a single candle. She had knitting in her hand, and her corncob pipe glowed merrily from the tobacco in it. The blinder goggles that had burnt out her eyes hung around her neck, and I could smell the lingering scents of oil and ozone that meant she'd flown a Double T recently.

Memories sprouted in the dank soil of my confused mind. My ankle throbbed, reminding me of the missing foot. A small price to pay when I'd expected to die. But it still hurt like hell.

"Libertas is safe?"

"Obviously," Maude said, waving a hand dismissively. "Use your head. Unless you think this is all a dream. In which case, make me a bit prettier and stop my joints aching, would you?"

The smile hurt, but I liked it.

A sudden fear cut through the fog in my mind.

"Maggie!"

My grandma nodded, taking a long pull off her pipe. "I heard. Henry warned me you'd try to run out the door first chance you got after her."

Terror gripped my heart as I remembered Trent, the dread promise of what he'd do to the Butler sisters heavy in my imagination. "Maude, we got to ..."

"Got to what?" she asked, blind eyes glittering in the shadows. "Get ourselves killed? You're smart enough to know that she's gone for now. We'll figure something out though to snatch her back. You got my word on it."

"I shouldn't have let her go in the first place," I said bitterly, laying back down and putting hands over my face. "Oh God, there must have been something I could've—"

"Stop that!" Maude barked, rapping me with a carved cane that was leaning against the rocking chair before resuming her knitting. "Could've, should've, would've. I won't have you whipping yourself with maybes. You did the best you could."

"But Trent took her. He's going to . . . going to . . . and here I am, still alive, while he's . . ."

"That's enough, son," Maude said. "It don't matter whether you won or lost, just that you fought your best and spit in the Devil's eye when he came for you. Sometimes all we got is survival, and there ain't nothing wrong with living through hell to see the other side."

There was no arguing with her tone. I'd spent most of my life trying to make my grandma proud, to live the way she'd taught me. To hear her say it was all right was like receiving a priestly benediction, a divine forgiveness.

But I had other crimes on my conscience too.

"Portland?"

Maude put down the knitting with a heavy sigh.

"It burned. For the better part of a week."

I tried to struggle up. Hunger and thirst lanced my guts. "I've been out that long?"

"Does a bear crap in the woods?" She grunted.

"Not if there's a werewolf around," I wheezed. The thought of a furback taking on a grizzly made me try to laugh.

Maude didn't join in the merriment. I settled back down, letting my aching body rest.

"That bad, eh?"

"Worse," Maude said, taking her pipe stem out to spit to the side. She took a long pull off the smoke, letting it seep out of her nose. "And better. At least better than those shitheels deserved."

I tried to shake my head in confusion. It was a terrible idea.

"Best to let the others explain," Maude said, grunting as she lurched from the rocking chair. "I'm only recently arrived. Couldn't set down until they cobbled together a grounding trestle. Only took two days of buzzing them before they finally lit up with the idea. Idiots. Speaking of . . ."

I raised a hand before she could leave.

"I . . . that is, thank you for coming, Maude."

"Yeah, yeah," she grumbled, feeling her way to the door. Her voice was gruff, but there was a deep sadness to it. "I missed you too, son. Even though you bring more trouble than a tent preacher at a saloon."

Maude pushed open the door, letting in a cold crackling light from outside. Even darkened by the rainstorm, it burned through me as if I were a creature of the night. I burrowed deeper into the blankets.

"Ouch."

"Shut it, sissy," Maude chided. She motioned to figures standing outside the door. "You three can come on in. But mind your manners or I'll bounce you faster than you can bitch about it."

A low rumble of protest outside that sounded like Neshomne made Maude snort.

"Even if you could fit in here, I don't want to smell like wet dog the rest of the day. Stay, Fido."

Sister Marie looked sideways through fresh bandages at Maude as she entered. "How lovely of you to tell me how to behave inside of my own house."

Maude moved the stem of her pipe on one side of her mouth. She gave a big, fake smile to Marie and patted the curved iron wall. "This is as much a house as you are a nun. And ain't nobody that can tell me how to act where my grandson is concerned, missy."

Marie didn't quite know how to take that, so instead made way for my other visitors.

Malakhai followed, taking his hat off after a sharp glance from Maude. Trailing behind him was Henry, replete with ozone smell from his constantly-charged lab coat. Even with just this many people the room was crowded, and Maude's impressive bulk only made it more so.

"Good to see you alive, young'un," Malakhai said, nodding to me.

"No thanks to the likes of you," Maude growled, staring hard at him with milky-white eyes.

"He did as he promised them," Henry interjected. "Would you expect any less of Eli?"

Maude sighed heavily. "I suppose not. Still, that's no excuse to take advantage of Eli's naive nature . . ."

"Maude!" I choked out, my cheeks blushing.

"It's true and you know it," she countered, taking her pipe out and jabbing the stem in my direction. "You've always been soft-hearted. Letting folks grab hold of you to float while you're all drowning. Full of useless guilt. People like to take advantage of that."

"Now see here, ma'am," Malakhai interjected, raising his hand to cut her off.

"Don't you 'ma'am' me, youngster," Maude snapped. "Ain't no one ever told you to respect your elders?"

The Judge looked flustered, his pale face lined with creases. What he didn't understand was that Maude was just covering fretting about me with anger. I'd been subject to more than one painful lesson in that when I'd worried her with my excursions on the moisture vanes of Wardenclyffe. Hadn't been able to sit down for a week one time.

"How's about we all just settle down," I said, hating how my voice cracked. "I'd like to get caught up on the news."

"These know-it-alls can handle that," Maude harrumphed, grabbing her knitting from the chair. "I've had my fill of this sweat box; you've got ten minutes to get dressed and on board before I leave all of you behind."

Maude stomped off, shoving her way through Malakhai and Henry and out the door. Those left looked at each other uncomfortably for a moment.

"Well?" I prompted.

"It's complicated," Marie said, moving to take the rocking chair.

"When isn't it?" Malakhai sighed, hooking his thumbs into his gun belt. "Short version: Libertas lives, Portland limps on, and Wardenclyffe flies."

"It worked then? Disabling the hive collars with Trent's control bracer?"

Henry snapped his fingers. "Ah, that explains it! I was wondering how that one mechanism superseded the others. So was that also his, uh . . ."

"Arm, yes," I nodded. "A parting gift from Maggie."

The other three shared worried looks.

"We suspected they were taken," Marie said. "Malakhai scoured the city looking for them, but in the chaos of the first few days . . ."

"What. Happened?" I said slowly, enunciating both words with as much force as I could muster. My belly rumbled with savage hunger, and my lips were parched. But nothing compared to how much I needed to know about the fruit of my labors.

The other two inclined their head to Henry. He cleared his throat, and although the respirator covered his mouth, I could hear the grimace in his words.

"It wasn't clean. When the hive collars went dead, it took a while for the Augmented to realize it. When they did . . . well, there was a lot of pent-up hate for what's been going on here over the years."

Malakhai glowered, but stayed silent.

"So, they turned on their former masters," I said, thinking of the Grant family. "Did any survive?"

"Oh . . . no, no, not that bad," Henry said, shaking his head. "Yes, there were killings. Quite a few, in fact. But overall the Augmented were more humane in their attitudes toward the city residents than the treatment they'd received. There were several groups that banded together to keep who they could safe. They weren't entirely successful, of course, but it wasn't the bloodbath you're imagining."

A weight I hadn't realized I was carrying suddenly got lighter. "But you said some did murder?"

"Some always do," Malakhai said. He looked tired in the dim light. "Don't worry, your Grant friends are fine. But enough Augmented went insane to set fire to the city, and more than one Returned ended up on the wrong side of steel claws. The Shadow Pack went on their own rampage, taking out targets they've had their eye on for months. But the others helped us get it under control. We even managed to dig out the survivors from the ravine trap y'all used on the Augmented army. A few got killed from being too close to the explosives, but the Libertas population damn near doubled overnight with those that lived. Any ire they had about being buried alive was countered by not being enslaved to assholes anymore. They were just sad they'd missed the murder spree against the Cabal flunkies.

"There's a shaky peace now between the citizens, Libertas, and a dozen Augmented factions that formed after the collars went dead. I put Judge Glover in charge of Portland for now, with a couple of trusted

Advocates near him with orders to shoot him if he falls out of line. He was a Cabal man, without a doubt, but he values his own hide more than any real allegiance to them. No one's innocent anymore. That guilt gives us a start to figuring it all out."

"I'm surprised the Augmented let any of the Cabal or their cronies live at all," I said, coughing as I struggled to sit upright. "The slaves have been freed. World's better. The end."

"But it ain't though," the Judge said, anger clouding his features. "Yeah, it's better that the chains are broken. No one's arguing that. But now what? Execute all the Returned who laid an unkind word or hand on those that were different than them?"

I stuck out my jaw stubbornly. It hurt, but my own temper was rising. "Seems fair to me."

"Does it?" Marie replied. She stroked the rosary beads hanging from her wrist, taking the small cross on the end in her hand. "Heaven knows I'm no champion of the Portland citizenry. But is a cold-blooded massacre really how we want to restart civilization? Is not forgiveness worth the risk? Killing those that disagree with us, that strike out at us in their ignorance and fear, cannot possibly result in a better world."

"Forgiveness is your business, sister," I said, shrugging off the covers with a grimace. "Not mine."

My lower left leg was bandaged from the knee down to the ankle. If I was an average werewolf, I'd just have to wait for the next full moon for my missing foot to grow back after the shift. But there was a price to pay for my uniqueness. Experience with the Tellurians told me that without a full transformation I was going to be a one-legged man for a very long time. The stormwolf offered limited healing, but its nature precluded the idea of my foot ever regenerating. I didn't know how, but somehow I was certain I'd never experience the normal transformation ever again. When the change came for me, my beast had left flesh behind rather than reshaping it. That was locked in now, and that was that.

"I take it that the *Heaven's Grace* is outside?" I asked. "Maude believes we'll be leaving with her. I thought that was forbidden by Steinmetz and the other Betas. Henry?"

"It was," he said, putting emphasis on the past tense. "Ever since the loop formed, things have been a bit different. The Tellurians are desperate for any help they can lay hands on."

"Backtrack a moment; the loop?"

"Ah, that's right. Sorry, Eli, got ahead of myself."

Henry cleared a section of floor and rolled out a sheet of paper. A simple map had been drawn on it with Portland and the Cascade mountain range marked, as well as a dot to the north marked 'Old Seattle.' He squatted down with a pencil and started sketching the wiggliest oval I'd ever seen.

"After the telluric backlash from bringing down the deadzone, the streams permanently altered their course," he explained.

I nodded. "Figured as much from the aurora."

"Well, when the flows settled out, they were disconnected from the rest of the world's electromagnetic energy. The Telluric society has been doing calculations and sending out Thunder Trains to map the new rivers the last few days. What they've discovered is . . . not good."

Malakhai snorted. "That's an understatement."

I groaned and rubbed my face. "Don't tell me there's another deadzone."

"No, not at all," Henry said, shaking his head. "In fact, it seems the event essentially condensed all the tributaries in the area into a single main flow, one that follows this loop from south of Portland to north of Old Seattle. There's enough ambient energy to keep Wardenclyffe aloft for centuries, if not more."

"So, it's good news then?" I asked.

The grim look on the others' faces was enough of an answer. Henry leaned back down to the map, marking a spot a bit east of Portland.

"Here's Wardenclyffe. It's trapped in the loop, and that's all there is to it anymore. It'll never deviate off the path without crashing. In about six months it'll follow the full circuit and return here, long after its wake has dissipated, thankfully. But there's no way to free it from its track. There's a huge gap to the closest telluric stream that it can never cross. Our long era of wandering is over; better or worse, we've found our home territory."

"And that's bad why?" I asked, looking around the worried faces. "Assuming they can figure out how to live in peace, that gives us a visit to Portland and Libertas every half year. For the first time ever, we got friends on the ground, and we can even come by for regular visits. Sure, we won't be finding any new supply depots to plunder, but those were drying up anyway."

"The problem is," Henry said, marking a spot above Portland, "Wardenclyffe is not the only salvation city caught in the telluric loop."

I stared hard at the dot on the map. "Menlo Station."

Marie nodded. "Indeed. They were caught in the same backlash event."

"So, are we to be dancing partners, fighting and cussing at each other as we circle round the Pacific Northwest like wolves round a fallen lamb?" I asked.

Marie nudged Henry with trepidation, but it was Malakhai that finally spoke up.

"You're assuming the two cities are going the same direction on the loop. They ain't."

"You don't mean . . ."

"Got it in one," Malakhai said with a nod. "The storm prophets figure in about three months Menlo Station and Wardenclyffe are going to crash into each other. Given the squirreliness of the flows, they think it'll be somewhere above Old Seattle."

Looking at the map, a chill ran up my spine. I'd done everything I could to keep the salvation cities from hitting each other. But it looked like all I'd accomplished was to delay the inevitable.

"Maybe if we create another backlash—"

"Jesus Christ, no!" Henry interrupted. "Do you know how badly Wardenclyffe was damaged by the last one? Another surge on the lines like that and there won't be anyone left to worry about fighting Menlo. We'll all be dead."

I shifted uncomfortably. "Ah. Sorry about that."

Marie shook her head. "There's nothing to be sorry about, Eli. You did the best you could with what you had. For better or worse, the choices you made have shaped the future. Now it's up to us, all of us, to finishing sculpting it into something better than the past."

An impatient pounding on the door startled us all. Malakhai opened the door to find Maude standing there, blinder goggles secured around her eyes. Outside, I could hear the tell-tale crackle of a grounding trestle building a charge.

"You ladies done braiding each others' hair?" she asked, spitting off to the side. Her pipe had gone dead, but she didn't seem to notice.

"We were discussing strategy, madam," Malakhai said, stiffening his neck.

"Is that what the young'uns call it now?" Maude cackled. "Henry, stop being lazy, boy. Go get your shoulder under Eli. We need to get airborne soon as we can."

Despite being decked out in his Tellurian regalia, Henry snapped to as if he were still part of the crew. He put his arm under mine, helping me to my one good leg as Marie handed me the carved crutch. It wasn't quite the right height, but it worked well enough for the time being.

Beyond the doorway it seemed like the world was made of cascading light and shadow to my oversensitive eyes. But the breeze from the rainy day felt good. The massive silhouette of the *Heaven's Grace* crackled with active squall tubes on a grounding trestle, lightning flashing in the darkness. It was like she was welcoming me back.

My thoughts turned to Maggie and Sarah, lost in the black clouds above. How long until Trent got them back to Menlo Station? How long until he started cutting into them, driving them insane with his mad experiments? What torment did he have planned for the women who had defied him, crippled him?

I'd get better. I would learn to control the stormwolf, to summon it to serve. Time healed the body, allowed a man to regain strength and will. But it wouldn't calm the mind. I would nurture the flames of my rage, the pain of my lost love. I would not let a day, an hour, go by without reminding myself of Maggie and Sarah, of the degradation and horror they were enduring. My fury was immortal, everlasting. But Trent and the Cabal weren't so lucky. They could suffer. They could die. Religion had better be alive and well on Menlo Station.

Because the Devil was coming for them all.

About Timothy Black

Born a modern-day nomad in the Deep South, Timothy Black wandered through most of the southern United States in an attempt to find his life, love, and home. After studying Geology, Astronomy, and the Occult, he found himself with a degree in Philosophy and a habit of writing odd things. A serial killer of coffee and whiskey sours, he has since found his den in the Pacific Northwest with two raucous bird ladies that peck him when he gets too far out of line. That's a whole lot of beaking.

Email the author at: sraelkin@gmail.com
Facebook: www.facebook.com/timothyblack.author
Twitter: @Tim_RFP

More From Dreamsphere Books

Realms of Valeron
Alison Cybe

When Roka joined the Realms of Valeron, he was a fledgling elven cleric with only a minor healing spell and a dingy brown robe to his name. But that was just fine, since it was the hottest fantasy MMORPG, with over a million players, and Roka could not resist the allure of this rich, bright fantasy world, eccentric NPCs, and ravenous monsters.

And best of all, he met his friends—a wild and eccentric band of misfits who would change his life forever!

Join Roka and his newfound guild as they face devastating Razor-Squirrels, confront the Labyrinths of Ancient Storylines, and rush to max level in order to take part in end-game content (while probably not reading any of the quest text as they go!). But the real treasure that they find isn't the Bejewelled Anklets of Monster-Commanding or even the mythical Pointy Stick—it's the friendship they make along the way.

Enter the Realms of Valeron, a tale of high humor and eager adventuring like nothing before!

Available in paperback and ebook

More From Dreamsphere Books

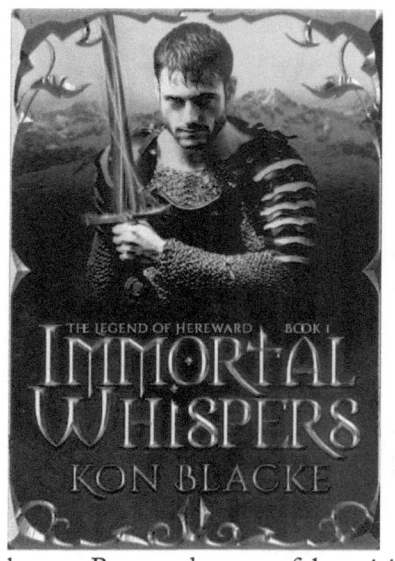

Immortal Whispers
Kon Blacke

The Whispering Monks have foretold change to the world, and it's fast approaching. They also speak of the mortals who'll be involved.

Hereward, a lord knight who only worships the steel at his side, as the mad magician Ealdræd has taken away everyone he had ever loved. Wymond, an oblate determined to find his true self, even if it means turning away from everything he has ever known. Beornræd, a powerful magician who fears to love again after the cruelties of his past. Kieron, a stable hand with dragon blood flowing through his veins and is the rightful heir to a realm of unimaginable beauty.

All four will travel their own paths, to destroy their pasts and rebuild their future, as they thwart the evil plans of Ealdræd and his conduit, the immortal Abbot Hosho.

The whisperings continue through epic battles, both on the ground and in the sky.

The whisperings shall continue beyond the aftermath.

As it has been foretold.

Available in paperback and ebook

More From Dreamsphere Books

An Angel Among Dogs
Charli Mac

Bethany is dead. It was horrible and violent, but it's over now. And she's still here, kind of, floating aimlessly in a vast nothingness, a mind without a body.

Kai Strand is First Hound. It's a heavy responsibility, trying to ensure the survival of his race against the men who have always seen them as second-class citizens. After his Hounds are instrumental in winning a battle for valuable new land, he is aston-ished when Price Faron offers him an unbelievable reward: a chance to stand before the Ether at the Solar Convexion—the first in a hundred and fifty years—and see if he is lucky enough to call forth a spirit to bind.

A strange doorway opens before Bethany, pulling her through. Is it the real world or something else? On the other side, she finds a riot of noise and confusion...and a handsome man whose tortured expression called to her through the portal. She clings to him as he whisks her away into the night.

This may not have been the wisest decision because it seems there's been a case of mistaken identities of epic proportion: he and his companions, Hounds, they call themselves, think she's an angel. A sacred being with all sorts of powers. Ha.

Available in paperback and ebook

More From Dreamsphere Books

Dragon's Breath: Black Flame
Kenla Nelson

Nihility the Harbinger feels a flicker of danger, a sense of impending doom. She is the black dragoness, Empath, and Weaver of the Dreaming.

Destined the Farseer has been too long away from his body in a place called the Between. He is Nihility's mate, bonded eternally through their heart of hearts. Known as the prophet, and Walker, he now finds himself at the center of an old danger.

The demons known as the Prem threaten their homeworld. Hurrying to her mate's aid, Nihility calls on Destined's other mate, the Watcher, Endrir the Broken. All must unite, and overcome their differences—even if it means Endrir must expose the secrets he has tried to keep from Nihility—for the three dragons face more than just the seven great demons who seek their freedom. Jezzar, the once great dragoness, leads the forces of darkness, and Nihility will need her strength to face her, as only she can.

For she is the wielder of the Black Flame, their only hope.

Available in paperback and ebook